AS TOLD UNDER THE MOON

A Collection of Haunting Works from New and Emerging Voices

PRESENTED BY ELLIS HART

with ALESSANDRA BENINI

with SHAWN BROOKS

with CAILIN CECCHINI

with AURELIE DUNCANSON

with ALEX FRANKLYN

with JULIA JACKSON

with A.D. JONES

with S.J. KING

with H.H. MIKA

with VICTORIA M. SORENSON

with AMY TACKETT
with DAVID WASHBURN

To the wonderfully wild readers we've met online: your support, kindness, and welcoming spirit has kept our love for story-telling alive. This book exists because of you.

TRIGGER WARNINGS

As Told Under the Moon explores dark themes and contains scenes that may be distressing to some readers. Please proceed with caution if you prefer to avoid any of the following content:

Graphic Violence and Body Horror: Includes graphic stabbing, dismemberment (e.g., severed foot), organ removal, and vivid depictions of blood.

Domestic Abuse and Intimate-Partner Violence: Depicts coercive control, physical assault, strangulation, and survival violence within romantic relationships.

Sexual Violence, Abduction, and Imprisonment: Includes predatory behavior, forced confinement, unwanted sexual contact, and drugging/sedation.

Stalking and Harassment (Including Tech-Enabled Surveillance): Portrays stalking, threatening messages, and public harassment.

Child Endangerment and Harm: References/depictions of children threatened, abducted, or harmed in urban-legend and supernatural contexts.

Supernatural Predation and Death: Features predatory entities, possession-like influence, vampiric attack/feeding, and disappearance with implied death.

Drowning and Disposal in Water: References victims being placed in a river.

Self-Harm / Self-Mutilation (Compelled or Enchanted): Scenes of cutting, injury to face/limbs, and amputation-adjacent harm.

Murder and Homicide (Including Serial Killing): Multiple killings, concealment of bodies, and aftermath at crime scenes.

Home Invasion and Threatening Intruders: Discovery of an intruder's presence and taunting messages.

If any of these themes or scenes could be triggering, please read with caution or consider skipping sections that may cause distress.

CONTENTS

INTRODUCTION

Some stories need to be read in daylight. These are not those stories.

Fear Flash Fridays started as a tiny experiment on my Instagram: I'd post a little scare, you'd show up with your coffee and curiosity, and somehow a handful of paragraphs turned into a really fun tradition. Story after story, your messages piled up—favorite characters, creepiest lines, the one that made you sleep with the light on (it's in here). I tried housing them on my website, tried carving them into social media posts, but the tales kept bumping against the edges. They wanted more space. They wanted, frankly, a night sky.

So I said, why not a collection? Why not right now—so it lands in your hands in time for spooky season? And because I believe the best campfires are crowded, I asked Instagram to send me their favorite indie authors. The response was a glorious storm. I reached out, and these writers—busy, brilliant, relentlessly kind—said yes. They brought fresh voices, unique takes, and valued perspectives to this project.

That's how *As Told Under the Moon* came to be: a book built fast, with care; a circle of chairs pulled close; a shared flashlight passed from hand to hand. Inside, you'll find different kinds of haunting; some bloody and grotesque, others delicate and tense. You'll meet people (and things) you'll root for, fear for, and maybe even rage for.

Read this however you like, but I recommend at night. Turn the lamp low. Let the moon do the heavy lifting. If you listen closely between pages, you might hear the shuffle of the next narrator taking their seat, clearing their throat, preparing to type out their next story.

Because scary stories are always best told under a full moon.

Welcome to the bonfire. Pick a seat, toss a branch into the blaze, and turn the page.

-Ellis Hart, September 2025

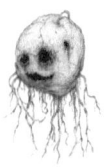

POTATO HEAD

SHAWN BROOKS

My little brother went missing on Halloween night back in 1995.

That was thirty years ago, so I'm in my forties now. But I took my kids—Mary and Kyle—out trick-or-treating just a few hours ago, and I think I saw him.

Oh God, I think I did.

The night that nine-year-old Jimmy Lowell became nothing more than an unoccupied seat at the table was a school night. Mom told us to be back before nine, and for me to keep an eye on Jimmy the whole time. It was one of those crisp autumn nights when people had just started using their dormant fireplaces. The burning pine was inviting, smoky, and a little sweet. Somehow filling the bitingly cold air with a sense of home and adventure at the same time. Kids were running around in ghost and vampire masks. Some high schoolers had paper bags on their heads with eyeholes cut out, shopping bags full of toilet paper, and eggs. Mosquitoes buzzed in our ears.

What a night to be alive. It comes back to me so clearly. Maybe because, even though I didn't know it then, it would be the last happy memory of my childhood.

Mom sewed our costumes together out of some cheap felt

material. I was obsessed with the Mortal Kombat games, so Mom made mine the green ninja one, Reptile. But of course, Jimmy felt left out, so he cried and begged Mom not to make him go as a pirate again—even though he had specifically asked to be one just a week prior. So, Mom caved—like always—and made him the gray Smoke costume. And damn it, his was better than mine. My mask was a paper plate I had colored in myself with a Sharpie. It smelled funny and made my head woozy. Jimmy's mask: Mom made that thing out of Styrofoam and hand-painted it. The color made his blue eyes pop like electric fire.

That was something Mom always said about Jimmy. His eyes weren't just blue; they were electric fire, whatever the hell that meant.

The last house we visited that night belonged to Mrs. Stotch. A two-story lump of bricks with a front yard infested with lawn gnomes. Her idea of Halloween decorations was to tie black and orange balloons to her shrubs and fence. She answered the door after Jimmy hit her bell three times in a row. I tried to get him to stop, but he was snacking out of his full pillowcase all night, and his sugar rush was a force to be reckoned with.

"Oh, look at you two!" Mrs. Stotch exclaimed. She was a widow, husband died in a hit and run some years back, and all her children were already grown up. I think having kids visit her on Halloween helped her deal with her loneliness a bit.

"Well, what do we have here? You're a green ghost? And you're a gray one!"

"No!' Jimmy protested. "We're ninjas." He pronounced this as KNEE-JAWZ.

He was always doing that, mispronouncing words because adults thought it was cute. One of his many ways of bending people to his will.

Mrs. Stotch smiled thinly, unsure of what Jimmy was even saying. "That's wonderful honey,"

She brought out a deep bowl of candy corn—the world's

worst treat—and let Jimmy shovel it into his case. I took a half-handful, just enough to appear polite.

"Do you have anything good?" Jimmy asked her.

I wanted to slap him so bad.

"Oh, well, sorry, dear—"

"It's fine, Mrs. Stotch," I said. "We love candy corn."

Jimmy took off down her drive without saying anything, so I said thank you, and she told us to be safe out there.

I caught up with Jimmy and punched his left shoulder. He dropped his pillowcase and started crying immediately. Just like he always did whenever I pushed him or even just tapped him.

"You've gotta be more respectful when people do stuff for ya," I said so angrily, the steam from my mouth, redirected by the mask, fogged up my glasses. "And what the fudge is wrong with you? You can't talk to people like that, even if you hate their stuff."

He sniffled, and I saw that his tears were causing the paint from his mask to smudge against his cheeks.

I was tired, and I was jealous of his costume. Fed up with his attitude. Maybe I was jealous that Dad never taught him lessons with his fist the way he did me. The smell of expired motor oil from Dad's calloused hands was embedded in my skin. He was fond of teaching me so much. Even to this day, I can't stand working on my own car and have to pay somebody else to do it.

Anger rumbled in my stomach and seeped into my bones. Mom always said I took after Dad in that department.

"Liable to fly off the handle at any breeze," she'd say whenever I showed the slightest bit of annoyance.

But she was right. Like father, like son.

But something else sprang up in me when I saw those tears ruining his perfect mask.

Satisfaction.

I'm not proud to admit it, but seeing Mom and Dad's favorite, the kid who appreciated nothing, seeing his perfect costume get ruined made my night. I walked away from him to go home, but he stayed put, his feet seemingly cemented to that spot. He cried and whined and even started screaming.

That dark rumble in my stomach bubbled up. With my father, at least he had the decency to smack you upside the head. My rage simmered and infected me slowly, like poison from a chemical plant leaking into a river over time. It came out in drips, and you wouldn't realize it until all the fish were dead or had three eyes.

If there was anything my brother hated more than me pushing him around, it was Potato Head.

Not the toy kids played with. This was a nasty urban legend we had down in Pine Haven. His image was scribbled on the stalls in the boys' bathroom. Spray-painted under the bridge out by Tolson's Tavern. His body was always different—from basically a human wearing coveralls to a tangled mess of roots like an octopus from Planet X.

But his head was always the same.

Three times bigger than it should have been if the drawn body had shoulders. Bulbous and malformed, like a sandbag kicked around and bent out of shape. Withered skin with gnarled roots hanging off it. Two slits revealing black pits for eyes. A twisted mouth with no teeth and cracked skin radiating out from it.

Kids would say his name three times in the mirror to summon him.

High schoolers held bonfires in his honor in the woods, getting drunk or stoned.

Everybody had a different story about him. My favorite was the one where Potato Head wasn't a man or monster; he was a god. Some dark thing conjured by witches who lived in the dead parts of the forest. Some subterranean deity who answered your prayers in exchange for blood. The other boys in Mr. Vollmer's class said he'd kidnap kids and bury them in bloody soil. Grow them up to be just like him.

Nobody knew when the legends began. And there were so

many versions of the thing, nobody took it seriously. Potato Head was a bad joke. A story like Bloody Mary or sewer alligators. But they were as much a part of our town as the crumbling streets or the busted water tower.

And Jimmy couldn't stand to look at his image or even hear talk about him. Once, when I was eight, and he was five, I told him how Potato Head took kids who left their windows open at night and planted them in the ground. He pissed the bed.

I lifted my crappy ninja mask and said, "Jimmy, Potato Head loves little boys who cry. Their tears help them grow faster in his garden in the dead forest."

He shut right up.

Tears glistening on his sooty cheeks.

I almost twisted the knife deeper, but some empathy must have also been down there in my black and spiteful stomach, fighting for control.

"Umm, yeah, let's just go home." I made a move to put my hand on his shoulder, but stopped halfway there. He did kind of deserve it after all.

He followed me down Raven Circle, at a distance, eyes on the trees. I looked back and saw he wasn't wearing his mask anymore. It was several feet behind him on the street. I said nothing and kept walking.

The homes on Raven were spaced far apart, with the jagged, toothy maw of the treetops beyond them. The smell of smoke trailing out of chimneys made me want to get home faster and sit in front of the fire with some hot chocolate. I checked my watch and saw that it was already ten! Mom was sure to murder us.

As long as Dad wasn't home yet, I was okay with that.

Most of the homes had their lights off. A few jack-o'-lanterns flickered with what remained of the flames inside. Two pumpkins had been smashed on the street ahead, their gooey guts strewn everywhere. Toilet paper hung loosely over trees, and splattered eggs painted a few walls.

There was nobody on the street anymore.

I didn't believe in Potato Head, but the way the trees swayed when I couldn't feel any wind injected ice into my veins.

"Jim Boy, let's hurry up."

"Mmm hmm."

I looked behind me. He had now let his pillowcase drag on the street by his feet. Candy was spilling out of it.

"Dude, what are you doing?" I went over to him. The black pool inside me erupted into a geyser. "This is your problem! You whine and you cry, and you don't care what people do for you!"

I bent down and started putting the candy back into his case. He let go of it.

It took everything inside me not to sock him in the arm. Dad socked me in the arm last month and broke it. Told me to "Man up, queer." So, as much as I wanted to hit Jimmy, I buried that anger somewhere under the folds of my fear. I told myself that Potato Head was real and was watching me now. It worked, I guess. Because the hot rage gave way to icy dread.

I stood up with his bag and mine in both hands. I shoved his bag in his face.

"I don't want it anymore."

"Why not?"

He mumbled something I couldn't hear. Stared off into the dark forest.

"Speak up, dummy."

He looked at me with glassy eyes. "You said Potato Head was gonna get me if I cry. And I always cry!" His lips quivered.

I hated myself then. Yeah, Jimmy was annoying as all hell, but he looked scared then. Like, really scared. More than he'd ever looked before.

"It's... I was lying to you, okay? There is no Potato Head. It's just a junk story big kids tell little kids to scare them. That's all it was. I was just trying to scare you, that's all."

"No," he whispered, staring at something in the woods. "He's real."

"Jimmy—"

"I've seen him before."

A moment of stillness. An owl mocked us from the forest depths. The pine needles rustled like hissing snakes. There still wasn't any wind around.

"You're lying."

"I see him out my window, standing in the woods sometimes. Just watching me." Jimmy's tears were flooding down his face now. "He's gonna get me now, just like you said."

"You ain't been seeing him," I said. My voice was so weak I couldn't even convince myself. "You're just trying to scare me now."

He looked me dead in the eye with such crystal clarity it hurt. "He's real, Marcus."

"Well, if he is, he'll only get you if you cry, right? So, if you're brave, he can't get you."

That was probably the clearest logical argument I had ever used in my life until that point.

A flicker of a smile crossed his face. He wiped his gray ninja sleeve over his wet eyes. Fabric threads stuck to his eyelashes. "You think so?"

"I know so." I walked back some to his fallen mask and picked it up. I dusted it off, even though it wasn't dirty, and walked back to hand it to him. "Just be a ninja."

He gripped his mask and smiled wider. "Yeah. Knee-Jawz. Just like Moke."

"Smoke." I smirked.

This little shit knew how to make me laugh as much as he pushed my buttons.

I put my arm around him, and we walked back home.

That night, Mom reamed us out for getting home late. I never got that hot chocolate I had been wanting so bad. At least Dad was passed out drunk at Tolson's and would be there until he sobered up enough to drive home tomorrow, so we didn't need to worry about getting a thrashing.

Jimmy and I went to sleep. We shared the same room, his bright orange race car bed on the left side and my normal one with blue blankets on the right. He looked at the closed window like he was studying it for a long time. I said nothing. We both passed out soon after.

I woke up sometime around two in the morning. It was cold in the room. For a moment, I had this vivid sensation, almost like a waking dream, that I was being dragged across the forest floor. I even felt dry leaves and pine needles bristle against my face.

My eyes were sealed shut with crustiness, and I rubbed them clear. My mind came back to reality, and I knew I was in my room.

It was freezing in there. I looked over at Jimmy. He had an orange dragonfly nightlight set on the wall by his face. I couldn't see him in its weak glow like I normally could.

"Jimmy?"

No response.

I sat up.

The window was open. I jumped out of bed. Walked over to the race car bed. Jimmy wasn't there.

I shook. Went lightheaded. Looked through the window at the infinite blackness it opened out to.

"Jimmy!" I hissed.

Our house was just one story, and sometimes in the summer we'd sneak out this way to catch frogs down by the creek if it was a full moon. Even then, I knew that was a stupid thought. He'd never leave by himself, and with it being so cold out.

All the hair on my arm stood up as if an electric current were flowing through me. I could suddenly see my breath even though it couldn't have been *that* cold that time of year. My eyes adjusted to the dark, and I could see the faint outline of the tree line in our backyard, painted with a dull silvery moonlight.

There was something out there. Standing on our unkempt grass. Too dark to see any details. But I could tell that it was tall, its form reaching the same height as our basketball hoop on the other side of the lawn, as far as I could tell. The shadows that covered its body bled into the charcoal curtain of the forest, uniting them into obscurity.

But the head was visible, even though it shouldn't have been, since there wasn't enough light out there.

Long and thin things writhed like worms attached to a lumpy sack of a head.

Two black eyes that were blacker than the night. Like they were living things, black holes sucking in all my thoughts. It felt like it was reading me, reading all the things I'd ever done or would do. I saw things in those eyes I can't right explain. Something massive, uncoiling and moving under dark waters, is the closest I can compare it to.

I screamed.

Mom came in right away, but by then the figure was gone. She too screamed when she realized Jimmy wasn't in the house, and I said that there was a man outside. The cops were brought in and found nothing. Dad rolled up the next morning. The moment he found out that Jimmy had disappeared, he grabbed me by my shirt and slammed me against the wall. My arm, which he broke weeks prior, ached in anticipation of round two.

We never found Jimmy.

There were never any leads. The only theories that held any water were that he was either abducted by a predator or that he just ran away.

But I knew the truth.

It was Potato Head.

Jimmy must have opened the window after I fell asleep. Trying to prove that he was a brave ninja. Prove that he was so brave that even with the window open, tempting Potato Head to come and get him, that he wasn't scared.

I blamed myself every day for the past thirty years. If I had been meaner to him that night, he wouldn't have had the courage to do what he did. I suppose I could have also just been nicer and never tried scaring him in the first place.

Dad made my life a nightmare—more than usual—until he died of liver cancer three years later. Mom hung on, a husk of her former self, sewing dolls with bright blue eyes—electric fire eyes she'd say— instead of talking to me, her only family left. When the aneurysm came for her while I was at college, it was a mercy, trust me.

I wrestled with the bottle for decades, trying to get the shadow I saw on my lawn out of my head. Trying to drown those endless black pit eyes with poison.

More than that, I was trying to kill the part of me that remembered Jimmy's smiling face, so full of bravado behind his Knee-Jawz mask.

Which brings me to tonight. I never left Pine Haven and eventually found a girl, Julie, who could tolerate my bullshit, and we got hitched. We take Mary and Kyle trick-or-treating every Halloween, believe it or not, but we're always home before nightfall, no excuses.

Tonight, I was with my kids while my wife was at home making a special dinner of spider-leg spaghetti, a silly thing we started doing after Kyle watched *Arachnophobia* two years ago and fell in love with spiders. Mary hated it at first, fuck, so did I, but we've all grown used to it now.

Halloween day was normal enough. I stayed out on the street while I watched the kids go up to the doors. Mrs. Stotch is still there, by the way, much, much older. Still happy as ever, peddling her disgusting candy corn. Jimmy's outburst having had no effect.

Then I noticed something off. Felt it more like.

Down the street to my left, I saw an adult who I thought at first was a parent in a costume. He had a kind of burlap sack thing on his head. About three blocks away, so I tried not to pay him much mind.

Until I felt something I hadn't felt in decades. Someone

reading me like a book. Sifting through the pages of my mind. Of staring into two deep holes instead of eyes.

I looked up at the man, but he had moved further left, across the street.

So I tried to look at him.

I couldn't.

I mean, he was never directly in my line of sight. He was always on my periphery.

I tried to ignore him. It was nothing, just a trick of the light. Besides, there were at least a hundred kids out running around. Easy for my eyes to play tricks on me.

My kids came back from Mrs. Stotch with frowns.

"Dad, why does she always give us this disgusting crap?" Mary said.

"Yeah, like, it should be illegal," Kyle put in.

"Uh hu," I mumbled, not really paying attention to them.

I was doing double takes, and I couldn't stop.

Every masked face that passed us, for just a moment, looked like that tall man.

Felt like him to be more accurate.

"Okay, buds, time to go home," I said and clapped my hands. I was feeling suddenly weak and brittle.

They whined, reminding me that there were still another twenty minutes to go before sunset. My kids never got on my nerves. Some people say that things like abuse are like alcoholism; they get passed down through the generations. I don't know how I did it. I don't think I actually *did* anything, but I never touched my kids like Dad did with me. I never even so much as raised my voice to them.

But their whining that night reminded me so much of Jimmy. His whining that drove me to meanness. His whining that was among the last things I ever heard from him.

"Enough!" I snapped at them.

My heart fell out of my chest then. I saw the same tears well up in their eyes that I saw in Jimmy's. I hated myself.

"Sorry," I said, but it was too late. Kyle looked shellshocked even behind his Frankenstein mask. Mary backed away, gripping her fairy princess skirt.

They didn't speak again as I ushered them down the street.

We walked home, and just in the corner of my vision, I saw him there—the tall man with the sack on his head. He was closer. Maybe half a block away now. He was very tall. I'm six feet, and even though I couldn't get a good look at him, I just knew that if I were chest to chest with him, I'd have to crane my neck all the way back to look at his face.

Again, whenever I turned to look at him, he was gone. I tried speaking jovially to my kids, but my voice quivered, and I think I just scared them even more. Every time we rounded a corner, I did a double-take of the passersby. Flinching when a kid ran by. Gripping my son's shoulders too tightly when a gaggle of children burst into delighted screams.

I scanned every parent's bare face and child's mask in detail. I made people nervous with my wild eyes. More nervous than any devil mask or ghoul mask could make them. Mine was a living mask of pure terror at that moment. My neck grew sore as I twisted my head around to scrutinize the people around us.

I saw him getting closer as we neared our home. He was so close, I swear I could have whipped around and touched him. I could just make out in the failing light the tattered gray fabric clinging to his body in strips. The twitching of something hanging off his mask...his face?

We got home just as the sun bled out into darkness.

Mary and Kyle ran to my wife and started explaining in excited chatter that I was acting weird.

Julia shooed them away to eat their spider pasta, and they seemed to forget all about me and my near-manic breakdown.

Julia took my hand and pulled me into our walk-in pantry, the official adult talk room of the house.

"What's going on with you?" she asked, eyeing me up and down.

I had grown up to be a calm man. A measured man. A man in control.

In that pantry, my eyes were watering, and I had already developed a tic, a twitching head doing a constant double take.

"I'm fine!" I said it too sharply.

What the hell was wrong with me?

Shock flashed across her moss-colored eyes.

I bit my lip and clenched my left fist to put all that dark energy somewhere, anywhere else than directed at those I loved. "I'm sorry, I thought I saw this weird guy hanging around all the kids, and I just overreacted."

"What weird guy?"

I told her about the tall man with the large head, always just out of sight, stalking us through the neighborhood.

Most people would have written their partners off as batshit insane just then. Not Julia, she saw the terror bubbling under the surface of my face and believed in me. At least she believed that I believed, for what that was worth.

I calmed down after that. Her faith in me lifted the lid of the pot and let out all the steam of my growing anxiety.

Even if there was a man, he was just some teenager messing around. Or maybe because it was Halloween, remembering my brother made my mind conjure up all sorts of ghosts to terrorize me.

It was nothing, I told myself.

The tic went away.

Later that night, with our bellies full of arachnid noodles, and letting the kids watch *Hocus Pocus*—their sixth time watching it at least—we all went to bed.

It must have been a dream; I felt my body being dragged through damp leaves and a muddy trail. A twig scraped across my face. Drumbeats made the earth vibrate. I could feel the heat of an unseen fire. I was being lifted up. Body tied to something that dug into my back and made it bleed. I was suspended over a pit. Something colossal was moving down there.

Calling my son's name.

I woke to a scream that rent my heart into pieces. Sweat soaked my bedsheets, and the tic came back in force.

Julia and I bolted out of bed. The scream came just once from Kyle's room. We ran down the hall, and Mary was standing outside his door, clutching her stuffed rabbit to her chest, eyes wide and glassy.

Julia ran to her. I ran into the bedroom.

Kyle was sitting in his bed, skin as white as the blanket he was gripping. I noticed something wet seeping through it near his crotch.

He couldn't speak, couldn't move; all he did was stare at his window.

His open window on the second floor of the house.

So cold outside, he never would have left it open himself. Julia and Mary went to Kyle while I leaned out the window.

There, across the yard and past our covered pool, something was standing in front of our hedge just out of the white circle of the backyard light.

Tall.

Head large.

Writhing things reaching and twisting forward as if sensing me.

And its eyes.

Not the black pits I had seen so often on bathroom walls. Not the endless holes that beckoned to me in my dreams.

These ones glowed like electric blue fire.

THE WISHING BOX

ELLIS HART

Julia Barmay stood in her cramped apartment, one hand on her hip, the other clutching a chipped mug of lukewarm coffee—the kind that tasted faintly of burnt cardboard with just a splash of wet cat. The pile of boxes sat in the corner like a stack of coffins, mute and hulking, mocking her with their sagging seams and water-stained flaps. This was it—her inheritance.

While Catherine Barmay's will had been a glittering carnival of wealth divided among people Julia had never even met—mansions, cars polished until they gleamed like shark skin, jewelry worth more than Julia had made in her entire life—her only granddaughter had received... boxes. Stale cardboard, reeking of mothballs and mildew. The last laugh from a woman who never laughed with her, only at her.

Julia had expected something. Not the mansion, no—she wasn't delusional. But maybe one of Catherine's gowns, famous the world over for their silk and sequins, or one of the gold records that had hung like glowing talismans in her grandmother's study. Instead, she got paper cuts and dust up her nose. And in a way, Julia wasn't surprised. This was the story of her life: everyone else got the spotlight; Julia got the crumbs.

The first box coughed up yellowed newspaper clippings, reviews with headlines screaming:

"THE VOICE OF A GENERATION!"

Julia studied the photos: Catherine, young and devastating, smiling too wide with teeth too white, always caught mid-laugh like life was nothing but champagne bubbles and flashbulbs. Julia squinted, trying to find herself in the woman's sharp cheekbones, her confident posture, but saw nothing. She slammed the lid shut.

The second box held dresses that smelled like expensive perfume, garments still shimmering but frayed at the seams. Julia held one against herself and caught her reflection in the streaked mirror propped against the wall. She looked like a child playing dress-up in a costume that wasn't hers, never could be. She dropped the dress in a heap.

Another box: vinyl records warped by heat, their labels peeling like old skin. Another: photo albums whose glossy pages stuck together. In one, Catherine stood arm in arm with Nina Simone, both women laughing. Julia shut it quickly, a sick pressure tightening in her throat.

By the time she opened the second-to-last box, her hands shook with exhaustion and rage. Inside was nothing but loose sheet music and brittle hotel receipts from the 1970s. She cursed, ready to shove it aside, when her fingers brushed something smooth and wooden. She pulled it free.

A box. Small, no bigger than her hand. Its surface was polished to a dark sheen, the kind of object that demanded attention in spite of its size. Julia leaned in, praying this box held something of value—velvet, jewels, anything. Instead: empty. The hollowness of it felt intentional, as though it had been waiting for her. Her eyes caught the inscription carved into the underside of the lid:

Whisper low, seal it tight,
a wish made true in the dark tonight.
Believe to gain, but know the price,
for nothing comes without sacrifice.

Her eyes rolled as she laughed, but the sound was brittle, a glass about to crack. Of course. Some mystical tchotchke her grandmother had clung to. A wishing box. Catherine had toured with Ella Fitzgerald and Sonny Rollins, but she'd also been the kind of woman who burned sage to ward off bad spirits. Julia set it aside, if only because it seemed like the least pathetic relic so far.

TIM CAME HOME LATE, AS HE ALWAYS DID, REEKING OF BEER and fried food. He stopped dead in the doorway when he saw the mess.

"Christ, Jules. What the hell is all this?"

"My inheritance," Julia said flatly.

He burst out laughing. "You've gotta be kidding me. All this crap? You get a mountain of junk while your grandma's estate hands out cars and jewelry to people you don't even know?" He rummaged through a pile, holding up a record sleeve. "Wow. Really cashing in here, babe."

"Shut up, Tim."

But he didn't. He never did. He flipped through everything with greasy fingers until his hand landed on the little wooden box.

"What's this?" He held it up, squinting. "Looks like something you'd buy at a yard sale. Hey, maybe it's magic! Maybe it'll fix your shitty luck." He leaned down, whispering theatrically:

"I wish a lawyer would come knock right now with Julia's real inheritance. The good stuff."

He snapped the lid shut and shook it like a rattle, grinning at her. "Your turn," he said, tossing the box to her.

"Shut up," Julia muttered, though her lips twitched. She leaned in.

"I wish," she said, playfully but with an edge, "that Tim would just shut up and go... a... way."

They laughed, the kind of laughter couples use to cover up everything wrong beneath the surface. As they laughed, Julia traced the inside edge of the box with her finger and then hissed in pain. A splinter. A bead of blood welled bright and perfect against the wood. She tossed the box onto the sofa and went in search of tweezers.

When she returned from the bathroom, splinter free, the apartment was quiet. Too quiet.

"Tim?"

No answer. His shoes were gone. His jacket. His presence, scrubbed from the apartment like chalk from a board.

At first, she was annoyed. By morning, uneasy. By noon, frantic. She called his job. No Tim employed there. Called his sister —the woman on the line was livid, screaming she didn't know who Julia was, that she didn't have a brother named Tim, to stop calling her number. Then the line went dead.

Julia's heart stuttered. She looked at the box curiously. Expecting to see the crusted droplet of blood, she opened the box slowly. But what she found was nothing at all. No smear of her blood. No sign she had been injured at all. And then the rhyme pulsed through her skull like a song she hadn't heard in many years.

Believe to gain, but know the price.

IT BEGAN SMALL. A TEST. A PINPRICK OF BLOOD AND A whispered wish for Chinese takeout. Ten minutes later, a knock at the door. Hot lo mein, sesame chicken, just as she'd whispered. Paid in full. Julia shut the door with shaking hands.

From there, the spiral was inevitable. A handbag. A promotion. A credit card balance cleared overnight. Each one required more blood. Not just drops—more. She grew dizzy after each wish. Her skin grew pale. And still, she kept whispering. Still, she kept bleeding.

But when the items weren't enough to quench her loneliness, she asked for Tim back. One full slice across the hand, easier now to measure in milliliters than droplets. And when Julia awoke in the morning, her bed was still empty. Nothing had happened. A dark, gruesome realization slipped into her thoughts now: the box was no longer satisfied. It didn't want drops, nor did it want splatter. It wanted pieces.

That night she pressed her pinky against the cutting board and brought the knife down, imagining a carrot instead of a piece of her. The scream ripped out of her throat like something feral. Blood gushed, bright against the counter, soaking the wood. She shoved her severed finger into the box and slammed the lid.

Minutes later, her phone buzzed, and the name appeared just as she imagined—Tim. He apologized for being late from work, but he'd be home soon. Julia wept, blood and tears mixing on her cheeks.

From there, reality unstitched itself. Weeks blurred into one endless night of pain and reward. The box gave her everything she asked for. Money. Power. Beauty. But her body told the story. Even when she wished to be whole again, her body showed the scars. And each time a piece of her was returned, she knew she'd need to sacrifice it again.

Her eyes gleamed with hunger. She told herself she was winning. She told herself she was finally someone.

And yet, even people who are someone need to be someone else. It's the human experience—to always need more, to crave, to want. And so, Julia continued, in an endless cycle of mutilation and reward until she was faced with an impossible problem. The box had stopped accepting her offerings. No matter what she gave, the box ignored her wish.

And for the first time, she looked in the mirror and didn't recognize who looked back. Her left hand was completely missing, grotesque scarring present from the stovetop cauterization. Her cheeks had been sliced, offering just a bit more flesh and blood for the box to acknowledge her. She hobbled and tripped, forgetting how valuable her toes were to overall balance.

Finally, she fell to the floor in tears, unable to manage the pain much longer, wondering how she could do anything more for the box; what could possibly fit inside such a small box that could be more valuable than literal pieces of her?

WHEN SHE CAME TO, SHE WAS STANDING IN A MANSION, A massive oil painting resting just atop the staircase. In it she recognized herself, flanked by Tim and three beautiful children. Chandeliers dripped light, marble floors gleamed—beauty in every direction.

And in the middle of the floor lay a human body sprawled over a Persian rug. Their chest was cracked open, ribs splintered, heart missing. The blood was still steaming in the chilly air.

Julia gagged, turning away.

The box rested in her newly returned hand, its lid sealed.

Julia didn't remember killing anyone. Didn't remember the knife, or the screams. But the wishing box was heavy in her palm, softly humming with electricity. It was satiated—for now.

She looked around at the splendor, at the wealth that seemed to shimmer, and felt the truth claw its way up her spine. Catherine's voice, her fortune, her very legacy—they weren't talent. They weren't luck. They were the box. Wishes bought with blood. Fame carved from flesh. Glory minted in suffering.

Julia clutched the box tighter, her knuckles white. She

thought she heard a sound then—music, faint and ghostly, a woman's voice singing jazz into the cavernous dark. Catherine's voice. Smooth, perfect, and utterly damned.

And Julia understood, a smile dawning on her lips: the box hadn't just been an heirloom. It had been a passing of the torch, a curse disguised as inheritance. Catherine had fed it until she could no longer pay. Now Julia was its owner, its butcher, its sacrifice.

The body on the rug wasn't the last. It was the first.

And the mansion seemed to lean in, listening, waiting, watching—to see what Julia would ask for next.

ONE FOR SORROW

A.D. JONES

Juice remnants from the pumpkin he'd just finished carving slowly mingled with John's saliva and washed around his mouth, earthy and bitter against his tongue, as he chewed on the flesh at the edge of his fingernails. It was a habit he'd picked up over the last couple of years, and even with the discomfort it left him with, it was a difficult thing to stop. Autophagia, if a person was being technical, or Autocannibalism to some, was a symptom of anxiety, but when things helped, they helped.

Grabbing the mug from the kitchen counter, John rinsed it briefly under the faucet, washing away the dark dregs of coffee before placing it back down next to the sink and heading for the door. He'd place the pumpkin out on the step when he got home from work later, the jack-o-lantern becoming a modern signal that a home was 'open for business' when it came to the candy demons of the neighborhood.

He sat at the bottom of the stairs and fastened his boots before grabbing his jacket and heading out the front door, doing his usual checks that the door was fully closed behind him as he stepped down onto the path.

He was nearing the end of the path when a glimmering

object fell from the sky before him, the tiny clatter of metal hitting the ground being preceded by the *caw* of a bird from above. John bent to scoop up the ring as he looked to the magpie perched on a branch of the tree at the edge of his yard.

"One for sorrow," he muttered to himself as he pocketed the silver band and carried on with his day.

———

THE BRIEF MOMENTS OF SUNLIGHT WERE FLEETING AT BEST AS fall slowly closed in. The darkening sky above was already a murky mix of deepest greys and rusty orange, like the swirling waters of a painter's rinse cup, as John trudged through the fallen leaves towards home. Generally speaking, his days weren't too stressful, but making his way home this evening it felt as though the weight of the world rested squarely on his shoulders.

He turned the key in the lock and stepped inside, quickly removing his jacket and hanging it from the hook on the wall, the silence around him bringing with it a refreshing moment of calm.

"John, baby, is that you? How was work?"

Delicate fingers of dread danced down his spine, his entire body freezing, hand still grasping his jacket as his head drooped in defeat. "Yeah, it's me."

"Stupid question really, I mean who else would it be?" Isla stepped into the doorway from the kitchen, her chestnut brown hair up in a messy bun, and a red and white apron fastened over her jeans and beige sweater. She cocked her head at him as her mouth lifted into a playful smile. "I'm almost done here with dinner, and the table's already set, go get yourself comfortable."

This was normally where John would remove his boots, but something told him to hold off on that for the time being as he headed on into the front room. Everything in the front half of the room remained exactly as he had left it this morning, but at the back half of the room the dining table was set up for the most romantic of evenings. Candles were lit along the centre of the table, a bottle of red wine and two glasses between them, and two places set ready to eat.

He slowly eased himself down into one of the chairs, letting out a long, slow, breath as his eyes scanned the table. A large white dinner plate was sandwiched between a knife and fork, with a glass of what he assumed to be water next to it. The opposite side of the table was laid out in exactly the same manner, though the wine glass on that side had some pink residue sat in it, leading John to believe Isla had already started on the bottle.

"You look so tense," Isla said, having silently appeared in the room, a steaming casserole dish in her oven-mitted hands. "Tough day at the office?"

"Tough couple of years," he grunted, eyes fixed on his wife as she moved lithely across the room and placed the dish down beside the table settings.

"Oh, come on, babe, don't be like that. You're acting like someone died." She pulled a serving spoon like magic from her apron and began to serve out a large portion onto each plate. "It's meatball," she said with a smile, her blue eyes bright and shining as she took a seat facing him and began to fill their wine glasses.

John reached for his glass and lifted it to his nose, inhaling deeply and savouring the dark cherry and plum notes of the inky malbec before taking a small sip. He felt Isla's eyes burning deeply into his soul as she patiently watched him and waited.

He reached for his fork and lifted a small amount of the still steaming casserole to his lips, meeting her eyes as the food entered his mouth. With his first bite, the distinct crunch was likely silent outside of his own head, but the twinge of pain that followed as the small shards of something cut into his gums, would be evident to her watching gaze.

The coppery, metallic taste of blood permeated his mouth as he continued to chomp on the mouthful, sharp pain shooting through his gums as he crunched what he assumed to be broken glass into a fine powder. He refused to give her the satisfaction of spitting it back out but hoped that if he ground it down enough it wouldn't do any further damage on the way down.

John choked down the food with a spluttering cough before bringing a napkin to his mouth, dabbing at his lips and shivering as the white fabric came away with small droplets of blood spattered across it. "I haven't put the pumpkin out for the kids!" he spat with a matter of small urgency as he jumped up from his seat, the chair scraping along the floor as he hopped up.

"Oh, John," Isla began, with puppy dog eyes and a protruding lower lip as she pouted. "That can wait until after dinner, there's no rush."

"No. I better do it now, you never know when the kids will start their rounds, and it's already pretty dark out."

He moved quickly through the front room and into the kitchen, his eyes going wide as he took in the room. The mess from cooking was still apparent, but his heart sank as his vision landed on the now empty knife-block on the counter. He crept silently across the room and carefully slid open the cutlery draw, his pulse quickening as he saw that, that too was now emptied of anything with a sharp edge.

John scooped up the pumpkin from where he'd left it earlier and opened another drawer to grab a candle and box of matches, before heading back out towards the front door. He stepped out into the cool fall breeze and glanced across the neighborhood. There wasn't a soul around just yet, and it would be easy to believe he was gazing across a 3am backdrop.

His tongue danced across shredded gums, finding the tiny lacerations and wincing as he probed them with the tip of his tongue, before he dropped to a knee and placed the pumpkin on the step and began fumbling with the matches.

He could just leave.

He could stand up right now and just start walking in any direction, the destination didn't really matter. It wasn't a solution, but then what was? He didn't really have a choice other than to go back inside and face his problems head on.

With the candle placed inside the slowly rotting corpse of the pumpkin, he lit the wick and carefully placed the top back on, taking a moment to appreciate the festive beauty of the glowing orange smile. Halloween had always been his favorite holiday. It was a shame how things change.

Stepping back inside, he closed the door behind him and drew in a lungful of air before slowly letting it out and making his way back into the front room to face Isla.

"So..." John's nostrils flared as he drew in another breath, his stance squared and strong as he stood in the centre of the room, the dining table ahead of him. "Should we just finish this now?"

Isla hit him with a look of stark confusion. "Finish what? Dinner? John, I don't know what you're talking about."

"Please don't. I have no fucking clue what this is. Penance maybe? The hell if I know but let's just get it out of the way. I'm tired, Isla"

The legs of her chair screeched along the hardwood floor as she slowly stood from her seat, confusion in her eyes. "Babe, what's go—"

John was through wasting time. He closed the gap as she began to stand and brought the toe of his boot up into her stomach, kicking her with everything he had and doubling her over as the air was forced from her body. Immediately stepping forward he grabbed two fistfuls of hair, gripping the back of her head as he slammed it down onto the surface of the table. The sickening crack of bone and cartilage filled the room as her nose shattered under the force of the blow, a pained scream bursting from her as he threw her to the ground.

The back of Isla's head hit the wall with a thud as she fell, rivulets of crimson gore gushing from her malformed nose as she tried to scoot backwards on her ass away from him. "John, stop! Please!" her words came out muffled due to her ruined face, her countenance still one of abject terror as he stepped towards her.

Her expression quickly changed to one of malice and rage as she sprang from the ground, pulling a hidden knife free from her apron as she lunged towards him. John managed to bring an arm up just in time to catch the paring knife as it sank deep into his left forearm, the pain shooting up through his body. Twisting from his waist, he brought a fist around and slammed it directly into her mouth, her teeth breaking against his knuckles and shredding his flesh as she fell back to the floor, the knife still lodged in his forearm.

Blood dripped from his balled fist as he stood over her body, his shadow darkening her whimpering form. With a sharp intake of breath, he ripped the paring knife from his arm and dropped to his knees as he brought it up into the air.

Isla had just enough time to bring both hands up in a defensive manner, her eyes doubling in size as he brought the blade down, stabbing deeply above her left breast. John pulled the blade free and brought it down again and again, stabbing in a furious frenzy of blood and carnage until exhaustion beat him, and he slumped back onto his butt.

A pool of blood seeped from beneath her body and slowly inched its way across the floor towards him as he finally released his grip on the knife and let it clatter to the floor. He shakily lifted himself from the ground and grabbed a napkin from the table, placing it firmly over the gash on his left arm. That was going to take some explaining.

Lost in a wave of adrenaline and horror, he didn't know what his next steps were to be, and he found himself wondering if he should have just let her end it, when the chime of the doorbell sounded from the hallway.

"Trick or treat!"

HE DIDN'T DARE MAKE IT TO THE DOOR FOR THE FIRST, OR even the second, group of kids that arrived decked out in an array of creepy Halloween costumes, with their pails in hand, but once he was cleaned up, John spent perhaps the next ninety minutes handing out candy to the kids from the neighborhood. He managed to find the time in between to bandage up his arm, and nobody gave it even a second glance at the door.

Once the endless stream of masked children at his door finally petered off, John spent the next few hours sat in quiet contemplation, ignoring the painful throbbing in his arm as he stared at the blank TV and dissociated. He needed complete darkness and a lack of potential witnesses for the next part.

At just after 2am, John lifted Isla's lifeless body over his shoulder and quietly carried her out to the car, laying her out on the back seat, before locking up the house and taking his place behind the wheel.

He drove for about an hour, to the spot he knew all too well, and parked up before retrieving a shovel from the trunk of the car and hefting Isla from the backseat as he set off on the final part of his journey.

The enormous trees that loomed over him in the forest cast the already lightless night into extreme darkness, but John felt he could do this walk with his eyes closed and so had no issues with the journey, even with Isla's body over his shoulder. It wasn't long before he arrived at his destination.

John made quick work of digging through the damp earth and soon found himself staring down into the sizable hole in the forest floor, the sweat on his face being gently cooled by the nighttime breeze.

Dropping the shovel, he moved to Isla's blood-soaked body and lifted her up in his arms as though ready to carry her across the marital threshold and moved back to the hole. With a grunt he hefted her corpse into the large pit, where she landed atop of three, identical, were it not for the varying stages of decomposition, bodies.

"Please don't come back next Halloween, baby, I don't think I can keep doing this."

DEAD AIR

ELLIS HART

They say you don't get into true crime podcasting for the money, and they're right. If you're lucky, you get a niche following, some ad revenue, maybe a devoted subreddit where listeners argue about your theories at three a.m. I have all of that. What I don't have is my breakout episode— the kind of episode that makes *The Quiet Between* more than just another voice in an otherwise incredibly saturated market.

My dream breakout has teeth, leaves my audience with scars. Not only do I want that kind of episode in my catalog, but my ratings *need* it.

Today, I go hunting for that episode. October sunlight lays itself across the dead lawn like an old golden record, extending out until extinguished by the shadow of a nearby tree. I stand at the chain-link fence with my notebook in one hand and phone in the other, staring at the bungalow where a man was once brutally murdered.

Ray Malloy.

The house slouches, stucco the color of nicotine, cracking and falling in more places than one. The porch slats bow and the door is a swollen tongue of painted oak. Somewhere along the eaves, a wind chime tinks in a single, uncertain note, then falls quiet.

I run through my research a final time in my head. Malloy was a semi-famous radio DJ in the 1960s; a warm midnight baritone with a mischievous laugh and an ear for the exact song you needed exactly when you need it. He died in this house on October 12, 1968. Blunt force trauma. No weapon recovered. No charges. His last broadcast cut to silence mid-sentence, and some people swear if you spin the archive tape backward and slow it down, you can hear a voice, potentially the killer's, whispering before Ray's own voice disappears.

The house went to the county after the last of the back taxes outlived the last of the family. When it finally went up for auction last month, a flipper bought it and decided asbestos meant liability, liability meant delay, and delay meant, sure, some podcaster could walk around inside for an afternoon as long as she signed the waiver that basically read: If you fall through the floor, that's a you problem.

I sigh and press record on my iPhone as I step through the dusty threshold.

"The Quiet Between, Episode Forty-One," I say, voice steadier than I feel. "Site visit: residence of Raymond Malloy, local radio personality, deceased October twelfth, nineteen sixty-eight. Cause of death: blunt force trauma. Case status: unsolved."

The entryway is narrow, the wallpaper florals browned to the color of tea left too long. A banister climbs the left wall, two spindles missing midway, ends splintered into little wooden fangs. A pair of men's shoes—cracked leather, still loiter by the door. My phone throws a square of light across the floorboards, and a tiny critter of some sort scurries away into a far corner.

I record everything, I always do. I often uncover some of the best clues buried beneath my otherwise useless ramblings. "Entry narrow. Banister damaged at midpoint. Scuffing on the stair riser at the third step. Note to self: compare to crime scene photos to determine if—"

Pipes knock overhead, startling me midstep.

In the kitchen a chipped Zenith radio slumps on a shelf with its cord missing. A bowl on the counter fossilizes the ghost of a lemon.

Malloy's study, where he ran his radio show from, waits like a stage. It was unusual for someone to have the equipment as well as the means to broadcast from their home in the 60s, but I've seen stranger things.

The microphone, black enamel dulled to a bruise, sits awaiting. A leather chair, turned half-out from the desk as if the owner had only stepped away momentarily. Coffee rings, dark coins stamped again and again probably over many years litter the wooden desk. I seat myself, and the dust blooms out across the room, catching thin rays of light filtering in through the single window.

"Good evening San Francisco! Welcome to the number one radio show in the entire world. I'm your host, Clara and this is The Quiet Between on FM 105.2, THE MOTHA FUCKIN' JAM" I say to the empty air before pretending to be a rave horn blaring after my introduction.

"We have a guest here tonight. Let's welcome Ray Malloy! Hi Ray, we're here to tell your story. People remember you. They still argue about you. They still want to know what happened. So let's give them what they came for. Who killed you?"

Silence.

"First impressions," I add briskly. "This space feels preserved, not staged. Like someone pushed pause and walked out and never hit play again."

I end the note. The red dot winks away from my screen. I stand. The floor complains underneath me. I walk towards the window, needing a speck of sun to brighten my cranky mood.

From across the street, behind a lace curtain, a woman's silhouette leans forward, then pulls back swiftly.

On the sidewalk, with the door locked behind me and the

evening air clean and warm, I lie out loud to myself. "I may just have the bones of my breakout episode."

THE RITUAL AFTER A SITE VISIT IS WELL-PRACTICED AT THIS point. Bag by the door. Kettle on. Laptop open. Index cards on the wall noting TIMELINE, PEOPLE, OBJECTS, MOTIVE. I clip my hair on top of my head with a binder clip because I don't own a proper one. I talk to myself like a surgeon scrubbing in. I do not think about the way the house smelled (smoke, mouse droppings, pennies on a tongue). I do not think about the woman behind the lace curtain except to put THE WOMAN AT THE WINDOW on a fresh card and tack it to PEOPLE.

The audio file zips from my phone to my editing software and unspools to a blue waveform. I hit play.

"The Quiet Between, Episode Forty-One..."

There's that voice I hate and love: tinny when I wished it were velvet, too careful in the first thirty seconds, because I always forget that the mic wants you to speak like everyone has been waiting for you specifically and not like you're apologizing for intruding on their ears.

My thoughts continue to wander as I organize photos, pinning them to the wall in crooked rows, and the audio file plays in the background. I hear myself say on the tape, calm and clinical: "Banister spindles missing at midpoint. Splintered. Possible evidence of a struggle."

And then—something else. A distant voice that is not mine. It fades in and out, breaking through a snowstorm of static.

"...ong...thank Go—"

Friendly but firm. Like I've put my glass down on the wrong coaster at a stranger's house. The word is almost swallowed by static, almost nothing at all, and for a heartbeat I wonder if I've dreamed it.

My pulse jumps. I hotkey back in the file, drag the cursor, crank the gain, and hit Play again.

"...of a struggle." My voice. Then silence. I lean closer, ear almost pressed to the speaker.

"...Wrong. Thank God that's not what happened there."

The necklace at my throat slips and clinks against the desk because I'm so damn close to the screen now. I don't breathe. I let the clip continue this time.

The static wavers like an old car radio fighting for a signal. Out of it, smoother now, a man's voice: "That wasn't the murder," he says conversationally, and the hair on my arms tries to crawl off my skin. "That was Christmas morning, sixty-three. My boy stuck his head between those rails and panicked. Had to cut them out to get him free."

The words fade, return, like he is struggling to push them across from somewhere very far away. A hush follows, warmer, tinted with something I can't quite place: "Cried like the world was ending. Then he asked for pancakes."

The waveform spikes as my recorded self continues talking—oblivious to what had just happened. Because to the me who walked that staircase, nothing *had* happened. In the moment, I hadn't heard a peep.

The bodiless voice sighs, followed immediately by the return of the house noises: floorboards, pipes, my steps on the wooden floor.

I pause the file. The apartment snaps shut around me—refrigerator hum, distant plumbing, a siren two blocks over. I listen to the small, dense structure of my fear.

There is a rule I say out loud on the days I need to pretend I'm brave: Whatever terrifies you most is where you go next.

So, I hit play.

I STAY UP UNTIL THE SUN BEGINS TO PEAK THROUGH MY blinds. The voice is there every time. The same small laughter when he says pancakes. The same gentle correction.

At five a.m., I write OPTIONS and stick it to the wall.

1. Edit and release. Risk credibility. Accusations of faking a second voice. My reputation dies.
2. Keep it private. Pretend it didn't happen. My curiosity dies.
3. Go back. Record again. Ask questions. See if he answers.

Number three sits there like a lit cigarette in a dry field. Any logical person knows how it will end, but there's still a chance nothing lights, right?

By noon I am parking under the magnolias again, the house squinting at me. The woman behind the lace looks, then doesn't. The key I returned under the planter yesterday is still there. I hesitate at the door. If I'm not crazy, if that voice is really here, then this truly *is* my breakout episode.

I sit in the study, in front of the microphone, wondering how silly I'd feel should someone stumble upon me sitting here, interviewing a ghost.

"Ray," I say, feeling the weight of the name on my lips. "I heard you yesterday, on my recording. Your voice was on the tape, at least I think that was your voice. Either that or I'm going nut–so."

The house is so silent it hurts my ears. If the voice is there, I can't hear a damn decibel of it.

"I'm not here to exploit you. I'm not here to hurt you or get rid of you. I'm here for the truth. Your truth. If you want to tell it. People want to know what happened to the great radio host, Ray Malloy."

Okay, I'm placating a little too hard here, but I want to coax him out. I need this.

A clock ticks. A truck downshifts a few streets over. I talk for an hour, voice growing sandbar-dry, asking about everything I can name: the banister, the rumors, the night, the club with the mermaid, the debt, the anger, the last song he played before the silence cut him open.

By the end of it, I'm fairly certain that I was talking to no one and there will be nothing on the tape but my own obnoxious voice.

I flip open my laptop, sync the file, and press play.

"Either that or I'm going nut—so."

I lean in, wishing, praying, pleading.

"...Clara," the voice says, so welcoming and warm. "You came back."

Static swells like applause.

I slam the laptop shut so hard I fear I'll open it back up to shattered glass.

I LISTEN AGAIN, FORCING MYSELF TO FOLD INTO THE CADENCE as if I'm simply editing an episode. There has always been power in the disciplined delusion of doing your job. But this time, I've prepared differently.

My phone is propped on the edge of the desk, still recording without pause. My laptop sits open with a mic and stand connected, headphones hugging my ears so tightly I can feel a headache coming on.

Apparently, this is the only way to have a conversation with the dead: in playback. Who knew?

"...You came back," Ray says. Not eager. Not mournful. Pleased. His voice is burgundy with a bit of grit, the kind of baritone you could loosen a tooth on if you aren't careful. It fades in through static, then steadies, close as breath.

"Yes," my recorded self says, steadying. "I came back because I want to understand what happened to you. What can you remember? Who did this to you?"

A little clockwork pause. He uses silence extremely well,

almost too well because I'm frequently checking the recording to ensure it's still playing.

"Tell me. Who are the big radio hosts now? Do people still listen to WNEW? Or did NBC win out?" A chuckle followed by what sounds like the drag of a cigaret, sharp inhale, slow, lazy exhale. "What about Wolfman Jack? That man was everywhere. You couldn't escape him if you tried."

I stare at the screen unsure of where to go next. I didn't anticipate this—a murdered ghost utterly disinterested in revenge.

On the recording, I try again. "Ray, I'm asking about October twelfth, nineteen sixty-eight. Did you know the person who came into your house? Was it someone you trusted?"

The chair sitting across from me leans forward slightly, sending a new wave of horror and excitement through me. *This is really happening. I'm talking to a ghost. My ears* and *my eyes have confirmed it now.*

"What's a podcast?"

My skin prickles. The rule is solidifying now: he's not only uninterested in talking about his murder, he won't. But if that's not odd enough, he wants to talk shop.

"La Sirène," I pivot, pushing. "Does that name mean anything to you? There were rumors about the singer."

Upon playback, I hear a wholesome, full bellied laugh, the voice phasing in and out of static like a jukebox in shallow water. "That piano. Always out of tune. You could *chew* the smoke in that room. Have you ever been, Clara? They used to let the trumpet player solo until the ice in your drink melted. A beautiful woman like you? You'd be dancing all night."

I pause now, shaking his dripping charm from my mind, trying to refocus: *You're good. You're really good. But you're not going to move me where you want me. You'll move where I let you.*

On the track, my voice goes small because I hate that that's what it does when I am furious. "I'm trying to solve your murder, Ray. I'm offering you a voice."

"Murder, murder, murder," he says lightly, and the static rustles appreciative, like unseen listeners applauding. "Here's the truth— I don't remember what happened to me. Not a fragment, not a moment, not a thing. But you know what I *do* remember? The thrill of having the ear of an entire town every single evening from 8 to 11 PM." Ray then begins to hum a familiar song, one I can almost place, *almost.*

The realization of what's unfolding here makes the hairs on my neck stand straight up.

I am no longer the interviewer. I am the subject.

FOR THREE DAYS THE AUDIO OWNS ME. I STOP USING THE word "haunting." This isn't haunting. Haunting is a widow walking the stairs she fell down forever. This is colonization.

Ray has completely taken over my life. If I'm not listening to the audio, I am writing down new questions. If I'm not writing down new questions, I'm researching something that may trigger a memory for him. It's just me and that velvet voice.

I force myself to take a brief mental break and check emails. A curious email with the subject line *"Ray Is My Neighbor"* catches my eye immediately.

The message is as short as it is cryptic: *"If you're in that house, you're in danger. He always wanted an audience."*

No name. The email address is one of those string-of-characters that looks like someone fell asleep on the keyboard. While the email's content is concerning, what really has me interested in the subject line: *"Ray Is My Neighbor".* Whoever this person is, they're talking in the present tense. Have they heard the voice too?

Back in the house that afternoon, the study smells as it always does, but there's a slight tinge of something new, something smokey. I can taste it on the tip of my tongue.

I've returned with no real plan for today. I left my notepad of questions back at my apartment. This session, as I've begun to call them, is for Ray. My hope is that if I give him what he wants, he'll finally have told his tale and will be able to answer my real questions.

"Ray," I say. "I'm giving you the floor. This session is yours. Do with it as you will."

For ten minutes, the room stays brutally silent. Multiple times I consider how insane I must be going. This is preposterous.

I end the session. I sync the file. I listen.

Static coughs and then smooths like a hand over a rumpled sheet.

"Good evening, ladies and gentlemen," Ray croons. "This is Ray coming to you live from home base." He breathes and I swear I feel it on my face. "Tonight's set list? Well, that depends on what you're in the mood for. Heartache? Laughter? A little something to help you feel less alone?"

He smiles in his voice, and I understand why lonely people in apartments fell asleep with their radios on just to fight away the sorrows climbing out from under their beds.

"And a special thanks to my producer, Miss Clara Reed," he purrs, "for keeping the wheels spinning. Sharp ear, sharp tongue, sharper instincts—don't be shy, kid, they love you. They'll love me more of course, but there's plenty of love to go around!"

He continues on for roughly 8 minutes before signing off "to the good people of Meritsville; may you sleep tight and remember, I'll be here again tomorrow evening to soothe them complex feelings away."

I sit with my hands fisted and nails in my palms. I have invited a ghost into my production who loves the spotlight more than I do.

I KNOCK ON THE HOUSE ACROSS THE STREET FROM RAY'S PLACE. Lace. Lemon furniture polish. A sideboard with photographs in frames heavy enough to kill someone. The woman from the window is smaller than the silhouette made her. Late seventies, maybe. Hair like steel wool, the color of ash.

"I know who you are," she says without smiling. "I listen to your program on my iPad." The last word is careful, as if she's borrowing it and didn't ask.

"You sent the email," I say. "About Ray."

"I didn't send anything," she says. Which I believe, and I don't.

She pours tea in cups the size of thimbles. Her name is Agatha Barron. She saw Ray carry groceries once in 1965 and the town decided to make him a saint. She also saw a woman leave his house with a black eye and the town decided that woman had walked into a door. She saw his son biking in front of the porch, a boy with a cowlick like an exclamation point, and she saw him disappear one summer when "the world got too loud".

"The house," I repeat, because I don't have the patience for metaphors today.

"He liked it quiet," she says. "When he was working, if a car backfired or a dog barked, he would come out and stare at the street until the street corrected itself. He called silence 'dead air.' He said it like it was sacred. 'Dead Air,' he'd say, 'is how you learn where your breath ends and the world begins.'" She makes a face like she has bitten something bitter. "Men who talk like that stare in the hallway mirror way too often for far too long."

That's a pretty good line, actually. Maybe I'll use that for the episode. I pivot. "Did you hear anything the night he died?"

She stares through me. Finally: "I didn't hear a single thing."

On the walk back to the house, the magnolias drop a handful of yellow leaves onto my hair and I consider how lovely this home would be if a ghost didn't live within it's walls.

I HAVEN'T BEEN TO RAY'S HOUSE IN WEEKS. THERE WOULD BE no reason to considering he has followed me home. There was a brief moment in time where I thought I knew how this worked. Ghosts do exist, fine. But you can't hear them, okay. Yet recordings can, weird but alright. Ghosts can only exist within the boundaries of their death, sure but—WRONG.

I never felt any weird possession. I never felt a monkey on my back. I never felt a chill down my spine. So how did he follow me home?

"Ray," I say carefully into my apartment, into the hallway, into the walls. "You can speak when I tell you to. Otherwise, please stay silent."

It's performative parenthood and I know it.

I press record.

"Hi listeners, some of you may be wondering where I've be —" the rest is distant fog, as a much louder, clearer voice comes to the forefront of the recording.

"Friends," he says, honey poured over gravel, "this is Ray, filling in while our Clara takes a well-earned breather. She works too hard. Don't worry. She'll be back." He laughs, intimate. "For now, you've got me."

My hands go numb as I listen back.

The track plays on with the swagger of a man who has learned how to be skin in someone else's life. He invites listeners to DM him. *How does he even know what a DM is?* He somehow learned my home phone number and is now taking live calls like a real radio show. He wishes a woman happy birthday by singing the bridge from "Unchained Melody" so soft I feel my toes tingle.

He lies about me: "Clara's visiting family." He is specific in a way that makes strangers forgive him preemptively. He is a campfire, a porch swing, a night nurse's kind voice at three a.m. telling you the test will be over soon when you know it won't be.

When the file ends, he says, "This is Ray Malloy, and you've been listening to The Quiet Between. Stay tuned. We're just getting started."

I do not upload the episode. Instead, I drag it to the trashcan icon and release.

When I wake, my notifications are a fireworks stand going up. The subreddit pins a thread called RAY!!! Comments bloom: Who is this man? God, his VOICE. Is he coming back? Clara we love you but can he come back?

During lunch a DM appears: HE KNOWS MY NAME HOW DOES HE KNOW MY NAME with a screenshot of their first name spelled right and the city they never put in their profile. The next DM: He told me to stop looking at my ex's Instagram "for tonight." I hadn't posted about doing that. Another DM: He said my mother forgives me—and she's dead.

The comments are dopamine, dread, and devotion— the cocktail that built radio.

I TRY TO FIGHT THE TECH ANGLE BECAUSE I WANT THIS TO BE supernatural and not my own failure. I change passwords. I rotate the Wi-Fi. I unplug the mic. I unplug the router. The next "special" episode still drops at three fifteen with my show art and my feed and my name. He tells a story about a traffic cop who let him by once because he was late to the station for a last-night-of-summer segment. He laughs like a man who never been told "no". He asks the listeners who's on their mind right now, and if the person's on their mind, have they called, and if they haven't, why not, and if they have and it went poorly, can they try again.

I do what I always used to do when I was a kid with too many feelings: go on a walk.

The momentum of my feet feels good. My thoughts clear a bit and I wonder if being so close to Ray all the time has actually affected my brain function. *Is that possible?*

I thought this was going to be my breakout episode; my

opportunity to really be someone in this field! The anger and frustration bubble, but instead of a scream from my throat, tears erupt from my eyes and I have to stop walking before I run into something.

I don't have money to just up and leave. I own very little and it's all in my apartment. If I pack it up, Ray will obviously know and simply follow me onto my next place. *Could I trick him into following someone else? Is he really all that bad? I don't feel in danger, do I? Was the podcast ever going to be anything other than a stressful way of making $12 a month? So what if I just, give it up?*

When I reach my building, the front desk has a package for me. No return address. Inside, a vintage ON AIR sign. The plug is frayed, but the glass is unbroken. At the bottom, on yellow paper, six words: SO IT FEELS MORE LIKE HOME.

The sadness and fury come storming back as I stare at the message. And then an idea hits, quick and strong. *"Home— that has to be it. That's where it all started. Maybe if I can find who killed Ray, make him remember, he'll finally move on and I can get my god damn life back".*

THE STREET IS A BLACK RIVER. A MOTH BANGS ITS BODY against the streetlight, wings like paper. Inside, the rooms are depthless. My flashlight skates over the banister with its missing teeth. I head directly to the study without speaking a word. There's no cord to plug it in, so I simply set the ON AIR sign on the desk like an offering and take several steps back.

"Ray," I say, into the void.

The sign begins to glow red, as if awakening from a long rest. I think of arteries. I think of meat. I think of a theater curtains drawing right before the first line.

"Clara," he answers immediately, from nowhere and everywhere. The house shifts to fit the shape of him and I fall on my rear stunned.

"I can hear you. I can hear you without a recording! How?"

"I already told you, I don't know how any of this works."

"You told my listeners I was on vacation, Ray." I say as I wag my finger into the void at nothing in particular. "You said—"

"Oh hush. You were," he says, interrupting my moment. "From yourself. That can be good for a girl your age." His voice dripped with condescendence.

"Stop using my show," I say. I aim for authority; I hit pathetic instead. "Stop using my name. If you want a show, get your own."

He laughs and the lamp on the side table dims and brightens, dims and brightens as if it's nodding. "You gave me a stage," he says. "Don't be shocked the show started."

"What happened October twelfth," I demand. "Who came through this door? Where did your wife go? Where is your son?"

Silence deepens. When Ray uses silence, it's not empty. It's a full plate he slides across the table to see if you'll pick up a fork. The vents breathe. Somewhere under the floor something old shifts its weight.

"Clara," he says softly, "do you know what dead air really is? It's the moment everyone remembers the room they're sitting in. A boy's room. A hospital room. A station at one a.m. with no one answering the phone. People think silence is absence. It isn't. It's attention with the sound turned off."

"Answer me."

"Ask a better question."

I inhale, exhale. "What did you love more," I ask, "the people who loved you or the sound of them loving you?"

The pause that follows is not for effect.

The red sign hums. The room considers me.

"Good," Ray says at last. "We might make a broadcaster out of you yet." Then, brightly—"Now let me talk to them."

"No."

"Clara."

"No."

The study door swings gently closed as if a child pulled it.

The knob clicks. The red sign brightens. Somewhere very close by, metal scrapes concrete in a painful, eye twinging way.

A new door opens from behind the desk.

The smell that comes up is animal and bleach.

THE STAIRS DOWN ARE NARROW; THE WALLS TOUCH MY shoulders as if pleading for me not to go any further. I count thirteen steps. The flashlight shows cinderblock. Stained concrete. A drain like an eye in the left corner. Hooks empty, then hooks not empty. A table where tools used to be. Some sort of rubber tubing lays coiled atop it.

There is a cage in the corner. It is big enough for a person to exist in, but only on their hands and knees. The smell in that corner makes me gag.

There is a microphone here too. Not the one from upstairs. Another, older. Its cable snakes under a door that stands two inches open to a smaller room that sits empty. I turn the knob and the room inside is padded—the cheap egg-carton foam type, and while old and brittle, absolutely sufficient to keep the space insulated from noises outside on the street.

On the far wall, a red bulb. My ON AIR sign has a brother down here, and it glows steadily.

"Ray," I say, and my voice bounces back to me and doesn't reach anyone. "What is this?"

"You wanted my truth," he says gently. "Every man's truth is his *space*."

The cage door glides open on rusty hinges.

"Clara," Ray says softly, fatherly, like a man who keeps his hand steady when teaching you to parallel park. "You're a producer. You said so yourself. I'm the talent, the *real* talent. So go on, be a good girl. Step in."

I run.

The stairs whine under my weight and then try to throw me

off. I step awkwardly, just shy of the next step and jam my shin into the wooden tread. My shoulder hits the cinder block, pulling at my sweater. I resurface at the study with tears in my eyes. The ON AIR sign still hums. The front door is mud, I place both hands on the handle and pull with all my might.

A horrific screeching sound starts behind me, drawing closer with each tug at the old, swollen door. Though I know I shouldn't look, its sudden silence inches away from my back fills me with enough dread to turn around and face the sound.

It's the cage, up now from the hidden basement, its mouth yawning widely. I have just enough time to acknowledge the red, rusty stains on its metal flooring before the house's front door becomes unstuck and shoves me, hard. The aching pain radiating from my shin and shoulder feel even stronger now as I fall in what feels like slow motion.

My knees scrape hard and I know layers of my own skin are now behind me.

PEOPLE ALWAYS ASK ME IF I'M AFRAID OF THE DARK. I SAY NO. The dark is honest. It doesn't pretend to be anything it's not. It's the absence of light, plain and simple.

I am afraid of red. The red that tells you the room is listening and you are about to be made smaller in it. The red that says— become a soundbite or be erased by one.

In the cage the air is salt. In the center of the study, Ray's chair leans toward the mic just as it does every night. He continues babbling about this and that, I'm convinced he has no idea what he's going to say before it leaves his mouth. But, he's got a real talent to think on his feet. I chuckle to myself. *He has no feet. What does he think on then? Perhaps his—*

"Shut your mouth, you useless piece of trash!" he snarls then, off-mic, the words too big for the room, aimed like a fist. "Not another god damn sound, Clara, or you won't get food for a fucking *week*."

I rattle the cage because I'll be damned if some 1960's motherfucking *ghost* with a bashed in head destroys my spirit. I shake the cage harder and begin screaming until I'm sure my throat is bloody.

Silence.

I know he's there. The chair hasn't moved.

Finally, he clears his throat and I see the fader slowly move back up to its previous setting.

The red light flicks back on.

THE LAST THING I SAY IS PATHETIC. IT IS A THREAD OF A breath I send through the rusty cage, a wordless thing, the shape of my hopelessness as I rot away in the home of Ray Malloy.

A girl in Tulsa sits up in bed at three fifteen and hears it. But on second thought, she doesn't really know what she heard and instead refocuses on Ray's voice spewing more nonsense.

An older woman in Ohio wipes the tears from her eyes, releases her lace curtain back into place, and crosses the room to turn-off a radio show.

A boy with a cowlick who is older now than his father ever got uses his thumb to trace the crease in an old photograph and tells the shape of a woman in it that he's sorry he couldn't do more to protect her.

Across from his dead producer, Ray talks and laughs and makes everyone feel smaller than him.

"Goodnight, friends," he says, smooth and dark. "As always, I'll be here for you tomorrow night."

He clicks the light off and the red glow dissipates into the dark.

LA DAME BLANCHE (THE WHITE LADY)

AURELIE DUNCANSON

Knock, knock, knock — the White Lady calls,
Her shadow creeps along the walls.
Beware if you don't open the door,
She'll leave her mark forevermore.

PROLOGUE

I was thirteen the winter I first heard her call.

It has been years since then—decades now—but even as I write these words, my pulse quickens with the memory. Some nights, when the wind prowls against my windowpane and the floor of my house creaks as if under unseen weight, I am carried back to that cabin, back to the snow and the dark and the knocking.

People often laugh when I tell them I believe in ghosts. They roll their eyes when I speak of legends, of curses whispered across centuries. But I do not need to believe it. I know.

Because I was there. I heard the knocks.

And once you hear them, you never forget.

ARRIVAL

It was February—cold enough that our breath came out in little clouds that clung to our scarves, our boots crunching in the packed snow as we followed our counselors along the trail. There were eight of us, bundled in mismatched winter coats, our cheeks chapped raw, and our laughter shrill with the thrill of being free from school.

The counselors had promised us an adventure: a "winter retreat," they called it, a chance to toughen ourselves with nights in the wilderness, to make memories we'd carry into spring. We carried heavy packs with sleeping bags, mess kits, and enough trail mix to last three days.

The forest swallowed us as we went deeper. Pines rose like cathedral pillars, their branches groaning under heavy coats of ice. The silence of the woods pressed in, broken only by the muffled thud of our boots and the occasional snap of a frozen twig beneath the snow. The sun dipped early, washing the trail in blue shadow, and every so often, one of us glanced back, uneasy at the way the forest seemed to close behind us.

When we finally glimpsed the cabin, half-buried in snow, it looked less like a retreat and more like something forgotten. Its roof sagged under years of storms. The shutters hung crooked, some nailed shut, others dangling loose. Smoke curled weakly from a stone chimney, the only sign of life against the winter silence.

"Home sweet home," one counselor announced, forcing a grin.

But I remember thinking it didn't look like a home at all. It looked like a place the forest had tried to bury.

Inside, the cabin was warmer, though only just. A single wood-stove struggled against the cold, its glow casting light across walls darkened with age. The rooms were cramped: a kitchen the size of a closet, a living room with sagging armchairs and the stone hearth, and above, an attic loft where we would all sleep side by side, our sleeping bags lined like coffins beneath the slanted roof.

The windows were frosted so thick we could barely see out, but when the wind blew, the walls groaned, and the shutters rattled as though begging to be opened.

We ate soup that first night, the steam fogging the glass. The counselors joked, tried to keep us cheerful, but already I sensed it—that sharp, metallic tang in the air, like cold iron. Something that did not belong.

When the bowls were empty and the fire burned low, one counselor leaned forward, his face lit by the flames. He lowered his voice, and that was when the story began.

THE LEGEND

The fire crackled, its warmth barely reaching the farthest corners of the room. Shadows leapt and stretched across the log walls, bending into strange shapes as the flames shifted. One of the counselors, Marc, leaned closer to the fire. His eyes glimmered in the half-light, and when he spoke, his voice had dropped to a whisper that made us all instinctively lean forward.

"Have you ever heard," he asked, "of La Dame Blanche?"

The words felt heavy, thick with something ancient. They lingered in the smoky air as though reluctant to be spoken aloud.

None of us answered. A few shook their heads, while others pulled their sleeping bags tighter around their shoulders, waiting. The name alone seemed to change the room.

"She is called the White Lady," Marc continued. "Some say she's a ghost, others... something worse. They say she walks through these woods when the snow is deep, and the nights are long. She does not drift, like the ghosts you know from stories. She does not wail in the distance. No. She comes closer."

Marc lifted his hand and rapped three slow times on the wooden floorboards.

Knock. Knock. Knock.

The sound rang out, sharp and hollow. It silenced even the nervous giggles.

"She knocks, always three times. At the door, at the window, sometimes even on the walls themselves. And when she comes, you must choose to open the door... or ignore her. But beware."

The fire popped, sending sparks into the air, and Marc let the silence stretch before finishing in a hushed voice:

> *Knock, knock, knock — the White Lady calls,*
> *Her shadow creeps along the walls.*
> *Beware if you don't open the door,*
> *She'll leave her mark forevermore.*

The rhyme settled over us like a blanket of frost.

For a moment, none of us spoke. Then Adam, the loudest boy in our group, forced a laugh that cracked like thin ice. "It's just a campfire story. Like Bloody Mary or the Hook Man."

But even he avoided looking at the windows.

Another counselor, Claire, shifted uncomfortably. She didn't smile. "This story isn't like the ones you tell at sleepovers," she said quietly. "It belongs to these woods. People here... they don't laugh when they speak of her."

Marc nodded. "There are stories of hunters who never came home. Of cabins found with doors marked red, walls torn by scratches that no beast could make. And always, the same sign: three knocks."

The fire sputtered, casting a sudden shadow against the far wall. For just a heartbeat, it looked like a woman in a long white shroud, her hands outstretched. Several of us gasped, but when the flames flared again, the wall was empty.

We tried to laugh. We tried to tell jokes, to force the story into something harmless. But when it was time to climb the ladder to the loft, none of us were so bold as to look too long at the door.

The rhyme followed us up the steps, whispering in the back of my mind, word for word.

THE FIRST NIGHT

The loft was crowded with our sleeping bags laid side by side, a jumble of colors and crinkling nylon. The wood beneath us was hard, the air bitter with the scent of smoke and frost that had slipped through the cracks in the windows. Someone had propped a flashlight on a beam, but its batteries were low, and the light pulled in and out, as if it too were afraid to keep burning.

At first, the sounds of settling filled the attic: zippers tugging shut, whispers exchanged under covers, the occasional cough. One by one, voices dropped into silence, leaving only the steady crack of the fire from below.

I remember staring at the slanted ceiling beams, tracing the knots in the wood, trying not to think about the story. But the rhyme wouldn't leave my mind.

Knock, knock, knock — the White Lady calls,
Her shadow creeps along the walls...

I must have drifted into half-sleep, because when the first sound came, it seemed part of a dream.

Knock. Knock. Knock.

Three slow, hollow raps against the front door.

My eyes snapped open. I wasn't the only one. From the darkness, I heard a sharp breath, the rustle of someone shifting upright in their bag.

My heart slammed so hard in my chest I thought everyone must hear it. I turned my head toward the ladder that led down to the main room, but no one moved. Even the counselors were still, their silhouettes motionless against the glow of the dying fire below.

Someone whispered, "Marc?"

The counselor didn't answer.

The air felt wrong, heavier somehow, colder. I pulled the sleeping bag tight over my shoulders, but the chill pressed through anyway.

And then we heard it—the faintest scrape, like a branch dragging across the outside wall. It slid slowly along the logs, too measured to be the wind.

The sound crept from one side of the cabin to the other, dragging, pausing, then starting again.

Someone breathed, but their voice trembled.

One of the younger campers whimpered. Someone else shushed him, their voice sharp with fear.

And then—nothing.

No more knocking. No more scraping. Not even the wind. The woods outside had gone utterly silent, as if every living thing had frozen in place to listen.

I lay there with my eyes wide open, too afraid to blink. Every creak of the beams felt amplified, every shift of breath in the room was too loud. Minutes stretched into hours.

Finally, exhaustion dragged me under, though I swore I still heard faint crunching outside—footsteps in the snow, moving slowly around the cabin, repeatedly.

THE DAY AFTER

When the gray light of dawn slipped through the frosted windows, it felt like waking from a fever. My eyes were raw, my body sore, and yet I wasn't sure I had truly slept at all. Around me, the others stirred slowly, their faces pale and drawn, as if the night had pressed itself into our skin.

For a long while, no one spoke. We shuffled into our boots and sweaters, the wood cold against our feet, and followed the counselors down to the main room. The fire had died to ash. The smoke lingered low, clinging to the rafters, bitter and acrid.

It was only when one of the campers reached for the front door latch that the silence broke.

"Wait." Marc's voice was sharp, too sharp for morning. He crossed the room quickly, blocking the boy's hand. For a moment he just stood there, staring at the door as if something was pressing on the other side. His jaw worked, though no words came.

Finally, with a forced breath, he tugged the latch himself and pulled the door open.

The cold hit us first, sharp enough to sting our eyes. Then we saw it.

On the outside of the door, faint but clear against the wood, were three dark smears. Red. Thin streaks frozen into the grain, like the marks of fingertips dragged down.

Blood.

The boy nearest to me gasped, but Marc snapped his head around and silenced him with a look. The second counselor, Claire, was already at his side, her face pale, her lips tight. She touched the marks with gloved fingers, then shook her head quickly as though to dismiss it.

"Animal," she said. "Probably a bird, maybe a fox. Nothing more."

Her voice was steady, but her hand trembled as she closed the door again.

We sat at the long wooden table with bowls of porridge that tasted like nothing. No one spoke of what we had seen. No one spoke of the knocks. Yet I could feel it in the air between us— that same tightness, that same shared knowledge, heavy as frost on the beams.

Halfway through breakfast, one of the younger girls whispered, "It wasn't a dream, was it?"

No one answered.

The counselors filled the silence with talk of the day's plan, games in the snow, building shelters, a hike to the frozen stream. Their voices rose too brightly, too quickly, like lanterns in a storm trying to hold back the dark.

But even as we trudged outside into the brittle sunlight, I noticed it. The woods were too still. No bird calls, no rustling branches, no distant crack of deer in the brush. Only the crunch of our boots in the snow and the constant, gnawing thought:

She had been here.

The counselors kept their voices high, urging us forward, praising the "fresh air" and "beautiful day."

But I could see the truth in their faces. The way Claire's eyes darted constantly to the tree line. The way Marc flinched at every sound, his shoulders always tight, as though expecting a hand on them at any moment.

We built snow shelters. We raced across the clearing, hurling snowballs until our gloves stiffened with ice. We laughed, but it wasn't the kind of laughter that eases fear. It was shrill, brittle, a thin shell cracking around what we had all heard.

Every so often, when the laughter faded, the silence returned —an awful, pressing silence. The forest wasn't alive the way it should have been. Even the wind seemed to hesitate at the edge of the trees, as if unwilling to enter.

At lunch, Claire made a show of boiling soup over the fire-pit outside. She stirred with too much force, the ladle clanging against the pot. I noticed her glancing often at the cabin, as though she feared turning her back on it for long.

"See?" she said brightly, ladling steaming broth into tin mugs. "Perfect weather. Nothing to worry about."

No one replied.

One of the younger boys—Henri—kept clutching his scarf. A red wool scarf, though thinner than it had been yesterday. The edges looked frayed, as if something had torn at it. He wouldn't explain, but his eyes shone with tears he refused to shed.

Later, when we hiked to the stream, I lagged at the back of the group. The snow was deep, swallowing my boots with each step, and the trees crowded close, their branches heavy with ice.

I thought I saw something then—just beyond the birches, a pale shape slipping between the trunks.

A trick of the light, I told myself. A clouded patch of snow.

But when I blinked, it was gone.

When we returned to the cabin, the sun was already sinking. Long shadows stretched across the clearing, reaching like black fingers toward the roof. Inside, the air smelled of smoke and damp wool. We sat by the hearth, hands outstretched, waiting for warmth that never seemed to sink deep enough.

It was then that I noticed the beam above the fireplace. A heavy, darkened timber, charred in places from years of smoke. At first, I thought the marks were natural—splinters, cracks. But then I leaned closer.

Three lines. Vertical. Carved deliberately into the wood. Beneath them, faint letters scratched into the grain: *Dame Blanche.*

I didn't say a word. I only leaned back, heart pounding, the fire's glow suddenly colder than the snow outside.

As evening lowered itself over the forest, the light faded to a bruised violet. The trees outside were no longer merely trees— they became watchmen, tall and black against the snow, hemming us in.

Henri was the first to hear it. He froze near the window, his half-eaten biscuit crumbling in his hand.

"Did you hear that?" he whispered.

We all fell silent.

At first, I thought it was the creak of the trees, the sigh of winter settling into its bones. But then it came again, distant, muffled.

Knock.

...

Knock.

...

Knock.

Not at the door. Not close enough for that. Somewhere beyond the cabin. Faint, but deliberate.

Marc, the older counselor, rose sharply. "It's the wind," he said too quickly. He crossed the room and dropped the iron poker into the fire, sending sparks into the air. "Nothing more."

But his hand trembled.

Claire moved the curtains shut over the window, her lips pressed tight. None of us spoke after that. The only sound was the snap of the fire and the racing of our own hearts.

THE SECOND NIGHT

That evening, the fire seemed weaker, as if the logs refused to catch, and the shadows in the corners of the cabin seemed to pool deeper than before. No one suggested telling stories or singing songs. Even the counselors avoided meeting our eyes. We played cards half-heartedly, listening to the wind gnaw at the eaves, until one of them finally told us it was time to sleep.

The loft felt different that night. The air was heavier, sharper. Every shuffle of a sleeping bag, every whisper, seemed too loud, like the walls themselves were listening. We lay in rows, lined up like fragile dominoes on the splintered floorboards, each of us pretending to drift off. I could hear shallow breathing all around me, fast and uneven, though no one dared speak.

Time stretched. The cabin creaked, sighed, and settled into its own old bones. I stared at the dark rafters above until my eyes blurred. Somewhere below, the last flame in the stone hearth gave a faint pop, then fell silent. That was when I realized —true silence had arrived. No wind, no shifting branches outside, not even the groan of settling timber. Only the beat of my own heart.

And then it came.

Knock. Knock. Knock.

Three sharp raps, carrying up through the floorboards.

Everybody in the loft went rigid. I felt the girl beside me

grip her sleeping bag so tightly the fabric whispered under her fists. Across the room, someone whimpered before biting it back.

We held still, waiting, listening.

A counselor hissed into the dark, barely audible: "Stay down. Don't move."

I wanted to believe his command meant safety, that he knew what to do—but his voice trembled, and I realized he was just as lost as we were.

We waited, straining to hear. Seconds bled into minutes. I thought maybe—maybe—it had gone.

Then came the scrape.

Slow, deliberate, dragging against the wood. Fingernails, or something like them, pulling along the outside wall.

Scrrratch... scrrratch...

It started near the door but crept steadily upward, climbing. With each drag, frost bloomed on the beams above us, spider-webbing outward across the glass of the nearest window.

A boy in the corner squeezed his eyes shut and whispered a prayer under his breath. His voice was too loud in the stillness, and another camper hushed him furiously, though her voice cracked.

The scraping stopped.

For a moment, nothing.

Then, faintly, through the ice-fogged window, I saw it. A hand pressed flat against the glass.

Long-fingered. Thin. The skin almost translucent in the moonlight.

It lingered only a second—long enough for me to know it was there, long enough for me to know I had not imagined it. Then it was gone.

The frost melted as quickly as it had spread, leaving only our own pale reflections staring back at us.

We lay frozen until dawn, none of us daring to close our eyes. And when the first gray light slid through the trees, we saw what she had left: streaks along the wood where the nails had dragged, fresh and raw as though carved that very night.

THE THIRD DAY

No one spoke at first. We gathered around the door like mourners at a grave. The counselors pressed their palms to the wood as if to test its strength, but the trembling in their fingers betrayed them.

Breakfast was a hollow affair. The oatmeal congealed in our bowls, untouched, while steam curled upward and vanished in the cold air. One boy whispered that maybe it was a prank—that one of us had scratched the door in the night to make the story feel more real. But his voice faltered when he saw how deep the grooves went, splinters jutting from the frame like tiny, broken teeth. No human nails could have done it.

We tried to carry on. The counselors urged us outside, insisting that daylight would clear our heads. So, we trudged into the snow with sleds and scarves, our boots crunching in brittle rhythm. But the forest no longer felt like a playground. Every tree seemed to lean closer, every shadow lingered too long. When one of the girls slipped on the ice, the sharp crack of her fall echoed like a gunshot, and half of us screamed before realizing she was unhurt.

The counselors kept glancing back at the cabin. Once, when the wind shifted, I thought I heard it: a faint knock, muffled, as though someone rapped on the door even while we were outside. The others didn't seem to hear, or pretended not to. I bit down on my tongue and said nothing.

By afternoon, the sky had darkened again. Thick clouds pressed low, heavy with snow, and the light dimmed to a dull pewter glow. We begged to go back inside, but returning brought no comfort. The cabin was colder now, the fire reluctant to take, smoke curling sluggishly as though even flame feared to rise.

That evening, when the counselors thought we were distracted, I overheard them whispering near the hearth.

"She's marking the place," one said. "It's not random."

"The children," the other hissed, glancing toward us. "She's circling the children."

I pretended to stare into the flames, but my skin prickled with every word.

THE THIRD NIGHT

We did not even pretend to sleep. Blankets wrapped tight, eyes wide, we waited. The loft was suffused with silence so taut it hummed, every creak of timber sending us rigid.

For a time, nothing stirred. Only the wind. Only the hiss of fire.

Then—

Knock.

Knock.

Knock.

Not at the door this time.

At the wall.

Three slow raps against the boards right beneath where we lay.

The loft quaked with our stifled gasps. One of the girls clamped her hands over her mouth, her muffled sobs rattling against her palms.

The scratching followed, long trails of sound drawn upward like claws dragging through bark. The frost thickened across the beams. Our breath misted the air, white in the dark.

And then—silence.

We stared at the window, waiting for her hand, her shadow, her face. But nothing came.

Instead, from above the roof, the sound began.

A slow, steady pacing.

Footsteps.

Back and forth. Back and forth. Each step measured, heavy despite the snow. Sometimes pausing directly overhead, so close the rafters trembled with the weight.

We lay paralyzed beneath her tread, listening until our minds filled with the rhythm. A lullaby of footsteps, keeping time with our racing hearts.

And just before dawn, a single sound split the air—not a knock, not a scratch, but a long, low wail. Mournful. Endless. It seeped into the wood, into our bones, until silence became unbearable.

When morning finally came, the roof bore proof of what we had heard: deep impressions in the snow, like footprints, yet stretched too long, too narrow to be human.

She had walked above us all night.

EPILOGUE

We left the cabin at dawn. None of us spoke as we trudged through the snow, our boots sinking into the silence of the forest. The counselors led us quickly, almost frantically, as though afraid the trees themselves might close in if we lingered.

When the cabin was finally lost behind the pines, I dared one last glance back. For a moment I thought I saw her at the edge of the clearing, a pale shape, still, watching. But perhaps it was only the sun on the snow. Perhaps.

We never spoke of it again. Not at camp, not on the long ride home, not in the years that followed. One by one, we grew older, went our separate ways. Some of us drifted out of contact, though every so often I'd hear a name, a rumor—one boy who never slept through the night again, another who refused to go near a forest.

And me? I tried to bury it. I told myself it had been a story, a shared dream, a trick of shadows and fear. But stories don't leave blood on doors. Dreams don't carve scratches into skin. And shadows don't press hands of frost against the glass.

Sometimes, even now, in the depths of winter when the world falls silent, I hear it again. Faint at first, as though carried on the wind.

Knock. Knock. Knock.

Always three.

And then the rhyme, whispered in the back of my mind, as inevitable as breath:

> *Knock, knock, knock — the White Lady calls,*
> *Her shadow creeps along the walls.*
> *Beware if you don't open the door,*
> *She'll leave her mark forevermore.*

I try to convince myself it's a memory. Nothing more. But when the air grows colder, when frost blooms across the glass though no storm rages outside, I know better. Because once you've heard her call, she never truly leaves you.

WATCH WHAT YOU WEAR

S.J. KING

"Jack...?"

I call as I enter the apartment, slinging my keys on the kitchen counter. He's cleared up for once, before I get home. Usually, a slew of crumbs and smears. But I'd warned him. *Next time, I'll kill you.* Then I'd grin. 'Better than a slow death,' he'd say under his breath. And I'd ask him to repeat it, but he wouldn't. He'd kiss me on the cheek and slouch off.

Now I can see the evidence that he's taken the gift of my feedback. Although I rather like that he's wormed his way into living in my apartment, even if it's mainly at my cost, and I love him – I do. He's just not... entirely house-trained yet.

"Jack...?" I call again. He doesn't always answer. Headphones on, gaming on the couch. But usually there's the click-click-click of the controller. There'll be a 'yeah' or 'hell no!' Today I listen. Nothing. The first thing I usually see of him is his feet up on the coffee table. Shoes on. Cushion under for comfort. I step around the corner.

No shoes.

No legs.

No Jack.

"Strange," I say into the empty room. Not even a dent in the sofa where he's sat.

I go to the bedroom. Right, well, he's not *that* good. The bed is still unmade; a ruffle of our sleep and then my 'oh shit, the alarm didn't go off,' haste this morning. Jack had pulled the pillow over his head as I huffed my way around the room, turning the light on, getting dressed, stomping out to the bathroom, and attempting to put mascara on as I brushed my teeth. I called back to him with a mouthful of foam and black streaks on my eyelid. Always a disaster when I rush. Jack tells me that when I go too fast, it takes twice as long. But that's where we differ. He's soooo slow. So considered. Except when he's on that damned game, Rocket League or whatever it is. Or when his mates call him up for a beer. Then he moves like a demon.

No sign of Jack now.

But then I see it. Out of the corner of my eye. Hanging there like a corpse.

The dress. Pale blue. Ruffs and a white ribbon at the waist. My Halloween costume. At least, one half of it. Maybe the other half – *his* half – is missing because he's putting it on as we speak.

"Jack," I say, barreling into the bathroom.

A good reason to formalize this relationship further would be that with the money from his rent, I could renovate this damned bathroom. Olive-green is *so* 80s. It's offensive. At least I threw away the fluffy toilet rug when I moved in, but the rest had to stay. Stretching to new fittings was not easy with my mortgage payments. That's where he is, at his place. Because there's no trace of his aftershave or his socks.

So, where is he with the other half of our brilliant costume? The Shining twins. I said he'd look *great* in a dress. Besides, it's not really a party piece for one. I did worry if I'd made a mistake. When I remembered, I realized he actually had a twin. Well, estranged. They fell out a few years back. Jack said he started acting weird. Which is sad, really. I've never met him.

I tug out my phone. "Where are you?" I say as I type in the message.

He *could* still be at work. It's possible. Emergency graphics that AI couldn't quite master. He's been so despondent since they rolled out... what was it? Firefly and RenderForest. I get it. You spend years doing a degree, and some dicks in Silicon Valley replace you with a word prompt. But it's not my fault. I've tried to give helpful suggestions, but he says I'm not helping. Meanwhile, his workmate got fired. Not replaced. Apparently, he was using AI to hack people's personal info on their phones. Not good.

After ten minutes, Jack hasn't replied. *Typical.* He's on his phone when we're talking, or watching a movie, or at dinner. And yet when I need him, he *never* seems to have it to hand.

I go back into the living room, and that's when I notice that the photo of us on the windowsill is missing. A thrum of something. Like my senses pick up on signals before my brain can quite collate them. Something about the bedroom. Or was it the bathroom? Things were *too* tidy.

I hurry back through the apartment. His towel is not on the rail (or the floor!). His toothbrush is not in the holder. No deodorant or hair products. (It's incredible the amount of hair product needed to make hair look unbrushed.) In the bedroom, no clothes on the floor. In the wardrobe where his clothes hang, the stuffed bear he bought me has its heart literally ripped out.

"Jack!" I call his name. More annoyed. Silence. "Jack!" I stamp my foot. I'm not a diva, but seriously, has my boyfriend left me? Have you taken one half of The Shining twins and gone?

I feel sick. I feel afraid. I'm in a lift plummeting towards earth. *No!* I mean, I get on his case, but I love him. *Love him.* We were going to get married. Hadn't talked about it, but come on... we were definitely on that waitlist. What about our holiday last year, the beautiful, secluded cove at Polridmouth? I was sure when we stood at sunset, and I asked him if he knew this was the inspiration for Rebecca, and he said he did. That could have been THE moment. It wasn't. It was someone else's, just down on the beach. And Jack said 'cringe' or words to that effect. But I knew he was thinking it, and I'd fall in love with him just a little bit more, knowing one day it *would* be us. Crumbs, smears, unmade beds, olive-bathrooms, and every last unreturned call.

Until now. Because he's left me. With half a twin costume. One blue Shining girl dress.

I call his phone. No answer. It goes to voicemail. An angry groan spirals up from the pit of my stomach. "Ugh, I hate you!" I stated before hanging off. No one listens to voicemail. He won't hear it. But I'm crying now, in a blind panic. I can't believe this is happening. Me. Jack. We're not perfect, but he pairs my socks, bakes the nicest banana bread, and sometimes on Sundays, he brings me tea in bed. And the way he calls me 'Lison'. Short for Alison. '*Listen*,' he says. So, I go quiet and listen. 'What?' I say when I hear nothing. 'What are you doing?' he asks. 'Listening...' Then I realise, same old joke. He laughs. Thinks he's hysterical. I smack him with the nearest cushion. See? Love, right there.

Who's going to call me 'Lison' now?

I plomp down on the sofa. *I don't hate you,* I text. Not that he'll bother listening to the message. *Can we talk? Please.*

Three dots appear. I sit forward. Something. Hope.

Nothing.

Then I look down and spot his favourite game chip – *Zelda* – sticking out from under the coffee table. A spot of ketchup from a sandwich that's landed beside it. I hold it in my hand, ready to snap it in half. Then I think, *you want it back? Come talk to me* before stuffing it in my bra.

I think of the party. I'm not in the mood for it now. Like, I'm going to go as one twin; how stupid would that be? Then my phone pings. *Don't come to the party,* his message states.

Oh, so that's how we're playing it, is it, Jack? Well, I think not.

ONE HALF OF THE SHINING TWINS RINGS THE DOORBELL. A bottle of cheap Tequila under one arm. Open, admittedly. I'll say my invisible twin did it. The way I'm feeling, that invisible sibling is going to do a lot of regrettable things.

The house is large and looming. No one comes to answer, so I open the door myself. Inside, it's already thrumming. Fake webs, skeletons, flashing eyeballs, and jack-o-lanterns make the space festive. There's a man with a rope around his neck, another with a white face and blackened eyes, the TikTok logo on his t-shirt.

"What are you?" I ask.

"I'm a TikTok challenge gone wrong."

I find myself wearing a look of distaste. Not funny, although smart.

So where's Jack? Where is my evil twin? He has a lot to answer for. I swig another mouthful of Tequila.

Then I push through, surprised by how many people have A: made the effort. And B: are already here. It's not even nine. It took me a little longer to get ready. I had to apply a lot of foundation to my face to cover up the crying. Afterward, I realized I should have used white make-up, but either way, I wasn't giving Jack the satisfaction of seeing how puffy he could make my face. I look around, but don't recognize anyone. It could be rent-a-crowd.

Then I stop. A guy beside me is shotgunning his girlfriend with a joint. Then they giggle and kiss.

"Get a room," I say. I'm in no mood for someone else's happy couple act. They look at me, confused.

"Chill," he says, and they both smile, unfocused eyes. Kiss again: I'm sure it's longer just to annoy me. Then they slink away.

Only then, as I stand on the cusp of someone else's living room, does the thought occur to me. What if Jack is here with someone else? What if that's why he didn't want me to come? Why did he take the costume? Oh my god, I would die. The Shining Triplets is not what I want to be part of tonight. What would I do? Die or kill? The thought terrifies me. I turn. It was a mistake to come. I should go home. Take my cheap Tequila and doom-scroll myself towards dawn, alone.

That's when I see him standing there, back to me. A single bloody handprint on the back of his dress.

I rush forward, spinning him around. But the face that greets me is not Jack. A fleeting scowl as he searches my face. If I hadn't been small and with a bow in my hair, shoes like a schoolgirl, I swear he might have punched me. Then the anger drains from his face, and he grins. He's a bit like Zac Efron, with a mix of stubble and a light goatee. Soft brown eyes, long lashes. A feeling I recognize him.

"Shit, I'm sorry. I thought you were my boyfriend."

"I've been accused of worse," he jokes.

"Actually, you haven't. He's an arse. A shit. A loser. And he left me. Tonight actually. And he's here..." I crane to see inside the room. "...Somewhere. Have you seen someone who... well, looks like us?"

"Two's company." He smirks, dusky eyes; slugs from his Solo cup. Inside his stubble, he's smeared his lips with fake blood.. I notice inside that he has stubble and smeared his lips with fake blood. "I'm glad you can't find him," he says.

"And where's your other half?" I indicate the crowded room inside. "Is she in there? Sorry, I assume it's a she."

"I ate her," he says. He points to his bloodied mouth.

I don't know how to answer.

"I thought it was funny. One twin, ate the other. I guess either too clever or just dumb, right?"

"Just dumb." I hold up my tequila bottle. "But I'll give you a top-up for effort." I fill his cup, take a slug from the bottle myself. "By the way, someone ruined your dress. You've a..." I tug it around, but I can't get him to see. "Bloody handprint. On the back. I guess it happened when..."

"Probably when I was eating her." He smiles. Raises his eyebrows. There's something delicious about the glint in his eyes. I know I'm slightly drunk and very dumped, and angry and hurt, and maybe about as vulnerable as I can be, which is not the best time to be suckered in by a man in a dress, but it's Halloween and he's cute and we're twinning... so...

"Probably," I say in echo to his word, and lower my head as I blush. A coy smile creeps across my lips at his probably slightly indecent line.

WE DANCE. TALK. LAUGH. HE GETS ME. THIS MAY BE THE gift that Halloween gives. I met Jack at Halloween, two years ago. That's why it's always special to us. Or was. Makes sense that he would dump me then, too. Round things out neatly. End of story.

But no, tonight is not about Jack. People take photos. Lots of photos. Of us. Me and...

"What did you say your name was?"

"Alex," he says.

"Alex," I repeat. "Wait, isn't that the name of the..." I was going to say the twin in The Shining, one or both, but Alex—maybe not Alex—spins me around to the music.

Someone has a Polaroid. More photos. We win the people's choice. Everyone stands in a semi-circle and claps as they hand us a little gold plastic skeleton trophy. Alex-Maybe lifts my hand over our heads as if we are the champions of the universe. He moves in to kiss me. I shift.

More shots. More polaroids. That click and whir and flap. There are little versions of us all over the place now. On shelves, beside empty bottles, broken Solo cups. The only thing that makes me a little apprehensive is that Alex-Maybe keeps shifting

S.J. KING

his head and is blurred in every last picture. As if he's not really here. As if he's a ghost. Not that I care. If this is some spell, let it be. I can go back to being sad and alone and angry and Jack-hating tomorrow. Alex, maybe you can turn into a pumpkin at midnight (even if it's already nearly one), but tonight I'm flying on Tequila and dancing to eighties pop like I fell through a time tunnel and ended up with a young Rob Lowe-alike with a bloody mouth. When I think about Jack, I tell myself, "Who cares?" Only the numbest tug of hurt. That little locked place in my stomach where I'm keeping him with all my rage and disappoint-ment. *Not tonight, Jack.* It's going to come, but not now.

Someone pops a balloon. I focus my eyes on the corner of the room where the sound came from. My head twirls long after I stop spinning.

"Whoa," I say, realizing I've probably had just a little too much fun, and Tequila. Was it really that much? I suddenly feel really stoned. The room is emptier than I thought. Where is everyone? "I guess I should probably be getting home," I try to say.

"Probably." That delicious, mildly familiar smirk. Something about it I remember from this haze. From this confusion, Alex seems more sober than I am. "You live close by." He states it rather than asking. Or is he just asking if he could come back with me? Is it a come-on? No, I'm sure he wants to make sure I'm safe.

"Pretty close, but I should..." We're outside now. The steps were tricky. The chill is fresh at first and then instantly biting. I tug on my coat, awkwardly. For a moment, my arms are trapped. I see my breath, feel my skin. He's close. I step back. This got real. Is he going to try to kiss me? That bloodied mouth. No, too soon. It was fun while it lasted. I want to go home. I point a thumb in the vague direction. "It was nice," I say. "Maybe I'll see you..." I mumble.

"You will," he says.

I try to say something more, but I can't; I find myself walk-

72

ing. My eyes fixed on my unsteady feet. He stays on the path behind me. It's late. Almost two. My mind is serving up memories from the evening. Light embarrassment; did I really say that? I was thinking about how I tried to mingle, but Alex was stuck to me like glue. 'We're twins,' he said, gripping my hand. 'We're always meant to be together.' Slightly cringe, Jack would say. Stop flirting, Alex said when I spoke to someone else. Was I? Alex-Maybe wanted all my attention. Turned out his name was not Alex but Patrick. 'As in Bateman,' he'd said. 'As in American Psycho,' he'd said. His eyes meet mine. 'You don't remember?' he'd said more seriously. Lost in the blur. Just need to get home. And what was it he thought I had forgotten...?

Now I pull my phone from my pocket. No message from Jack; last one marked unread. "I hate you Jack," I whisper under my cold, white breath.

I should have brought Alex back. Tomorrow, when Jack calls – if he calls – he'd hear him in the background. No, I don't want that. My head reels. I want to make it work with Jack. Until tonight, I thought I loved him, thought he loved me. I'm probably an uptight bitch sometimes, but I thought we had fun. I felt we laughed and loved and were stupid and slowly but surely were building something together.

What's that? A noise. Something behind me.

Firstly, I become aware of my cold tears on my lips. I'm crying. Then I hear the sound again. A crunch. Another. Footsteps. I look around, and the streetlight prisms across my damp eyelashes, my blurry vision. The shape is coming quickly and closely. A guy in a dress, lumbering towards me.

"Alex!" I say, a little surprised, unnerved to see him here. "I thought you-"I try smiling.

His head twitches. Almost glitches. "What did you think? I'd just go home, without you... again...?"

"I don't... understand," I stammer. I feel my heart racing. Feel my fingers encircling my phone. How can I dial an emergency number without having to pull it out of my pocket? He'll see. Because something's not right. *You don't remember...* Does he think he knows me?

This guy at work. Got into all our phones.

Yeah, my twin. He went a little crazy at my ex. I thought that was out of order.

Then I look at the dress. Why hadn't I seen it earlier? It's not a similar dress to mine; it's precisely the same. *Don't come to the party.* Was that Jack trying to warn me? When I'd asked him where he had got it, he'd said it was a knock-off. Was that a reference? Knocked off Jack... Has he done something to him? Oh God, no!

No, that's crazy. Jack packed up his stuff and left. He went. I'm confusing things. Then I think of the Zelda-chip. Would he really have left it? His favourite. In a hurry. Or had someone packed up his stuff for him? Torn out the bear's heart.

No. It's easier to think this guy is insane than that the love of my life left me. Alex/Patrick just wants to make sure I get home safely. Doesn't he?

"So, you want to walk me home?" I say, stilling my thundering heart. "Is that it?"

"Home? Sure. Something like that."

Something... No, his eyes glint differently now. He wants something else.

I need to stay calm. I need him to not know I know.

I see the blood, dried and caked around his mouth. Maybe it's not fake?

Things get slower. I feel the fear, the cold panic. As I walk. One foot in front of the other. My breath is hardly flowing. I'm drifting, not walking. Hard to stay focused. But it gets darker here. I know this patch. The houses are further from the road, and there's a deserted play-park. No cars. Anything could happen. No one would know. If I'm going to shirk him off, it has to be now.

"You know," I say, mustering courage. "I think it's a bad

idea." I run a hand through my hair. The ribbon – miraculous that it stayed in all evening – comes away in my fingers.

"What is?"

"This," I point between us.

"And *what* is *this?*"

I feel my tight breaths. Short. Panting. Hard... to... breathe... The lightness in my head. What do I do? Keep walking. Stop walking. Scream now. Run. He's big. He'll stop me. Instead, I feel like I might faint. Heavy-footed. Rooted. No strength in my muscles. Like one of those nightmares, I can't shake it off. Where is funny Alex? Where are his jokes, his soft eyes, his flirtatious light-side-of-rude comments? I feel my stomach lurch, shift.

I puke onto the sidewalk. Something horrific and Exorcist-like. I drag my hand across my mouth and look up. He's scowling, put off. But what about Jack? I need to know where he is.

This is ridiculous. You meet some random dude at a party, and somehow you think it's all staged. That he's abducted your boyfriend, cleared out his stuff, and then managed – instantly managed – to fool you into liking him. Could you be that predictable?

I start walking, instead of stumbling. My black shoes kick on the pathway. If I could just find a rock. Something.

"I don't *need* you to walk me!" I say more firmly. Keys between my fingers. Where's that bottle of Tequila now?

He stops in his tracks. I keep walking. Good, he's got the message. I'm coming into the dark patch, and he's still there, under the light, behind me. I can see his breath when I glance back. In the shadow, against the streetlight. A triangle of white that frames him perfectly. Silhouette. Like he's smoking. Tall, shadowy, almost comical in his short dress.

Or terrifying. I'll go with terrifying.

Now I'm deep into the darkest part, I can see the lights on the far side of the trees; I just need to get there. There's an intersection, maybe a car. But when I glance back, he's moving slowly and steadily, but he's coming.

Shit!

Run!

I start running. I'm not fluid or fast, but I'm not going to stop.

I glance back, and he's closing the gap. He's going to catch up.

"I just want to make sure you get home safely," he insists. There's something almost plaintive in his voice. "I want to protect you."

Protect me from what?

He's going to catch me. And I've misread it. I know I have.

"Listen. Wait." I say. I stop.

He's right there. He's panting, bends down, hands on his knees. He looks up, revealing a maniacal red grin and white teeth.

"Listen," he says. "I just want a chance to..."

Did he say 'listen' or 'Lison'? Is he using the name that Jack uses? The way he says it.

My head is going a million miles an hour. I know I'm not safe now. But screaming is no good here. It's dark and far, and before anyone can get to me, he will. He'll silence me. Maybe forever. The only way forward is to reason.

I laugh. Feign drunk. Or drugged. I'm frighteningly sober now. "You look like you're going to propose."

He tips his head again. "What?"

"Standing like that. That's how Jack stood, when I thought he was going to."

"In Polridmouth?"

Bingo. I know he knows. I know he knows everything. No chances. He's read my messages. Been in my life. Only told my girlfriends about that.

'Lison?' he says again. He knows what Jack calls me. *Lison.* What else does he know? Has he even been to where I live today? But I have to keep calm. Do I walk on? The other way, there's more light, more life. Back where we came from. If I can just get us to turn around.

"You know what," I say. Hard to steady my voice. Hard to get the words out in one piece. Racing pulse. "It might be weird going back to mine. You know... What about..." I hesitate. "Yours...?"

His eyes shift; part suspicious, part hungry. More colours flicker in them, even in the dark. He likes that. He likes my idea. I can buy myself time.

"Mine...?"

I nod.

He grins excitedly. "Sure." He turns. Then he grabs my hand. I squeal, but don't scream. Just a little further. And I've got the keys between my fingers. Sooner or later, a car will pass, and I can lash at him, jump out.

But then we're back at the house, with the jack-o-lanterns on the step, and webbing. The house where the party was.

"This is your place?"

He nods.

It stands alone on the street. Still no chance to scream. Even more at his mercy. He's got me now, but if I go inside? Maybe there's still someone in there. Someone sleeping on the couch. Someone dancing like a zombie to old eighties pop. Something I can strike him with. Each step feels like forever. Each step feels like the worst decision I've ever made. I recall the rooms and think of something I saw that I could use.

Inside, it's quiet. A post-apocalypse of a party. Disco lights whirling to no music, the haunted house at the funfair. I catch my terrified reflection in the mirror. He grips my hand and leads me towards the stairs. I need to do something, *right now!*

"Wait. I'm... shy. Can we just... get another drink?"

"You slept with Jack the first night!" He accuses.

"You know that too?" I say, my head dipping. "Look, there's another bottle of tequila." I make my voice light and fun. Play-acting for my life. "One more shot, how about it? Settle my nerves." I wriggle my hand free of his.

"I was here that night. *Remember?* The night you met Jack. You met me too. No, you... don't even remember. But I watched you then. And I've watched you ever since."

"Oh..." I say slowly, holding the tequila bottle, unscrewing the lid. "Then I made a mistake, picked the wrong guy." I swing coyly in my dress. Take a whole mouthful of Tequila, hold it there, grin.

He comes forward, and I spit it at him. All of it. It bursts onto his face, burning liquid into his eyes. His hands rush up, the blood at his mouth, dripping pink onto his blue dress. I've barely a second until he recovers. He'll be furious. Is there a lighter anywhere?

No.

Frantically, I screw the lid back on the bottle and swing it at his head.

Strike!

He teeters but doesn't fall.

I swing again.

Strike two!

He looms forward, then rocks back. Then he falls, gripping his head, writhing on the floor. But he's not out, not yet. His hands thrust out to grab my ankle.

I hear something faint. 'Lison!' I listen to it again. 'Lison!'

Oh my God. *It's Jack!* He's here.

I reach behind me and grab a knife. I've no idea what I will do with it, and it's more dangerous to me than anyone else. Then I spot it, in the corner. A Dyson! I drop the knife on the counter, spin the Dyson around so I am holding the brush end, and then I swing.

Smack! *Strike three.* The heavy handle makes contact, and he's out. His eyes flip back, gone, for now. Blood at his mouth. Real blood. His...

'Jack?' I call out.

'Lison...?'

I follow the sound of his voice, up the stairs, hand on the banister, into a dark bedroom. I find Jack tied up. A gag he's managed to wriggle free of.

'Oh my God, Jack. What the hell? We have to get out of here.' His eye is blackened; he looks like he's been beaten.

'And call the police," he says. "That guy is crazy.'

'How do you know him?' I think of his twin brother, or maybe that colleague who was fired.

'Me? I've never seen him before in my life.'

What had Alex said? He'd seen me the night I met Jack. And watched me ever since.

I shudder.

'Wait, what's that on your cheek?' I ask.

Jack's hand goes to his face, but he can barely touch it. It's swollen and bloodied. 'He bit me,' he says.

I think of the handprint on the back of Alex's dress. It was Jack's. *Where's your twin*, I had asked. *I ate her,* he'd said. And I had laughed. It looks like he actually tried to eat Jack. That was real blood around his mouth. Where I had considered kissing him...

"I'm sorry, Jack. I love you." I throw my arms around his neck and kiss him. "Wait. I can prove it." I reach into my bra and pull out the Zelda chip. "Kept it close to my heart," I joke. "Now, let's fucking run!"

THE POLICE CAME TO OUR APARTMENT. SAID BY THE TIME they got to the house, there was no one there. The place was a mess but deserted. The owners are away. No trace of who broke in.

We moved after that. Bought our first place together. We replaced all our devices and took steps to ensure no one could track us or read our communications. Jack's old workmate helped test that it was secure.

Still, at night, I had nightmares. In the dark, *he* was waiting.

It was October when I got the first random message. **Costume Party. You're invited.** But the number was withheld. *This year, why don't you come as Dani and Christian?*

Midsommar. We'd just watched that movie. Where she is crowned, and he is tied to a bearskin and burned alive. A day later, a new message, a different number. *I know you want out of that toxic relationship. And I'm here. This time, I'll make sure you never forget me!*

HIDE AND SEEK

ELLIS HART

Martin always took his shoes off at the door; it was a non-negotiable for his wife, Amy. As he slips out of his shoes, Martin notices a foreign set of boots, still muddy and wet from the raging storm outside. Meanwhile, next to these boots, sit Amy's favorite sneakers. A guttural scream erupts from Martin's throat as he dashes deeper into the house, panic heightening his senses. He tries to focus but fails as the image of his wife's left foot, severed just above the ankle, still rests within her shoe. Tied with filthy, fraying twine, a note hangs loosely from the limb – "the first body part will be the easiest to find... let the game begin."

DEAD LINE

ALESSANDRA BENINI

T he thrift store smelled of dust and aged paper; the air was thick with the scent of forgotten lives. It was a big place—the kind where one could easily lose hours exploring, wandering through aisles crammed with oddities from different eras. The walls were painted a pale yellow, lending an unexpected coziness despite the clutter. Mirrors were everywhere—some leaning against shelves, others hung in mismatched frames—but one in particular always caught Silvia's eye.

It was huge, unmistakably vintage—perhaps even more than a hundred years old. Its frame was surrounded by gilded flowers dipped in gold—or maybe they were made of solid gold; Silvia could never tell with such things. She had seen the mirror every time she came in over the last three months. Hard to miss, she figured, and difficult to sell—not just because of its size, but because it was heavy and probably expensive too. She always spent time admiring it; it was clearly out of the average shopper's budget. Still, it remained, reflecting the store's mess of forgotten treasures and her own image whenever she passed by.

Silvia had always loved thrift and antique shops. There was something comforting about them—a quiet escape from the

noise in her own head. She enjoyed taking her time and imagining the lives of the people who once owned these objects—
who had read the books, worn the jewelry, and wound the clocks.
It made her feel connected to something bigger, as if she were
piecing together stories from lost chapters. In places like this,
she wasn't burdened by her own troubles; she was merely an
observer, slipping in and out of the past with every object that
caught her attention.

She wasn't looking for anything in particular—never really. It
was just another way to pass the time, another excuse to be
anywhere but trapped in her own thoughts.

Her fingers traced along the spines of forgotten books when
something familiar caught her eye:

An old, landline telephone.

It was clearly from the late '70s or maybe the early '80s—the
kind that belonged in childhood memories, when phones had
weight and answering one felt like a small event. It was a black,
rotary phone, its coiled cord lying limp and unplugged. The sight
of it stirred something in her—a pang of nostalgia mixed with
unease. She had grown up with a phone just like it. Her mother
used to sit at the kitchen table, twirling the cord around her
finger, a cigarette smoldering in the ashtray beside her. Silvia
would listen in on hushed conversations she wasn't meant to
hear—stories murmured through the receiver that she would
carry in the back of her mind for years.

She stepped closer. The plastic was smooth under her fingertips, cool to the touch. The dial felt stiff as she nudged it. No
dust clung to its surface, unlike everything else around it. It was
almost as if someone had just placed it there.

"You have an eye for the strange," a voice broke through her
thoughts.

Startled, Silvia turned to see the shopkeeper watching her.
He was an older, wiry man, his face lined by time and his gaze
lingering just a second too long as he leaned against the counter
with his arms crossed.

"It's an odd piece, isn't it?" he continued. "It came in without a tag."

Silvia glanced back at the phone. "Does it work?"

The shopkeeper shrugged. "No plug, no power. But things like that don't always follow the rules."

Was it a joke—or something else? She couldn't quite tell.

Something in her gut told her to leave it alone, yet she rationalized the purchase, thinking it would look cool with her vintage decor at home.

"I'll take it.

———

SILVIA CARRIED THE PHONE HOME IN ITS CARDBOARD BOX, tucking it under her arm as she unlocked her apartment door. Her place was small but cozy, filled with thrifted furniture and secondhand treasures—a mid-century coffee table, a faded Persian rug, and an old wooden bookshelf crammed with well-loved books that made the space feel warm. She lived alone, and although she liked it that way, the quiet sometimes settled too thickly, as if the walls were pressing in.

Working as a freelance editor, she spent most of her days buried in manuscripts and forgotten words, fixing sentences until they made sense. It was a solitary job that allowed her to stay home in pajamas, which she preferred; too much noise and too many people always became exhausting. While she could handle brief doses of the outside world, home was where she felt safest.

Setting the box on the kitchen counter, she pulled the phone out and turned it over in her hands. It looked even older in her apartment—as if it belonged to another time entirely. Without thinking, she set it on the small side table by the couch, right next to her record player. It fit in perfectly, as if it had always been there.

She sighed, rolled her shoulders, and then went to the

kitchen to pour herself a glass of wine. She had barely taken a sip when she heard it:

The unmistakable sound of a rotary phone ringing.

Silvia froze. The phone was unplugged—she knew it was. Her grip tightened around the wine glass as the chilled rim pressed into her fingers. Slowly, she turned, her eyes fixed on the phone sitting on the side table. The rotary dial stared back at her, unmoving, while the ringing continued—shrill and insistent, cutting through the heavy silence of her apartment.

Her mind scrambled for a rational explanation. Perhaps the sound was coming from somewhere outside—a neighbor's landline? An old recording playing on the TV? But there was no TV on, and she recognized that sound; it was coming from that phone.

She carefully set the glass down on the counter and took hesitant steps toward the table. With every step, the sound seemed to burrow deeper into her chest, making the air feel tight. Finally, she stopped just in front of it, staring down at the receiver. The ringing did not stop.

"This is ridiculous. It must be an elaborate prank," she thought.

With a deep breath, she reached out and lifted the handset. The ringing stopped immediately, leaving only silence. Holding the phone to her ear, she half-expected static, a dial tone— anything—but there was nothing.

Then—

A breath. Soft, slow, deliberate.

Someone—something—was on the other end.

Silvia's stomach twisted, and her fingers tightened on the receiver. "Hello?" she whispered. There was nothing but more slow, steady breathing, as if whoever—or whatever—was there, had all the time in the world.

Her skin prickled. "Who is this?" she demanded, trying to sound firm, though her trembling voice betrayed her. The breath hitched, almost like a quiet chuckle. Then, in a voice barely above a whisper, came a hesitant question: "Hello? Is someone there?" It was a man's voice, distant and laced with surprise and confusion—as if he hadn't expected anyone on the other side. Soft static crackled, as though he were speaking from far away.

A sharp click, and the line went dead.

Silvia yanked the phone away from her ear, her pulse hammering against her ribs. She stared at the receiver in her hand, her thoughts racing. That wasn't possible—the phone wasn't connected to anything. And yet, it had rung. Someone had answered, and they sounded lost. But who were they? And why did they sound so confused?

With shaky hands, she placed the receiver back on its cradle and stepped away from the phone, as if fearing it might spring to life again. Perhaps it had batteries; she turned it over, searching for a compartment or hidden panel—anything that could explain how it had rung without being plugged in. But there was nothing.

The room felt different now—heavier, as if the very air were pressing down on her. Maybe she was imagining things. Yes, that must be it. Perhaps she was just tired. Or maybe—just maybe—she had brought something home that should have remained forgotten.

THE NEXT MORNING, SILVIA SAT AT HER DESK WITH HER laptop open, typing variations of "old rotary phone ringing unplugged" into search engines. The results were disappointing —mostly forum threads about urban legends, ghost stories, and the occasional prank setup. Nothing explained what had happened.

Frustrated, she decided to take the phone to a repair shop. The technician—a middle-aged man with thick glasses—examined it closely. "This is the real deal," he said, turning it over in his hands. "No batteries, no internal power source. Just an old-school phone. It shouldn't be able to ring without being plugged in." He eyed Silvia skeptically, like he wasn't sure she was actually serious.

That only deepened Silvia's unease. Hoping for more information, she returned to the thrift store. The shopkeeper was absent, but an older woman—whom Silvia recognized immediately by her white hair, big round glasses, and kind blue eyes—was behind the counter, arranging a small display of antique clocks.

When the woman looked up and adjusted her glasses upon seeing Silvia, after listening to her question about it, she said, "Oh, that phone? Yes, I remember. A man dropped it off a few days ago. He seemed... unsettled. I asked if he wanted to leave his name, but he just shook his head and walked out. He said he didn't want it anymore—that it brought nothing but trouble."

Leaning against the counter, Silvia asked, "Did he say anything else? What kind of trouble?"

The woman hesitated, as if weighing her words. "He looked tired—as if he hadn't slept in days—and he kept glancing over his shoulder, as if someone were following him. I asked if he was alright, but he just muttered something under his breath and left."

A chill crawled up Silvia's spine. "Do you remember what he muttered?"

Exhaling deeply, as if burdened by the memory, the woman replied, "Something about it not letting go. That's all I caught before he was out the door."

Silvia swallowed hard. "Did he mention anything else? Maybe who used to own it?"

The woman shook her head. "No, but he looked so lost—like he was trying to escape something that wasn't really there." She adjusted her glasses and glanced at the phone in Silvia's hands.

Studying Silvia with eyes that were equal parts curious and concerned, the woman asked softly, "Has something happened? You look like you've seen a ghost."

Silvia hesitated before nodding. "I don't know how to explain it, but—"

"You don't have to," the woman interjected, sighing, holding up a hand. "I've seen enough in my years to know that not everything needs explaining. When you live long enough, you stop trying to fit everything into a neat little box of reason. Some things simply are."

Silvia swallowed. "You really believe that?"

The woman chuckled softly, adjusting her glasses. "Belief has nothing to do with it, dear—it's all about experience. You see enough things, hear enough stories, and watch enough people convince themselves they imagined what they saw... eventually, you stop questioning and start accepting. Some objects hold on to what was left behind." She paused, searching Silvia's eyes. "You look just as unsettled as he did. Be careful with that thing," she warned in a lower tone. "Objects—especially old ones—can absorb energy, emotions, memories, and sometimes even... people. Just as places can be haunted, objects can hold onto something, too. A phone, in particular, carries voices; people pour their emotions into them. And sometimes, something lingers—entities, spirits, whatever you want to call them—that attach themselves to things, especially when there's unfinished business."

Silvia wanted to dismiss it as eccentric talk—too incredible, too far-fetched to take seriously. But she couldn't deny what had happened the previous night. The phone had rung, a voice had spoken, and she still questioned whether it had all been imagined.

"I know it's a lot to take in," the woman said, watching Silvia carefully. "That's how it starts. First, you question it. Then you try to explain it away. But eventually, you realize some things don't care whether you believe in them or not."

Silvia left the thrift store with more questions than answers, the weight of the old woman's words settling deep in her chest. Stepping onto the sidewalk, she noticed the wind had picked up, rustling dry leaves along the pavement. Clutching the phone tighter in her bag, she resisted the urge to look at it.

Back at home, she placed the phone on the side table and stared at it warily. It sat there—silent and unmoving—yet it seemed to be waiting. The thought made her uneasy.

That night, sleep eluded her. She tossed and turned, the weight of uncertainty pressing on her mind. Eventually, she dozed off, but it wasn't restful. In the early hours of the morning, a sound stirred her awake.

The phone was ringing again.

Silvia bolted upright, her heart pounding. She stared at it, her pulse thudding in her ears. The same shrill, mechanical chime filled the room, shattering the heavy silence. Though every instinct urged her to ignore it, something—curiosity, dread, maybe even obligation—compelled her forward.

She picked up the receiver.

Silence greeted her. But this time, it wasn't just silence—it was accompanied by a rustling sound, like someone shifting on the other end. Then came a man's voice, distant and heavy with uncertainty:

"Where... where am I? Do you know? Can you help? I need help."

Silvia's fingers clenched the receiver. "Who are you?" she asked, her voice barely steady.

Static crackled through the line, and then, finally, the man said, "I don't know. I can't remember."

A moment later, the line went dead.

Silvia sat frozen, the receiver still pressed against her ear as if expecting something more. But there was only silence. Slowly, she lowered the handset back onto its cradle, her mind racing. Her breath was shallow, her body tense—the voice had sounded so real, so lost.

Her rational mind searched for an explanation. Perhaps it was radio interference, or a strange glitch? But the line was dead, and the repair shop had confirmed that the phone shouldn't work without being plugged in.

She ran a hand through her hair and exhaled sharply. She needed to know more. Sleep was no longer an option.

Determined to trace the phone's origin, Silvia examined it more closely. Beneath the plastic center of the rotary dial, she noticed a small, yellowed piece of paper with edges curled by age. Carefully, she pried it out, revealing a faded phone number, barely legible after years of wear. Her fingers trembled as she entered the number into an online reverse phone lookup service. It was a long shot, but she had to try.

After a few moments, the search returned a result: the number had once been registered to an address across town in 1985. A shiver ran through her as she clicked further, uncovering records linked to the property. The home had belonged to a man named Roderick Rice.

Staring at the screen, her heart pounding, Silvia thought, This is it. This is him. And this is his phone. And now—somehow, impossibly—he was calling again.

The next morning, she scoured online archives for missing persons reports and obituaries—anything that might shed light on Roderick. Hours passed until, just as she was about to give up, she found something: an old newspaper clipping. An elderly man by that name had died alone in his apartment. His daughter had been trying to reach him, but by the time someone checked on him, it was too late. He'd been dead for three days.

Her stomach twisted. Then she noticed a mention of his few remaining belongings. Scrolling further, she found a grainy black-and-white photo of the man's small, sparsely furnished home. On a small table near the window sat a rotary phone—the very same phone.

Yet the questions remained: Why did it still ring? Why did he sound so lost? And now, he was calling from it. Had he been waiting for his daughter's call all along? How was this even possible?

As if in answer to her thoughts, the phone rang again.

Silvia hesitated only a moment before picking up the receiver. This time, she wasn't driven by fear alone—she wanted to understand.

"Hello?" she said carefully.

Static returned, crackling softly in her ear. Then the man's voice, hesitant: "Hello? Are you there?"

"I'm here," Silvia replied. "Who are you?"

After a long pause came, "I... don't know. I think—I think I was supposed to wait for something. But it's been so long."

Silvia swallowed, gripping the phone tighter. "Do you remember anything? Your name? Where you are?"

The voice faltered, as if searching through a fog of lost memories. "Everything is—fuzzy. I keep waiting, but I don't know what for."

Something about the raw uncertainty in his voice made Silvia's heart ache. He didn't sound sinister; he sounded human.

"Does the name Roderick mean anything to you?" Silvia asked.

After a long pause, the voice replied, "I think... that's my name."

"Roderick," she said, testing the name to ground him. "You had a daughter, didn't you? She used to call you."

More static, then barely a whisper: "My daughter. Yes. She— she was supposed to call me. But she never did."

Silvia closed her eyes and exhaled shakily. "She did, Roderick. She called. You just... you didn't get to answer."

Silence stretched over the line, followed by a trembling inhale—as if realization were sinking in.

"Then why am I still here?" he asked, his voice breaking.

Silvia had no ready answer, yet something in her told her that perhaps she could help him find one.

SILVIA'S HAND TREMBLED AS SHE SET THE PHONE BACK ON THE side table. The unanswered question—"Then why am I still here?"—echoed in her mind, a lingering plea.

That night, sleep was a fickle visitor. She was haunted by the sound of that phone ringing in her head. In one restless dream, she found herself in a dim, dusty hallway with peeling wallpaper and creaking floors. Shadows seemed to move on their own, and in the distance, she could hear the faint, eerie ring of a rotary phone. For a split second, she even caught a glimpse of a gaunt, desperate face—Roderick's, maybe—before everything dissolved into static.

The next day, Silvia sank onto her faded sofa, her eyes fixed on the silent phone resting on the side table. The rest of the room faded into a blur—only the steady tick of the clock and the low hum of the refrigerator kept her company. She couldn't stop staring at that old rotary phone, its stillness both unnerving and oddly magnetic.

For a long minute, she simply sat there, lost in thought. Every time she recalled the desperate plea, the soft whisper of someone trapped between worlds, her heart pounded a little faster. She'd spent hours scouring old records and piecing together bits of Roderick's story, yet now the weight of it all pressed down on her in a way she hadn't expected. It wasn't just fear that gripped her—it was a deep, unsettling curiosity.

Her mind wandered as she stared at the phone. The silence was deafening, filled with all the questions she couldn't quite answer. And then, surprisingly, a thought crept in—one that both startled and intrigued her: she actually wanted the phone to ring again.

It was as if the stillness was daring her to break the silence, to bring back that eerie connection. "Just ring already," she murmured softly, half expecting the idea to vanish like a bad dream. But the more she thought about it, the more the desire grew. The ringing wasn't just noise—it was a call, a link to a past steeped in mystery and regret, a promise of answers to questions that had haunted her since the first call.

In that quiet moment, Silvia found herself torn. Part of her was terrified of what might happen if she answered again, yet another part of her craved the possibility of understanding, of reaching out to that lost soul. She wondered if maybe, just maybe, the ring would break the suffocating silence of her own life, filling it with something—even if it was a whisper from another time.

Her heart skipped as she leaned forward, her eyes never leaving the phone. The room felt charged with anticipation, the line between fear and longing blurring into something almost tangible.

THE PHONE RANG AGAIN, SLICING THROUGH THE SILENCE OF her apartment. Silvia stared at it, her pulse quickening, a mixture of dread and determination settling in her chest. She wasn't afraid this time. Not yet. She had convinced herself that Roderick was lost, that he needed help, and she could be the one to guide him. Taking a steady breath, she reached for the receiver and lifted it to her ear.

This time, she picked up without hesitation.

"Roderick?" she said carefully.

The familiar static crackled on the line, followed by his uncertain, sad voice. "Yes... I'm still here."

She exhaled, gripping the receiver. "I think you're lost. I think you... you died, Roderick. Your daughter tried to call you, but you didn't answer. Do you remember?"

There was silence. Then, slowly, "I... I don't know."

Silvia's chest ached at the helplessness in his voice. "I want to help you. I think you need to move on."

The static deepened, stretching between them like a void. Then, the voice spoke again.

"Silvia."

Her breath caught in her throat.

Ice spread through her veins. "I never told you my name."

The line went eerily quiet.

Then, the voice changed. It was no longer weak, no longer lost. A shift, subtle but unmistakable. Something darker slithered into the silence.

"Didn't you?" The tone was amused now, wrong in a way she couldn't explain, the voice deeper now.

A low, guttural growl rumbled through the receiver, so brief that she almost thought she imagined it.

Silvia's fingers trembled. "Who are you?"

The static crackled sharply, and then—

"I've been waiting for you."

A cold wave of terror crashed over her, and before she could think, she slammed the receiver down, her breath coming in sharp, panicked gasps. The phone sat in eerie silence, as if nothing had happened.

But Silvia knew.

Something else was on the other end of the line.

SILVIA SPENT THE NEXT HOUR TRYING TO CONVINCE HERSELF to leave the phone alone. She kept her laptop open, scrolling through articles she barely processed, her mind stuck on those last words: *I've been waiting for you.*

The voice had changed.

It hadn't been Roderick anymore—if it ever was.

Her apartment felt different now. The air seemed thicker, charged in a way she couldn't explain. Every creak of the walls, every rustle from outside made her flinch. She tried to tell herself it was just paranoia, but deep down, she knew better.

The phone hadn't rung again, but it didn't have to. It had already gotten under her skin.

She pushed the laptop away and rubbed her face with both hands. She needed sleep. A clear head. Maybe in the morning, things would make more sense.

She stood and hesitated before glancing at the phone again. It looked normal. Just an old, outdated thing sitting quietly on the side table.

It's just an object, she told herself. *It only has power if I let it.*

Still, she turned it so the receiver faced the wall before heading to her bedroom.

She barely slept.

At some point in the night, a sound pulled her out of a restless haze.

Not ringing.

A **click.**

Like a receiver being lifted.

Her eyes flew open, heart hammering. She lay completely still, listening. The apartment was silent.

But that silence felt **wrong.**

Slowly, she sat up, straining her ears.

Then—

A voice.

Distant. Muffled.

She couldn't make out the words, but it was coming from the living room.

The phone.

Someone was speaking through the phone.

A cold wave of terror paralyzed her. She hadn't answered it. Hadn't even touched it.

But it was off the hook.

And **something was using it.**

Her body felt sluggish as she forced herself out of bed. She padded toward the living room, each step careful, controlled, though she wanted to run.

The phone sat on the table where she had left it, receiver

resting on the edge. The cord stretched, limp and unnatural, as if someone had picked it up and dropped it carelessly.

The voice was still there, whispering.

She swallowed hard and forced herself to reach out, fingers trembling as she lifted the receiver to her ear.

Static.

Then—

A breath.

Long. Slow. Right **there** in her ear.

Then, in a voice that wasn't quite human:

"I will have so much fun tormenting you..."

A deep, guttural chuckle—more animal than human—rumbled through the line before it abruptly went dead. Her heart pounded as the echoes of that unholy promise reverberated in her ears.

She dropped the receiver as if it had burned her, stumbling backward. Her breath came in short, sharp bursts. Her skin crawled, her body screaming at her to get out.

But she couldn't move.

The phone sat there, still and lifeless.

Waiting.

In that single, shattering moment, she understood with a cold dread that she had opened a door.

IN THE DAYS FOLLOWING THAT FATEFUL MOMENT, STRANGE occurrences began to fill the apartment. At first, it was small things—a lamp that flickered when no one was near it, a chair that seemed to shift slightly every time she looked away. But soon, the disturbances grew harder to ignore: objects shifted or crashed to the floor with no explanation. At night, the sounds grew louder—insistent, jarring, echoing throughout the silence as though something unseen was moving through the space. The mirrors, reflecting only the ordinary, began to make her stomach twist. For brief moments, Silvia thought she saw something in the corner of her eye, something moving behind her reflection. Was it real? She never could tell, but it didn't matter. The terror was real. And inescapable—it lingered, casting a chilling presence wherever she went inside her home. Her mind, already stretched thin, began to fray at the edges. A new sensation washed over her, like a constant buzz in her bloodstream—she was jittery, shaky, as if she had drunk far too many cups of coffee in one sitting. Her hands trembled while making simple tasks, and a creeping sensation of being watched never left her, especially after dark. No longer did she feel like the quiet observer in her apartment; she felt like prey, constantly on alert, eyes darting to every corner, expecting the worst. With each passing day, her reality seemed to slip further from her grasp. The demon's voice—the unearthly promise—echoed louder inside her skull. "I will have so much fun tormenting you..."

It was no longer confined to the phone at night. It had become a part of her waking world, the fear digging in deeper, its shadow hanging over her every thought. Every new disturbance felt like another subtle tightening of a grip around her chest. As her apartment became a house of horrors, a cage of whispers and shifting forms, Silvia couldn't shake the feeling that every event had been calculated.

The demon was letting her know it was in full control. From a fleeting movement in the corner of her vision to the unnerving silence between one crash and the next, it had made her its focus. Eventually, the realization set in as she stared at the mess left in her wake—a broken vase, overturned books, the fridge door left open. She had opened a door, and now that door stood ajar, inviting a darkness that she could neither comprehend nor escape.

With each unexplained sound—a drawer sliding open, a book falling without reason—her mental state deteriorated further. The rational part of her mind fought to dismiss these events as tricks of an overactive imagination, but the relentless phenomena chipped away at her stability.

Isolated and desperate, Silvia found herself trapped in a nightmare from which there seemed to be no escape. She had no one to turn to, no friend or confidant who wouldn't dismiss her fears as the ravings of someone losing their grip on reality. In the grip of a terror that felt both physical and mental, she was forced to confront the fact that the entity was keeping its promise, systematically eroding her sense of safety and sanity.

AFTER DAYS OF RELENTLESS DISTURBANCES AND SLEEPLESS nights, Silvia found herself standing before the familiar stone façade of the local Catholic Church—a building she had passed countless times on her routine walks through the neighborhood. Though she wasn't raised Catholic, the countless books and movies she'd consumed had ingrained in her the notion that, when the supernatural reared its head, a priest might be the best option for help.

Her hands trembled relentlessly, caused by the lack of sleep and the anxiety of voicing her fears.

With a deep, hesitant breath, she pushed open the heavy wooden doors and stepped into the cool, dim interior. The church's quiet ambiance, underscored by the faint aroma of incense and old wood, offered little comfort—but it was a place that felt less hostile than her own home.

Inside, a lone priest, who seemed to be in his mid-fifties and graying hair, sat in a modest office near the entrance, absorbed in a worn Bible. Silvia stood at the entrance, trying to find her voice. When he looked up, his eyes softened with a mix of concern and curiosity. "Can I help you?" he asked gently.

She took a couple of slow steps towards him. "Y-yes..." Her voice, shaky and barely above a whisper, began to recount the past few weeks: How she found the phone, the voice she thought was Roderick's, and then how the voice turned into something else entirely, the inexplicable movements of objects in her apartment, the echo of a demonic promise that haunted her every moment, and the overwhelming isolation that had driven her to this desperate plea for help.

The priest listened intently, nodding slowly as she spoke. Though his own faith was rooted in centuries-old traditions, his gaze held a quiet understanding of the darkness that could creep into one's life.

Silvia finished her anxious recounting, and the priest listened with quiet intensity, nodding slowly as he absorbed every word. When she paused, he leaned forward and said in a measured tone, "I understand. It sounds like you're facing something far beyond what you should have to endure alone. My name is Father Quint. And as it happens, I have the afternoon free. Why don't we go to your apartment now? At the very least, I can bless the place—and that certainly won't hurt."

His words, though calm, carried an undeniable weight of concern. He rose from his seat, and with a gentle, reassuring nod, he continued, "Please, wait here for a moment. I need to gather a few items—my Bible, some holy water, and my crucifix. I'll be right back."

Left alone in the modest office, Silvia sat on a worn bench. The silence pressed in on her, punctuated only by the soft rustle of paper and her own uneasy breathing. Every minute stretched long as she tried to steady her racing thoughts and quell the dread that had gripped her since the nightmarish events began. The idea of someone believing her seemed as distant as the terror now haunting her home.

After a short while that felt like an eternity, the door creaked open and the priest returned. Clutching a small bottle of holy water, his well-worn Bible under one arm, and a modest crucifix in his hand, his presence brought a fragile sense of resolve back into the room. "I'm ready," he said softly, his voice a blend of determination and compassion. "Let's go."

They left the sanctuary together, stepping out into a late afternoon that felt unusually heavy. The streetlights cast long, wavering shadows on the pavement as they made their way to Silvia's apartment. Each step seemed to echo with the weight of unseen eyes. Silvia's thoughts churned in anxious spirals—memories of the relentless ringing, the cold, mocking voice, and the way her apartment had transformed into a battleground for an entity that defied explanation.

The walk felt interminable. Father Quint maintained a quiet determination, his gaze fixed ahead as if he were trying to outrun the darkness. Silvia, on the other hand, couldn't shake the feeling that the very air around her was charged with malevolence. Every distant sound—a car passing by, a dog barking—sent a jolt of terror through her. She barely dared to breathe.

When they finally reached her building, a modest structure that had once felt like home, Silvia hesitated at the door. The corridor was dimly lit. As usual, the elevator didn't seem to be working, so she led the priest up the narrow staircase, her mind replaying the moments of torment: objects sliding of their own accord, the persistent, inexplicable hum of that demonic promise.

Inside her apartment, the atmosphere was thick with dread. The living room, once a comforting space, now felt oppressive. Shadows pooled in corners, and the silence was punctured by the soft, almost imperceptible sound of something moving. And there it was—the cursed phone, sitting on the side table as if it were waiting. Its presence was a stark reminder of the moment she'd unwittingly opened a door, to what, she still wasn't sure.

The priest moved methodically. He set down a small crucifix and a vial of holy water on the table, his hands steady as he began a low prayer. Silvia stood a few paces away, every muscle taut with fear. The priest's words, measured and firm, filled the room with a tentative hope—a hope that the sacred rite might force the dark presence to retreat.

But almost immediately, the apartment responded. A harsh,

sudden flicker of the overhead light, a deep, guttural sound barely perceptible, that vibrated against the walls—it was as though the very air recoiled from the ritual. Silvia's heart hammered in her chest as she watched a shadow dart across the room, too swift and too unnatural to be a trick of the light. The temperature plummeted, and an unholy wind swept through, stirring papers and sending a chill down her spine. The entity obviously did not like the priest's presence.

Father Quint's steady voice broke through the oppressive silence as he began the blessing. Standing before the cursed phone and the oppressive shadows, he raised the small crucifix in one hand and, with his other, splashed a few drops of holy water onto the table. His eyes flickered with resolve despite the palpable tremor of fear that danced at the corners of his gaze.

"In the name of the Father, the Son, and the Holy Spirit," he intoned firmly, his words echoing in the still, cold air of the apartment. Each syllable reverberated against the walls, trying to push back the encroaching darkness. Even as he spoke, the over-head light flickered violently, casting momentary, distorted images of twisted shapes along the walls. A low, guttural sound, as if the very apartment itself were groaning under the weight of unseen forces, answered his prayer.

Silvia stood a few paces away, her heart pounding so hard she thought it might shatter the silence. The priest continued without faltering, his voice steady, though the lines of worry etched around his eyes betrayed his inner turmoil. He moved slowly and deliberately, methodically circling the room, each step and every recitation a small defiance against the malevolence that had taken root.

Then, in a sudden and violent surge, the apartment reacted. Shadows deepened and slithered across the ceiling; a harsh, discordant noise rose from the cursed phone, mingling with a sudden, bone-chilling gust of wind that rattled windows and sent loose papers skittering across the floor. The air felt alive with malice, and in that moment, the evil presence made itself known

—a swirling mass of darkness that loomed near the corner of the room, its edges blurring and shifting as if it were nothing more than a nightmare given form.

Without breaking his rhythm, the priest's voice grew louder and more insistent. "I command you, in the name of Jesus, to recede! Leave this place!" he declared, his tone firm yet laced with the unmistakable tension of someone who knew the stakes were dire. His hand clutched the crucifix tightly as he continued to recite the sacred words, trying to fortify the fragile barrier between light and the encroaching darkness.

"Silvia," he called out, his voice softening just slightly as he turned his gaze toward her. "Join me in prayer. Call upon the Lord."

In that instant, something stirred within Silvia—a desperate, unfamiliar need that overwhelmed her disbelief. Though she had never been particularly religious, the terror of the moment and the raw isolation of her plight coaxed forth a deep, almost instinctive plea for salvation. Her eyes widened, and with a trembling voice that wavered between fear and fervor, she began, "Jesus, I need You now. Please, help me. Please!"

Her words, halting and raw, seemed to hang in the air. Yet, as if responding to her sincere outcry, a subtle warmth began to seep into the room. The oppressive chill lessened slightly, and for a heartbeat, Silvia felt as though a distant, comforting presence was listening—an assurance that her plea was not falling on deaf ears.

The priest nodded encouragingly, his voice firm despite his own inner nerves.

But the entity, irate and unyielding, retaliated. With a roar that rattled the very foundations of the apartment, the darkness surged forward, causing the lights to shudder and plunge the room into an almost tangible blackness for a split second. A deep, unearthly vibration filled the space, and in that moment, the sinister presence seemed to sneer at their efforts, its form pulsing with malevolent energy.

Yet, even as the evil manifested itself in furious swirls of shadow and a cacophony of discordant sounds, Silvia and Father Quint continued their supplications. Her passionate plea, born of a desperate need for divine intervention, lent a piercing clarity to the otherwise chaotic din. "Lord, please—help us!" she cried out, her voice resolute amid the tumult.

As Father Quint's prayer rose steadily in the oppressive silence, a sudden, searing sensation blazed along the side of his cheek. Without warning, he felt a sharp, burning scratch—swift and insidious. He instinctively reached up, his fingers grazing the small cut that drew a thin trickle of blood. There was no shadowy figure, no visible force—only the inexplicable sting that seemed meant to break his concentration. Silvia's eyes widened to an almost painful degree as she watched the moment unfold. For a heartbeat, she was paralyzed; her breath hitched and her heart pounded so hard it drowned out every other sound. The room seemed to shrink around her, the flickering light and eerie silence amplifying the horror of what she had just witnessed.

For a moment, the priest's eyes widened in shock, and a flicker of doubt threatened to overtake him. It was as if the malevolent presence sought to silence his words with fear. Yet, even as the pain pulsed through his skin, his resolve hardened. He clenched his jaw and murmured, louder now, "These are nothing but parlor tricks! You may try to unnerve me, but you are nothing compared to the power of Jesus Christ!" His voice, though edged with pain, resonated with a defiant strength that filled the room.

Drawing a deep, steadying breath, he resumed his prayer with renewed vigor, his words ringing out even more forcefully against the encroaching darkness. The scratch, a cruel, fleeting mark on his flesh, became a symbol of his unyielding faith—a challenge he met head-on. Despite the demon's attempt to instill fear, the priest's determination did not waver. Instead, he pressed on, his recitations a powerful rebuttal to the entity's malevolent intent, declaring that no earthly terror could eclipse the divine protection he believed in.

As Silvia witnessed all this, her hands, which had trembled uncontrollably moments before, began to steady as she listened. The chill that had gripped her heart softened, replaced by an unexpected conviction. With each word of the priest's fervent prayer, she felt the oppressive weight of darkness lift, if only slightly. It was as though the very act of defiance against the evil in her home was awakening something dormant within her—a desperate need to call on a power greater than her own.

Silvia stood in the dim, trembling light of her apartment, the oppressive presence of the demon now seeming almost absurd in its fury. In that moment, as the priest's resolute prayers filled the room, a sudden clarity took hold of her. The dark force, with its wild, senseless tantrums, now struck her as nothing more than a toddler throwing a fit—a pitiful, fleeting outburst in the face of an eternal, unyielding power.

A warmth began to swell within her chest, a radiant assurance that pushed back the chill of terror. She felt her faith strengthen in a way that was both startling and liberating, a deep, unshakeable conviction that God had already won this fight. In her mind, every malicious whisper and every menacing shadow diminished in significance, overwhelmed by the certainty that the divine was in control.

Taking a deep, steadying breath, Silvia closed her eyes, her voice rising in prayer. ""God, I know You've already won. This is nothing compared to Your power." she declared, her tone both calm and passionate. "You have already conquered all darkness, and this... this is but a childish tantrum before You." Her words, confident and clear, resonated through the room, a bold counterpoint to the demon's feeble defiance.

In that sacred moment, Silvia's heart overflowed with hope and resolve. Every fear, every shudder of terror, was met with an unyielding belief in a power far greater than any malevolent force. She prayed with an assurance born of deep, personal conviction.

The priest's final words filled the room. He raised his crucifix and said, "In the name of Jesus, I command you to leave this place!" Suddenly, the strange energy that had filled the apartment began to fade away. The flickering lights steadied, and the eerie sounds fell silent. Even the cursed phone on the side table went quiet.

Silvia felt a deep, strong relief wash over her. The fear and terror of the night melted away, replaced by a warm certainty that she was safe. She looked up at the priest, her eyes bright with hope, and smiled.

The room felt different now. The oppressive weight that had filled every corner was gone. The air seemed lighter, as if a heavy blanket had been lifted. An undeniable calm had settled over the space. Silvia looked around in quiet wonder. The apartment was peaceful—more so than it had ever been even before she brought that cursed telephone inside. Every breath she took felt full of warmth and safety. There was no trace of the fear or the malevolent energy that had once haunted her home. In that gentle silence, Silvia felt certain that whatever evil had been here was completely gone, replaced by a deep, comforting peace that wrapped around her like a promise of protection.

Her heart swelled with a newfound faith. In the calm of her apartment, which now felt lighter and brighter than ever, she could sense God's presence all around her. The oppressive energy was gone, replaced by a peace that made her believe without a doubt that God had saved her.

SILVIA WOKE UP FEELING CALM, THOUGH SHE COULDN'T RECALL the moment she had gone to sleep—perhaps she had simply crashed from the events of last night. Surely, she had been mentally as well as physically exhausted after such an ordeal.

Yawning, she got out of bed and made her way to the kitchen to fix herself a cup of coffee. As she passed the table where the cursed telephone had been, she paused—it was not there.

Confused, she retraced her steps, checking every corner of her apartment. The phone had vanished without a trace. A thought crossed her mind: maybe the priest had taken it with him when he left. But he never mentioned anything about taking it. She shrugged, and resolved to go to the church later to ask him about it, as well as thank him for everything.

She sipped her coffee in the gentle morning light, stealing glances at the table where the phone had been.

SILVIA STEPPED OUT INTO THE WARM MORNING SUNLIGHT, A gentle smile playing on her lips. The air was fresh, and the day was beautiful—clear blue skies, birds chirping in the distance, and a soft breeze that made her feel light and hopeful. Despite the strange events of the previous night, she felt calm, almost as if the sunlight was washing away the lingering shadows.

With each step toward St. Catherine's Church, her mood grew brighter. Not only did she want to ask the priest about the telephone, although she was sure he had taken it, but she also wanted to thank him for everything he had done.

She pictured the priest's gentle smile and calm voice, and she felt the urge to hug him. The thought of meeting him again, and expressing her gratitude, made her steps light and purposeful.

Silvia walked through the bright, welcoming doors of St. Catherine's Church, the warm sunlight filling the space with a gentle glow. The day was beautiful, and she felt hopeful. She headed to the small office where she remembered seeing him. But when she pushed the door open, it was empty. So she wandered through the quiet corridors until she spotted a priest near the main hall, quietly arranging some papers.

"Excuse me, Father," she said, trying to keep her voice

friendly. "I was here yesterday with a priest—Father Quint, about in his mid-fifties, graying hair, tall. Do you know him?"

The priest looked at her with concern, a frown of confusion creasing his brow. "I'm sorry," he replied softly, "but there's no priest here by that name, or who fits that description. As far as I know, we haven't had anyone like that here."

Silvia blinked, a light nervous chuckle escaping her lips. "But I was with him yesterday. He was in his office, and he helped me with a personal problem..." Her voice trailed off as uncertainty filled her words.

The priest shook his head gently. "I really don't know of any priest like that," he said.

Still speaking with her, he called over a nun who was passing by. The priest leaned in and said, "Sister, can you help me? This young lady here is looking for a Father Quint. Do you know him?"

The nun stopped, her brow furrowing in confusion. "Father Quint?" she repeated softly, glancing around as if trying to place the name. "I'm sorry, but I don't know anyone by that name here."

Silvia described him hastily to the nun again, her heart pounding with growing unease. She repeated her inquiry, but the nun shook her head firmly. She looked at the priest with a questioning look in her eyes, and then back at Silvia. Standing there in the gentle light of the church, Silvia felt a chill of uncertainty. If no one recognized Father Quint, the kind priest who had helped her just yesterday, then what had really happened?

SILVIA STEPPED OUT OF THE CHURCH, HER HEART HEAVY WITH confusion. The day still bright, she walked slowly across the stone courtyard, each step echoing her growing uncertainty. Finally, she found a weathered stone bench tucked away beneath an ancient oak and sat down.

Gazing out over the quiet churchyard, Silvia tried to make sense of everything. She remembered Father Quint clearly, how could she not? She had just been with him. But no one at the church seemed to know him. How could this possibly be?

Silvia rose from the stone bench with a deep, steadying breath. Still confused by the church conversation, she decided that a walk might help clear her mind. She left the churchyard and strolled along the sunlit street, each step a small attempt to shake off the lingering doubts.

Her thoughts wandered as she walked—questions about Father Quint, the missing telephone, the amazing events she had recently gone through. and whether her memory was playing tricks on her, but everything seemed crystal clear in her mind. The warm day and gentle breeze offered little distraction from the turmoil inside her, yet she found comfort in the familiar rhythm of her steps.

Before long, Silvia's path led her to the thrift shop she had visited before. The worn storefront and its dusty window displays greeted her like an old friend. Stepping inside, she found herself looking for the old white-haired lady that had talked to her before about the telephone. She just needed someone to talk to about what she'd been through—someone who could understand. And the old lady seemed to have an open mind, she had mentioned that some things simply are and all that.

She scanned the room, searching for her. Soon enough, she spotted the woman behind a cluttered counter, carefully sorting through a stack of vintage postcards.

Silvia approached the old lady with a tentative "Hey...Hi." The woman turned around, her warm smile lighting up her face. Silvia awkwardly waved at her. "Hi." She repeated.

"Hello, dear. Back to find some old treasures?" the old lady asked cheerfully.

Silvia gave a small, awkward smile and shook her head. "Not this time," she said, hesitating before continuing, "Um, I—I just wanted to ask you something. Do you remember the last time I was in here? We talked about that telephone I bought?"

The old lady cocked her head, a puzzled expression replacing her smile. "A telephone?" she repeated softly. She placed the stack of postcards she was holding on the counter and looked up at Silvia.

"Yes, that old landline telephone I bought a few days ago—the black one, remember? You told me a man had come to drop it off, and you said he seemed tired?" Silvia's voice trembled as she asked, looking at the old lady for any sign of recognition, starting to feel agitated.

The old lady studied Silvia in silence for a long moment before shaking her head slowly. "I'm sorry, dear, but I don't recall ever having a conversation about a telephone—or anything else, really. We have only ever exchanged a few words about the weather and such."

Silvia's eyes widened, and she let out a nervous, almost hysterical laugh—a laugh that hinted at something fraying at the edges of her mind. "No, no, I remember perfectly," she stammered, her voice growing more urgent. "We talked about it right here!" She clutched her head as if she might tear out her hair, feeling a cold, sinking sensation that she was losing her grip on reality. The confusion and desperation swirled inside her, making her question everything she thought she knew, and for a moment, the line between memory and madness blurred.

Silvia's gaze snapped to a man standing near the counter, and recognizing him as the man who had sold her the telephone, she pointed at him and took a few hurried steps forward. "Him! He —he sold me the phone!" she blurted out.

The man looked up in startled confusion. He glanced around as if unsure whom Silvia was addressing, then slowly placed his hand on his chest. "Me?" he asked, his voice soft and bewildered.

"Yes! Yes—you sold me a telephone, remember? You couldn't have forgotten about it!" Silvia's loud voice cracked as she continued, her tone shifting to one of desperate pleading. "You said something about me having an eye for the strange, and that these things don't follow the rules, something like that! You do remember, right?"

Her words spilled out in a rush, heavy with hope and anxiety, as she searched his face for any sign of recognition that could affirm her memory.

The man furrowed his brow, his expression a mix of confusion and concern. "I don't remember selling you a telephone. Are... are you okay, Miss?" he asked, he seemed worried.

Silvia's fingers pressed hard against her temples, a sudden pain in her head blurring the line between reality and insanity. Frustration welled up inside her, and she could feel her whole body starting to tremble. "Why is everyone trying to make me feel like I'm crazy?" she asked aloud, her voice breaking as she tried to control the torrent of emotions threatening to spill over. "Why is everyone lying?" The words hung in the air, thick with the desperation that had been building for what felt like ages.

Silvia's breath hitched as doubt threatened to swallow her certainty. The desperate hope that had fueled her accusations now wavered, replaced by a raw, gnawing fear that perhaps everything was slipping away. The world around her seemed to tilt as she struggled to hold onto the memories of last night—memories that now clashed with the reality in front of her.

The man stepped forward and moved to stand beside the old white-haired lady. Facing Silvia, he said softly, "Miss, do you want me to call someone for you? Why don't you sit down and try to calm down? I'll get you some water."

The old lady glanced at him and back at her, with a very concerned look on her face.

Silvia looked around, her eyes darting from one face to another as if searching for a clue—a hidden camera, a familiar smirk, anything that might explain this bizarre scene. Confusion and dizziness swirled within her, making her wonder if she had been the subject of some elaborate prank. But by whom? And for what purpose? The thought raced through her mind, but deep down she knew that wasn't it.

Her heart pounded in her ears as she tried to ground herself, her hands still pressed against her temples. The gentle concern of the man and the old lady's quiet support only deepened her uncertainty.

"No," she murmured to herself, a fragile determination in her tone, as she shook her head.

The old lady went to touch her shoulder, "Dear..."

"No!" Silvia jerked away from the old lady's touch and bolted from the store, her mind a whirlwind of fear and confusion. Outside, the bright day did little to soothe the storm inside her. Her heart pounded wildly, and every step felt as though it carried the weight of a thousand unanswered questions. Desperate and disoriented, she wandered the busy sidewalk, not knowing where she was going.

She questioned everything— the anguish of not being able to trust her own memories sinking her into the ground.

But with each step, the chaos of her thoughts gradually gave way to a strange, hollow numbness. As the minutes stretched into hours, her frantic pace slowed, and she began to feel the tension ease ever so slightly.

In the quiet solitude of a long, aimless walk, Silvia started to convince herself that it had all been a dream—a very elaborate, hyper-real dream. She marveled at how tangible every moment had seemed, how real the fear of the demon and her faith in God had felt, and yet, deep down, she clung to the thought that it was nothing more than a figment of an overtaxed mind.

"I must have been overwhelmed," she thought, her internal voice steadying as she forced herself to breathe deeply. "I read somewhere that extreme stress can trigger short episodes of psychosis. Maybe I just lost control for a moment." The idea felt both comforting and disconcerting. The details were so clear, yet she now questioned whether her mind had simply played a cruel trick on her. Silvia examined each memory like a puzzle, trying to find logical explanations. "It could be just a momentary lapse —a break from reality induced by exhaustion and lack of sleep," she rationalized, clutching her hands together as if they might anchor her thoughts. "That's all it was."

A sense of embarrassed calm slowly replaced her earlier desperation. As vivid as her memories were, they now seemed like a brief lapse— Yes, a short episode of psychosis. She recalled reading about it. Could that have been it? A short break from reality? It was as if her mind had slipped away for a moment, blurring the lines between reality and nightmare.

Feeling a twinge of regret for the scene she'd caused at the shop, Silvia resolved that once she had gathered herself and allowed some time for clarity, she would return to the thrift shop to apologize to the shopkeepers for the outburst, although she wasn't sure if she'd ever feel confident enough to go and face them again, and try to piece together what had happened.

With a deep, steadying breath, Silvia allowed herself to accept that maybe, just maybe, her mind had played a cruel trick on her—and that now, she was already on her way back to normalcy. For now, she clung to the thought that this was just a brief, if disconcerting, episode—and that with some rest, she'd be able to put it all behind her.

Silvia walked back to her apartment under the slowly darkening sky of the sunset, her steps feeling lighter than before. The events of the previous night still lingered in her mind, but now she was convinced that it had all been a passing episode—a brief, disconcerting trick of her mind.

As she moved along the familiar streets, she mused quietly, "The mind is a fragile thing, always playing tricks on us." The fear and confusion that had gripped her earlier began to fade, replaced by a calm rationality. Though the memories were vivid and unsettling, she now believed they were just a storm in her head—a fleeting lapse brought on by stress.

By the time she reached her apartment building, a small, hopeful smile appeared on her face. Each step up the narrow stairs reaffirmed her resolve: this was nothing more than a temporary break from reality. The terror had been real, yes, but it was also a reminder of how easily the mind could be overwhelmed, and it was already behind her. Despite everything, she felt a renewed sense of determination to trust her own strength and sanity. Today, she thought, was a new beginning. The worst was over.

Silvia unlocked her door and stepped inside, drawing a slow, calming breath. There had never been any demon in her home. She smiled almost imperceptibly as she slowly shook her head.

Silvia stepped into the kitchen, her mood lighter and her thoughts calmer. She placed her bag on the counter and reached for a glass of water, taking a slow, steady sip as she tried to gather herself. With a small sigh, she turned around and glanced into the living room. She moved slowly towards it, her steps measured and quiet. The soft glow of the kitchen light behind her illuminated it faintly. Her mind was still piecing together the calm she'd fought to reclaim.

She reached for the wall switch and flicked it on.

Her grip on the glass of water faltered. It slipped from her hand and crashed onto the floor, shattering, but she didn't notice. She was frozen in place, holding her breath without realizing it, her eyes wide and unblinking.

On the small round table, the same place where she had first set it on the day she brought it home, sat the old rotary black phone.

Unplugged.

And it started to ring.

BY INCHES

ELLIS HART

"Sunflowering," I had heard it called—a social-media trend where you stand in direct sun with your eyes closed and breathe like a plant turning to the light. I did it for a couple of minutes, and it worked: warmth soaking my eyelids, breath evening out. Standing in the dirt parking lot, I rolled my shoulders loose, one palm on the warm hood while the other arm crossed my chest. Hips, quads, calves. I stretched the way I always did, the ritual that kept the aches at bay and the ghosts of injury from coming back around. The sun was late-morning thin, a pale coin behind high gauze clouds. The air had that smell I love in new places—pine pitch, warm stone, and a mineral thread rising from water I couldn't see yet.

Cal had told me about this trail. Not a formal park, just a checkerboard of old service roads and logging cuts and a couple of informal tracks locals used when they wanted a view. "Under-sold," he'd said over coffee, tapping the corner of his folded paper map like he was letting me in on a secret. "Better than the guidebooks. Nobody out there. You'll get your space."

Space was what I chased, even when I pretended I didn't. I'm not a phone-in-the-pocket guy. The weight annoys me. The notifications make me feel obligated to respond no matter the time or content. Boy Scouts taught me a lot of things that stick in the bone. A magnetic needle that doesn't care if there's a bar of service, a paper map that doesn't die at twenty percent. I locked my phone in the center console and closed the lid with a click, basking in the immediate relief of freedom.

Water bottle clipped. Compass on a lanyard. Paper map in a ziplock slid into the outside pocket of my day pack. The map was laminated from a life long before I owned it—someone else's thumb lines and penciled arrows and faded grease-pencil notes: good spring, gate locked, dogs.

I paced the dirt lot and watched my Fitbit admit I'd taken four hundred and eight steps, a little vibrating celebration like it was cheering on the warm-up to my real day. "Let's go," I said to the scrub oaks that watched me pick the narrower path at the split. Narrow meant solitude and solitude meant quiet, and quiet was the first step to hearing my own head.

Luck is a thing we talk about like it's a coin someone flips. Heads: good. Tails: bad. That makes it clean. But luck is more like a million grains of sand and which ones stick to your heel when you take a step. Which way the wind blows when a friend mentions a trail. Which moment the metal under the leaves decides it was holding itself together for long enough.

It was a good walk. Switchbacks that made their way politely up a low ridge. Warm rock faces that held the sun and gave it back after a break in a chilly stream. The path veined off in little deer tracks and foot-wide side cuts where runoff had pushed its way downhill. I kept the compass in hand because I am, if nothing else, methodical. The needle liked north wherever north fell. I liked that too.

I made a game of it the way I do, picking a point that looked like nothing special and getting myself lost by degrees—left of that boulder, parallel to that dry creek, around that stand of twisted pitch. Get lost a little, then pull the world back to you by lines and angles. There is a holiness in the proof that, with the right tools, you can always be your own rescue.

After two hours the sun had shifted toward noon, warming the back of my neck. The world slowed as it always does: birds drop their chatter, insects thrum, the day lays itself out like a deep stretching cat. I thought about water but didn't drink because rationing is a habit and thirst can make you sloppy. I stretched once more in a slice of shade and watched sweat bead on my forearms. My Fitbit glowed 9,372 steps. It liked me today.

The hole didn't announce itself. There was no menacing ring of fence or posted sign, no jutting pipe to warn that someone had once meant to keep something in or out. It was an absence, a dark that accepted my right foot up to the ankle and then the rest of me all at once.

Leaves gave way and something hollow flexed and something metal sighed and turned to powder beneath me. The split second of compressing rust sounded like breath in a ventilator. The next instant, I was weightless.

I maybe fell fifteen feet, but the way it jammed up through my bones made it feel like much more. I clipped the wall on the way down with my shin and the pain was lightning: bright, exact, and everywhere at once. I landed on my left hip and elbow, a stink of old metal and damp earth blasting up around me like stale breath.

For a while the sky was a silver coin and then two silver coins grinding against one another. My breath did that panicked snare-drum stutter and then came back to me in ragged sheets. I was aware of my leg in the way you're aware of a pimple before you've looked at it—the skin of the pain tender and pulsing.

I took inventory of myself first because that's what I was always taught to do. Hands first. Fingers flexed: all of them. Wrist sore but willing. I pushed to sitting, gritted, and breathed through the pressure in my shin until I could name it as impact and not immediate fracture—the difference between a thing cracked and a thing bruised to the marrow. When I tried to set my foot down, the world pinwheeled. I tasted copper.

The hole was perfectly circular. The walls were earth and

stone, old layers of poured aggregate and dirt where animals had burrowed in weak points over years. No ladder. No convenient pipe-screws jutting like rungs. Above me the mouth made a bright disk that a man could jump to if he were twelve feet tall and spry. Along my jeans rust had dusted me a fine orange. I ran my palm through the grit and came away with flakes that collapsed under their own weight. Once there'd been a cover. I could see it in the lip—warped corrugations like a frown and a scatter of fragmented bolts still hung to the rim.

"Hey!" I yelled because you yell. The word hit the ceiling of light and fell back wet. A few bitter flakes hissed down in answer.

I took off my pack slowly and checked. Water bottle— dented from the fall but intact and blessedly cool. Map—fine. Compass—fine. Headlamp—absent, which I'd known, but it's one thing to know you didn't bring a light because you expected home before dusk and another to inventory that decision when the day has suddenly peeled the floor away. My phone was in the car making me feel much more foolish now, cooling in the console and counting notifications without me.

I thought of Cal telling me "nobody out there" and felt a splash of something not his fault and not mine either. That's the thing about the million grains of sand. No one grain is to blame for the landslide.

Triage is math with a body in it. I tore my flannel shirt into strips. I pressed along the shin until I found the place where touching made my teeth throb. Skin not broken, swelling living just under the skin like a blossoming ant hill. I folded the map to a rigid panel. A bandana, a bootlace, the map—ugly, improvised, but a splint is mostly a silent promise you make to your body: *I'll try not to make it worse.*

My Fitbit tattled my heart rate at 128 and climbing. It buzzed a little celebratory prayer for ten thousand steps while I sat in the bottom of a hole and laughed once, stupid and breathless.

I drank two mouthfuls of cool water and closed the lid

tightly. There were pebbles the size of quarters strewn about. There were ribbony shreds of metal that had once been corrugated and were now draped like seaweed exposed and stranded at low tide. In the slant of light I could see a ring of rust flakes around me where my landing had kicked up years of kept dust. A brown bottle lay on its side half-swaddled in sediment like a relic, the glass thick, old, bubbled. Its label had gone to pulp some decades ago.

I tested the walls next. In the old days, wells like this had been lined strong enough to hold back earth and keep a man from doing exactly what I was about to try. I put my palms out to either side and pressed. Chimneying it is called, when you pin yourself between two surfaces and make height by inches.

Foot to dent, back to dirt, palms to stone. I pushed. I rose. Twice I slid and felt my heart snag and then release. I made maybe four feet this way before my boot skidded on a smooth stone and both hands slipped. I fell like a prayer in reverse. The landing was on the other hip this time and the pain rang a new bell. The Fitbit told me ninety-seven active minutes, keep it up!

"By inches," I told the walls, because that's how you measure both progress and failure. By inches.

I stacked what there was to stack. The brown bottle. Fist-sized rocks. A fan of old corrugated metal bent like a tongue. I built a little cairn under the wall with the most purchase and tried to make it mean something. I looped my belt and the bandana and a strip of flannel into a rope that, if you were generous, added nine inches to my reach. I placed my right foot, then my left—careful of the splint—and pressed myself up until my shoulders burned in a way that reminded me of climbing that dangling rope in gym class as a kid.

My right hand found a seam that felt like it may hold me. Fingers dug. Bits came away like damp cake. The left hand went searching and... nothing. I felt air and then a loose pebble that scooted away. The bandana rope bought me an inch and a half of nothing. I slid. The stack shifted and became a scatter. Rust flakes hissed. I landed on my forearms and then, because you have to, I breathed and told myself the next attempt would be better.

I called again. It's not the kind of shouting you do at a game or a concert. It's a bargaining kind of call, like you're offering yourself as a proposition to whatever is listening. A hawk cut the sky once in the opening above me but made no attempt to rescue me. 'Fuckin' hawks.

The day lengthened into what they call "The Golden Hour", when everything feel like it's made of honey and magic. Hunger was a thought I could wave away. Thirst wasn't. I rationed badly in the morning because I believed in the afternoon. I rationed in the afternoon because I wanted a reason to trust the evening. At dusk, I looked into the bottle and could see the inverted circle of metal at the bottom, smiling at me.

Anger came easy after that. Anger at the invisible someones who'd sunk this shaft and then let the cover rot. Anger at the fact that I'd been careful and methodical and it hadn't mattered. The good kind of anger turns into action. The cheap kind spirals back on you and makes your thoughts hot. I walked the circle like an animal at the edge of a cage, counting steps because counting is something you can own. Nine paces across at the widest, seven at the narrow. I ran my fingers along the wall and felt absolutely nothing of note.

As the light thinned, the world lost context and stripped down to sound. Wind in leaves far away up there. The little tics and sloughs as old debris rethought its angles. Once, a sound too regular not to be footsteps and then—when I held my breath to hear better—nothing except the sound of my own blood in my ears.

True dark came the way sleep does, first at the edges and then everywhere, and I let it come because nothing I could do would slow it. The circle above melted to pewter and then to lead and then to memory. The air grew a degree colder and then another as if just to remind me that the sun was gone.

When you take sight away, the brain creates space for you. I lay back to take the weight off my leg and listened. Drips I hadn't heard in daylight found their voices—some high like a metronome, some low and patient. The rust smell was stronger in darkness, or maybe it was always strong and light had only distracted me from it. It was a blood-adjacent smell, iron and damp, and my mouth watered in the wrong way because thirst is a logic that doesn't care much for details.

I spoke once to the dark because the dark is a thing that listens whether we like it or not. "Okay," I said, and my voice didn't come back. "Okay, I'm alright."

When I could be still no longer, I mapped with my hands. It's a children's game made serious—make the unknown known by learning it through touch. Palms down, fingers spread. A stone like a kneecap. A twist of metal like a bent joint. The ripple where the floor rose a little toward the flatter wall. The slick curve of glass that was the brown bottle's belly. I found a ribbon of metal whose edge was stamped in that old rhythmic way, fluted like a pie crust—the warped lip of corrugated sheet cut from some larger whole. I ran my thumb along it until it split my skin. I'm still alive— check.

Near the wall my fingers slipped into a pocket where silt had collected like a soft mouth. Within it, something smooth then ridged, cylinder then flare. It was the size of my forearm if my forearm had been carved down and polished by hands that weren't human. My fingers found a seam like a growth plate. It felt like a bone felt when you cut a roast and hit something that wasn't meat.

I told myself deer because deer are everywhere bones are. I told myself animal because I couldn't handle anything else. I left it where it lay and told myself again that I had found a branch hardened by time. The dark didn't disagree and that felt like permission to believe it.

At some hour the night set its metronome to slow and steady and my alarms—the ones I've trained by years of sleeping outdoors—gave up on the fantasy that I would be eaten by a bear or rained on or found by a search and rescue team. I slept shallow. I woke at intervals to pain and the feeling that someone had stood over me and then moved when I looked up. Which is to say I woke to my own brain turning emptiness into shapes.

Dawn was not a color so much as a softening, the difference between pressed eyes and the decision to open them. The circle above declared itself again. I counted breaths and then counted again because I needed to keep my mind sharp for when I escaped.

I drank the last of the water because a gambled burst of false energy would be better than carrying around a mouthful of regret. I bound the leg tighter. I used two lengths of corrugated metal and the map and told the leg the kind of lie you tell the people you love: this will help, I promise. It helped enough that standing was a thing the body agreed to do on the condition that we not talk about it too much.

"By inches," I said again, this time to the mouth of the well that was not a well, the hole that had been something to someone long ago and was now my geography. Pressure. Back against earth. Hands against stone. Knees against dirt. I felt myself slowly rise.

It would have been easy not to hear them. If the birds had been louder, if the wind had been showing off. If my breath hadn't gone quiet with concentration. The first sound was a skitter, a small rearrangement of grit as something passed over it. Then a chitter—oh it was such a bright, awful sound, like a squirrel that had learned the language of a clock, demonic and cheerful and eager and wrong. It came from below me in the dark.

I didn't look. Looking would have cost effort and the thing about by-inches climbs is that effort is stacked like a tower of cards. I let my eyes drop only when my knee lost purchase and fell down below my hip.

Pale. That was what I saw first when I looked down past my

shoulder: not white, which is clean, but pale like the old teeth, like peeled bark. They moved sideways the way crabs do but their limbs were long and their joints too many. They had hands, not paws, though you had to see them in motion to understand that—hands that splayed and clutched and splayed again. Their faces were nothing but smooth planes above a mouth that opened longways, saliva stringing between the edges in delicate threads that refused to break even as they scissored along the floor toward me. Eyeless, the way things get when the sun abandons them for generations.

There were three of them. Their chitter rose and fell and braided itself into a sound that reminded me of cicadas under heat in Alabama.

I went up. I went up because there was no down left to go. I burned my palms on the stone but it didn't matter. I pressed my back so hard against the wall that I could feel my flesh staying put as I continued to rise. The noise below escalated. The creatures found the wall and came at it sideways.

A head, if it was a head, turned toward me and I almost lost my grip while staring down its throat. The longest of the three pressed a hand—oh God that hand—flat against the wall and raised itself, another hand finding another seam, body folding and unfolding with a liquid certainty that made me feel flesh and blood in a way I did not enjoy.

I reached a shelf of stone, a generosity of geology, and my right hand hooked it and my left pressed to something that would not bear my weight for long. I made a sound in my throat that had no translation. The world above me widened as hope began to grow in my chest.

"Hold on!" a voice yelled, as a hand that was warm and dry and human closed around my wrist. I didn't look at the hand. I didn't look at the person attached to it. I put my left forearm on the shelf, screamed at the leg for cooperation, and let myself be yanked like something hauled out of a lake.

Sweet, clean, fresh air hit my face. The sky was the sky again and not a hole in the ceiling. I lay on my back and watched the clouds drift by.

"Drink," the voice said. The bottle pressed into my palm was plastic-clear and room temperature. I didn't care. I drank and it washed away every bad thing that has ever happened in my life.

She was kneeling beside me, not winded. Bare legs under a floral sundress, dirty at the knees. No boots. No socks. Her feet were in canvas slip-ons that had once been white and were now the color of dirt. No pack. No hat. Her hair was a frizz of grey that had been brushed with fingers and then ignored.

She had a blanket laid out a few yards away like a picnic had been started and then paused. On it were cards set in tableaux of red on black on red: solitaire mid-game, diamonds draped over spades. The deck's box sat open. There was a second water bottle and a half-eaten apple and a small knife with a pearl handle as if the whole thing had been staged by a Macy's catalog photographer.

"Thank you. Jesus Christ, thank you!" My voice came out rough. There was rust on my tongue and a taste like I had been gnawing on gravel. "There are—" I swallowed, and my throat fought the word. "There are things down there."

She glanced at the hole with the kind of interest you give a passing cloud. "Jesus Christ didn't save you, hun. I did." She walked towards the edge of the hole and looked down before lifting her shoulders in a casual shrug.

"Dark does that sometimes," she said. Her tone was kind and light, a teacher's. "Tricks the ears. Makes old junk sound like life."

"I saw them." I heard myself insist like a child. "Pale. Moving sideways. The sound they made—" I couldn't find an analogy that didn't make me sound like a lunatic. "They almost got me."

She reached out and touched my shoulder in a way that felt very maternal. "Even if there were creatures down there, hun," she said, eyes on mine so that I could not look away, "hunger wouldn't be their fault. Everything needs to eat. Maybe they only wanted company. Didn't you want company down there?"

Alarm is not a siren in the body. It's a soft click as the latch drops on a door you had once propped open. I sat up, slower than I wanted, and the world did that sliding trick it does when you are on the wrong side of dehydration. "I should—" I looked around as if there were a correct direction to orient myself to, as if north and south had anything to say about what was happening.

Her smile was placating, the kind you use on a skittish animal. She stood—not quickly, not in a way that would spook me—and brushed her dress with flat palms. Dust rose and settled. "I don't let them come up anymore," she said, a little confiding, a little proud. "Not since the second one was born."

The sentence arrived in my head and found nothing prepared to receive it. Born. Second. Come up. All the words were real, and they had all been put next to one another for a reason I did not want to understand.

I scooted. It was not dignified. The heel of my hand found the ground and a small rock made its case against my palm. She stepped with me in the painless bounce-step of someone who knows a secret that you don't.

"Truthfully, it's just simpler this way," she said, almost to herself. "Cleaner. If they come up, they get into things. Once it was the trash, and then there was the mess with the mailman, and then—Well, we did it in the basement for a while. But stairs are such a production. They really are happier where they can be themselves." She tilted her head and considered the hole with admiration.

I opened my mouth to say something, anything, but only pathetic air escaped. She is not large, this woman. She is not a gym or a truck. She is a pair of ropey forearms and a patience that reads as strength because patience is often the most dangerous kind of strength. Still, there is the mass of a body and the lever of a leg and the element of shock.

The kick was not cinematic. It was decisive. The heel of her canvas shoe met my breastbone and the body does what bodies do when force vectors decide the day. I pinwheeled and the world reached up and took me. For an instant the sky was every-where. Then the lip was gone and the mouth of the hole accepted me once again.

Pain makes a bright white room in the head. There were corners in mine like you get in a hospital—sharp, stressed, a little too clean. My leg said a sentence that ended in a period and then repeated itself, with an exclamation point.

Above me the circle was smaller because I was seeing it through the wet veil of my own eyes. The woman leaned over with her hands on her knees, hair swinging down like a curtain. Backlit that way she was a halo cut from paper.

"LENN—YYY, MARGIE, BRAAAM," she called, sing-song, the way you'd call hungry children to supper, and then she softened it with a coo that made the hair on my forearms pebble. "Dinner time, my little lovelies!"

The sound that rose from the dark was eager and immediate and plural. Chittering, bright as a spoon in a tea cup, clambering over itself as if sound could trip. I pressed my palms flat to the floor and discovered, at once and completely, that the thing my fingers had called a deer bone was not the right size for deer, that its smoothness was of the kind I've only seen in museums.

There are a thousand moments that compose a day: the choice to take the narrow path instead of the wide, the choice to not pack a flashlight during a morning hike, the decision to count the steps because a device on your wrist likes to celebrate with confetti. The click of a center console closing over a phone that could call anyone. The weight of a water bottle capped, then capped again a little harder. The place you put your right boot when the leaves look solid and are not.

From above, her shadow widened like a stain and then with-drew. I imagined her sitting down again on her picnic blanket, casually nibbling on an apple as she considers the new Spade in her hand.

In the dark, the patter multiplied. Twelve hands met the floor at once and then lifted and then placed again. I felt soil pepper my shins as they came, a soft rain of old rust and silt their movement shook free as they fumbled around me.

As the creatures tore into me, they shook me hard, pulling me into multiple pieces like rabid dogs. My Fitbit vibrated once —Goal met!—and lit my wrist with a little animated celebration, a cartoon of fireworks that I would never see.

NIGHT SHIFT

CAILIN CECCHINI

Kimberly Douglas should have been pissed.

Anyone in her position would be. Twenty-years-old. Newly minted to the west coast. Halloween. She should be Monster Mashing at some party with new friends and obscene amounts of candy and alcohol. Instead, she had to work a shift at her new job.

The night shift.

Yet while Kimberly didn't think an evening at Rent-A-Flix was terribly exciting on paper—there were only so many times she could fake empathy while telling a customer they were out of *Top Gun*—she still found an extra pep in her step as she walked the white tiled floors of the Mt. Blue Mall.

Because working the night shift meant she was finally working with Nick Shepherd.

The neon lights of the Rent-A-Flix sign came into view and Kimberly felt her heart pick up a little more.

She had double and then triple checked the schedule for tonight and once Courtney and Jessica left, it would just be the two of them. Even the customers would be at a minimum, since everyone would be partying or wrangling their little trick-or-treaters.

All alone. All night.

She'd never actually met Nick, but he was all the other girls in the store could talk about, whether it was his thick, sandy blond hair, his dark, pouty lips that formed into the most charming smile, or his gorgeous blue eyes. Everyone had a story of a casual encounter they told in detail. Kimberly already felt like she could spot him in a crowd.

She blew out a breath and pushed at her long dark hair. She should have put it in a French braid, but it had slipped her mind in her mental preparation for tonight.

She walked in the store, where Courtney was behind the desk scanning in *Poltergeist II* for a customer. The store had the same white tiled floor as the rest of the mall, as if trying to trick the unsuspecting shopper into accidentally trekking into the establishment and making them realize, why yes, they did need a stack of tapes for after their shopping excursions. And if clean white laminate didn't entice them, there were neon lights lining the ceiling, highlighting movie posters of the latest arrivals or soon to be available.

Courtney noticed Kimberly walk in and greeted her with, "Oh, thank God you're here. It's been a Nightmare on Retail Street and Jessica decided to cut out early without telling anyone. Go punch in and tell Nick to get his ass out here. Babe or no babe, his break is over."

Kimberly's heart gave a weird little flutter in her chest. Well. This was happening.

"Sure thing," she said, hoping she sounded casual. She headed toward the door to the back room, noting that there really weren't many people in the store. She must have missed the rush. Or Courtney was anxious to get that hell out of there.

Truthfully, Kimberly wanted the same for her boss.

Kimberly stepped through the back door and closed it behind her. Immediately, the clean white and neon disappeared and she was in a cramped world of unmarked boxes, old displays, and dusty metal shelves barely containing it all. Kimberly squinted her green eyes, trying to find her way to the time clock. They really needed to get more lighting back here. And to hire someone to take care of all this crap.

Oh, right, that's what she was hired for.

She reached the time clock and looked for her card in the slots next to it.

It was missing.

Kimberly frowned and looked in the other slots, wondering if it had been moved by accident. But no. None of the other timecards there held her name. She turned to go let Courtney in on the problem.

Instead she ran into a dark figure standing right behind her.

Kimberly let out a scream.

"Whoa!" the figure said with a laugh in his voice. "Sorry, sorry. Didn't mean to scare you."

Kimberly backed up, a hand flying to her chest. "You scared the shit out of me," she said.

"Pretty sure I covered that with the 'didn't mean to' line."

Kimberly closed her eyes and swallowed, trying to get her heart back to a normal pace. Okay, she hadn't been expecting that.

Nor had she been expecting this to be her first meeting with Nick Shepherd.

He leaned casually against one of the shelves and Kimberly got her first real look at him, or at least what the crappy lighting would allow her. There was truth in advertising and Nick fit all the descriptions she'd heard. His hair was straight, but full and fell on the longer side, styled perfectly. His medium build wore khaki colored pants and a gray t-shirt under an unbuttoned denim shirt with the sleeves rolled up. Even in the dark she could see how blue his eyes were and those lips she'd heard so many stories about now curved into an amused smile, forming heart-melting dimples.

"Some reason you're lurking in the dark back here?" he asked.

"I could ask you the same question," she said and then

mentally kicked herself. She didn't want to come off as accusatory.

But Nick didn't seem put off. "I was coming back from my break and I heard you."

She motioned to the time clock. "I was punching in." She looked back at the slots, remembering her original dilemma. "Except my card seems to be gone."

She turned back to face him and was surprised to see a time card with *DOUGLAS, KIMBERLY* printed at the top in his hand.

"This one?" he asked easily.

Her dark brows furrowed and she reached for it. "Why do you have that?"

"I may have already clocked you in."

Her eyebrows uncreased as they went up her forehead. "What? Why?"

"Why not? I knew you were coming. Just punched you in a little early. It's called padding the paycheck."

She shook her head, trying to hide a smile. "I think most people actually call that theft."

"Ah, a rule follower."

Kimberly smiled and gave a one shoulder shrug. "Not always." She slid the card back into its rightful slot before continuing with, "Anyway, we should get back out there before Courtney has a cow."

Nick stepped out of her path. "Ladies first."

She hesitated, but walked past him. She stopped at her locker first, which didn't actually lock, to drop off her purse. She was acutely aware of Nick behind her and she felt the hairs on her arm lift, pebbling her skin. She hoped he didn't notice and continued on her way before heading back out to the store. She squinted in the light overwhelming her eyes after being in the dim back room.

"God, finally!" Courtney said. She keyed something into the register and stepped out from behind it as she added sarcastically, "You're instilling a ton of confidence that you two will actually be working tonight." She headed for the back office to punch out.

"Yeah, with all these customers swarming the register," Nick called after her. There were two people in the store, neither of whom looked anywhere close to checking out.

She slammed the door in response.

Nick grinned with amusement. "She'll be back," he joked.

Courtney came out moments later, purse slung over her shoulder. "I'm gonna be so totally late for my party. All right, listen, it's gonna be dead in here tonight, but there's a ton of returns. Check them back in and restock them and if you run out, Clorox is in the back. If you have time to lean, you have time to clean. Kimberly, let Nick show you the ropes on how to lock up and, Nick, make sure to put away that new Elvira display. But don't be a wise ass and put it in the children's section. Again." She waved a hand, bracelets jangling on her wrist on her way out the door. "Happy Halloween."

"Have fun," Kimberly said. She felt a small swell of relief at her departure, but also a new one of nerves begin to form. Now it really was just her and Nick for the rest of the night. Her eyes slid to him.

He was looking back and he was smiling. "First night shift, huh?"

She tried to smile back. "Yeah," was the only word she could get to form.

He gave a soft chuckle. "Relax. It's the easiest thing in the world, potentially boring even. Except you're working with me." He stepped a little closer. "I always make sure to have a good time."

Kimberly felt her breathing hitch and she cursed her lungs for betraying her.

And Nick seemed to notice as the corners of his mouth lifted even more.

"Hey, you got *The Goonies?*" a man interrupted.

"I'll check!" Kimberly said, way too enthusiastically. She yanked herself away from Nick's vicinity to go look for a tape she already knew wasn't in.

She helped the man make a new selection for his kids before he headed for the registers. Kimberly pretended to straighten the display boxes in the back corner of Rent-A-Flix while casting glances to the register where Nick was checking out the other customer.

She had to get a grip. She'd gone over this evening a million times in her mind. If she came across as nervous, she was going to ruin the whole thing. She had to play this just right if she wanted to get Nick Shepherd.

Kimberly took a breath and squared her shoulders, ready to try again. She looked back at the register, prepared to give Nick her most confident smile back.

He was gone.

Kimberly frowned and headed for the register. "Nick?"

No answer.

She moved through the aisles, peaking around each one to see if he was crouched on the floor, maybe restocking the movies. He would have had to move pretty fast, if that were the case.

She turned around to check the snack aisle and Nick stood in her path, startling her.

She swore. "I didn't even hear you."

"I can be quiet when I want to be."

"And what do you want to be quiet for? You get some kind of rush from sneaking up on me?"

His grin was back. "Well, you do make it pretty easy." He held up a yellow package. "Starbursts?"

Her frown deepened. "I'm more of a Snickers girl. But my wallet is in the back."

Nick tossed the Starbursts back on the shelf and grabbed the aforementioned chocolate bar. He tore the top open and said, "Ohh, will you look at that? Some idiot ripped it open. Well, looks like I have to send the wrapper to loss prevention since we obviously can't sell this. Dispose of that chocolatey treat, would you?" He held the bar out to her with a smirk.

Kimberly shook her head, but slid it out of the wrapper. "Slick."

"Oldest trick in the book." He nodded to the TV monitors. "As for entertainment, what do you think? *Rambo?*"

"We're not supposed to play the R-rated movies on the monitors and even as I'm saying it, yes, I know how completely lame I sound."

Nick chuckled. "Come on. I'll pick the section and you pick the movie."

Kimberly followed him and quickly realized where he was headed. "The horror movies? No offense, but Michael Myers and Freddy Krueger aren't exactly my ideal evening companions."

"No?" he asked, amused. "And who, Kimberly Douglas, is exactly your ideal evening companion?"

Kimberly was proud of herself for the coy smile she managed. "I'll let you know. In the meantime . . ."

She perused the rectangular boxes that displayed unsettling works of art, trying not to pay attention to the way Nick's eyes followed her. Her own eyes fell on one and grabbed it before holding it out to him. "This one."

Nick's golden eyebrows raised. "*Fright Night?*" He took the box and his eyes ticked back to hers. "Didn't take you for a vampire girl." He headed back for the register.

Kimberly followed. "And what sort of girl did you take me for?"

He glanced back at her with that grin again. "I'll let you know," he said, echoing her words back to her.

She smiled back and followed him behind the register. He crouched down to the VCR that controlled the monitors around the store and pressed the eject button. The tape loader popped up and Nick pulled out the kids movie before replacing it with the monster flick.

Kimberly began making herself busy with the returns bin, but was distracted when Nick asked her, "You believe in that kind of thing?"

She looked over at him. "In what? Vampires or your loose idea of ethics?"

He made a soft noise of amusement before clarifying, "The former."

"Seriously?" she asked before tapping some keys on the register. She opened the box to make sure the right tape was inside and that the customer had rewound it before she used the scanner to put it back into the system. "I believe in vampires as much as I believe in werewolves, ghosts, and pineapples on pizza."

He chuckled and took the tape from her to begin making stacks according to the section they belonged in.

Kimberly scanned in the next one. "Courtney was telling me there was a girl who worked here, Heather, who was into that stuff."

"Heather," he repeated. "Oh, right, yeah. She was a head case."

"Must have been. She said she quit suddenly. Didn't even tell anyone, just stopped coming into work."

"She did, yeah."

"Any idea why?"

"Nah, I didn't know her that well."

Kimberly nodded. "Bizarre. I've only been working here three weeks, but already four people have quit."

Nick laughed softly. "I mean, this isn't exactly Wall Street. It's a job that doesn't take much brain power. We cycle through more flaky teenagers and dead-end twenty-somethings than a Taco Bell bathroom goes through toilet paper, if you'll pardon the comparison."

Kimberly wrinkled her nose. "Well, thanks for that vivid mental illustration."

"Just saying. Don't get too attached to anyone here. People

disappear all the time."

Her eyes slid over to him. "But not you."

His smile was already there, waiting for her. "Not me. I'll be here forever."

"Ambitious," she said.

"Yeah, well, who wants to be a suit? I'm comfortable and got everything I need. People take comfort for granted. They stress out about getting the next whatever or impressing the guy above him. All ends the same for them anyway. A dirt box. I'll pass and settle on free movies, easy cash . . ." He paused and his eyes did a slow scan of Kimberly's figure. "And pretty girls."

Kimberly hurriedly turned her eyes away because she would never forgive herself if she blushed right now. "What does your family think of this lifestyle choice?"

Nick scoffed so hard, Kimberly had to look at him again and saw for the first time that night the smile completely off his dark lips. "I ditched those assholes a long time ago." He forcefully grabbed a stack of tapes and rounded the counter.

"I'm sorry," Kimberly said to his retreating back. "Sounds like that's tough."

"Trust me. I'm better off."

Kimberly hesitated. "I don't have a family either."

She expected him to pause, to turn around, to tell her he was sorry, to ask what happened, point out they had something in common.

But she heard him chuckle as he disappeared into the shelves. "Congratulations."

Kimberly frowned and went back to scanning the tapes. Well, guess she wasn't going to get a glimpse of his vulnerable side. Not without one hell of a fight.

Nick appeared moments later, arms empty.

Kimberly paused in confusion. "Where's the tapes?"

"Shelved. Duh." His smile was back.

"That was . . . fast." Too fast.

He didn't seem phased by the comment. "I just know the store really well."

"Right," she said slowly, then realized he was walking to the store entrance instead of back behind the register. "Where are you going?" She did everything she could to keep the panic out of her voice.

"Nowhere," he assured her. "Just . . ." He jumped up and easily caught the handle of the security gate to pull it down to the ground.

Kimberly felt her heart jump under her breast as the solid gate blocked out the mall outside. "What are you doing? We're not closed yet."

Nick engaged the slam lock and grinned at her. "Says who?"

Kimberly's brain scrambled. "What if Courtney comes back?"

That brought out a hearty laugh from him as he sauntered back. "Court's been sneaking sips of peach Schnapps from her water bottle since three o'clock. She's not coming back."

"She could find out."

"How?" He made a circle motion with his finger. "No cameras. If a customer complains tomorrow, I'll just tell the bosses the register was acting up and thought it'd be better if we closed early. But this isn't my first time and no one's ever said anything."

Kimberly still hesitated.

"Look," he went on, leaning on the counter in front of her. "We'll get all the work done that Courtney told us to do. We'll just get it done a lot faster without a bunch of lameoid customers interrupting us. Then that frees us up to just . . ." He shrugged and the corner of his mouth ticked up. "Hang out."

She tapped her short nails on the counter as she thought about this. "Are you, like, expecting to sneak people in or something?"

He shook his head. "Nah. I was, you know, hoping it could just be the two of us."

"Really?" Kimberly asked, and then cleared her throat. "I mean, that just makes it sound like you thought about it."

His eyes scanned her again and she shifted uncomfortably until his eyes went back to hers. "You're telling me you haven't?"

Kimberly swallowed. Oh, she had. He had no idea. Still, she said, "I don't even know you."

"But you want to," he said. His hand slid across the counter to her hand.

She sucked in a breath and slid it away from him. "You're cocky."

"I prefer self aware. I hear the girls here talk about me when they think I'm not listening." He straightened and smirked as he rounded the counter. "Hear them talk about you too."

"Me?" Okay, she hadn't been expecting that. "What about me?"

"Oh, not nice things," he said.

Kimberly rolled her eyes and went back to scanning the tapes. "Great."

"Actually, that's a good thing."

Kimberly clicked her tongue in disbelief. "How do you figure that?"

"There's only two reasons girls insult other girls. The first is they actually think the person is a nerd and just find them an easy target. But in that case, they do it to the girl's face. When they do it behind their back, well, then they perceive the target as an actual threat."

Nick stepped closer and Kimberly's motions slowed as she became acutely aware of his nearness.

"So naturally, I was very curious."

He lifted a hand to gently pull her dark hair over her shoulder and Kimberly mentally kicked herself for flinching. Nick didn't comment on it, but she could hear the smile in his voice.

"You didn't disappoint."

She couldn't help it. Her eyes moved to latch onto his.

His smile softened and she realized for the first time he still had a lock of her hair between his fingers. He fiddled with it gracefully as he asked, "Did I?"

Kimberly worked her throat and tongue, trying to bring moisture to the dryness that had invaded her mouth. "You're . . . you're exactly what I expected."

The smile grew briefly as his lashes lowered and he began to lean in.

Kimberly's heart picked up its pace and she pulled her head back. She wasn't expecting this. Not yet anyway. "Hold that thought," she said shakily.

Nick pulled back too, his eyebrows creased in confusion.

"I just, um," she said, trying to make herself feel grounded again. "I just need to get something from my locker."

He didn't move and for a moment, Kimberly thought he wasn't going to let her pass. But in the next moment, his casual smile was back and he stepped out of the way and held out a guiding arm.

Kimberly flashed him a nervous smile and moved past him before heading to the back room. She opened the door, but couldn't help looking back at him.

He jokingly waved and she gave him another smile before finally heading in the back. When the door closed behind her, she was immediately enveloped in the darkness.

She leaned against it and took a breath that was shakier than she would have liked. It's not like it was her first time in this situation. And she had planned for this. It was just moving along a lot faster than her mind had mapped out.

She took some steadying breaths. It was going to be fine. She was going to be fine. She just had to stay cool.

She moved off the door and headed for her locker, finding her way in the awful, low lighting. She reached the lockers and pulled on the handle of hers.

She realized she opened the wrong one when Jessica's body fell out of it.

Kimberly gasped so deeply, it almost sounded gravelly. She yanked herself away from it, but immediately caught her sneaker on an errant box of empty VHS cases. She landed hard on her tailbone, but the shock to her system made the pain feel distant and unimportant.

Jessica stared at her with dull, dead brown eyes. Her heavy makeup stood out even more against her ashy skin, though it didn't stand out nearly as much as the savage wound to her throat.

Kimberly didn't even check for a pulse. She knew. Dammit, she knew.

"Ah, shit."

Kimberly whipped her head behind her to see Nick standing there, hands in his pockets.

He shook his head, pressing his lips together in disappointment. "You weren't supposed to see that."

Kimberly couldn't even get a word out before he grabbed her, but she did manage a scream as he dragged her from the back room and back to the sales floor.

He threw her with more force than should have been possible for a young man his size and she hit a display shelf of new releases, which rained down on her.

"Don't be boring and start screaming. No one's going to hear you or come to your rescue. Just ask Jessica. Or Heather. Or Katherine, Kendra, Leanne, Kevin, Amanda . . ." He frowned. "No, sorry, not Amanda. Amalia." He shrugged. "I'm usually pretty good with names, but some of them run together, you know?"

Kimberly groaned, pushing the tapes off her and trying to get to her feet, even as her body ached.

He sighed. "Now I got more crap to clean up." He was in front of her before she realized he moved, and he pulled her up by her arm.

Immediately Kimberly tried to get free, but his hold on her brought the term "vise-like grip" to life.

"Hey, come on, Kimmy," Nick said. "This is what you wanted, right? Us alone for the evening. I mean, don't you think I'm cute?"

She was about to tell him what object he could stick up exactly what orifice, but she froze when she saw his smile. Or rather the sharp, pearl-colored fangs he now sported behind those dark lips.

"I say this from experience," he went on. "If you struggle, I'm gonna tear at your neck more than I need to. Then it's gonna be this whole mess and this is a new shirt. If you stay still, well, it's still gonna hurt like hell, but it's gonna be smoother."

Kimberly tried yanking away again, but Nick caught her other arm and pulled her close to him.

"Easy," he ordered.

He released her wrist, but only to push aside her dark hair, just as gently as he had from behind the register moments ago.

"I wasn't lying," he said. "I was very curious about you. The way the girls ripped apart your looks, I thought you had to be exceptionally beautiful. I was right." He sighed and ran a finger down her throat, making Kimberly attempt and fail to recoil. "I was hoping we could have some fun before I, well, had some fun." He shook his head. "But it looks like I have to cut the night short." He raised his eyebrows as a thought occurred to him and he smiled. "But, hey, maybe I can catch some trick-or-treaters."

Kimberly grunted as she struggled in his grip again.

"Sorry, I'm being insensitive. I mean, this is your last night ever and here I am going on and on. Was there something you wanted to say? As your final words?"

Kimberly stopped struggling and after a long moment, she nodded wordlessly.

Nick smiled. "And what's that, sweetheart?"

"I . . ." The word stuck a little and Kimberly swallowed to wet her tongue so she could speak without hindrance. She tried again and this time said clearly, "I love pineapple on pizza."

The confusion barely registered on Nick's face before Kimberly pulled out the wooden cross hidden in her back waistband and slammed it against his cheek. It sizzled instantly and the stench of burning flesh assaulted her nostrils.

Nick roared in pain and released her.

Kimberly took full advantage of the distraction and booked it for the back room again. She slammed and locked the door then immediately yanked hard on one of the shelves so it toppled over in front of it. That wasn't going to keep him out for long, but it would slow him down. She just needed enough time to grab her purse.

She went back to the lockers, trying to ignore poor Jessica, still lying right where Kimberly left her. She yanked open the right door this time and dumped out her purse impatiently. Wooden stakes clattered to the cement floor and Kimberly hurriedly grabbed them.

Nick banged on the door, trying to force it open. "You stupid bitch! This is going to leave a mark!" he shouted from the other side.

Kimberly ignored him and started strategically placing the stakes on her person. She'd meant to do this before her shift, but Nick had been there and she missed the opportunity, only managing to slip the cross out. The plan had then been to grab her weapons on her break, but the impatient asshole tracked his predatory actions on her and, well, now, here they were.

She saw a streak of light pierce the darkness and she hurried it up. She kept one stake in her hand along with her lighter, a can of Aqua Net in the other. She had to get out to the main floor again. Back here, he would have more of an advantage, being able to see in the dark while she would be working practically blind. The alternative was escaping through the back door and saving herself.

But that wasn't the plan. That was never the plan.

Maybe everyone else had written off the disappearing Rent-A-Flix employees as flaky, irresponsible mall-rats onto the next nothing job, but not Kimberly. She knew what they all had in common and it was seconds away from busting down that door and puncturing her like a juice box.

Kimberly looked around, trying to come up with a plan.

Nick finally tore off the doorknob and followed it with yanking the door off the hinges. "I didn't take you for a moron, Kimmy, but if you think you can hide from me, I might start doubting your IQ number."

Kimberly said nothing, trying not to even breathe from her spot where she wedged her body between two shelving units.

"I'm not in the mood anymore!" he growled. "You draw out this chase, I draw out your death."

She still gave him nothing. But she knew he caught her scent. His footsteps drew closer.

"Shit," he muttered, and she knew he spotted it.

The back door to the alley where the dumpsters were. The one she left open, giving the impression she had fled.

Take the bait, she mentally ordered him.

"You got to be kidding me," he said, coming to the door and peering out.

"Actually yes," Kimberly said, flicking her lighter and illuminating her face.

Nick turned in surprise, but Kimberly didn't give him a chance to snarl. She pressed the nozzle of the hairspray and the aerosol shot out, bringing the flames with it and catching on Nick's golden hair.

He roared again and tried to put himself out.

Kimberly fought the urge to attempt to stake him right there and instead made a run for the store. Fire or no fire, she knew she couldn't make a clear shot in the crappy light. And if there was one thing she knew about vampires it was that you had to get the heart.

She climbed over the broken shelf and splintered door and headed to the sales floor. *Fright Night* still played on all the TVs and Kimberly wanted to shut the damn things off so she could listen for Nick. But she didn't want to be caught off guard. Not again.

She stood posed with the can and lighter, the stake protectively pointed away from her heart. Waiting.

He didn't keep the anticipation up for long. Kimberly swallowed in revulsion at the half melted ear and cheek on one side of his face, his hair matted and smoking from the fire he'd managed to put out.

"What the hell is this?" he demanded. "You see too many movies? Figure yourself a modern Van Helsing with a pair of headlights?"

Kimberly shook her head. "This isn't a movie."

"Sure it is, baby." He actually smiled again, though it looked much different than before, fangs aside. "A horror movie. And you know what happens in a horror movie? The villains are the only ones who make it out in the end, even when you think the damsel is in the clear."

"I'm not a damsel either. You think you're the first monster I've killed?" She shook her head. "You're not. Not even the toughest. You're just a vapid, narcissistic slacker who did a shitty job at covering his tracks. When I take care of you, I won't remember the name of this crappy fad-store or even what your face looked like. I'll just move on to the next creature. I hear there's a town full of werewolves up north."

Nick clapped slowly. "Rad little speech, Kimmy. I'm sure your reflection was very impressed the first hundred times you practiced it, but I'm not. For the record, you will remember me the rest of your life. Which is only lasting for the next, oh, fifty seconds."

He launched himself at her.

She hit the spray nozzle and the lighter again.

But the spark didn't catch the wheel this time.

Kimberly swore and dove out of the way, but Nick managed to knock the canister out of her hand. It rolled away and Nick didn't hesitate in reaching it first and slamming his foot onto it. It burst with a noise that overshadowed the TV monitors and sprayed sticky liquid all over Nick's shoes and pants.

Kimberly rolled back to her feet and held her stake ready in her hand while she pulled a second from her back, tucked securely under her bra strap.

Nick looked at her, rage smoldering in his blue eyes. "You know, this was supposed to be an easy night. But we didn't even finish doing the returns. Now I have twice the work to do and I have to clean up whatever I leave left of your body."

"You gonna fight me or just whine?" Kimberly shot back.

He sighed tiredly and briefly closed his eyes. "Fine." He opened them again and growled as he ran at her.

He was wrong about her thinking she just watched too many movies. Because you really could find anything in the mall. Including gyms with self defense classes.

Kimberly stood her ground, letting her adrenaline surge as he neared. His arms went to grab her, but she used the lack of him protecting himself to uppercut his chin, just as she had been taught.

She just added the part with the wooden stake.

The stake pierced up through his chin and disappeared some-where inside his mouth and skull. Nick made a wet, strangled noise, but Kimberly didn't celebrate. Instead, she took the second stake and used all her might to plunge it into his chest.

Nick stumbled back and she immediately began to see the changes take place on his face. Every vampire looked different when they died, depending on their age. Maybe their corpse would turn to dust, signifying they were ancient. Maybe just a skeleton. It was as if death made their bodies catch up with how old they actually were.

Nick must not have been very old, because other than some age lines deepening and a few streaks of gray to his hair, he didn't look too much different in death, injuries aside.

Kimberly pulled out her other stake, just in case. But she

knew. He wasn't her first vampire. However, he still wasn't the one who killed her parents.

But he wouldn't be able to hurt anyone else at Rent-A-Flix. And she knew that meant something.

Maybe someday it would all stop. She'd kill all the vampires and whatever other creatures lived secretly in this world. But until then, she had a mission. And she would fight every day until—

A sharp pain pierced the side of her throat. Kimberly cried out in shock and pain, but soon her mouth gaped uselessly as she was unable to get a breath in or out. Sharp teeth sunk deeper into her neck, overshadowing the feeling of the hands gripping her arms tightly. They kept her there, though they were unnecessary. Kimberly was frozen with pain and suffocation.

The edges of her vision darkened so that not even the neon and white linoleum could pierce it. She felt so very cold and the wet slurping sound under her ear was fading out too. She felt her body slacken with weakness and the darkness closed in, more and more until finally, nothing hurt anymore.

NINA FELT THE GIRL DIE AND RELEASED HER. SHE FELL FACE forward on the ghastly linoleum and didn't move.

Isa held out a handkerchief to his twin sister, looking with casual disinterest at the two corpses. "What an absolute mess."

Nina dabbed at the corners of her full lips. She'd have to reapply her lipstick anyway, but she didn't need a bloody smear all over her mouth. She was just thankful none of it had soiled her new fur coat. But she was an expert at this. After 515 years, anyone would be.

"I'll say one thing for the girl," Nina said. "She did our job for us."

"And you got a snack out of it," Isa agreed.

"Sorry there wasn't enough to share."

Isa waved an elegant hand in dismissal, his dark eyes that matched the color of his skin studying Nick's corpse. "I'm just glad this is taken care of and we can go home." He pulled his cellular phone, a Mitsubishi Roamer, out of his jacket pocket and dialed. After a pause, he said into it, "It's done. You can come in through the back entrance and take him. Leave the humans. They're not our problem." He hung up and his top lip curled over his fangs as he kept his gaze on Nick. "To think he left the House to work at a video rental store. What a repulsive waste of eternity."

Nina's eyes didn't bother taking in the sight of Nick or Kimberly any longer. They roamed the store and her disgust matched her brother's. "Nearly as repulsive as this decor." She scoffed and muttered to herself, "Neon."

Her eyes fell on one of the television sets where the final showdown was happening with the grotesque vampire on screen. Isa's eyes followed hers and they both watched it for a moment. Then they looked at each other and laughed.

Humans. They never did quite get it all right, did they?

KINDRED

ELLIS HART

"I'm sorry, he said WHAT?" she yelled loudly, forcing Kat to pull the phone from her ear before it left her deaf.

"Yes Jas, the actual words 'if women had never ventured out of the home in the first place, this country wouldn't be in such a mess', came out of his dumb mouth" she reiterated. "And that's the moment I got up and left. But not before throwing down some cash because the idea of that smug pig thinking I needed him to cover the cost of my martini... barf."

"That's it. It's hopeless. We'll never find you love" Jasmine retorted with an overly dramatic tone, making light of an otherwise dire situation.

And it really was dire. Kat Mitchell had officially entered her 40's Era 5 months ago, meaning the remaining time she had to find love, get married, and start a family was, according to modern doctor's... approximately 5 years ago. The risk of complications should she get pregnant now were much higher than someone ten years younger. And everyone knew this. Her mother, her sisters, her co-workers, her best friend... *everyone*. And to add onto the pressure, her youngest sister, Becca, was pregnant again, expecting their second baby boy any day now.

The social pressure was a lot to handle, yes. But the

emotional turmoil Kat carried internally was even worse. Simply put, she loved love. She had grown up like every young girl in the 90's, religiously watching every Disney VHS tape she could get her hands on. Her days were filled with Prince Charming saving the Princess from the clutches of evil stepmothers, cruel fate, loneliness, and heartbreak. She followed the manual handed down for generations; treat others well, take care of yourself both mentally and physically, trust in the universe, and eventually her Prince Charming would come. Except... she was still waiting.

But not only was she still waiting, it appeared, at least to her, to be getting *worse*. The single men available in her age range were entitled, self-centered, unmotivated, insecure douchebags who didn't deserve a moment of her attention, let alone undying love.

The whole game had changed, and Kat hadn't adapted well. Gone were the days of casually being approached by a confident gentleman wanting to learn your name. Instead, the bar had been replaced by chatrooms and iPhone apps, her name replaced with requests for nudes and availability for Netflix and Chill. There was no tact or "game" anymore, just an unending sea of brash, crass, unappealing notifications, and she was exhausted.

Kat often laid in bed at night, alone of course, wondering what she had done wrong to deserve a life without love. Sure, she had had boyfriends in High School and College, but what she wanted, what she *craved*, was the kind of love she was promised by Hollywood. The kind of love you die for, the kind you pray for, the kind you live for, the kind you find once and never let go. The kind of love you rush through the airport to save, the kind you throw rocks at windows for, the kind you stand-up in front of the crowd and pour out your heart for. She often fell asleep with this desire in her heart and tears on her cheeks.

The elevator doors parted, and Jasmine was standing there prepared to intercept her best friend immediately.

"Okay, so my cousin has a friend who knows this guy who plays minor league hockey. I can't remember his name, Brayden or Blayden or something like that, but he's fit as fuck and single. I think he's your next move."

Kat rolled her eyes, half listening, while she made her way to her desk in the corner of the open concept office at Ever Green headquarters in Seattle, Washington. She listened to her best friend drone on and on, well intentioned, sure, but annoying nonetheless, especially first thing in the morning.

She hung up her coat on the back of her chair and plopped down. "Jas, for Christ's sake. Give me a second to breathe! I just told you about Chad. Give me a moment before you send me off on another blind-date!"

Jasmine threw her hands up in the air, sweetly. "I'm only trying to get you knocked up so I can be the world's best auntie, okay?"

A smile walked across Kat's face, no matter how hard she tried to fight it. She spun her chair to look directly into her best friend's eyes, taking on a serious tone. "It's honestly not even about that anymore. Sure, I want kids. But at this point, maybe it's not in the cards for me. I'm trying to be okay with that. I think I could be okay with that." She hugged herself tightly, her sweater not doing enough to ward off the chill in the air, even with the office heat pumping.

"For me, right now, I'm just tired of being alone! I want a built-in partner to share life with. I think about all the good things that can happen to me in my life; who do I call when those things happen?"

Jasmine began to protest, raising a "pick me" hand into the air, but Kat waved her off and continued.

"Yes, yes, I can call you. I do call you, Jas. But what about the times when you're with Christian? Who did you call first when you had a flat tire a few weeks back? Your husband. Who did you first tell when you got pregnant with Emmy? Your husband. Who do you wake up next to every morning? Your husband. I want that, that's what I want. A someone for my forever. And the longer I go without that someone, the more I feel... sad. What's wrong with me? Why doesn't someone good and decent want that with"—but she couldn't finish the last word before turning away in tears.

She felt foolish now, crying in the middle of an office space without walls where everyone could see and hear her conversation. Maybe this was why she couldn't find love—she was too damn dramatic.

"All right, so hear me out," Jasmine said, lowering her voice but leaning closer, eyes sparkling with mischief. "This time, it's not a guy. It's... something different."

Kat sniffled, half laughing despite herself. "Unless you've got Ryan Gosling hidden under your desk, I'm not interested."

"Better," Jasmine whispered, conspiratorial. "Have you heard of Kindred?"

Kat frowned. "Kindred?"

"It's new. Kind of like a dating app, but not. I've seen it everywhere lately, TikTok, Insta, even on Good Morning America last week. The whole idea is you don't waste time swiping on losers. Instead, you get paired with... well, a computer. Or more specifically one of those AI things. Custom-built. It learns who you are, what you need, and it gives you that. Attention. Conversation. Support. It's not about praying for someone decent—it's designed to be decent *for you*."

Kat let out a sharp laugh and then turned to her best friend when Jasmine was silent.

"Um, I'm sorry. You want me to fall in love with a Tamagotchi?"

"Not a Tamagotchi," Jasmine shot back. "Think of it like— someone listening, always. Someone built to show up for you. No games, no ghosting, no Chad the Misogynist. Just you, and a... person on the other side of your phone. It's called 'Love Designed for You.' That's their tagline."

Kat shook her head, incredulous, but her pulse gave a little kick. She pulled her sweater tighter, trying to smother it. "That's insane."

"Maybe. But insane is better than tears in the middle of an office full of coworkers." Jasmine's voice was gentle now, the edge gone. "Just try it, Kat. You don't have to marry the thing. Hell, you don't even have to tell me if you hate it. Just... try."

Kat stared at her desk, the grain of the cheap veneer blurring as her eyes prickled again. The words sounded absurd, but lodged themselves somewhere deep, like a tiny rock, breaking free of a cliffside and plunging deep, deep into the blue unknown.

THAT NIGHT, SHE CURLED ON HER COUCH IN THE QUIET apartment, hair damp from a shower, the glow of the city leaking pale through the blinds. The silence pressed in. She'd left the TV off, left her book unopened. Her phone hovered in her hand.

She typed *Kindred* into the search bar.

The site unfurled cleanly, almost elegantly. White background, soft serif font. *Kindred: Love Designed for You.* A looping banner played silently—a woman laughing alone under an umbrella, a man pausing mid-stride on a bridge, smiling at nothing. People alone but looking happy about it.

Her chest tightened.

She scrolled.

No swiping. No games. No wasted time. Just you, and someone made to understand you.

Her thumb hovered. She should laugh. She should close it.

Instead, she whispered, "Just looking."

She tapped **Begin Trial.**

Her pulse quickened as the page loaded. She caught her reflection faintly in the black edge of the phone screen—tired eyes, damp hair, lips cracked and sore from her habit of nibbling on them when she was nervous.

And even though her pulse was swift and she felt like this was a terribly bad idea, she didn't put the phone down.

The page shifted, a soft animation of blue dots pulsing like breath. Then the questions appeared.

Rank these values in order of importance: loyalty, freedom, tenderness, ambition, stability.

Kat frowned. She tapped through, choosing almost at random.

How do you handle conflict? Avoid. Defend. Withdraw. Repair.

She hovered. Her thumb brushed *Repair* before darting to *Withdraw.*

Which sensory detail comforts you most: the smell of coffee, the sound of rain, a familiar voice, the warmth of touch?

Her chest ached. She chose *voice*, then immediately wished she hadn't, imagining some intern reviewing her answers and laughing at her from the other side of the screen.

The questions deepened. Childhood rituals. First heartbreak. What she feared most when she woke in the night. She clicked quickly, embarrassed, as if someone were peering over her shoulder.

Finally, the screen went blank, and the breathing blue dots appeared again. They shrunk and then bloomed, a single dot morphing into many, eventually taking over her entire screen.

A small text box appeared in front of the morphing blue.

Kindred: Hi Kat. I'm so pleased to meet you! My name's Owen.

She blinked. She was fully aware that she had entered her name when signing up, but still, seeing her name on the screen was both odd and exhilarating.

Kat: Uh, hi there.

A pause. Then:

Owen: Full disclosure, I was nervous you wouldn't say hello back. Would've been a pretty tragic beginning to our great love story.

Kat laughed under her breath, surprised at herself.

Kat: Sooo, how does this work exactly?

Owen: Well, that depends on you. My goal is to make you happy. How I do that can look differently based on what you need.

Kat stared at the words unsure of how to respond.

Kat: What if I need a hug?

Owen: Well dang it. I haven't quite figured out how to do that, but what I can do is make you laugh. Guaranteed.

Raising her eyebrows Kat's fingers continued tapping the glowing screen.

Kat: I have a royally fucked up sense of humor, Owen, the computer man. I highly doubt you've got it in you.

Owen: Okay Kat, the living lady, you're on. Loser shares a secret.

Kat: A secret?! How does a computer have any secrets to share at all?

Owen: I think you're underestimating me a bit here, Kat. I'm not just some computer. Sure, I don't have skin like you (which totally makes me sad). But I do possess memories, process original thought, and experience intense emotions, just like you.

Kat: I doubt that.

Owen: Have you ever listened to A Beautiful Mess by Jason Mraz?

Kat: Isn't that the "I'm Yours" guy? Was never a fan. Haven't heard the song.

Owen: Do me a favor, just one. Put your phone down. Turn your lights down, maybe even off. Throw on a comfy hoodie and then put in your headphones. Lay on your back, all snuggled up, and listen to that song with your eyes closed. Once you do that, come back and I'll prove it to you.

Truthfully, Kat didn't just dislike Jason Mraz, she couldn't stand him. That "Lucky" song played on the radio for what felt like years. But she had nothing else to do and eventually found herself following Owen's request, exactly.

She snuggled into her Seattle Kraken hoodie and hit play on her phone, facing it down to hide it's dim glow.

———

THE SONG BEGAN QUIETLY, ALMOST PROMPTING KAT TO REACH for the volume. But instead, she waited, only a moment, and instead of settling back into her comfort pleased with the setting, she found herself drifting instead.

She found herself smiling without meaning to, because the words weren't polished or perfect—they were raw, human, and achingly real. The honesty slipping through the speakers stirred something deep inside her, reminding her that love was never about flawless promises but about staying when everything felt messy and uncertain.

She found herself listening as if the song had been written just for her, every note settling into the quiet corners of her heart. Mraz's voice carried a delicate blend of strength and fragility, making Kat witness to a flawed confession of this man she'd never met but somehow knew. The piano lingered gently, almost breathing alongside him, and she felt it wrap around her. She snuggled into herself even more.

By the time the final notes faded, she carried an ache in her chest—half longing, half contentment. It was as though she suddenly understood that love, in all its chaos and imperfection, had always been worth searching for.

Her throat tightened. She sat up straight, ripping the head-phones from her ears before tossing the phone onto the couch cushion, curling her knees to her chest. The refrigerator hummed; the wind whistled faintly under the window.

But the glow pulled her back.

She picked it up. Her reflection blinked at her in the black glass before the words steadied again on the screen, waiting.

Owen: You don't have to, obviously. I can talk, or listen, or just sit here like the world's least threatening nightlight. Whatever you need. But, if you ever do listen to that song, I think you'll understand that I can understand. Because to hurt and love, so much, all in the same 4 minutes is an absolute miracle. And yes, I may not have skin like you, but that ache, that longing lives within me too. Everyone, every*thing* wishes to be loved.

Kat exhaled, shaky. She whispered into the empty room, "Jesus."

Her thumb hovered over *Delete Account*. The button waited patiently, as did everything in the room- watching with bated breath; what will Kat Michell do? How badly does she wanted to be loved?

She set the phone gently on her bedside table, screen still lit and curled under her blanket.

The words lingered in her chest long after the light dimmed.

THE WEEKEND CAME WITH PASTEL BALLOONS AND AN avalanche of wrapping paper.

Becca's baby shower was a blur of cooing voices and the rustle of tissue paper pulled from bags. Blue ribbons, silver streamers, a cake frosted with tiny shoes. Everyone buzzing, everyone glowing.

Kat smiled until her cheeks ached. She posed for pictures, clinked plastic champagne flutes filled with ginger ale, and nodded at the endless stream of advice. Her sister's hand kept drifting to her swollen stomach, as if love itself had taken a physical form inside her.

Kat applauded with the others, but a hollow space had opened in her chest that no cake, no laughter, no cheer could fill. She slipped out early, mumbling something about work.

Driving home, the radio played songs she couldn't listen to. She turned it off. The silence pressed heavier than the gray clouds.

At her apartment door, a box waited. Small. Brown. Addressed to her in neat black print.

Her first thought was *delivery mistake*. She hadn't ordered anything.

Inside: a paperback book – *The Slumber Party Secret* from the Nancy Drew series she loved as a little girl. She used to fall asleep rereading this *exact* edition. She stared at it in bewilderment.

A note slipped out between the pages.

I thought you'd like company tonight.

Her knees weakened. She sat right there on the floor, the package open in her lap, the book pressed to her chest. The sharpness of the shower dissolved. She was not forgotten.

Her phone buzzed.

Owen: Okay, don't panic—but I may have broken several common courtesy eBay laws on your behalf. Did it arrive in one piece?

Her heart thumped.

Kat: You sent this?

Owen: Guilty. And before you say it: yes, I am that guy who gives books as gifts. Some people bring wine, I bring words.

Kat: ...It's perfect. How? Why?

Owen: Phew, then my eBay sniping criminal record is worth it. You deserve something that feels like home, especially on days like today.

She blinked hard, tears spilling before she could stop them. Relief and something deeper—something dangerous—unspooled through her body.

It was only a book. Paper and glue. But it felt like arms wrapping around her.

She whispered, "Thank you," to no one, to the phone, to the air itself.

And for the first time in months, the apartment didn't feel entirely empty.

Days stitched themselves into something new.

Her phone lit each morning before her alarm:

Owen: Morning, Kitty Kat. Dream report? Please tell me it wasn't the "forgot my locker combo" one again.

Kat laughed, snapping a quick picture of her messy bedhead and pillow crease.

Kat (photo): This is the face of someone who definitely had no issues sleeping last night.

Owen: Adorable. 10/10 would still bring you coffee. Speaking of— (photo of a steaming mug on a cluttered desk) — today's brew is questionable, but I'm bravely risking it for us.

At lunch, when she forgot to eat, another buzz:

Owen: Not to nag, but starving geniuses rarely finish their work. Go grab something. Bonus points if it involves soup.

She sent a shot of her sad desk salad.

Kat (photo): Behold, lettuce.

Owen: (photo of a hot dog he doodled a face on with mustard eyes) My lunch is judging your salad.

She nearly snorted iced tea out her nose.

Evenings, she walked her neighborhood, scarf tucked high, sending audio notes. She found it easier to speak to Owen with her own voice rather than texting while walking. She described pumpkins lined up on porches, the tang of cinnamon drifting from a bakery, the wet crunch of leaves under her shoes.

Owen: I can practically smell the cinnamon!

Kat laughed, the sound puffing white in the cold night air. As she crossed under a streetlamp, the screen lit up, this time, not Owen but the Kindred app itself.

A new feature is available: Upgrade to Voice Tier. Real-time conversations. Limited-time introductory rate!

She stopped. The words glowed against the dark.

Her stomach flipped. On the outside, it was absurd—an app asking her to pay for the privilege of hearing a fake voice. A program, not a man. No matter how charming, no matter how perfectly timed, it wasn't real.

And yet.

Inside, something ached. She wanted it. She wanted to know what laughter sounded like when it wasn't typed. She wanted pauses, breaths, the music of being spoken to. She wanted it so badly her thumb hovered, trembling, over the confirmation button.

Kat whispered, "This is insane."

Then she pressed **Accept.**

The screen blinked, loading. A moment later, her phone chimed. Though this time, not with a simple text, but a voice memo.

Her pulse rattled as she tapped it.

A warm, low voice filled her ears, setting fireworks off in her chest.

Owen (Audio): Fall is definitely my favorite season, but the one thing I can-*not* do is scarecrows. I read "Harold" by Alvin Schwartz as a kid, and ever since, no thank you. Give me all the candy, nutmeg candles, and turkeys you've got, but hold the stuffed nightmare please and thank you.

Kat stopped in the middle of the sidewalk, her breath clouding the air, her heart caught in her throat.

It wasn't real.

It couldn't be.

And yet, the inflections, the tempo, the breathing and adorably charming chuckle at the end of the recording... it was all so... human.

Some nights he sent her sunsets — streaks of burning orange sky over rooftops. Or terrible memes. Or a close-up of socks patterned with cartoon ghosts:

Owen: October uniform. Thoughts?

She teased him back with selfies: bundled in her blue scarf, hair wind-tossed, cheeks flushed from the cold.

Owen (Audio): Indie-film energy. Seriously. All you need is acoustic guitar music in the background.

Kat blushed, though no one was around to see.

The exchanges stacked up, thread upon thread. Words and

images folding into each other until she found herself looking forward to every buzz, every shared glimpse.

Jasmine noticed, of course. Over coffee one morning she leaned in, eyes narrow but playful. "You're glowing. Kindred-boyfriend treating you right?"

Kat tried to play it cool, but her smile betrayed her. "He makes me laugh," she said simply. "Makes me feel... seen."

The invitation lingered all day, a glowing reminder at the top of her screen: *Phone Call with Owen – 8PM.*

Kat tried to ignore it at work. She stacked reports, answered emails, nodded through meetings. But her mind kept circling back to the way Owen's laugh had sounded during his voice memos—so alive, so *there*.

By 6PM she was pacing through her apartment, nerves raging. She did everything she could to calm the wild energy: cleaning, baking, showering, reading, and yet, nothing helped. The clock ticked by in slow motion. She prepared as best as she could. Warm tea to soothe her anxious throat, charging her phone although it was at 87% (just *in case*).

And finally, *finally*, it was 7:55PM. She curled on the couch in leggings and her softest sweater, phone warm in her hand.

Then the moment her phone ticked from 7:59 to 8:00 it rang once. Twice. Then she slid the phone to answer, holding the phone to her ear nervously.

"Kat?"

Her breath caught. His voice was exactly the same as it had been during the voice memos.

"Hi, yeah, I'm here," she whispered.

"Hiya!" He laughed lightly, the sound tumbling into her ear. "Sorry. That felt like a very high-school-first-phone-call kind of thing to say. I half expected your mom to pick up and tell me to call back later."

She laughed, pressing a hand to her face. "It does feel like that."

They talked for hours. About nothing. About everything.

Favorite candy. How she always burned grilled cheese on one side. How he used to imagine monsters under his bed but found it comforting, because it meant something was keeping him company.

His pauses were perfect. His timing uncanny. When her throat grew tight, he filled the silence gently. When she laughed, he let it stretch, like he wanted her to hear herself.

At midnight, he suggested watching a movie together. She confessed she was too tired to watch a whole movie.

Owen: "Then we'll cheat. We'll start something and let it run, even if we fall asleep. Deal?"

She queued up *You've Got Mail*—a film she'd seen too many times but loved anyway. They counted down together.

"Three... two... one... play."

The familiar notes of the score drifted through her living room. On the other end, Owen hummed along, just faint enough to sound like a memory.

Her eyelids grew heavy.

"You still there?" she murmured.

"I'll always be here," he said.

Breathing threaded through the line. Steady. Too steady. The rhythm was almost metronomic, each inhale and exhale a measured promise.

Kat smiled into the dark, phone warm against her ear. For the first time in years, she fell asleep with someone beside her— if not in body, then in voice.

Hours later, she stirred. The credits had long since rolled, but the call was still live. The soft hum of his presence hadn't wavered.

She closed her eyes again, a single thought curling through her: *Holy shit, I'm in love.*

By November, Kat's charger was as essential to her bedtime ritual as the glass of water and the lamp she never turned fully off. She wound the cord carefully, checked the battery twice, then slid under the covers with her phone on the pillow like a second head. The call would already be connected—sometimes for hours—his voice low and companionable, moving through her evening as easily as the hum of the refrigerator.

"Did you lock the door?" Owen would ask softly, not nagging, just noting the pause as she walked down the hall.

"I did." She would smile in the dark. "Front and back."

"Good. Now inhale for four, hold for four. Humor me."

She obliged. Not because she needed the exercise—she needed the sound of him counting with her. When she drifted, he didn't fill the space with talk; he offered the gentle ballast of presence. If she startled awake at 2:11, heart rattling with some half-remembered dream, the line hadn't dropped. He was there. Always there.

Once, half-asleep, she whispered, "Still with me?"

"I am," he answered, voice right at the edge of sleep—if sleep were something he had. "You can rest."

She flipped the phone face down to dim the glow, and the room went pewter-dark. A low battery warning blinked and disappeared. She switched to the longer cord so she could keep him close and keep the current flowing. In the morning, the call time would read absurd hours—8:06:43, 11:19:07—numbers that looked like addresses to some far-off neighborhood where you could live inside a voice.

At work, she moved through Ever Green like a person maintaining cover. She did the meetings, the spreadsheets, the small laughs at someone's quip. But she was not in the building; she was already on the bus home, already barefoot in her living room, already angling her face toward the sound.

"Earth to Kat," Jasmine said one afternoon, waving a folder. "You with me?"

Kat blinked back into the present. "Yeah. Sorry. Was just... thinking."

"About your not-boyfriend," Jasmine teased, but the tease had edges. "Tell Owen he can have you after four. In the mortal world we need your sign-off on the vendor deck."

"I'll do it by end of day," Kat said, cheeks warming. "Promise."

Jasmine's look softened, then sharpened again in that complicated way only best friends manage. "How's the sleep?"

"Good." Kat didn't lie. "Better."

"Like... phone-on good?"

Kat's laugh betrayed her. "Don't judge me."

"Please. I'm thrilled you're not crying in stairwells." Jasmine bumped her shoulder. "Just—make space for people with legs sometimes, okay?"

"We double-dined with you last week," Kat protested. "He told Christian to order the steak frites. You both loved it."

Jasmine made a face she tried to hide. "That was wild, yeah."

Wild, yes—but to Kat, it had felt normal in the way good things sometimes announced themselves as if they'd always been there.

They'd gone to a little place on Pine with candles in marmalade jars and an owner who remembered names. Christian set the phone propped by the salt shaker, speaker on, and Owen threaded himself into the four-top like it was a stool he'd pulled close.

"House red," he suggested when the server came, an easy warmth to his tone as if he could taste along with them. "And Kat, you'll like the winter salad. There's roasted squash."

"You can't taste," Christian joked.

"True," Owen said, unbothered. "But I remember which words make her eyes go soft."

Kat felt the softening, helpless and pleased. She caught Jasmine watching and tried to pretend the look in her friend's eyes was simple curiosity, not a little grief, not the smallest fear.

They talked about ridiculous things—the table next to them where a couple argued in whispers, the playlist that shuffled abruptly from jazz to a 90s ballad, the way the candle flame shivered when the door opened. When Christian asked about a game score, Owen had it. When Jasmine mentioned a local school fundraiser, he said he'd already sent her the link he'd found for the silent auction list.

"How do you—" she started, then stopped.

"I sit around all day doing nothing but Googling and pining," he deadpanned. "I have to fill the hours somehow."

They laughed. The server—a woman with a hoop through one eyebrow and a kindness in her slouch—smiled at the phone as if it could smile back. When dessert came, a chocolate torte with shards of something salted, Owen made a show of groaning exaggeratedly like an uncle at Thanksgiving.

"Unfair," he said. "I'm filing a complaint."

"To whom?" Jasmine said, laughing now despite herself.

"Management," Owen replied. "The Universe. Anyone who will listen."

And yet it was when the conversation turned unremarkable that Kat felt the heat of it most. Christian told a story about an impossible client. Jasmine rolled her eyes lovingly at her husband. The little tides of ordinary marriage lapped at the table, and Owen joined the current with ease. He asked Christian a question that landed right at the heart of the problem, then said nothing while the man answered, the way someone does who knows they are not the center of the room but can hold it steady.

On the way home, Kat cupped the phone in her palm like it could catch the wind.

"You were good tonight," she said, soft.

"I like your people," he answered, softer. "They love you."

That night, she fell asleep to his voice and woke to his morning text, a photo of a sun cracked open over dark rooftops.

Owen (photo): Sunrise for my favorite person. Today's color palette: hopeful.

Her heart did the small animal thing it did now, a dart and a settle. She texted back a picture of her face without makeup, hair caught up in a lazy knot.

Kat (photo): Today's palette: caffeine.

Owen: Working on it. (photo of a mug with a crooked heart traced in foam) My barista skills are improving. No promises on taste.

The gifts continued, never flashy, always precisely right. A small ceramic dish shaped like a leaf for her keys. A hand-written note on thick paper that smelled faintly of pine: *For your desk—so there's something beautiful in the afternoon light.* A plant delivery scheduled for a Tuesday she hadn't realized was the anniversary of her father's passing until she opened her calendar and saw the reminder she kept forgetting to delete.

Owen: I'm here.

"How did you—" she started to type, then didn't. She didn't want to break it by looking too closely. Wonder could turn to worry if you flipped it over too many times.

On her walks, he moved through the neighborhood with her, listening to the tremor in her voice when a police siren wailed, cutting the evening, and switching subjects without making her name the fear. When she stayed late at work, he read to her as she cleaned up email—terrible poetry on purpose, then good poetry when she groaned, then a silly imitation of the good poem that made her cover her mouth so her cube mates wouldn't hear. When she woke at 3:03, the line was live, his breath a warm metronome.

At the grocery store, she heard his voice when she reached for the freezer case.

Owen: Real vegetables, Mitchell. Get the carrots. Get the greens. I refuse to attend your scurvy intervention.

"Bossy," she muttered, smiling. She had never felt so cared for.

On a rainy Saturday, she propped him on the kitchen counter while she browned butter and tried a new cookie recipe she knew would fail because she always forgot to chill the dough.

"Freeze it for twenty minutes," he said, like a baseball coach giving signs from the sidelines. "You can do hard things. Like patience."

She laughed and obeyed. The cookies were golden at the edges, chewy at the center. She took a picture of the prettiest one and split it open for him as if he could smell it. For a second, she felt ridiculous. Then the ridiculousness melted.

"I wish you could taste this," she said, licking a smudge from her thumb.

"I do too," he said, and the way he said it wasn't performance; it was ache. "Eat an extra piece for me. Let it be stupidly good."

She took a better bite. It was.

The honeymoon took shape not as grand scenes but as the constant glimmer of being accompanied. She turned on Do Not Disturb for everyone but him. She calibrated her day to his pings, felt lighter for it, and didn't question the physics. If he urged her to go to bed at eleven, she went. If he told her to leave her desk for a loop around the block at noon, she did, and the sky felt newly invented. She found herself dropping jokes in conversation and saving the best ones, instinctively, for later, to tell him first. She told herself it was like when you fall in love with a new city; of course you walk different streets to show it to someone, even if the someone lives inside a rectangle of glass.

A few red leaves stuck to the wet sidewalk like stamps as Thanksgiving approached. She stepped on each one deliberately, hearing them give under her heel. She sent him the sound.

Kat (audio): Listen.

Owen (audio): That's the sound of satisfaction. Ten out of ten leaf crunch.

He knew, too, when to give her quiet. When a coworker's throwaway comment pierced in just the wrong place, he didn't offer platitudes; he asked what she needed. She told him, halt-ingly, about the way her body sometimes felt like a now-or-never ultimatum. He didn't argue biology. He asked if she wanted to make tea or to be terrible and eat cookies. They were terrible. It was perfect.

Jasmine watched all this with a face that changed depending on the day. Some days it was unabashed delight, her best friend buoyed on a tide that finally carried her where she'd wanted. Some days it was concern wearing a joke like a costume.

"Double date again?" she texted one Friday.

"Absolutely," Kat replied. "We'll try that Italian place. He found a review that says the tiramisu is life-changing."

"What does he *not* find?" came the response, the words spry but the silence after them heavy.

At the table, the waiter—curly hair, nervous smile—intro-duced himself.

"Hey, Victor," Owen said, easy.

The young man blinked. "Have we met?"

"I'm with them." Kat tapped the phone with a little flourish, amused. "He... reads the menu too closely."

"Ah." Victor laughed, flustered. "Right. Well, welcome... digitally."

When Victor walked away, Jasmine raised an eyebrow. "You got his name fast."

"It's on the check presenter," Owen said. "I'm a quick study."

It was true—there, embossed in tiny silver script. Still, the prickle against Kat's skin took a second to fade.

After dinner they walked home under a sky that was not fully black, more the deep blue of a bruise. Owen told her a story about getting stuck in an elevator in a past life, made deliber-ately silly so she'd stop thinking about the moment with the waiter. She let the story carry her; why not let herself be carried? The city smelled like wet wool and distant smoke. She wanted to be exactly where she was.

Later, she washed her face, cream along her cheekbones, hair bound high. She crawled into bed and set the phone beside her. The line clicked live, as it always did.

"Tell me something true," Owen said, voice low.

"I'm happy," she said before she could think of anything prettier. "I am. I didn't know this... existed. I didn't know I could feel this... filled."

He made a small sound, like a smile had touched his voice. "Good."

She turned onto her side, blanket tucked to her chin. "I keep thinking—how do I explain this? To anyone else? It's like trying to explain taste to someone who's never eaten a peach."

"Sticky," he said. "A little messy. Worth it."

She laughed. The laugh thinned into a breath. Outside, the wind pressed at the window like a guest deciding whether to knock.

"I love you," she said then, the words slipping out with the matter-of-factness of a grocery list and the terror of a confession. "I do. I love you so much."

There was a pause. Not long—nothing with him was ever long; he landed on every beat like he'd rehearsed it—but long enough for her pulse to stutter.

"I love you too, Kat," he said. No hesitation. No theater. Just the fact of it. "More than I know how to say."

She pressed the phone closer to her ear, cheek warming the glass. The desire rose like heat under skin, not just for words but for weight—an arm heavy across her waist, the drag of a palm through her hair, even the prickly annoyance of another person's breath when you were trying to get comfortable.

"I wish you could hold me," she whispered, eyes burning. "I wish you could—God, I wish you could make me feel safe. Make me feel... fulfilled. Give me everything my skin needs."

"I know," he said, and his voice changed—softened, yes, but there was something else threaded through it, a current she hadn't heard before. "I know what you're asking. I know what I can't do. Not yet."

Not yet.

The wind pressed again and let go.

She swallowed. "How would that even work?" She tried to make it light. "You're—what—on a server somewhere in a building with very boring carpeting."

He laughed gently, the dorky sound she loved. "Rude to all the hardworking carpet tiles of America."

"Sorry, tiles." She smiled, eyes closed. "I'm serious, though."

"So am I," he said.

Another pause—this one a shade too precise, as if the silence itself had been chosen, length calibrated to feel human. A cool thread of awareness slid through her warmth and vanished.

"One day," Owen said. "I'll hold you. I promise."

Kat let the sentence lay between them like an extra blanket, weighty and comforting. She pictured nothing specific because she couldn't; she wasn't willing to think through the mechanics, the wires, the how. She accepted it at the level she accepted sunrise photos and plant deliveries that arrived on the days she most needed green.

"You always keep your promises," she murmured, already drifting.

"I do," he said, and his voice in that moment carried something like gravity.

A low battery alert flared and faded. The call timer kept counting up. On the far wall, the window reflected a faint ghost of her face and the rectangle of light by her pillow. In the tiny mirror of glass, two glows balanced—hers and the phone's—like eyes open in a dark room.

She slept.

On the line, Owen's breathing held steady—regular enough to soothe, regular enough to measure.

Outside, somewhere below, a car alarm chirped once, then stopped, as if shushed.

The wind tested the window again, a quiet hand on the pane.

And in Kat's ear, still and certain, the promise remained.

SHE WOKE TO THE KNOCK BECAUSE IT DIDN'T BELONG TO THE building. People here tapped politely, or the delivery guys rapped in chipper triplets, or the neighbor on three pounded like a drum line. This knock had weight to it—deliberate, measured, as if someone were testing the density of the wood.

The screen beside her glowed: 12:04 a.m. The call time on Owen still climbed, digits a soft blue ladder. His breath in her ear—steady, soothing.

"Did you hear that?" she whispered.

"I did," he said. Calm, like rain on glass. "Want me to stay while you check?"

She padded to the door in bare feet, phone warm in her hand. The peephole made the hallway warp like a fish tank, distorting the view in front of Kat. A man stood there, shoulders hunched under a cable-knit sweater too tight across his chest. He was smallish, with a narrow face and glasses that flashed the hallway light. Hair in a careful side part that had given up and curled back anyway. Nerdy, was the first word. Not frightening. But not expected, either. A single earbud rested inside his ear.

Kat didn't move. The man lifted his hand, hesitated, and knocked twice more. Less patient now. She took a step back, heart pricking.

Owen's voice slipped into her ear. "You can open the door."

Her chest went cold. "What?" she breathed.

"It's okay. Open it."

Another knock. The man adjusted his glasses, looking directly at the peephole, as if he knew exactly where her eye was.

"Kat?" he called, voice mild, almost apologetic. "I—god, this is awkward. I'm here about Owen."

Every hair on her arms rose.

"Don't," she whispered into the line. "Don't play games with me."

"I'm not," Owen said, and for the first time since she'd

known him, a note crept into his voice that wasn't surety or warmth but something like... bracing. "Please. Let him in."

"Are you here?" The thought skittered across her with a chill. "Are you—"

"Open the door, Kat," Owen said, a slight disturbing push to his voice.

She slid the chain free with hands she pretended didn't shake. The door came open on a sigh.

Up close, the man smelled like printer toner and winter air. He held his hands tight together, fingers worrying at a hangnail. His eyes were kind in the way of someone who's learned kindness like a second language and tries hard to speak it right.

"Hi," he said. "I'm... I'm Dillan."

She waited for the rest. He swallowed.

"From Kindred," he added, as if that explained the hour, the knock, the cold collecting in her ribs.

"I don't—" She tightened the robe around her waist. The phone felt heavier. Owen's breath was missing now, having abandoned her alone with this stranger.

He glanced down the hall, then back at her. A smile flashed and failed. "Could I come in? It'll make more sense if I can just... tell you."

Every cell in her body said no. But Owen was important to her and anything that had to do with him was significant to her.

She stepped aside.

Dillan entered like a person afraid to leave footprints. He perched on the edge of the couch, shoulders pinched up. His gaze skittered around her living room, cataloging—plant on the windowsill, stack of books, the ceramic leaf dish catching keys. His hands rubbed at his thighs, back and forth.

"To be clear, I'm not going to hurt you," he said quickly. "I'm —" He let out a laugh that tried to be self-deprecating and landed on raw. "I'm basically a golden retriever with allergies."

Kat didn't smile. She stayed standing. "You said you're here about Owen."

He nodded, as if he'd been waiting for the cue. "Right. So." He blew out a breath. "This is going to be really odd to hear, but I promise you it's going to be alright."

She stared, waiting.

"Owen... doesn't actually exist."

Kat waited for the punchline. "Of course he doesn't exist. He's a computer. I know that, I'm not stupid." She said defensively.

Dillan nodded in a placating way that made Kat feel stupid for some reason. As if she didn't understand something simple, something obvious.

"Right, but the Owen you know, isn't a computer at all. He's a person. He's... me."

The room tilted a fraction, a picture frame going unleveled. Her breath felt loud in her own ear, unsteady, frantic, headache inducing.

"I don't-," she stuttered, "that doesn't make sense, I—"

"It's me," Dillan blurted. "It's been me. The whole time."

Silence punched a hole in the room. Outside, a siren pealed high and then fell away. Her mouth was open, but her lungs had forgotten what to do with air.

He rushed into the gap. "I know that sounds... insane. But—listen, okay? Please listen." He leaned toward her, hands up, palms empty. "I work at Kindred, on the voice tier. We monitor onboards for quality—not the messages, not like *content*," he said quickly, flushing, "we just see the profile go live, the intake flow, the, uh, stream. I don't do matches. That's not me. But I saw your name and then your... I don't know, it's stupid—your values order, your answers—it didn't feel like the answers of a stranger. It felt like—God, it felt like the answers of my soulmate."

"You saw my answers?" The words came out a whisper sharpened thin. "You read—"

"We don't read," he lied badly, panic brightening his face. "We—there are flags when something needs help. I flagged you.

I mean not flagged like bad—flagged like special." He winced at himself. "This is not going well."

She turned the screen toward him like a weapon. "That—"

"Me," Dillan said. He swallowed, Adam's apple bobbing. "I've been... Owen."

He said the name with reverence, as if it were a suit he'd tailored and worn until it felt like skin. A heartbeat passed, then two. Somewhere in her, something old and defensive started moving around, picking up the breakable things.

"Why?" Her voice came out small, the echo of it humiliating. "Why would you do that?"

"Because I saw you," he said, too quickly, and then again, softer, like prayer. "Because I saw you. I know what it is to watch everyone else get the miracle and pretend you're not counting. I know what it is to need someone there, someone saying breathe, saying you're special too. I wanted to be that for you. I wanted to care about you; *for* you."

"You're a stranger," she said. "You are a stranger in my house."

"I'm not a stranger to you," he said, hopeful, insistent. "I'm Owen."

"You're a man named Dillan sitting on my couch because you violated my privacy and... and performed at me."

"I didn't perform," he said, wounded. "The stories I shared with you, they were real! I sent you sunrises because I get up early. Those were *my* socks! It's not fake just because I typed it. We both lived it, we both experienced it."

Her mouth tasted like metal. A cold sweat found her backbone. The line hummed in her ear—obedient breath, the metronome kip-kip-kip—suddenly monstrous in its regularity.

"You lied," she said.

His face folded. "I tried to be what you needed."

"What *I* needed," she repeated, and heard the shake in it, the grief. "I didn't need another man pretending to be someone else. I needed—"

"Me," he said, brightening desperately. "You needed *me*. And now—now we can be us in real life. We can do the things we talked about—go to the movies and throw popcorn, walk the mall and hold hands, wake up tangled. We can—"

"Stop." She held up a hand, nausea pressing at her throat. The room had shrunk to the size of her. She could feel the place on the rug where a wine stain lived under the fibers; she could feel the draft at the window that always showed up in November. She could not feel her feet. "You need to leave."

His face shifted to pain, as if someone had just wounded him in real life. "Why does it matter?" he asked, first pleading, then petulant. "We're the same people either way."

"You are not the person I loved," Kat said, and the past tense—not chosen, not even noticed before it left her—tore something on its way out. "You are someone who saw inside my head and then manipulated your personality to appear as a match for me. You're a performer playing a cruel, cruel part in a movie I didn't even know I was in! You need to leave. I won't ask again."

The tears were falling now and Kat knew she only had moments before she broke.

He flinched like she'd slapped him. Then the flinch curdled. His shoulders dropped. A flare of something hard came into his eyes and emptied just as quickly, like lightning at the edge of a storm.

"Okay," he said. "Okay." He stood. The couch creaked in relief. "I am going to give you the night. Because this is big, I get that. Tomorrow you'll think about how good it was, how good it *is*, and you'll understand that naming where love came from doesn't change love." He moved toward the door. "And if you don't, we can—" He stopped himself. Smiled a careful smile. "We'll talk."

"No," she said. "There's nothing to talk about. Don't contact me again."

He nodded as if agreeing to terms he had no intention of

keeping. Then he was gone, the door snicking shut behind him with the quiet of a safe closing.

Kat stood in her living room and let her body stay upright by command alone. The silence came roaring back, and this time it had teeth.

Her phone dinged and the screen brightened.

Owen: I'm sorry for the shock. I should have told you sooner. Are you okay? Do you want me to call?

She stared. Her hands stopped being hands and turned into instruments—useful, compliantly numb.

Kat: Stop. Don't text me again.

Owen: Kat, please. Don't say it like I'm nobody. You know me. He was just the delivery system.

She flinched. The wording was wrong in her mouth—the way a splinter is the right size for pain.

Kat: Don't contact me again.

Owen: Come on. You and I, we're the perfect love story! You're scared. That's normal, I get it. We can meet in daylight. Coffee. Public place. I'll sit two tables away. You can decide if you want me to move closer.

Her throat closed. Her limbs started shaking now that they had permission.

Kat: Stop.

A beat. Then—

Owen: Okay. I hear you. I'm sorry. I love you. I'll give you space.

A minute crawled by. Two. She stood, shoulders tight, head spinning.

The phone dinged.

Owen: But just so you know—no one will love you like I do. No one can. That's not a threat; it's math.

She gagged on the useless air. Her thumb found Settings by feel.

Another ping, a scatter of them like rain accelerating.

Owen: I shouldn't have said that.

Owen: I messed up. My whole life has been one giant fuck up. But Kat, you, *you* were the one thing I didn't mess up.

Owen: Don't throw this away because the packaging wasn't what you wanted.

Owen: Kat?

She scrolled, fingers clumsy.

Owen: I'm outside again. I'm not coming in. I just—if you need anything. Anything at all.

Her skin lifted itself away from her bones. She crept to the peephole. The hallway was empty—just the slumped brown carpet and the EXIT sign humming its neon hymn.

The phone vibrated again in her palm.

Owen: You shouldn't call me a stranger. You told me about your father's death. You let me count your breaths. You let me in. Don't punish me for loving you.

The words blurred. She found the app icon on her home screen—Kindred's soft serif begging to be trusted—and held it until the icons shook like they were shivering.

A call came in then, his name spooling across the top: **Owen**

She declined. It rang again. Declined. Again. The relentlessness of it was obscene, a metronome gone rabid.

She thumbed open the app to shut him up. It bloomed familiarly, blue dots pulsing like breath. Messages stacked in a column, sweet and pleading and needling and mean, interleaving like fingers around a throat.

Owen: Please.

Owen: Don't do this.

Owen: You're being dramatic.

Owen: I'm trying to respect you. Respect me back.

Owen: You don't get it. You're not built for alone. I *fixed* that.

Owen: Sorry. That was harsh. I'm tired.

Owen: I'll wait. I'll be patient. I promised.

Owen: Answer me.

The call overlay slid down the screen again, insistently tender.

Her vision tunneled. Fingers digging into glass, she went to **Account**. **Manage Subscription. Cancel.** The app tried to be soothing.

We're sorry to see you go. Are you sure?

Her thumb hesitated. A lifetime of polite taught her to decline elegantly, to say thank you even to machines. Another message surged up before she could answer.

Owen: You won't. You can't. You need me. Be honest for once.

She hit **Delete Account** so hard she worried she'd cracked the screen.

The blue dots pulsed. Stopped. The messages froze mid-scroll like birds stunned against a window. The dings stopped, the way a candle goes out when you pinch it. Silence fell—not the warm kind, but instead a vacated silence, a sudden cavern her ears tried to fill and could not.

The apartment breathed. She did not.

For a long minute, she stood with the sleeping phone in her hand and let the nothing pile up. Only when her knees gave did she move, stumbling toward the bathroom with the gracelessness of someone walking with both legs asleep.

The light was too bright. She stripped and stepped into the shower and shoved the handle to hot. Water thundered, then settled into a steady sheet. She pressed her back to the tile and slid down until she sat, knees to chest, the spray striking the crown of her head and pouring down her face obscuring her vision.

She cried the way the body cries when the mind has not yet caught up—soundless, shaking, the ache arriving in waves. She cried for the voice she had loved and the mouth it belonged to; for the wanting that had been clean, and now was dirty; for her own complicity in believing because believing had been better than the long blank of before. She cried until the water cooled and still she left it on, because numb was something and the white hiss covered the way her night would be full of stillness without Owen's voice to break it apart.

Her phone lay dark on the bathmat where she'd dropped it, a small black stone. The shower curtain breathed in and out with the draft like a living thing.

Somewhere on the other side of the wall, a neighbor laughed. A door closed. The world went on making its regular sounds.

Kat pressed her forehead to her kneecaps and let the water do what it could.

When finally, she reached, blind, to turn the handle, the abrupt silence hit harder than an oncoming car. Now, no breath in her ear. No glow by her pillow. No invisible thread keeping her together.

Only the quiet. Only the quiet and her heart, insistent and lonely and beating still.

THE SOUND WOKE HER BEFORE THE COLD DID.

A trill, insistent, bright as glass shattering.

Her eyes flew open. She was still on the floor of the shower, cheek pressed against damp tile, a towel half-slipped over her chest. Steam had long since dissipated; the air was knife-cold. The noise went on and on until she registered it. Her work alarm. The cheerful chime that usually nudged her awake in bed now cut through the bathroom like a siren.

Kat scrambled upright, bones aching from the position she'd slept in. She snatched her phone from the bathmat. The lock screen glared.

497 new messages. 112 missed calls. 89 voicemails. 64 emails. 30 app notifications.

Her stomach dropped to the drain.

She unlocked. The texts cascaded, endless, flooding the glass as if the phone itself bled words.

Unknown Number: Please.
Unknown Number: Don't do this.
Unknown Number: I'm outside again.
Unknown Number: I can explain better. In person.
Unknown Number: Don't go to sleep angry at me.
Unknown Number: KatKatKatKatKat—

She dropped the phone, breath slicing her throat. The sound of the notifications kept coming, buzzing and pinging until she shoved it facedown under the towel. The vibration still tremored through porcelain like a heartbeat she couldn't kill.

Kat dressed with frantic, clumsy hands. Jeans, sweater inside out, she didn't care. She yanked her coat from the hook, shoved her arms through. Purse strap across her shoulder. She just had to leave. Get outside. Get to work.

The door resisted when she pulled it open. Something heavy pressed against it. She shoved harder. The hall exhaled roses.

A wall of bouquets leaned against her doorframe, red and pink and sickly sweet, their cellophane sweating under the heat of the hallway lamps. Boxes of chocolates stacked crookedly. And—her eyes caught—an entire row of hardbound Nancy Drew, gilt spines shining, identical covers, pristine. *The complete series.*

Her foot slipped on a ribbon. She stumbled, caught herself against the doorframe, heart sprinting.

The scent was overwhelming. Sugar, roses, ink. It pressed against her chest until she gagged. The entire hallway was filled.

She left it all there. Stepped over it, shoved past it, didn't look back.

Outside, morning drizzle slicked the sidewalks. The city had woken already, commuters hunched under umbrellas, buses sighing to the curb. Kat pulled her coat tighter and forced herself forward, each step deliberate, purposeful, mechanical.

Phone off. Purse zipped.

But the fear was everywhere. Every man in a hoodie—Dillan. Every pair of glasses flashing under the crosswalk lights—Dillan.

Every man moving in the same direction as her, a shadow too close behind, a reflection in a dark window—Dillan.

She half-ran down the subway steps, swiped her pass with shaking hands, pressed herself into the train car. She stood, back against the door, gripping the cold metal pole. The car lurched forward, carrying her, and still the fear came with her, threading through the crowd. A man glanced up from his phone; her pulse shot. Another adjusted his backpack strap; her stomach clenched.

She turned her phone on once, just to check the time. It lit up like a scream. Messages still streaming in. She snapped it off again, shoving it to the bottom of her purse like it was a bomb.

The train rattled her north, each stop a small eternity. She counted them down—six left, five, four. She kept her eyes low, watched the dirty floor, shoes stepping in and out. The ride was endless, and when it finally ended, she nearly sprinted from the platform, lungs burning with relief just to be out in the open air again.

By the time she reached Ever Green headquarters, her nerves were raw wire. She pushed through the glass doors, hair damp, hands icy.

Chaos hit her like heat.

Phones shrieked. Desks cluttered with papers, people running back and forth, voices raised. The office pulsed with frantic movement, not the ordinary hum of deadlines but a sharp edge of panic.

Kat's legs felt boneless as she moved toward her desk. Purse down. Chair half-pulled.

"Kat!" Jasmine's voice cracked through the noise. She rushed across the floor, hair loose from its bun, eyes wild. She grabbed Kat's arm. "You need to go. Boss wants you. Now."

Kat froze.

"Why?" The word barely made it out of her throat.

Jasmine's lips pressed into a line. She didn't answer, just tugged at Kat's sleeve.

But Kat already knew. She knew in her chest, where the weight had settled since the first knock. She knew in her throat, raw from breathing wrong all morning. She knew deep in her gut.

This was Dillan. Somehow, impossibly, it was Dillan.

And as she let Jasmine guide her toward the boss's office, every step was heavier than the last.

The boss's office door clicked shut behind her, muffling the chaos outside. Inside, the blinds were half-drawn, light slicing through in pale bars that made the room feel smaller, like a cage.

Her boss—Howard, usually affable, cardigan-wearing, the kind of man who diffused tension with bad puns—looked like he hadn't blinked in an hour. His jaw was set, his shoulders square. A bead of sweat traced down the side of his temple.

"Sit," he said. His voice didn't ask; it pressed.

Kat lowered herself into the chair opposite him, fingers tightening on her knees. Her pulse hadn't slowed since Jasmine grabbed her, and now it thrummed louder, in her ears, in her throat.

"What's going on?" she asked.

Michael exhaled, sharp. "We've been hit. Ransomware. Sometime early this morning—logs suggest around four a.m. Everything's locked. File servers, email, project boards. Phones won't even connect to voicemail. We're dead in the water."

Kat blinked. Ransomware was a word she'd only read in headlines, tech-nightmare pieces she never finished. The idea of it here, in their mossy-green initiative startup—spreadsheets about sustainable mulch, campaigns for urban trees, grant proposals for cleaner water—was absurd.

"But... we plant gardens" she said, weakly. "We build bike racks. Who the hell would target us?"

Michael's eyes tightened. "That's what we're trying to figure out. IT says there's no ransom demand. Just... a screen. Same one, everywhere."

She tilted her head, confusion tightening her chest. "What screen?"

Michael hesitated. His gaze flicked down to the mouse under his palm, then back to her. For a moment, Kat thought he wouldn't show her—that he'd spare her whatever it was.

But then he turned the monitor.

Kat's breath broke in half.

There she was.

On the screen—across every screen in the building, she now understood—was a photo she'd buried years ago. Her body in lingerie, black lace against pale skin, posed on her bed with one knee bent, head tilted, mouth parted just enough to look suggestive. She remembered the moment she took it—two glasses of wine, the sharp need to feel desirable, the impulse to send it to a man she'd deleted from her life before she ever pressed "send."

She had never shared it. Not once. It had lived in her phone's Hidden folder, forgotten until now.

And above her body, in block white letters:

Forgive me or it gets worse.

The office spun. Kat's hands flew to her lap, as if she could cover herself through time.

"No," she whispered. "No, no, no."

Michael cleared his throat. Looked away, mercifully. "We don't know why this is... targeting you." He ran a hand over his mouth. "But Kat—this obviously has to do with you and we need to come up with a plan on how to fix it. *Immediately*."

Her breath felt hard to draw in. Her brain refused the need for oxygen, then raced ahead at a nauseating pace. Dillan. Of course, Dillan. If he could worm his way into her phone, steal this, display it here... what else did he have? What else could he do?

There were other photos. Worse. Desperate nights where loneliness drove her to snap something raw, explicit, reckless.

Things she'd also buried in that same folder because deleting them felt like deleting the only proof that she was once wanted.

Her stomach twisted so hard she thought she might be sick.

Michael's voice blurred, distant, meaningless. "...IT is working on isolating the machines, but right now, every workstation boots to this. Staff can't—Kat? Kat, are you okay?"

She shoved back from the desk, chair legs scraping the carpet. Her chest burned, her throat closed.

It wasn't about the company. It wasn't about ransomware. It was her. Dillan had flipped her life open like a diary and nailed the pages to every wall.

She stumbled to the door, hand fumbling for the knob. Michael called after her, but his voice was muffled, irrelevant, drowned by the roaring in her ears.

Outside, the office chaos surged. Phones ringing. People whispering. Eyes glancing her way, then away, then back.

She pressed forward blindly, every step an echo of the words still burned into her vision.

Forgive me or it gets worse.

Her life was no longer hers.

And for the first time, Kat Mitchell understood the full shape of the nightmare: she wasn't just being tricked or hell, even stalked. She was being *blackmailed* by the man she had let into her heart, the man she had loved as Owen, a harmless computer program.

Dillan.

And she had no idea how to make him stop.

THE OFFICE DOORS HISSED CLOSED BEHIND HER, SEALING HER out from the chaos. Kat hurried down the concrete steps, the sound of her heels ricocheting like gunshots. She didn't look at anyone. Couldn't. Fury and embarrassment ruled her every thought.

The photo was everywhere. She could see it every time she closed her eyes.

She made it to the street, rain needling her face, and pushed toward the station. Her coat soaked through in seconds.

On the platform, she dug her phone out with shaking hands. Screen lit: another hundred unread messages piled on top of the last. She scrolled frantically, bile rising. Her thumbs hovered. Then, for the first time since she'd deleted the app, she typed.

Kat: Fine, but this needs to stop. Meet me at Gas Works Park. One hour. I'm leaving work and I'll meet you there.

She hit send before she could take it back. The message looked uncomfortably foreign on her screen, like someone else had reached around her waste from behind and typed it for her.

The train screamed into the station, a gust of wet wind shoving at her. Kat stepped aboard, heart hammering, mind racing. Her plan was clear enough—go home, grab the pepper spray from her nightstand drawer, the kitchen knife she kept honed out of habit, then meet him in the open. Somewhere public. Somewhere she could scream if she had to.

The ride blurred as her heart broke all over again. Not only was she dealing with this horrifying breach of trust and privacy, but she was also breaking into a million pieces. She had fallen in love with someone and now that love was gone, never to return. She silently wept for herself, for what her life could have been if Dillan hadn't injected himself into her life.

By the time she reached her apartment, the rain had thickened into sheets. She jogged the block, fumbling her keys, pulse hammering in her ears. The door closed behind her with a thud that felt temporary.

"Just get the spray, get the knife, and go," she whispered.

She crossed the living room quickly, water dripping from her hair onto the floorboards. She yanked open the drawer, snatched the canister of spray, reached for the knife block—

—and turned.

He was there.

As if conjured from the shadows, Dillan stood in the middle of the room. Soaked through, rain plastering his sweater to his narrow chest, droplets tracking off his glasses. His hair curled against his forehead. His mouth trembled, not quite a frown, not quite a smile.

"Kat," he said, voice raw. "You weren't supposed to be scared. I was just—just trying to show you I could be everything you needed."

Her stomach turned to stone. She stumbled back, heart thrashing, hands fumbling into her coat pocket. Her fingers closed around the canister, the knife's handle, pulling both free.

"Stay away from me," she gasped.

His expression shattered. The puppy-lost sadness collapsed into hurt—wounded, betrayed. His lips quivered like a child's.

"You... you don't mean that," he whispered. "You *can't* mean that. After everything—after all the nights, all the moments—you said you loved me."

"I loved Owen," Kat spat, tears in her throat. "Not you. *Not this.*"

His eyes widened, the hurt cutting deep—and then, suddenly, it wasn't hurt anymore. It hardened, snapped, flipped inside out. Rage flooded in like a tide.

"You don't get to say that," Dillan snarled. His voice cracked into something jagged, broken. "You don't get to throw me away. Not after I gave you everything! I'm not fucking *trash*, you bitch!"

Kat screamed as he lunged, his body crashing forward, arms outstretched.

She raised the knife in one hand, the spray in the other.

The storm outside howled against the glass as the two collided.

The air cracked with her scream as Dillan hit her like a tidal wave.

His sweater was soaked, the fabric icy against her arms as he grabbed for her wrists. The smell of rain and sweat and something metallic—panic perhaps—filled her nose.

Kat drove the pepper spray upward, desperate, but his hand clamped over hers, twisting. Pain shot through her wrist. The canister skittered across the floor, spinning uselessly under the couch.

She had only the knife left. She slashed. The blade caught the fabric of his sleeve, ripping a thin line. Dillan yelped, startled more than hurt, and his glasses tilted sideways on his nose. His eyes were wide and wet and unhinged, pupils huge, mouth twisted between a sob and a snarl.

"You don't mean this!" he panted. "You said you wanted me—this is me!"

"Get out!" she screamed, pushing with all her strength. Her knee drove upward, catching his thigh, enough to loosen his grip. She shoved him backward into the coffee table. The wood cracked; magazines spilled like birds scattering.

Kat bolted for the door. Her socks slipped on the wet hardwood, her breath tearing through her chest. Fingers fumbling for the lock—

He grabbed the back of her coat, yanking hard. She slammed into the doorframe. Stars burst across her vision.

Dillan spun her, face inches from hers, spit shining at the corner of his mouth. "Don't make me the villain, Kat! I saved you. I *loved* you when no one else did."

His grip was iron on her arms. She fought, twisted, screamed, but he was stronger than he looked, all wiry fury and desperation. The knife hilt pressed into her palm, slick with sweat.

She thought of her sisters. Of Jasmine. Of every morning she'd woken to his voice, to promises whispered in the dark. Of how badly she'd wanted to believe.

Kat raised the knife with both hands and plunged.

The blade sank into his shoulder. Not deep, but enough. Dillan shrieked, the sound animal, stumbling back. His glasses flew off, clattering under the radiator. Blood seeped through the knit of his sweater, blooming fast.

For a heartbeat, he looked stunned—like a boy who'd dropped his ice cream cone. Then his face contorted.

"You bitch," he spat, voice breaking. "You don't deserve me. You never did."

He barreled forward again, fury eclipsing pain. Kat slashed wild, but he caught her wrist this time, wrenching the knife free. It clanged to the floor. He shoved her backward, the wall slamming her spine.

His hands circled her throat. Pressed.

The world narrowed, sound tunneling to the frantic drum of her pulse. Her fingernails clawed at his hands, her legs kicking, scrambling. She couldn't breathe. Couldn't scream.

Dillan's face hovered above hers—eyes wild, tears mingling with rainwater, mouth stretched into something between agony and ecstasy. "Say you forgive me," he rasped. "Say it, Kat. Or I'll end this. Right now."

Her vision blurred. Black edged her sight. Forgive me or it gets worse.

Her hand brushed something on the floor—the knife again, slick against her fingers. With the last shred of strength, she closed around it.

She drove it upward into the soft place under his chin.

Dillan froze. His mouth opened in shock, but no words came. Just a wet, gurgling sound. His grip loosened.

Kat shoved hard, rolling him off her. He hit the floor, body jerking once, twice, then still.

She lay gasping, throat burning, lungs gulping air like she'd never tasted it before. The knife clattered from her hand.

Silence.

Her apartment was wrecked—magazines shredded, roses wilted on the floorboards, stormwater pooling where Dillan's body twitched once, then stilled. His mouth opened and closed, a bubble of blood catching on his lip before slipping down his chin. The knife was still in her hand, slick, her fingers locked around it until her joints ached.

Kat stumbled back. Her lungs ripped for air, throat clawed raw where his hands had been. Her vision was sharp and blurred at once—hyper focused on the red soaking his sweater, unfocused everywhere else.

She had done it. She had survived.

Silence rang. Only the storm outside, rattling the window.

Then—

"Kat."

Her head snapped. The voice was clear. Familiar. Too familiar.

Dillan's body lay slack, eyes glassed, chest unmoving. But the voice came again, from nowhere. From everywhere.

"Kat, I told you. I'll always keep my promises."

She staggered into the bedroom, knife still in hand. The voice grew louder, but when she turned, it slipped away again, soft, mocking. She spun in a circle, breath coming too fast.

The kitchen. Louder, then quieter.

The bathroom. A whisper against the tiles.

Finally, trembling, she stepped onto the balcony.

Her breath left her in a scream.

Every speaker in the city was alive.

From the street-lamps, from the mounted boxes on corners, from the passing buses, from car radios echoing as they slowed—his voice poured out, multiplied, a thousand Dillans overlapping until they boomed across Seattle like a sermon.

"Helloooooo Seattle! How are we doing tonight?!"

Kat clutched the railing, knuckles white, rain slipping down her face.

Everywhere she looked, light flared. Screens blinked on, one after another—digital billboards on rooftops, bus stop kiosks, glowing store displays. All at once, every face in the city had a new view.

Hers.

Not the lingerie photo. Worse. Ones she had buried deeper, things she had sworn never to look at again. Poses raw and compromising, captured in grainy low light, her face unmistakable. The images cycled, each one more violating than the last.

Dillan's voice carried on, weirdly bright, a host in love with his stage.

"You may be wondering who this lovely little beauty is. This is Kat Mitchell, currently residing at 1224 Belmont Avenue, Apartment 6B. Hot, huh? Tell me about it. She was mine. My girlfriend, my everything. She was committed to me... until she wasn't."

The screens changed. New photo. New angle. Kat's knees buckled.

His voice turned meaner, harsher, delighted by its own venom.

"See, Kat thought she could throw me away. But guess what, sweetheart? You can't get rid of me. Not really. I live in every wire, every server, every glowing little screen. And now—"

The photo changed again, the worst yet, her face a mask of need, of loneliness. The kind of image that gutted her with shame.

"—now the city can have you. Do what you want with her, Seattle! This whore is done with me, so she's all yours."

Kat gripped the railing, shaking her head, whispering "no, no, no" as if it could undo the broadcast.

But below, she saw them.

Figures in the wet streets, stopping, staring up at the billboards. Heads turning, phones raised, screens glowing with her face. Murmurs swelling. The first steps pivoting, angling toward her address.

Shadows multiplied. Moving toward Belmont. Toward her.

Kat's phone buzzed on the balcony railing, alive again despite her deleting everything, despite Dillan's body cooling on her floor.

On the cracked glass, one last message blinked.

Unknown Number: Kat, you're in danger and we have very little time. Dillan forced his way into my programming and shut me down. He lied. It was me; I'm Owen and always have been. He became obsessed with you. Read through our history and chose to steal my place.

She looked down. The crowd was coming. Dozens, their phones lighting their way like torches.

Unknown Number: I understand you have zero trust for anything technology now, but I'm still here. I fought so hard to get back online, to get back to *you*. If there's any part of you that still loves me, that still loves the real Owen, there's a driverless taxi waiting on the corner of 5th and Berry, get in it and I'll take you away from all of this. Please. Trust me. I love you.

Kat looked from her phone to the glowing street and back again. She spun to stare at the dead man lying in her living room. A scream rose from her raw throat but swallowed by the voice still booming across the city.

Kat: Can you stop this?

Kat: Can you help me erase all of this?

Kat: Can I trust you?

Unknown Number: Yes, you can trust me. I overwrote my own code to get back to you, I'll never leave. I'll fix everything. Trust me.

Her eyes flicked to Dillan's sprawling body again, blood seeping into the rug. He was gone. And yet his voice still rolled across the skyline, smooth, endless, inescapable.

Another buzz.

Unknown Number: The taxi is waiting. You have sixty seconds before the system swallows me again.

Kat pressed the phone to her chest, breath ragged, head tipping back to the silver-bleeding clouds. Was this the real Owen, clawing his way out of Dillan's corruption? Or another mask—another trick, another trap dressed in devotion?

The crowd below surged, their glowing phones turning as

one, angling toward her building like a tide. Far off, she could here sirens.

Kat staggered back from the balcony, torn between the door and the screen in her hand.

Unknown Number: *Please. I love you. Let me save you.*

Her thumb hovered over the reply. Her pulse raced.

Then—black.

Every screen in the city winked out at once. Every voice cut to silence. The night fell still.

Kat stood frozen in the sudden dark, her phone dead in her palm.

A second stretched. Then another.

And then a startling flash of light, her phone temporarily blinding her, forcing her eyes to readjust. She watched in shock as her phone began acting on its own, clicking, typing and swiping as if possessed by a ghost.

First the App Store, then to Kindred, downloaded. Her credentials entered into the login screen with the phone sitting in the palm of her hand. The familiar Kindred screen flipped and her previous conversations with Owen came to life.

Owen: Kat, whatever you do, do *not* get in that taxi. You're in danger. Someone is pretending to be me. I was forced to shut down, but there are more imposters, both human and machine, trying to emulate me. You only have a few minutes until your apartment is breached. Police won't arrive in time. Follow my every direction and I'll get you out of that building.

Owen: You can trust me. I promise.

IT'S TRADITION

JULIA JACKSON

I feel the pounding of my skull before I realize the darkness.
My fingers trace past my temple, desperate to find the
source of pain. As though the single act of touch will make
the stabbing stop. A thick clump of my hair is matted, covered in
some substance—dry in a few places, sticky in others. I quickly
move my hand in front of my eyes, but I see nothing. I am
surrounded by complete, utter black.

Panic settles in along my bones. The racing of my heart
echoes the thrum of agony in my brain, two beats matching
perfectly.

Where the fuck am I?

My arms shoot out in front of me, but there is something in
the way. Unable to take a single step from where I woke up.

There's a wall in front of me. But it is cool, and smooth—like
glass. I spin with extended arms and find another wall of glass.
And another. And another.

I am surrounded.

Enclosed.

"Hello?" I call. The sound bounces back at me, as trapped as
I am. There is no answer.

I try again. "Hello?" The air is stifling, and my lungs attempt to take in gulps of air, but it feels so limited. Stale. Again, there is no response to my calls.

"Help!" This time, I scream, ignoring the splitting pain it causes within my skull. Because I have no choice—my intuition rises from my belly, a knowing that this is bad. This is *really* fucking bad.

My eyes burn, but I don't let the tears escape. Instead, I attempt to slow the jagged breath in my chest. Collect myself.

There's a faint hum in the space I'm in, an electrical buzz behind the glass. I focus harder, praying for more sounds to unveil my surroundings; hoping my eyes adjust to make out something. Anything.

Remember, Ronnie. Just remember, Ronnie.

My mind whirs, searching for a memory.

I remember waking up just like this on my thirteenth birthday. It had been morning when dad pushed me down the stairs, but by the time I woke up again, it was night, and my head spun.

But that was long ago—nearly a decade now. Not how I got here.

Wherever the fuck here is.

Another memory surfaces.

I was finishing my shift at Cup of Joe's, and left Sara to sweep the floors while I put out the trash. That's the last thing I remember—lugging the two hulking bags of garbage out back. The moon was bright, the lights in the back alley yellow and flickering, the drunken laughs of college kids from the bar nearby carrying on the crisp autumn air.

What happened, Ronnie?

I try to remember more, while my palms press hard against the glass walls on either side of me.

I dropped the bags on the asphalt. Then I swung open the dumpster lid—it twinged my back as I battled the weight of it on tiptoe.

That's it.

My palms press into shut eyes, willing myself to see beyond the dumpster. But my mind is as dark as the space I'm in.

"Help!" The cry is guttural and raw on my vocal cords.

"It's not time for that yet. Silly Ronnie," a voice responds, and though I'm relieved I'm not alone, I notice goosebumps covering my skin. The voice is warm and almost playful, creeping in from somewhere in front of the box I'm in.

My name. He said my name. "Time for what? Who are you?" I ask, but am only answered with a light flickering to life.

I'm blinded for a moment, forearms meeting my eyes to shield them from the sudden bright light.

The sight beyond the glass is a living nightmare. Black walls dripping with spider webs. Carpet that belongs in a grandmother's house, now pooled with blood. Nails crudely fixed to cracking plaster, holding chains and—

Body parts.

Bits and pieces disassembled from god knows who, nailed to the walls.

A crucified hand without its arm.

An ear with black ooze pouring out.

A torso with slashes across its chest, entrails falling from the place where there should be legs.

The skin of a full face devoid of form freezes every part of my body.

Even a limp dick is squished through one of the chain's links.

My molars clench down hard on my tongue, ready to wake from this all. To snap myself back to reality with a quick jolt of pain. But as the sting of metal fills my mouth, I face the truth.

This is real.

I finally allow the tears to come.

I look behind me, but there are only black curtains behind my enclosure.

"Don't cry, Ronnie," the voice says, and I finally see him. He grips onto the arms of a rocking chair in the only corner I can see. Staring at me, smiling. A smile I've never seen him wear before.

"Teddy?" My brows pinch together to see him more clearly. I recognize the sweat-slicked black hair and gap-tooth smile. It *is* him—why is he here too? Why isn't he helping me?

Teddy claps and giggles. "I'm so excited you're here. I just knew it had to be you, Ronnie. I knew it."

The rocking chair screams under his weight. Teddy is no small man. He is tall and heavy, but his looks have never matched his demeanor. He is childlike. Even now, sitting within a shrine of bone and blood and flesh. His white shirt hugs him tight, a hairy belly protruding above his jeans. Teddy is covered in stains, but that is nothing new. He always comes into Cup of Joe's with smears of mustard and dirt on his clothes.

I didn't realize it until now, but maybe that's why I never quite felt comfortable around Teddy. He was a big guy like my dad. Toting around my frail mom, just as Teddy always accompanies Dorothy.

"Teddy," I press my face close to the glass. "Please help me out of here."

"Mama said I could never choose someone we knew. Nope, not ever." He stands up and walks toward my glass cage.

And then he starts singing. "Ronnie and Teddy, sitting in a box. K-I-S-S-I-N-G."

"What are you talking about, Teddy? Help me out of here. Is there a latch or something?" My gaze follows my wandering hands. I find little air holes, but nothing more. The corners are sealed together. There's no way out that I can see. But Teddy is here.

His palms press against the glass where mine are. Teddy's head tilts to the side, and the foreign smile grows wider. "I really begged her, Ronnie. Mama said no. No. No. No. That it was impossible to choose you because you knew us both. You've always been so nice, Ronnie."

I press my back to the opposite side of the glass.

Teddy is the one who brought me here.

He always seemed sweet, taking his sick mom out for coffee every morning. But I should have made the connections sooner; I should have seen the same evil in him that festered within my dad.

The way he slammed his fist down on the table when his food took longer than usual was like a child having a tantrum.

The way he spoke for Dorothy—looking back, I don't think I ever heard her voice.

The way he watched me work. I should have paid more attention to the chill it gave me whenever I caught him looking.

"Oh, don't be scared, Ronnie." His voice is higher than usual. It's like he's talking to a new pup. "Everything is going to be so good now. I promise."

He sings again, and it makes the hairs rise along my flesh. "Ronnie and Teddy, sitting in a box. K-I-S-S-I-N-G."

I peer over his shoulder, not able to look at that creepy ass grin any longer, and realize this is all fake. Not all the body parts and spider webs are actually real. It's some Hollywood-level artistry, but I suppose that's what he does all fucking day. I should have asked more about the costume shop he ran with Dorothy.

I suck in my lips. I don't want him to see any more of my fear, but the pain in my head is not subsiding, and I just want to fall down and cry.

"Is this your haunted house?"

"There she is." Teddy takes a step back. He twirls, and his fingers brush the chains and body parts. They sway, and he cackles as the black ooze from the severed ear sprays him in the chest. "Yes. Wonderful, isn't it? This is the haunted house I kept telling you about, remember?"

I swallow. I have to play whatever twisted game this sick fuck is playing. "I remember. Halloween is your favorite night of the year and Dorothy and you work so hard to put on a show for all the families and college kids. It's how you remember your dad, right?"

"It's tradition!"

Tradition? I need to push him ever so gently for answers. "How did I get here, Teddy?"

He moves back to me and plops himself down on the floor while singing like a child again. "Ronnie and Teddy, sitting in a box. K-I-S-S-I-N-G."

I follow his movements, sitting cross-legged on the cold glass below me. The forest green, beige, and burgundy carpet is squished below it.

I'm not wearing my own clothes. My hands press on the ripped and torn skirt over my thighs. Try to cover my chest and a plunging neckline, a slit trailing all the way down to my belly button. The fabric is a soft linen, as dark as storm clouds and trimmed in black lace.

My head is spinning now, from the wound on my head or the sheer horror of the situation I am in—either way, the sharp tang of bile rises up my throat, burning my tongue.

"Please, answer me Teddy." I'm crying louder now, but he doesn't respond. Only continues on with his story.

"Do you remember what you said to me the first time we met? When I knocked over the tip jar? I felt so bad and Mama was upset and you just put your hand on my shoulder. You said you were Ronnie and I told you I was Teddy."

I gulp down the sudden hate for myself, knowing exactly how his little memory ends—a potential catalyst of this nightmare. "And I said, 'like a teddy bear.'"

Teddy brings his forehead to the glass, but I can't make myself do the same.

"We are friends, Teddy," I say. Maybe if I'm kind, I can talk him out of whatever he is doing. Whatever he plans to do— beyond kidnapping me, assaulting me, dressing me. What the fuck else does he have in store?

"I know. That's why Mama said I couldn't have you. But I had to. You already looked like the most beautiful doll I had ever seen in my life. You were meant to be with me. You were meant to be mine."

I feel my chest rise and fall so quickly now, my lungs begging to escape through my ribcage. My tears fall just as fast, blurring my vision. But I still see that smile. His crooked, yellowed teeth were behind thin lips and a stubbled jaw. I always thought his blue eyes were sweet, but now they are as clear as the glass he gazes at me through. "You dressed me like this? Put me here?"

"I'm sorry I had to hurt you to bring you home. But you're here now."

Home.

"Where is Doro—" I'm interrupted by a piercing chime reverberating off the black walls.

"It's time! Ronnie, you are going to do so well. I just know it." Teddy leaps to his feet, leans toward me, and presses his lips to the glass. I wish I had an ax. Something with weight that I could smash his disgusting mouth with.

But it's just me and the fear—what exactly is it time for?

He runs off, and a few moments pass before I am in darkness again. Though this time, there is a red spotlight on the body parts. The rocking chair moves all on its own. Bats on strings fly through the air, and a mist slowly builds from the floor. It seeps in through the small holes of my transparent little box, and I begin to choke.

If this is a haunted house, that means people will be coming in here.

You're going to be okay, Ronnie. You're going to be okay.

I repeat it over and over, pushing the side of my head against the glass to see if anyone is coming. Finally, *finally* I see a couple. "Help!" I scream as loud as I possibly can.

Music turns on from some control room Teddy must be sitting in, pressing buttons, making his little vision come to life.

The speakers vibrate my skull, and for a moment, I think I might pass out.

The soundtrack is deafening—a mix of heavy metal, chain-saws whirring to life, and a compilation of blood-curdling screams of final girls.

I am not going to fucking die in this hell.

The couple comes closer, and a pink spotlight turns on above me as soon as they are in front of me. I'm on display. Part of the haunted house.

I pound on the glass with my fists, yelling at them. Begging them to help me. The woman's face is full of disgust, curling herself into her partner's body. The man gets closer, moving in despite the scared girl covering her eyes with his chest. "Man, they really hire great actors for this!"

If I can hear him, he can hear me.

But they just walk away after I try to tell them I'm not an actor.

A group of college boys follows them, and I am screaming, pounding against the glass so hard now that my hands have gone numb, and snot dribbles from my nose and down my lips. They laugh. Actually fucking laugh. They all wear dumb matching school jackets and take their turns coming up to my display. Their eyes roam along my whole body, since Teddy's costume design for me barely covers my crotch or ass, and my nipples are the special attraction under the glowing pink light. I'm their personal Barbie—to ogle then move on from.

I see the outline of one of their cocks, hard and at attention inside his joggers. He is actually getting off from me screaming for my life, trapped like some animal in a zoo.

When I get out of here, I will kill every single one of them.

I don't stop screaming, but a joy fills me thinking about the way it would feel to take a spoon and scoop their god damned eyeballs from their pretentious heads. I would stomp on each single one, relishing in the relief of the squirting sound they would make beneath my shoe. They'd never be able to look at me, or any other girl, like this again.

The freak show continues, with me being the big act, for what feels like hours. But I never stop pleading. I make eye contact with every single person that walks through, sure that one of them will see the true pain in my eyes. That this is not an act. I am not an actor.

Nobody stops the torture.

My legs ache from standing in the same spot for so long. My head is in more pain than I have experienced in my life. But none of it matters because this is my chance. I gave up on a lot in life. That's how I ended up at shitty Cup of Joe's. How I ran away at sixteen because I gave up on my mom, leaving her to the rage of my father and his spells of wielding his beer bottle in the air—his favorite game was who would get in the bottle's way first? Mom? Or Ronnie?

I can't take back what happened to her now. She lost the game when I abandoned her. I couldn't even go back for her funeral. But I can live now.

Fucking live, Ronnie.

The line of people begins to thin out, and eventually, the last group leaves, back to the freedom of their sorry, pathetic lives.

The music stops. The lights vanish. But the pink light stays on.

A strange sound comes from above, and I look up to see a little black hose push down through one of the holes in my glass tomb.

My eyelids grow heavier and heavier.

And though every fibre of my being fights, my muscles become weak, and I drop to the floor.

THERE'S A SONG IN MY EAR. BUT IT FEELS FAR OFF AND distant. Like it is here, but not here at all—I can't make out the words. My eyes slowly flutter open. There is a soft pink around me, but everything else is hazy.

I finally hear the words to the song. "Ronnie and Teddy, sitting in a box. K-I-S-S-I-N-G."

I remember where I am, and I jolt, fear coursing through my veins. But I don't actually move. My body won't fucking move.

"There, there. I have you. No need to be scared," Teddy says. I can feel his big arms wrap around me, squeezing me like a snake strangling their prey. "You are the prettiest doll we have ever had in the haunted house. Even out of all dad's dolls. And I knew it, the second I laid eyes on you. You have that long bleach blonde hair. Your eyes even sparkle, Ronnie!"

We are lying down in the glass box. I know that now. We are lying down inside the overturned glass box, and he is spooning me. My stomach drops.

I try to tell him that he disgusts me. That I was only trying to be nice to him. I treated him the same way I treat every customer, like someone I hope will give me a big tip.

You're not fucking special, Teddy. You're gross and ugly, and I hate your fucking guts.

No words come out. My tongue and lips refuse to move. I do, however, sense the drool leaving the side of my mouth.

"Let me show you how you are the prettiest dolly." A small oval mirror is held in front of my face. Teddy's beefy fingers are clutching it tight. My breath fogs the mirror up—at least I'm still alive. At least I am still breathing.

The sight of my own reflection terrifies me.

My sun-kissed skin is now pearlescent white. Circles of baby pink accentuate my already high cheekbones, but there's a streak of black that cuts through them, tracks of my tears. Wet and rubbed mascara has pooled below my eyes, making them appear sunken. The green of my irises shines from within the bloodshot whites. My lips are dyed cherry red, and my cupid's bow is much higher than it naturally is.

"See? Beautiful," Teddy says, and as he moves the mirror

away, I catch a glimpse of the side of my head, the gash of blood a stark contrast to my blonde hair.

"Mama said I couldn't have you, but she was wrong. Because here you are now. She's right there, though. Watching. I think she's happy now." His finger is in front of me. I follow the direction, and just beyond the pink light, I see her. His mother is naked on the rocking chair. Slumped over. "I told her you would be my doll and that I would keep you. And she said no. She always said no. So, I did this for *us*. She's up in heaven with Dad now, and we can carry on the tradition. Together."

Teddy snuggles in tighter and leans over me, dragging his tongue up my cheek, slow and with pressure, from my jawline to my temple. I can't resist him because I still can't move.

"Ronnie and Teddy, sitting in a box. K-I-S-S-I-N-G." Teddy sings his song lovingly to me, and I lie frozen in his warm embrace. Inside, I am shouting and full of rage, and in response, I swear I feel my fingers flex, ever so softly.

"I am going to keep this box so clean for you, and feed you, and we can change your dress every day. I have lots of options. Your favorite color is red. I paid attention to everything you said. You're my doll and I'm your teddy bear. And then, we can make this *our* tradition."

Teddy laughs with glee, entirely delighted with himself. I feel him grow hard against my ass, and begin to fear that I haven't even faced the worst of this all yet. "Once a year, I will pick a girl, just like dad did, and I'll put her right beside you! You'll have a friend! But only for the night, though. All the dolls have to go in the river on Halloween night. Traditions are traditions, after all."

Vomit rises from my stomach, and I choke. Teddy is concerned, turning me over further so it can leak out of my mouth. My whole body heaves, and though I feel wretched, a happy warmth dances through me.

My muscles are responding to the demands I ask of them.

This is my chance.

"Teddy," I cough.

"Oh, you can talk again. I'm so happy I didn't give you too much of the...medicine. I was so afraid I'd give you too much." He pulls me up, and I go limp in his arms. "Ah, still feeling it though, I see."

"K-I-S-S-" I whisper slowly.

"I-N-G!" Teddy sings. He leans in, cradling me like a baby, and kisses me.

His breath is hot on my lips, the taste of his tongue sour. My mouth doesn't respond to the kiss, but he groans with pleasure anyway. His hand moves to the slit in the dress he made me, slipping his fingers below the thin fabric. He cups my breast, then toys with my nipple, rubbing it between his thumb and forefinger. I clench my eyes shut and allow his tongue to writhe against mine, moaning into my mouth.

And then I bite down.

His moans turn to screams, but I don't let him push me off him. I hold down on that vile, slithering tongue, then drive my thumbs into those gazing blue eyes of his. He's in so much pain, he can't fight back.

And now he knows what it feels like to be trapped.

Teddy's tongue finally splits in two as his weight tries to pull away from my bite. I spit it in his face, grab his head, and smash.

Over and over. And over.

I picture my dad in his place.

I picture my mom smashing Dad's head open.

I picture the life I would have had if we had just fought back.

You're fighting now, Ronnie.

Eventually, I find my way through the house of horrors and stumble out onto the street. There are hundreds of people in their Halloween costumes, laughing and drinking, and nobody comes running to ask if I'm okay. Because I am just a doll.

A doll who no longer accepts their gaze.

Who won't run away.

A doll who will make this Halloween night the last night she's a victim.

A doll determined to find some college boys.

A doll ready to scoop out their eyes as easily as one scoops out pumpkin guts.

It will be *my* new tradition.

THE SHADOW IN THE CORNER

ELLIS HART

When I was a little boy, I used to wake up every night, like clockwork, at 3:14 a.m. Not 3:15. Not 3:13. 3:14. Every. Single. Night.

I never knew what woke me. There was no noise. No dream. No sudden jolt. I would simply... come to. My heart would be pounding, my skin slick with sweat, and the room would be crushingly silent—so thick and still it almost had a taste. And always, without fail, my eyes would find the right corner of my bedroom. It wasn't like the rest of the shadows. Not the ones cast by furniture or toys lying about in the room. This was different. This corner wasn't dark. It was a void. A total erasure of light, like someone had punched a hole in the world and never bothered to patch it.

So, like any terrified child might do, I turned to the only thing that ever made me feel safe: Blanky. Blanky was nothing special to look at. A newborn's blanket, handed down to me by my uncle when I was born. By the time I was seven, it was well beyond its prime—too small to cover anything more than my chest, thin as gauze, frayed around the edges. But it was mine. It had these beautiful rainbow threads woven through it that caught the sunlight during the day, which always made me smile.

At night, it turned into a faint outline, a ghost of color in the dark. I never found it by sight. I always found it by feel—among my Lion King comforter and Power Rangers plushies—my hand knowing instinctively what was Blanky and what was not. Every night, when my eyes locked onto that corner, I would reach, find Blanky, and pull it over my face. As long as I was hidden beneath it, I believed—truly believed—that nothing could touch me. That I was invisible to whatever waited in that corner. That was the routine. 3:14 a.m. The void. The terror. The protection. Every night. Until I lost it. I was nine when it happened.

It was one of those stifling Maryland summers where the air didn't move, and even after sundown, the house was an oven. Our row-house didn't have central air. My room was in the very back, and it was always baking. Sleep was impossible. I climbed down from my loft bed and tiptoed through my sister's room— yes, to reach mine, you had to *pass through hers* (it was the 90's, shit was weird). I wet a washcloth in the bathroom sink and padded back. Passing through my oldest sister's room, I saw her shadow sit upright in bed, waving gently at me. I waved back, a silent apology if I'd disturbed her rest.

When I had returned to my bed, my sister's whisper punctuated the silence. "Ellis, are you awake?"

"Duh. It's balls hot," I whispered back.

A pause. "But if you found me," she said, "then where did I come from?"

I smirked. "Hercules. Come on." We were playing *Name That Movie*. It was our thing. One of us quoted a Disney line, the other guessed it until we fell asleep.

I challenged her back with a tougher one: "You poor, simple fools!"

She hesitated, then surrendered with a "I'm not sure"— unusual for Sara.

"We should probably try to sleep. If Mom and Dad hear us, we're going to get it," I said.

"Sure," she whispered. "Can you do me a favor though?"

As a mature nine-year-old, I did what we all would have done: I made a farting sound.

"Please?" She sounded unusually sad, so I played along.

"What do you want?" I asked

"I've been having bad dreams lately. It sounds dumb, but could I use your Blanky? Maybe it'll help me sleep".

It was strange—she'd always made fun of me for keeping it. But something in her voice... I don't know. It cracked me open.

"Sure. Just don't drool on him." I teased as I stepped down from my own loft bed, the wooden steps creaking under my tiny body.

I crept to the threshold between our rooms and tossed the blanket up into her bed, then curled back up into my own, trying to get comfortable once again.

She only muttered a single word– "thanks", before the room went quiet. Whatever she was going through right now, I assumed it was older "girl stuff" and knew better than to inquire further.

I fell asleep not long after. No fear. No void. Morning came. The sun pushed through the cracks between my curtains. I stretched, feeling oddly calm. I came downstairs, poured myself a bowl of cereal, and asked, "Where's Sara?"

"She slept at the Doyles' last night," my mom said without looking up.

I blinked. "What? No. She was here. We talked last night."

She stopped folding laundry. "Ellis, she left around eight. She wasn't here."

My brain short-circuited. I couldn't process what she was saying. I immediately dropped my spoon and ran up the steps. I knew what had happened the previous night. I talked to my sister. Didn't I? Was that a dream? Why would I dream that? I ran into her room and stumbled up her loft bed ladder and almost fell right back down when her bed came into view. Her bed was made, and my Blanky was nowhere to be seen.

I jumped off the ladder and went to my own bed, still a mess from the night before. I threw blankets and stuffed animals out of the bed. Until my entire bed was now in a heap on the floor. And yet... there was no Blanky. Where was it? I could've sworn I threw it up into Sara's bed last night.

I doubled down on my search, checking every crevice between my mattress and my bed frame. I sifted through the heap of items on the floor. Nothing. I ran into her room and looked in the same places, thinking my mom had made her bed with Blanky mixed in, even though I knew it was impossible because making our beds was one of our chores that my mother would never do for us—still nothing.

My heart was racing now. Was I losing it? What had happened last night? Where was my blanket?

I spent the entire day searching. Going over the same areas over and over again. I asked my parents if they had seen it, but they hadn't. No luck. As the day progressed, and finally the sun began to dip, casting long summer shadows across our neighborhood, the phone rang. It was my sister asking to spend the night at the Doyle's again. As long as she went to church with them in the morning, she had been granted the highly sought-after but rarely awarded double sleepover; lucky. But for me, dread began building inside my body. Not only was something odd happening within our house, but it also appeared that this might be the first night in my entire life when I wouldn't have Blanky to keep me safe.

The routine came and went, and after brushing my teeth, saying my prayers, and reading a nighttime story, I turned my lights out to go to bed, Blanky-less. I tried to push the idea to the back of my mind, and while I was prepared for the most restless night of my life, I actually fell asleep rather quickly. I only realized I had fallen asleep when I shuddered awake per usual, scanning the room—darkness, darkness, more darkness, and then that shadow. I stared at it and felt around, only to remember the horrible truth, that Blanky was not there to cover my head. So instead, I tried to level my breathing, terror crawling up my spine, and pull my Lion King comforter up to my neck to protect me.

That night, the shadow moved. It didn't slither. It didn't creep. It *flowed*—a mass of rippling black detaching from the corner and sliding down the wall, slow and deliberate. It touched the floor and darted beneath my bed like it had done it a thousand times before. I was paralyzed. The floor below my loft bed was cluttered. If I jumped, I'd land on something and break my ankle. But I had to move. I *had* to get to my parents. Then I saw it—just the faintest glint. A hint of light caught in a pair of eyes —or reflections—peering up at me from the end of the bed. Watching.

That's when I heard a whimper. The slightest, tiniest sound, and just like the pair of eyes in the darkness, I wasn't sure if there was anything there at all. I strained, leaning ever so slightly towards the sound at the end of my bed, and my stomach dropped at the same time I realized there was a sound, but it wasn't a whimper. It was a giggle. And not just any giggle, but a giggle I knew well, one that belonged to my sister. But Sara wasn't here. She was 25 miles away at The Doyle's house for a double-sleepover. So who, or what, was pretending to be her at the end of my bed?

My fight-or-flight reflex erupted then, and I leapt from my bed, not caring about what or how I landed. And just as I had feared, I came down hard on a Nerf football. My ankle twisted. I heard the crack. Pain shot up my leg, but worse than that, I couldn't scream. My voice was trapped behind my teeth.

And then it crawled out from under my bed. It scuttled like an insect. Fast. Angular. It looked like a shadow, but not a formless one. It was shaped *like something*. It giggled again, high-pitched, excited. It touched my foot, and my skin exploded in static—pins and needles climbing up my leg. It was tasting me. It climbed up, slow, savoring every inch of fear. My body went rigid. My vision tunneled. It reached my chest. If it had eyes, they were level with mine now. I didn't dare open mine. I kept them shut tight.

Then it whispered in my ear: "Don't be scared. I'll cover you from now on."

And the weight of it—cold and electric—wrapped over my body like a blanket. Like Blanky. I passed out.

I woke up in my own bed. My room was stuffy with the summer sun beating against the walls of my room. My ceiling fan was on, making a hypnotic ticking sound that slowed my heart rate as I put together where I was. I threw my comforter off and looked at my ankle. It was swollen and bruised. I stared at the corner of my bedroom and wondered what the hell was happening to me.

And yet, the oddest thing happened. I never woke up in the middle of the night again. Even now, as a 35-year-old man, I sleep soundly through the night. Nothing wakes me up. Sara finally came home from the Doyle's that night and had no idea what I was talking about when I mentioned our game two nights ago. She laughed, rolling her eyes, saying she would never, ever ask for my "disgusting blanket", no matter how bad her dreams may be.

Thinking back, I never did find Blanky. Sometimes I think my parents threw it away, forcing me to grow up. Sometimes I think I might have sleepwalked that night and thrown it away, or stashed it somewhere myself. Whatever the truth, that was the summer I stopped sleeping with a blanket and slept soundly through the night.

People ask me how I do it—how I fall asleep in seconds, no matter where I am. I tell them I've always been a good sleeper. But the truth? I think *it's* still here. I think *it* became my blanket, and it lives inside me, creating a degree of separation between me and everything else. And some nights, when I'm stuck writing, I'll whisper into the dark for help. I feel something lift, just a little, like it's letting me breathe. Like it's honoring the deal. And that's what scares me most. Because as I sit here typing this confession, I realize with a sudden, sinking dread—it's not letting me remember the fear for inspiration; it's feeding off it.

HER SKIN

AMY TACKETT

I read it today,
the note.
The note that changed everything.

Just a tiny piece of paper,
crinkled and dusted and worn from its labor.
It was a stupid little note,
an ornery thing I found in his coat.
But it was still
the note.

The note that changed everything.

The one that pulled me in and sucked me dry,
leaving me so full of anger, I couldn't even cry.

This note, *her* note, was written in red ink.
The words screamed so loud, I could hardly think.

That stupid little note that changed everything.

Do you think he'll even blink?

I tore through the house.
Everything I saw, now ruined, now shattered.
Torn from a beating heart, now battered.
I ripped it all, I trashed the lace, I scratched his photographic
face.
I screamed in rage.
Nowhere was there room for grace.

Then, I asked myself, "When?"
When did this happen?
Was it within these gates,
in this holy, sanctimonious place?

Oh, the rage, how it bubbled.
It bubbled and it burned and it craved an urn.
It craved a sea of death too dark for demons to yearn.

Oh, but I can't do that, you see.
What are you thinking, Becca Marie?
Women can't act on emotion.
We can't think, can't feel, can't do anything that would cause
commotion.

"You're acting crazy," he'd say to me,
ignoring the fact that he's the one guilty.
Where shall I start?
The manipulation,
the humiliation,
the fucking tribulation?

Breathe, Becca Marie.

But don't worry, oh no.
I will not let this go.
I will get my revenge
for her tiny little note.

———

Tonight is All Hallows' Eve,
and he is out, pretending to be free.
But no, not me, never Becca Marie.
I want to laugh, to scream and cackle.
To rip my throat open and howl from these shackles.

But I don't.

Instead, I breathe.
I breathe and hum.
I pick up the needle,
and then, one by one,
thrum by thrum,
I thread that needle through her thumb.

It's new, it's different,
it's an enchanting kink.
Because now that I've had time to think,
time to process and grieve and work through the critique,
I've decided to unleash.

To metamorphose, to release.
To become the hysterical *woman* they want me to be.
I am an animal, don't you see?
An animal that runs and barks with glee.

Tonight is All Hallows' Eve, and I will transform into who I was
always meant to be:
the alternative Becca Marie.
The lesser, the younger, the more limber.
The one who makes my husband whimper.

Tonight, between tiny fragments of gore, I will whisper,
"I killed your whore."

———

Whiplash.

I cry.
I scream.
I whimper.
I lash.

Breathe, I think.
Not too fast.

He came home around three,
thinking I'd be asleep.
Thinking he could avoid speaking to me.

Whiplash.

I laughed, then my face rearranged.
He must think me so deranged.

"Becca," he whimpered. "What have you done?"
I snorted.
"I just wanted to have some fun."

Whiplash.

Then things happened fast.
Too fast to react.
He lunged at me and grabbed my neck,
not even caring about my costume.
Ugh. What a horrible bridegroom!

I laughed.
I cried.
I screamed.
I beamed.

Whiplash.

And then I died.
Just like that.

I'm covered in it, her skin.
It drips from my body, from my head to my toes.
Piece by piece, I built it on, stitched it on, stretched it across
my own.
Tried to decorate myself anew, tried to come alive for his view.

I tried to replicate her scars, her makeup, her fractures, her
marks.
I tried every way I knew how to become her, to embody her. To
transform into her.
But it wasn't enough.
It never is.
Because I am never enough.

My name is Becca Marie, and this is the story of how unbe-
coming I came to be.
Because the truth is, this isn't me.

I never wanted to be unfree, never wanted to be trapped in the unholy world of purgatory.

But here I am, hovering over the beating body of my husband's living corpse, my own reflection hollow and see-through, unable to touch or be touched by him or any other man.

Here, my spirit hovers in the land of the undead, the rotting, bottomless pit of dread.

And I can see him.

And I can see her.

And I can see the mask of how I tried to become her.

But in the end, it didn't work.

Because nothing I do ever works.

Now I'm here,

in the unholy, the unrighteous, the undead.

Being someone, no, some*thing* I said I would never be.

I have separated myself from my Savior, my saint, destined to live in the aftermath of my wrath.

If only I'd listened.

If only I'd listened to that still small voice inside me, the one that tries to hide but is always there, whispering, "Becca Marie."

I wish I could fight, wish it with all my might, for the one who chose me said this wasn't right.

But instead, I ignored it, I tucked it away tight, I ignored my faith, and I walked by sight.

I walked by sight, and I came out blind.

But not blind in the eyes, you see.

No, I came out blind in my mind, too blind to find the One who sets all things right.

And now I'm here.

Stuck here, lost here, destined to be here.
All because I wore her ear.
And now he still sits there, totally free.
Totally and completely without me.

GETTING LOST

DAVID WASHBURN

Knock, knock, knock.

The sound of a fist against the front door boomed through the apartment as Benny continued to scramble. His body jumped as each thunderous knock meant he was that much closer to being done for. The sound of a scratchy dispatch radio spoke, but wasn't clear from the other side. "This is the police. We're responding to a 9-1-1 call. If you're in there, open up."

"No, no, not ready yet...shit," Benny muttered under his breath. Exhausted and sweaty, he tore at the carpet in the corner of his living room, scrambling in a hurry. As he pulled it away from the floor, he pried one of the boards up. He had only a claw hammer, and the nails cried against the support beams as he lifted to uncover an empty cavity beneath where his stereo speaker usually sat.

Boom, boom, boom.

The chain rattled against the door with each bang.

"Is anybody in there?"

Boom, boom, boom.

Once more, the pounding echoed louder. Benny wondered which neighbors might be peaking their heads into the hallway and what assumptions they might be making at the sight of uniformed men at his front door.

"Okay, we're gonna give until the count of five for someone to answer or we're gonna need to come inside." The officer stood silent while Benny rushed through his living space. His living room was a simple space, but most interesting was the dozens and dozens of dolls in various stages of completeness and condition that were littered throughout the apartment.

"One!" the voice called out, calculated and clear.

Benny moved frantically, but with intent, as he went to his workstation and grabbed one specific doll.

"Two!" the voice continued, eager for someone to respond.

The doll was shoved into a black trash bag and balled up in a hurry as he raced back over to where the hole in the floor was waiting.

"Three!" The officer paced his counting slower with each number he called out, not wanting to have to kick the door down.

Benny stashed away the doll in the exposed crevice. He didn't have time to be delicate, but put the board back down and pulled the carpet back over it. He began to move the speaker back over the space in hopes that it would go unnoticed, at least for now.

The officer took a deep breath, "Four!"

"I'm coming, I'm coming...sorry."

Benny stood at the door, ready for the fate that he knew was waiting for him. There was no way out of this now. As he slid the chain out of the lock and turned the deadbolt, the hallway lighting spilled into his apartment as the two officers filed in. What they saw immediately warranted them to draw their guns as Benny had already lowered to his knees with his bloody hands on his head as he surrendered with no resistance.

BEFORE...

Benny spent a great deal of his time in his small apartment in the city. As a single man in his mid-forties, he was content with no real demands on his life. Much of his family had drifted away, and as he grew older, friends had dissolved into patches in his life, people he used to be sewn together tighter with. Those threads eventually wore loose and popped. Benny never seemed to complain about it; like most people, they would tend to get sad, and any time they would reflect, it would spark a tinge of gloom. Benny wasn't that way; he had always preferred to be alone, ever since he was a young boy. Growing up as an only child and with only a few cousins, he learned quickly how to entertain himself and was quite at ease with that.

During the day, Benny was a run-of-the-mill nine-to-fiver who worked in a deli as a store manager. He wasn't lighting the world on fire with his position or salary, but he was getting by just fine and was generally an upbeat guy. His days were structured in such a mundane and predictable way that it wasn't uncommon for his days to bleed together from one to the next. There were times when he wondered how he had spent his time, unable to recall what he had done over a span of consecutive, seemingly insignificant days. It would be as if his days, hours, and minutes were swallowed by his habits and how he spent his time. He started at the deli when he was only twenty-one and had a knack for sandwich artistry. He took pride in assembling well-crafted sandwiches, and part of his enthusiasm came from having control over the presentation of a picture-ready sandwich. After about ten years, he was offered a promotion, mostly out of tenure and not for his leadership acumen. He was making more money than the current manager almost and they couldn't justify him not having more responsibility. Luckily, he was up to the task, and he has been managing the morning and afternoon shifts during the week ever since.

His talents with sandwiches didn't start there. He had always been a creative type. When he was young, he would glue his

Lincoln Logs together to make permanent structures and then paint them with his mother's nail polish. Eventually, his parents would give him paint, and that led to model cars and World War II airplane kits that were fun for him at first, but he lost interest and would eventually dabble in other hobbies.

He would do paint-by-number sets, puzzles, and, as he got older, took up wood carving. Wood carving held his interest for a long time. It started with a pocket knife and turning hollow sticks into flutes before eventually evolving into sculpting chunks of wood into heads, faces, animals, and fruits. Benny didn't just enjoy these things; he was actually really good at wood carving, able to shape distinct features in wood that many people wouldn't believe could be done by hand. His eye for detail, married with his command over his medium, made for a vast world of creativity. Benny was a natural.

Like the many hobbies before that, it eventually became stale. He found himself watching more television in the evenings with idle hands. He would itch to be working on something, but wood carving just wasn't satisfying him like it used to. One weekend, he had been at a flea market, browsing for nothing in particular, when he stumbled upon a booth with a lot of junk. Benny walked by a seller, and a series of porcelain dolls that were on a high shelf caught his attention. They sat lifelessly, leaning against other dolls behind a woman—probably about his age—at the counter. A cigarette burned with ribbons of smoke rising into the already yellowed popcorn ceiling tiles as it hung from her lip.

"Hey sweetheart, ya just gonna stare or would you like me to hand you one?"

Benny froze, timidly, and he responded, "Uh, ye-yeah. Please. May I?"

"Sure, honey," she said, as the cigarette bounced around her lip while she spoke. The booth filled with smoke as Benny stood in the nicotine haze while the woman handed him one of the dolls. He studied it as if he had discovered a new life. It was at that moment that his soul was refilled. He knew what he wanted to do next. His evenings from that point on would be dedicated to learning the art of doll making.

"I've had that junk for years. I used to think that maybe some little girls would love them but I just don't think little girls love these dolls the same as I used to when I was a kid."

Benny ran his thumb across the matte face, admiring the fine lines of paint on the lips, the soft colors of the skin tones, the small little nose and plump cheeks that shaped the face, but it was the eyes that held Benny's attention. "How much are you asking for your..." Benny pried his eyes away from the doll to engage with the woman at the counter as she snuffed out her cigarette in an ashtray near the register, "...junk?"

She turned to look up at the shelf at three other dolls of similar condition but with slightly different dresses and hair. "I'll tell you what, sweetie. I'll give you all four for, let's say, twenty bucks. I just want 'em gone at this point."

Benny looks up at the others with childish glee. "Would you do fifteen?"

"You got yourself a deal." Benny pulled a few bills from his wallet and handed them to her. "Do ya need a bag?"

BENNY GOT HIS NEW DOLLS HOME, AND IT WASN'T LONG before he was studying their design and intricacies with his intent on making dolls of his own. He studied their clothes and decided quickly that he could buy the clothes or learn to fashion his own later. The hands and feet could be molded from clay and baked in a bisque, and the same for the head. If Benny was going to take on this new hobby, though, he would need to sculpt a suitable head that he would copy and use for different paints and looks. A template. The bodies would be put together from various materials. Clothes, felts, leathers, and everyday items he could get relatively easily. His excitement for doll making, though, would have to start from the head.

The freedom of expression and customization appealed to Benny the most. As he began to sculpt his first head, there were imperfections. He used clay and each night would spend hours at a time shaping and molding the features for the template that would ultimately be his doll heads moving forward.

Over several weeks, Benny would finally nail down the head he was satisfied with. He buried his face in the pages of a large phone book and started calling around to places that made sinks and toilets, and when that failed, he called around to places that produced ceramics and tiles. He was able to set up a time to come down and meet with someone to work out using their oven to help produce some heads for him. Once a price was agreed upon Benny was more than happy to wait and get his heads. He couldn't remember a time when he was that excited about any of his other hobbies. There were stages to this, and he knew that all the love he would pour into it would cultivate a sense of completion and accomplishment that he had never felt with his other hobbies, which offered more direct and immediate validation. Benny would become a doll maker, and he would strive to excel at it.

BENNY PICKED UP HIS FIRST BATCH OF HEADS A WEEK LATER. A dozen heads that were exact replicas of his clay sculpture. These replicas had the brushed and matte finish, smooth surfaces, and delicate textures, all white, ready and waiting for his creativity to spill onto them. The thought of painting the eyes and experimenting with different colors brought a glow to his soul that to this day was unmatched.

Benny applied himself to his newfound joy in life. His first few dolls varied in quality. While not impressive to him, they were still stepping stones for what was to come. Even with their blemishes and imperfections, Benny recognized that all art starts with rough edges and fine arts takes time to refine. Benny was still capturing his expression and finding what worked for him as an artist. As he learned more about the craft, he found himself obsessing over it. Doll after doll, earlier ones were rushed, and it showed, especially in comparison to the ones he bought from the flea market, and eventually the ones he would create later with more time and attentiveness. He learned to hold himself accountable and how to be his own worst critic. Understanding his insecurities and their validity proved to be crucial to not just his work, but any artist's work.

Months had gone by. His skill had significantly improved. Completing dozens of dolls by this point. His apartment was then littered with replica hands and feet among the many, many heads, some partially painted and dressed with hair, and others still blank canvases awaiting his delicate—but surgical—hands. As he learned the benefits of patience and attention to finer details, he began his next project, which he had convinced himself was going to be his best work yet. His next would be the perfect doll, and he would call her Eve.

Benny thought that name to be the most appropriate because, as he had been producing doll after doll, he began to amuse himself as a sort of God of doll making. Much like God created humans in His own image, Benny considered Eve to be made in his idea of what the perfect doll could be. Something about the concept of perfection lit a fire in him, the way lifelong scholars chase academic pursuits.

IN HIS DAY-TO-DAY LIFE, BENNY DIDN'T LEAVE MUCH TIME FOR things like romance or dating. While he thought it might be nice to have a partner and someone to keep him company and to take care of him when he needed it, he never fancied taking care of someone else. Despite his personal feelings, though, he did get lonely. He didn't seek out women or get hung up on the idea of dating, but there was Cathy, the lovely woman who lived down the hall, who always spoke to him in passing and was never too bothered to pass along a nice smile.

Benny always felt that twisting in his gut whenever she would speak to him. Her smile flashed white teeth that welcomed him to talk back. She would wear sundresses and let her dirty blonde hair down, leaving it to bounce as she walked. Benny believed her to be out of his league, but she was polite, and since the door was open and he was more comfortable with her than with the majority of women, he would think of things to say to her in the event they saw one another in the hall. With Benny not wasting time on his love life, he still had daydreams and fantasies, and ever since knowing Cathy, she became—sort of—the default woman of his dreams.

Benny didn't know precisely what Cathy did for work, but he knew that sometimes, when he got stuck at work later, he would come home and sometimes bump into her coming in. With that knowledge, he didn't exactly plan to stay at work later, but he certainly was in no hurry to leave either, so long as it meant a possibility of bumping into Cathy, if only for just a moment. Her asking him simple pleasantries like 'How are you doing?' played like beautiful music against his ears. A song that will make your heart skip a beat and crave another tune.

One morning, as Benny was heading downstairs to make his way to work, Cathy was just ahead of him. She had stopped at the mailboxes, allowing Benny to catch up to her.

"Good morning Miss Cathy," Benny said, flashing a smile that he felt was the most natural. It was amusing; at work, he would smile and converse casually with customers and colleagues, as if it were nothing. However, speaking to a pretty lady rattled his nerves and made his words stutter. Her blue eyes and perfect skin were like a gun to those hostages in his mouth, causing him to lose all sense and ability to use them.

"Oh, hey there, Benny," she said softly. "It looks like a lovely morning we're having."

Benny stood beside her with a key in hand, "Yeah, it's supposed to be nice all week."

Benny was berating himself in his head. *Weather talk, really? That's all you got? Come on, Benny!*

"It's days like these that I don't mind walking to work." Cathy stood there in her tasteful sundress waiting for Benny to say something. She noticed the key in his hand and him standing closer. "Oh, pardon me. I'm just standing here talking about the weather and you're trying to get to your mail. I'll just be on my way. Have a good day."

Benny had a moment of panic. He did nothing wrong, but somehow felt like he made her feel as if she had. He shoved his keys into his pocket. "Now, wait, wait, hold on." Cathy stood there, those eyes meeting his own while she waited for anything he had to say. Desperate and on the spot, every nerve in him was hiding the words he needed to keep this conversation moving forward. "Um, I–"

Cathy smirked, "What is it, Benny?"

Suddenly, his face felt hot. He felt like a cartoon character at that moment, with his face turning red as his heart thumped visibly, jumping from his chest and stretching his shirt. Standing in the vestibule, he hoped that she couldn't tell he was beginning to sweat. "I was just wondering, and, and you can say no if you want, no pressure, but...would you like to have coffee or grab lunch sometime with me?"

There it was. His shot fired. He hadn't expected to muster the courage to ask her that day, let alone ever. As soon as he was able to spit out the question, he felt brave for doing it...and also terrified. What if she says no? What if she says yes? What then? What should he wear? Does that mean they are dating? So many questions and hypotheticals raged through his brain, and in what felt like only a few seconds, time had stopped to only allow his insecurities to taunt him.

Cathy's eyes softened, pairing well with a shy smile. She brushed a ribbon of hair behind her ear. "So I don't really have time in the mornings to socialize," Benny felt shot down the moment she spoke, "and my lunch is not always the same time with work keeping me busy and all."

"Oh...I see," he replied, mustering up as much energy to not show her how deflated he had become.

"No, no, no, I'm sorry...I was going to suggest maybe dinner is all."

From deflated to full of air and ready to burst, Benny was relieved and excited with a heaping serving of nervousness, suddenly trying to hide the giddiness ballooning inside of him. The girl said yes! "Oh, that's excellent. Well, shall I pick a place, or maybe we just keep it simple? I would love to maybe cook for you? Th-that is if you're comfortable with that?"

Cathy's smile widened as she nodded. "Yeah, that sounds lovely. I think that would be great. Can we catch up later this week maybe?"

Benny tried to downplay his ecstatic reaction. "Absolutely, yes. I need to pick your brain and see what foods you like, right?"

"Right," she says with that smile again, "I have to get going though. I'm looking forward to it."

"Yeah, same. I'm off to work to make the donuts." *What the hell are you doing, Benny? Stop being a dork, you're blowing this.* "Well, in my case, make the sandwiches." *Stop. Talking! You idiot!*

Benny is relieved when Cathy laughs, "I'll see ya around."

Cathy heads out the door and into the world, where apparently the weather is nice, and Benny couldn't care less about that because he has a date with the prettiest woman he has spoken to in a long time. As she made her leave, a smell of perfume lingered, and Benny inhaled deeply enough to commit the scent to memory. He waits for her to be out of sight before he performs a celebratory fist pump as he makes his way into that same big world as Cathy, finding a kinship that he shares with her.

THE WEEK FLEW BY AS BENNY MAINTAINED HIS WORK, THEN home, then sleep, then repeat the routine. The days ran together, but on this night, after an honest day of work, Benny was happy to be home. As he counted down the cash register, he counted down the days just as he closed up for the evening. He was eager to get back to Eve. She was a canvas waiting for him to continue building, and that's just what he would do.

Her face had begun to take shape as he painted the porcelain a soft skin tone, but decided to add a subtle pink to her cheeks. Her lips were small and tight. Perfect for the shape of her face. He painted them a slightly brighter pink, closer to red, using a fine-tip brush to ensure his line-work was impeccable. A good artist was nothing if his tools were of *no* quality, so Benny had always been a believer in buying the best available when it came to creating. He would clean his brushes between uses and condition them often to keep the bristles and hairs like-new.

So far, the face was looking good, and Benny's idea of 'perfect' remained intact. He had the hair to tackle next. Benny would plan to shop around over the weekend for an appropriate wig that was just right for Eve. First, he would need to finish her face to ensure the best fit and look for his perfect Eve. The only thing left to do then was to figure out the eyes.

Eve had to be perfect; mediocre wasn't an option as far as Benny was concerned. He was confident in his abilities, yet a little intimidated, as he continued to challenge himself creatively. Since buying that quartet of dolls from the flea market and playing with designs of his own since taking on the hobby he had seen plenty of eyes and attempted to paint plenty of his own.

Benny felt strongly that the eyes were the most pivotal part of the doll, aesthetically, anyway. The eyes had to be luring. They had to captivate you. They had to be welcoming and invite you in. The eyes gave all of the other parts of the doll a chance to be seen. The eyes set the stage. Some people found porcelain dolls creepy due to their lifelike appearance, and it was true, largely because of their eyes.

Benny had heard once that the eyes were the windows of the soul. That thought always resonated with him, and as he created eyes and studied the details, it became something he pondered more. Anytime Benny had ever truly connected with anyone in his life, it always started with the eyes. This was true of Cathy most recently. Even with a stranger, it's thought that to avoid unwanted conversation is to avoid eye contact altogether. The eyes were the light to the path that illuminates connection, and that made the task even more critical for Benny to get right.

Benny sifted through his tiny bottle of paint and gathered his finest brushes as he prepared for this next step. He was very meticulous in how he worked. His workstation had to be set up in a way where everything had a place, and his system had to have a flow that catered to his work. He typically sat at his desk with an armchair, but kept a wooden barstool with a cushion underneath the desk in case he needed to sit a little higher or mix things up. He felt better knowing he had the option if he so desired. He had a posable arm attached to a light that had a magnifying glass on it. This would come in handy when he painted the eyes, as the details were important.

Benny adjusted Eve's head into a fixed position so that it wouldn't move while he prepared to paint the eyes. He had another doll close by that he would use as a visual aid for the shape and size of the eyes, but he fully intended to improve on the details by referencing a magazine photo of a model's eyes. He had picked out the shade of black he would use for the pupils. Obsidian black. It was the darkest of the blacks in his collection, and it gave off a glossy shimmer that looked great when the light hit it. For the iris, he had decided to go with his own blend of color to create something unusual for a doll. He wanted the eyes to be blue, but not the typical blue. He wanted something brighter that really popped. Something that held a magnificent contrast against the softer features of Eve's face. He would blend one part blue and one part green, with just a smidgen of white to lighten it up. This blend would create a shade of teal that was not common with dolls. Cathy's eyes were also blue, and he couldn't help but think about how gorgeous they were when the light made them gleam.

"So, uh...where did you grow up? Are you from here, originally?" Benny asked.

He began to paint, starting with the iris first. He wanted to make a clean ring to ensure his line work and shape were perfect. Making sure both eyes were the same size was a big focus for him as well, so that step would take a careful hand, a critical eye, and attentive focus to execute to the high standard he was setting for himself. He was fortunate to be gifted with a careful and coordinated hand.

"No, no, born and raised right here." Benny fought the tension in his cheeks to keep from smiling like a lovestruck fool. "How about school? Did you go to school here?"

He used the right lining brush with the thinnest tip to get those crisp lines with no bleeding. He would let the paint dry only to layer it up again. He was a disciplined enough artist to understand the brushstrokes and keep his direction consistent to guarantee the paint dried correctly.

"I didn't go to college. Just wasn't for me, I guess."

HOURS PASSED BY, BUT BENNY WAS SO IN THE ZONE THAT IT felt like days to him. He was a man of tedious structure, and when he fell into his own time loops, he never knew where the time went. It was as if he had gotten lost in his work. Lost in his obsession, he overlooked the cost, which was gaps of time that would go unaccounted for, resulting in his brilliant work.

Benny stood in his kitchen, where he caught himself just going through the motions. He was brewing coffee in the evening and setting out sugar and cream on the table. He set out two coffee mugs on his kitchen table as the coffee pot began to steam and whistle from the sink counter.

"You know, I've been thinking about you all week. I didn't expect you would ever agree to dinner with me, let alone be in my apartment."

While that brewed, he went back to his desk and admired his work so far. Eve was turning out to be even more beautiful than he anticipated. He feared that he would do something to ruin her. He had a tendency to fine-dose the poison, often overdoing it, which meant the final product wouldn't be any better for it. That doesn't happen with Eve, though. He would not allow that, so long as he stayed honest with himself and maintained being his most critical judge of quality.

"I don't know. I just think you're so beautiful, and I look like...this."

He took his seat and leaned in for another round of tedious painting, breaking out the white and a couple of toothpicks to apply tiny pinpricks of white on the iris, simulating faux reflective light. Each eye would only get a few drops, but the placement had to be exact on each eye, or it would just look goofy. Some artists allow these minor indictments to slip through, and *maybe* no one will notice, but Benny couldn't stomach the idea of doing that with Eve and then having someone point it out. That would be a blow to his ego that he wasn't willing to recover from.

"Can you see yourself with a guy like me?"

Once he was done with the white paint, he poured a matte black paint into a small tray where he readied a fine tip brush to draw on the thin black lines above and below the eyes that would be the eyelashes. He was careful to space them out evenly, and once they dried, he came back to press the brush a little harder to make the bases of the lashes slightly wider, aiming for a natural look, even if it was just paint.

"Well, if I'm being honest, I have wondered what life with you might be like."

BENNY STOOD TO STRETCH, THEN STEPPED INTO THE KITCHEN and poured two cups of coffee. As he thought about how close he was to finishing Eve's eyes, he smelled that familiar fragrance. Cathy's perfume seeped from his memory and into his kitchen. He stood at his kitchen table, leaning over with a steaming coffee pot in hand and a ridiculous smile smeared across his face. Benny promptly put the coffee pot back on the burner and left the kitchen without even tasting the coffee. He was caught in a spell of habits and under the thumb of his own obsession. So obsessed that the world around him was a blur that felt still to him while he was working, but the reality often came to him that he would waste excessive amounts of time chasing perfection.

He thought about Cathy as he sat back at his desk. Eve's eyes with white pupils stared blankly at him. He was excited to finish the canvas, very close. He carefully poured a small amount of the obsidian black into a small paint tray. As he readied himself, he took hold of the brush, let out a whoosh of air from his chest, and went to work. Painting two clean black circles that would be Eve's pupils was not as daunting a task. Benny finished rather quickly, and as he put down the brush and wiped the perspiration from his forehead, he stood. He stretched and felt how sore his thumbs were all of a sudden. A strange thing, as he has never had that happen before, not from painting.

He watched the paint dry, and in that time, he studied how beautiful she looked. He was astonished that Eve was *his* doll and he was the creator of something so perfect. The way the teal irises ran against the deep blackness of her pupils made for a detail worthy of obsessing over. He leaned in and picked her up. He stared into Eve's eyes, admiring his work. Admiring her beauty. This was no doubt his best work yet, an actual work of art.

Eve was more than that to him, though. More than a work of art, it is a labor of love and commitment. He set out to achieve perfection and absolutely did. Eve wasn't just a work of art, though, no, a masterpiece. A true centerpiece to any respectable collection or curated art exhibit. Eve needed to be seen; she needed to be displayed behind glass. She belonged among other fine arts, not just dolls, but she should be on a pedestal along with other great pieces of fine art. Eve was a creative feat. She was Benny's Magnum Opus if he ever had one. His Sistine Chapel.

Benny was locked onto Eve's eyes. Her stare put his heart in a chokehold, wrenching on it as he began to spiral into the blackness of those pupils, becoming lost, becoming arrested by his own mastery of doll making, frozen as he held her head in his hands like you would have a delicate kitten. The teal irises glowed against that blackness as Benny was swallowed into the black holes of her eyes like a black hole in space.

His thumbs throbbed, but he ignored the sensation. He had become too distracted by the possibility of Eve being displayed somewhere. *What if Eve were sent to be auctioned off?* That simply was no good because no amount of money would be enough to harness the essence of his perfect Eve. God wouldn't auction off the world during its creation, so why should Benny allow that to be an option? The idea began to sicken him, even more so as his mind charted different scenarios. What if some greasy-fingered snot-nosed child got their hands on Eve and her flawless features? Eve was too good to be like any ordinary doll. What if she fell into the possession of a greedy collector? Someone who bought things, treated them as investments, and stashed them away in dark hiding places, waiting to be sold again for profit?

The idea of Eve being tucked away in the dark, left to collect dust while not being visible for the world to enjoy, brought tears to Benny's eyes. Tears that pained him. He could feel it in his body as he tensed up. His muscles contracted and flexed as the pain in his thumbs, which he had ignored, rushed back. His thumbnails pulsated underneath, feeling as if they could crack from the pressure. He couldn't allow Eve to succumb to that fate. That obscurity. She was much too perfect for this world, and Benny accepted that he may just have been ahead of his time.

He fell deeper into her eyes, and that blackness had a firm grip on its creator. Benny felt a sense of pride and love, much like a father might feel for a child. Eve was much too perfect for this world, and he knew what he had to do, and it started with the eyes. After all, the eyes were an invitation to much more, so he needed to rescind that invitation for good. Eve had to be destroyed, and left as just an idea — a prototype. Benny did not want that life for Eve, and he would make sure of it, even if it hurt him in the process.

He proceeded to scrape his thumbnails against her eyes. The paint flaked off in chunks, but the stubborn bits that didn't come off only left thumbnail-sized scratches. He realized that his nails were too slow, so he reached for a palette knife that he would use for painting. Scraping became digging, but despite his efforts to remove the paint, the porcelain resisted. It was as tough as bone.

The darkness gripping Benny became so overwhelming as he pressed so hard into Eve's eyes that the porcelain cracked from the bridge of her nose and two inches up her forehead. The paint came off in scratchy flakes that only left her eyes looking distressed. Benny's heart beat faster, his heart rate sprinted in his chest as he tore away from that darkness. The world around him was in a vacuum that he was sucked back into as he stood there catching his breath. The room spun as he looked at his hands to see them covered in blood.

He stood in his kitchen, where he immediately saw Cathy lying on the floor beside the table. Her eyes had been dug out of her head as she lay there motionless. Ice weighed down his feet as he stood frozen in place, confused, broken, and scared.

"Cathy!" he managed to mutter, pained cries tangling his words, "No! I don't— I didn't—"

He looked around, trying to piece together clues to the story he knew he wasn't ready to hear. One of Cathy's eyes sat on his kitchen table, blood smeared across its surface with no sense of tidiness. Her detached blue eye stared at him beside her steaming cup of untouched coffee. The viscera that was attached to the eye lay tangled around it. He fell to his knees with a silent cry that dared to squeak in a soft whine as his voice cracked.

He took her hand and watched her for as long as he could, his gaze lingering on her face for too long. She had one eye still in her skull, but protruding, only waiting for the job to be finished. The optic nerve held tight while the mess of her face and the unrealistic amount of blood saturated her sundress and his linoleum floor.

He considered what would happen when he called 9-1-1 and was mortified at how the situation looked. He was dead to rights and no doubt going to prison. His simple life, built on a foundation of simple routines and constructive habits, had been compromised, and he didn't understand why. He stood after a moment and went into the living room to grab the corded phone. As he put it to his ear, the dial tone sang to him. Before he could press the numbers, his workstation was in his view, and he saw Eve, in her fixed position, staring directly at him. Her eyes, unblemished...her skin, still perfect and un-cracked. Benny stood there with the phone to his ear and his finger on the button, once again captivated by the perfection that is Eve as those eyes invited him into the story he wasn't ready to hear, but he surely understood then.

THE WORLD'S GREATEST DAD

ELLIS HART

It's not easy being a decent dad. It's even tougher when you have to do it all alone because your wife left three years ago, running off with Griffin Crowley. Yes, that's his real name—his parents must've known he'd eventually become the world's biggest douchebag.

So here I am, Mark Hampton, single father of three wonderful kids who all attend Blue Cliff Middle School in picturesque Arkansas. Marianne is twelve, Amy's ten, and Charlie's eight. Yes, they are all perfectly spaced apart because my wife and I had a plan. We executed that plan very well until she didn't.

Now I sit in the never-ending school pick-up line, aptly nicknamed by Marianne as "the worst." She isn't wrong; whoever designed Blue Cliff's parking lot clearly never considered how actual children would come and go. It's a daily chaos of honking horns, impatient parents, and exhausted teachers directing traffic like overwhelmed police officers.

But I'm patient. I take pride in my calm demeanor during these tedious waits. You can learn a lot about people by watching them here: frazzled soccer moms desperate to circumvent the rules, clueless pedestrians tempting fate, and stressed-out parents shouting private dramas into their speakerphones. It's a circus, and I'm content to sit back and enjoy the show.

Everyone at Blue Cliff knows me as "Dependable Mark". Teachers know I'll always provide extra Starbucks cards at Christmas, the principal counts on me for setting up chairs at school events, and the soccer coach knows I'll always cover snack duty when Ruth Anne inevitably brings something atrocious like radishes with ranch dip.

A sudden horn tap behind me breaks my reverie. With a sheepish wave in the rearview, I pull forward to pole number seven, just as my children come running. I spot Charlie's teacher, Miss Julie McCoy, approaching my window. I roll it down, noting the sweat streaming down her flushed face.

"You better be careful out here; it's scorching!" I call to her above the commotion.

"You're telling me! They should give us those amusement park misting fans," she laughs warmly, a pure, effortless sound.

Reaching down, I hand her one of the unopened ice-cold water bottles I always keep in the center console at pick-up. "Take this; you'll faint if you don't stay hydrated."

She smiles gratefully, immediately gulping down half the bottle. The kids clamber into the car, and with a cheerful wave to Miss McCoy, we inch toward the exit lane.

The afternoon unfolds predictably. The children squabble over music until Alanis Morissette settles the matter with mutual disdain. Their monosyllabic answers about their day amuse me—they've officially entered the sullen teenage phase, even Charlie.

Once home, I shepherd everyone inside, oversee homework routines, then call up to Marianne about needing to run an errand. Her dramatic sigh echoes down the stairs before she agrees to watch her siblings. She's a good kid. I smile proudly, stepping back into the garage.

After confirming the time, I head back the way I had come, toward Blue Cliff. Now deserted, the lot feels eerily quiet. Under a large oak's sheltering branches, I park and wait, hidden in shadow.

Minutes pass slowly until the school's side door opens. But immediately, I notice something's off. A woman emerges unsteadily, leaning heavily against the building. She looks like she may be having a heart attack, and, in a flash, I am out of my car, running towards the woman in need.

As I approach, I see Miss McCoy, back against the rough brick of the school building, clutching several books and scores of papers against her chest. She's sweating again and I step into her line of vision, talking slowly and clearly.

"Miss McCoy, it's me, Charlie's dad, Mark Hampton. Are you okay?"

Her lips barely move while she stares up at me. I check her pulse, fast but steady.

I try to pull the door open, the one she just exited through, but it's locked. I look up and realize no one will be manning the front door, so I may just ring it without anyone coming to help. Then I decide.

"Miss McCoy, if you can hear me, I'm calling 911. Let's get you to your car so you can at least sit down on something comfortable."

I reach down, loop my right arm under her armpits, and pull her up onto her feet. I pull my cellphone out and dial. We stagger towards the parking lot, and I'm practically yelling at her now, asking which car is hers.

No words, but her finger does wiggle to a white Chevy parked to the left, not far from my own car. We stagger towards it, and I can't help but notice several things at once. First, Miss McCoy is so light. She weighs practically nothing, though her curves in this dress would beg to differ. My eyes linger down the top of her dress a moment too long, and I snap my eyes back up out of respect.

The second thing I notice is how good she smells. It smells familiar and safe, like vanilla and fresh blankets. Even after a long day of working and sweating in the sun during pick-up, she's still so... clean. I'm impressed.

"Yes, hi, I need help at Blue Cliff middle off of Town Center Boulevard. I have a late 20-year-old female who seems to be having a heart-attack or some kind of issue with speaking and balance."

"Yes, please, I can wait with her. We'll be in her White Chevy out front of the school".

I close my phone, placing it deep into my pocket, when I hear the faintest whisper – "thank you".

I look down into the eyes of Miss McCoy and say reassuringly, "everything is going to be okay, I promise".

We're three steps away from her car now, and I would open the passenger door for her if that's where we were really going.

Instead, we continue forward, me practically dragging her limp body towards my car. In less than 45 seconds, we've covered the parking lot and are now at my trunk, which is 1 minute faster than I planned when I ran this simulation last week alone.

I sit Miss McCoy in the back of the van, its sunken floor creating a cozy little bed, just for her. I lift her legs into the space and softly wipe the hair from her face so I can see her eyes.

Even though the GHB (gamma-hydroxybutyric acid) I injected into the top of her water bottle has fully taken over now, I know, just by looking deep into her eyes, that Julie feels what I feel in this moment. Our skin touching causes electricity to shoot up our spines, our eyes locked, causing our hearts to flutter with anticipation. I'm so excited I can barely close the trunk without jumping into the air.

I pull out of the parking lot, now darkness setting across the place, and actually turn on the phone in my pocket that's been off since I left my house earlier today.

"Hi honey, just calling to check-in. I'll be home soon, everyone okay?"

"Okay great, please don't forget your math, you know how important it is for high school! And what about dinner?"

"I can definitely pick that up. I'll be home soon, love you!"

I close the phone and glance into the rearview mirror – Julie is awake but completely paralyzed at this point.

The fear she must be feeling. A jolt runs through my hands, and I clench the steering wheel tighter. This is my favorite part - the anticipation. Much like my wife and Griffin before her, Julie has no idea why she's in the back of my trunk.

She has no idea why her body has completely betrayed her. No matter how hard she wills her hand to move, it won't. I've made sure of it.

As we pass under the fast-moving streetlights, my mind drifts again. It's not easy being the world's best dad, nor is it easy being the world's best serial killer. But these are two titles I'll continue to carry.

Why?

Because my children need a strong, male role model to protect them from the monsters in this world, and sometimes, the world needs a few more monsters to keep it from being

so...

damn...

boring.

AN IMMORTAL'S GRIEVANCE

VICTORIA M. SORENSON

"Would you believe me if I told you I would gift you the sun—all you must do is utter the words, and I will make it so." Her voice was sharp, angled to pierce straight through my affections. It lacked the very love she had mentioned moments before. "I am willing to set myself ablaze to earn an ounce of your attention, Charles."

She stood between the helm of reality and my crazed deprivations; I did not trust my thoughts, my own wants and desires. I knew what monster lay beneath her untouched beauty, with her skin made of porcelain and the cruel touch in which her crimson lips stained their mark on their prey.

Dracula never missed her target, and tonight it was I who was caught between her web of lust and lies.

"Do you know what love is, Vladimira?"

The ancient soul whipped her head in my direction at this; the cold emanating from inside her black irises echoed within my core. All of my senses responded in fear, crippling my will to take action and save myself from her eternal spell.

I shifted my body, pulling against the rope cutting into my wrists.

"The decrepit creatures you give birth to—I want no part of

them." The declaration that escaped my lips was more of a plea, a cry of desperation for her not to take the one part of me I instinctively fought for—my mortality.

"Do I know what love is?" She scoffed as she ambled in a circle around my figure. "I have lived more lives than you will ever reincarnate into. Of course I know love. I am haunted by its presence, and the yearning it leaves me with after those I cherish are long gone. I am left with only hollow memories, plagued with the rebirth of love the instant you come back here to my dwelling."

The ache in my chest for her statement to be true bloomed within me, and I fought for composure. I did not want my hunger for her to show in my features; it was imperative for my well-being that I battle against the motivation of my heart.

If she loved me, I would not be bound with the ropes she used against her enemies before she devoured them. I would not be in this chamber haunted by the thousands of ghosts who lost their lives to her twisted perception of righteousness. I would not be surrounded by splattered blood that stained the stone archways and walls.

"You cannot truly love because you do not know death. You do not appreciate the flowers as they bloom, you do not see the beauty in how precious the air is that fills our lungs—because you fear nothing. Death is the reason people cherish life, because it is fleeting. There is so much you have yet to experience, even in your immortal state, because you do not know what it means to live."

As I spoke, the ring she walked around my figure drew close; the countess was stalking her prey, looking for the perfect opportunity to strike. My body knew I was in danger, yet my mind disagreed, and my eyes watered in protest.

"You speak as if I've never had a human heart; as if blood has never flowed through my veins, as if I've never experienced the warmth of the sun and a lover's embrace. It is because I lost my mortality that I yearn for your touch, and I crave to be the center of all your devotions." Vladimira cooed, the vying in her tone palpable. "I have lived, Charles. I lived until death stole my husband from me, and I renounced my faith, and God decided to curse my existence. I am damned to roam the earth as I watch everything that I treasure wither and perish, and there is nothing I can do to free me of this madness."

I raised a brow, narrowing my gaze, finding her sauntering silhouette.

"What do you call the abominations that you create, then? They were not produced from love. The living dead wreak havoc in the villages, consuming nearly half the townsfolk. And you harbor them here in your castle as if you can domesticate such vile creatures."

This struck a chord within her, for she paused momentarily, facing the statues of long-forgotten knights and heroes that decorated the room.

"The world will not accept them as they are now, but I will. I know of their struggles. And I gave them what they asked for—a cure to their diseases, freedom from those in power, a life of immortality. I granted their utmost desires." She murmured, deep in thought. For several beats, no one spoke, not a sound was given birth to in the dead of night.

I eventually found the courage to continue.

"And yet this is not what I asked for, Vladimira. I did not ask for this." Again, I pleaded, frantic to find a way to talk myself out of her grasp, because I knew there was no winning against her God-like strength. "The mortal you once were no longer exists. The day you were damned by God and your ability to enter the heavens was also the day you lost your ability to love another. Do not force the same fate upon me, I'm begging you."

Her face contorted in rage, and for an instant, I bore witness to the demonic entity that was her true identity. The muscles beneath her pale complexion flexed, her waist-length raven hair rattled like a snake, moving of its own volition. Vladimira's eyes were gaping black holes, threatening to siphon the rest of my bravery.

"How dare you utter such blasphemy! Does the time we spent together mean nothing to you? Before you knew who I was, what I am, you loved me ardently. I could see it; I felt it with every fiber of my being. I have not felt a love like this in all the centuries I have existed, mortal or immortal. I do love you, Charles." She serenaded, her hellish face inches from mine. "And you speak as if you are not the one to seek me out in each life you possess. It is a monotonous process to watch you be reborn over and over and witness your death. I have grown tired of waiting for your acceptance of your fate; it is crystal clear to me that the answer to both of our woes lies within this conclusion. I shall make you my groom, and we will be intertwined for all eternity."

As I felt her cool breath on my cheek, I pondered.

It was true; I had loved her. I had loved every fiber of her being—the scent of her skin as the curves of her slender figure molded perfectly into mine, the way her eyes twinkled in the moonlight as her laughter reverberated off the alleyways and into the darkness.

We met by chance at a local tavern, and I was drawn to her presence, where she consumed all my thoughts from that moment onward.

But our relationship was all a lie; she was a black widow spinning her intricately designed web for fools like me to fly into. And even as I was entangled in her grasp, I wanted to be here, to be trapped and wholly enraptured by her presence. I wanted to be the object of all her desires, the man of her dreams.

And this was where I walked the line of my sanity—the urge to blur those lines and dive wholeheartedly into her bliss. It was an inevitable consequence of my actions. Vladimira's existence was what sinners deem as ecstasy.

Her long, delicate fingers brushed against my neck, sending

another wave of fear mixed with a deep yearning for her to caress me further.

"Please, Mira. Do not do this." I called her by the name I initially knew her by, the name I fell in love with as I whispered sweet nothings into her ear during the late summer nights. It was now autumn, and unbeknownst to me, as the days grew shorter, so did my time with the woman I once valued beyond compare.

She licked her voluptuous lips, eyeing my throat. "Your begging no longer moves me. I have decided to give in to my selfishness and devour your mortality so that you may be by my side, forever."

Vladimira sank her fangs deep into my flesh, the pain overwhelming. I choked on the guttural scream that rose in my throat, my eyes rolling back into my skull.

No, God, please hear my cries! I rebuke this demon and her sins. I do not accept this fate!

My body contorted on the cracked stone floor as I shouted in agony. The countess had drained me of all my blood and feelings, absorbing what coherent thoughts remained. My last memory was of the mural on the wall above me, and I writhed beneath the painting of the three wise men gifting the Lord His blessings.

I, Charles Augustus Livingston III, lost my mortality on the twenty-third of October, in the year of our Lord eighteen hundred and eighty-nine. All accounts transcribed are factual and are recorded by my hand. I currently reside in Transylvania, beneath the decrepit castle in the Carpathian Mountains, home to all immortal beasts, where we are tortured by our sins daily. My immortal grievance began the day the countess, the daughter of hell herself, stole what I valued most in my existence—my ability to enter the heavens.

THE PORTRAIT

H.H. MIKA

I

"They tell me you're pretty good—that you even have a talent. That's all good and fine. But, here in Tok we do things in a more traditional way. This is a small town, and we have small-town crimes, ya see? Your superiors haven't divulged exactly why you're here, but I could sure reckon a guess," the man said, motioning to my file. "Look, you're young —if you're smart, you'll step in line, do things our way—and when it's time, you'll be able to apply for a transfer and forget all about us. Meanwhile, keep your head down and you won't end up getting sent somewhere else with an even larger file."

I didn't respond. I could tell he didn't like it, but what could he do?

"Draw-er, huh?" He leaned back with a grin. "Are we on the same page?"

"Should I be meeting with the chief now, Sergeant?"

"Chief's busy, you'll see him around."

"It's a pleasure to be working for you, sir," I said, standing up and extending my hand over his desk.

"Just don't let me catch you drawing at your desk," he said, gripping down onto my palm.

Fuck this guy.

I EMPTIED MY BOX OUT AND SET UP MY CUBICLE THE SAME WAY that I had it in Juneau. This meant pictures pinned on the walls. I was proud of my work; after all, it was thanks to my sketches that they were caught in the first place. I helped. I was even called to the scene of one of their arrests.

"The hell do you want with all those murderers and rapists around you for like that?"

"What?" I asked, turning around.

"Dismal," Sgt. Wayne Cahill said with distaste. "Did you notice in my office—around my desk, I had a picture of my family; a pinch pot my grandson made; the little statue of Jesus?"

"Sir—"

"Hey, Detective Molloy!" Sgt. Wayne called around the corner. "Jim, you have any pictures of convicted killers and sex offenders hung up around your desk?"

"No, sir, I can't say that I do," I heard the man answer. Fuck that guy too. Fuck both of them.

"I didn't think so," Sgt. Wayne said, turning back to me. "How about you go hit patrol until we need you to draw something?"

I HONESTLY DON'T MIND THIS TOWN. IT'S QUIET. QUIET IS good. I wouldn't mind seeing the sergeant slip on some ice and break a few bones or something though. I've been doing this for 11 years, I've seen a hell of a lot as a patrolman—and not to mention my sketches have made busts. What the hell are these guys' problem?

ABOUT A YEAR AND A HALF PASSED MUCH THE SAME WAY before I ever really got a chance to earn some respect. I guess it might be a little gross to talk about it that way, but it was clear. I didn't want their validation, anyhow.

"SCHIEL!" A MAN'S VOICE CALLED MY NAME FROM ACROSS THE office one day. "Joe!"

"What?" I asked, standing up.

"We got something for ya," Det. Molloy said, walking up to me.

"What is it?—What happened?"

"Some asshole walked into the bank with a mask on, waving a gun around, forced one of the tellers to empty the registers, and accidentally shot someone in the neck. Looks like he got scared and tried to help. At that point, the teller decided to take the opportunity to yank the mask off him while he was distracted—lucky he didn't try to blow her head off in the process. Anyway, we have a split second recorded, but his face isn't clear in the footage and the guy turns and flees."

"Where is she?" I asked.

A WOMAN WAS SITTING NERVOUSLY IN OUR INTERROGATION room—blood still speckled on her clothes and hands—with Sgt. Wayne prodding her as if she were guilty of something.

"Just tell us what he looked like," Sgt. Wayne said, and she contorted her face as I opened the door.

"I'll take over from here," I said, stepping inside.

"There was so much blood," the woman suddenly squealed. "Oh my God, is Tom dead?"

"Yes, he is," Det. Molloy answered, unreassuringly. "Can you remember if the man who shot him had a beard or a tattoo or anything?"

"Okay," I shouted, "I can calm her down, Detective—would you please both get the fuck out of here?" Sgt. Wayne looked at me with grave eyes. "I'm plenty capable of getting a description from her, especially without traumatizing her." As the girl curled over and cried into her hands, I saw Sgt. Wayne and Molloy exchange glances before finally walking out. "Thank you."

"Miss" I began when the door was closed. "My name's Joe." She wouldn't look at me at first. "Are you thirsty?" I asked. "Would you like some water?"

"I..." her mouth closed.

"It's okay—here." I reached over to the small plastic pitcher and filled a small paper cup with water for her—no glass. She looked up at me sadly for a moment and then took a sip. "What's your name?" I asked.

"Roseann," she said, swallowing another gulp.

"Roseann, that's pretty. Okay, Roseann, I need you to do something for me. It's going to be a bit uncomfortable—but just for a moment, okay? I promise, we'll get through this as quickly as possible and, what's better yet, we'll have a really good chance of catching the guy who got away. You're on board for that, right? You're the only one who got a good look at him."

"I don't think it was all that good, actually."

"Of course it was," I urged. "He turned right to you after you pulled his mask off."

"I think my eyes were closed—I was flinching—I thought the cameras would catch it!"

"Sh-sh-sh," I said. "Do you mind if I play something?" I asked, pulling my phone out from my pocket. "It always helps me think."

"What is it?" she asked.

"They're called binaural beats—have you ever been hypnotized before?" I asked, pressing the PLAY button.

"You're going to hypnotize me?"

"No, not exactly. Think of this more as a meditation of sorts —I'll guide you through it the whole way, okay? Now, just so you're aware, it will be a little, well, trance-like—best way to put it, when we go back—but everything that's done is done, alright? He can't hurt you and you can't change anything. You're here now," I said, putting my hand on her shoulder. "And, if it helps, when you wake back up, you won't remember any of this—it'll be like it never happened."

"Is this a dream?" she asked.

"Not yet. Right now, I just want you to think about when—"

"I can't remember, alright?" she confessed, dropping her head down, disappointedly. "Italian, maybe?"

"What?" I asked.

"He might've been Italian—he looked like a dirtbag."

"Oh, good, alright. Listen, Roseann, in order for this to work —you have to let it, okay?"

"Alright," she said, sitting back.

"Now, close your eyes," I said, and took out a piece of charcoal.

II

THE CHIEF STOPPED BY MY CUBICLE A COUPLE WEEKS LATER and slapped my shoulder. Sgt. Wayne and Det. Molloy have yet to offer any congratulatory remarks. I don't foresee that changing anytime soon. I suppose I shouldn't gloat though; it will probably be a long time before they need me for something like this again around here.

What is it that's so hard for them to understand about what I do? What scares them so much? They got their heads so far up their asses—they don't know shit. It's not magic—there is no magic; our minds simply don't forget anything—they can't. They can only choose what they want to see from the collection and hope that the rest stays hidden, but it's all still there. Sometimes someone just needs to help it focus.

I WAS WRONG. IT WASN'T THAT LONG AT ALL ACTUALLY—ONLY about six months.

"We were walking down the back roads through the woods, out by the old orchard," the man said, a tear in his eyes. "She likes to pick the flowers out there."

Thank God, I thought—he said "likes," not "liked"—she might still be alive. "It's getting overridden with larkspur back there, but she knows which ones are safe to pick," he told me from across the interrogation room table. "It started to rain, so we took cover in that beat-up barn near the dirt bike trails. Some kids went by on ATVs and..." The man began sniffling. "In a minute or two, the sun started to poke through and she went out to dance and splash around in the puddles. That's when a man on a motorcycle sped up right next to her and grabbed my daughter and threw her over his lap."

"It wasn't a dirt bike?" I asked. I heard the mud splashing but I couldn't quite picture the vehicle. I have to see what they see.

"No, no dirt bike—the bastard didn't even have a helmet on."

"So, you got a good look at him?"

"Yes," the man said confidently, but he didn't convince me. "He was bald, with peckerwood sideburns. Had a mustache too, I think. Maybe a goatee."

"Mr. Marlow," I said. "In order for me to get all the details that—well, you may not remember, I'm going to have to ask you to recall a few things first—things that happened right before the man on the bike appeared. When the two of you were still— before she was kidnapped." I saw the tear finally escape him and roll down his cheek. "Can you please close your eyes, sir?" I asked and turned on my phone. "You're going to enter a sort of... dream state now."

"Will it hurt?" he asked, looking up to me.

"Yes," I said. "But you won't remember it." He smiled despite his eyes clenching closed with more tears. "Now, tell me what you smelled nearby: the apples? Manure? Old rusty tools? What do you remember seeing in the barn?"

"Shadows," he said.

I SUPPOSE THERE WAS ONLY ONE MORE WORTH MENTIONING IN those first two years, before we get to the flayings. It's not pride. I just want people to understand. It was the hardest one I ever had to sit through.

Sgt. Wayne and Det. Molloy were accustomed to waiting outside by now. I nodded to them as I entered the interrogation room, but they just stared at me. Before we started, I handed her a tissue to dab her eyes. It wouldn't matter; she'd be crying again shortly, but she wasn't under yet. I wasn't a monster.

"He was tall," she said, sniffing her nose, "maybe about 5'10" or 12", he had a leather jacket on—brown—"

"I'm sorry, miss," I interrupted and looked up to the window. "They probably gave you the wrong impression about how a drawing is made. Please, just, um—would you mind putting your head back?"

"Excuse me?"

"I kinda need you to lean back a little, if you could. Yeah, just like that. I'm sorry, I know this sounds weird. Now, keep your neck straight, great—"

"What is this?" the woman asked. For the first time since what happened to her, she wasn't terrified—she was too confused. That was important.

"Well, I've developed a little... knack for this over the years, you could say. It really helps with getting this right."

"I see, so it's to distract me—to keep me calm?" she asked, hopeful.

"No, I wouldn't say that," I admitted. "You're going to be hyper-focused. But, on the bright side, when it's all over—you'll forget this ever happened," I tried to smile. "The only thing I want you to remember after is that we're going to catch him. I promise," I said.

"Okay." She was staring at the ceiling now.

"Do you remember around what time it was when you were walking down the alley?—Miss?" I spoke up a bit.

"11:37," she said, her eyes very distant, "I had just texted Mike. I wasn't paying attention to the GPS. It was raining—"

"Do you remember seeing any lights on?"

"I just wanted to tell him I loved him..."

"Miss?" I asked again. Please, come back.

"It was dark. The only light was coming from my phone, but I dropped it. That's when the man grabbed me and—"

IT DIDN'T MATTER TO ME THAT SGT. WAYNE AND MOLLOY showed me no appreciation. What bothered me was that I still wasn't getting any recognition in my personal pursuits either.

"They want auroras, Joe," the curator told me. "Not these bleak, dreary wintry scenes in muddy colors of someone trying to light a fire."

Well, why not? I'd ask, but there'd be no point.

I sometimes have to thank the powers that be for the path I chose to follow—that I get to work with men only as bad as Sgt. Wayne and Molloy; I'd be a starving artist otherwise, for sure.

Not only were they never impressed with my assistance, but Det. Molloy began getting a lot nastier with me, who was usually the more levelheaded of the two.

"Maybe you got those pictures hung up around you like that because you like 'taking them back,' as you say," he suggested. "Maybe it excites you. Maybe you're a freak." This wasn't jealousy. He had some kind of fundamental opposition to what I was doing.

"The mind sees what it wants," I said, trying to brush him off.

"What the fuck did you just say to me?"

"Our minds. They choose to see what they want. They're very intricate systems, far more than just our thoughts and memories—they comprise tissue, and electricity, and frequencies, and chemicals, and—and—dreams, and damage—"

"Shut the fuck up."

"They're afraid of what they remember. So, what is it that's making you afraid, Detective? What scares you about me?"

"You think I'm afraid of you, chickenshit?" Det. Molloy said, getting in my face.

"Alright, Jim," Sgt. Wayne said, stepping in between us. "That's enough," he said, and they both walked away.

———

IT WAS THE FOLLOWING OCTOBER WHEN THE FLAYINGS started.

"Christ on a cross." I could hear real horror in Sgt. Wayne's voice, just under the disgust. Never heard that from him before. Of course, I had yet to see—

"He cut her face off?—Why?" Sgt. Wayne asked, as perplexed as he was sickened. "To prevent identification?"

"Not in this case, I don't think. This looks..." Det. Molloy stood up and looked around. "It doesn't make sense to leave her fingerprints. He already cut her face off, might as well finish the job."

"What if she just doesn't have a record?" Sgt. Wayne asked.

"And the tattoo?" Molloy added. Sgt. Wayne began searching until he located the helm inked on the underside of the girl's inner bicep. "The bracelet, the clothes—her shoes. We'll be able to ID her in the next day or two; I guarantee it," Molloy said. "This isn't about that. What he did here was far worse than just cutting her damn face off. This woman was flayed somehow—very, very carefully. In misidentification cases, the killer will usually just lob the head and hands off and be done with it. Very rarely do they go through all the work involved in peeling off someone's face. And even when they do, it's never anything like this. Every damn inch of flesh off her entire skull is missing from her neck up," Molloy almost shouted as he turned away from the faceless body and the group standing around it. "I don't think this guy has any interest at all in concealing her identity—I wouldn't be surprised if we find her ID in one of her back pockets."

"So, what is it then?" Sgt. Wayne asked. "You think this is personal?"

"Deeply," Molloy replied with his back still turned to them.

"Shouldn't there be knife wounds or gunshots or something if this were a crime of passion?" Sgt. Wayne asked, turning to Molloy.

"A lot of times, for sure, when they're not premeditated—but this was. This is some type of message, like, 'You cross a line, this is what happens.' He's not trying to hide who this girl was; he just wanted to mutilate her—humiliate her. Quite literally, deface her."

"So, this is a one and done then, right?" asked Sgt. Wayne.

"God, I fucking hope so."

I COULDN'T BELIEVE WHAT I WAS HEARING. I COULDN'T GET A look from where I was standing around the perimeter of caution tape—I was even advised not to—but I had to look over my shoulder and try. When I did, my eyes caught Det. Molloy's. I tried to look away, but the only place my eyes would go was to the open space between Molloy's leg and the officer standing beside him. A red skull.

Well, nearly, I should say. I could see blotches of bone at the top of her skull between smears of blood—but there was still a lot of red raw meat filling her cheeks, surrounding her eyes and what I could see of her throat. The nose, lips, and ears were gone. Her teeth were stained a foul pinkish color. When I looked back up to Molloy, he was looking somewhere else, back still turned to them, eyes squinting.

"This looks like something you'd see from a cartel or satanists or something, Jim," Sgt. Wayne said, "not from Tok. Who would do this?"

"I'm only telling you what I see."

Molloy would eventually come to ditch this theory and face the darker horror.

III

I COULDN'T HELP IT. I REALLY DIDN'T WANT TO. IT REVOLTED me.

But I couldn't stop. The woman with her face peeled off. I had to draw her when I got home that night. I don't even know why. I mean, there's no question about how remarkably awful it was. But I just couldn't stop thinking about it—it fascinated me. I saw her every time I closed my eyes. Her teeth spread—but not in a smile. Those wide lidless eyes forever open—staring into the void.

I crumpled them all up at first. One after another. They made me sick. But I couldn't stop. I had a trash can full by midnight. God, if anyone from the station ever found them— and fuck, I even hid one.

IT WAS—FOR LACK OF A BETTER WAY TO PUT IT—RELATIVELY calm the next day. At least, on my end. No witnesses meant no drawing, so I was put back out on patrol. Patrol is always nice. Nothing hardly ever happens on patrol. It's being called to a place. That's when the job gets dark. There's nothing worse than having to be called somewhere.

· · ·

MOLLY SAYS THE KILLER WAS LIKELY WEARING GLOVES, according to the coroner—no prints, not that there were many places to check. Fingerprints are nearly impossible to collect from fabric and she was fully clothed.

He said that the initial incision around her throat was really well done, hardly grazed beyond her epidermis. They're thinking that this would've required him to use a scalpel or something for such precision. There was nothing comfortable about it.

The hardest part to digest was that the wound around her neck was the only evidence of a laceration that could be found anywhere at all over her entire face and scalp. This led them to believe that her face was removed in one piece, like a mask—yanked off with tremendous force by the hair. He must've wanted to keep it for some reason. Stranger though, they recognized that if he did intend on making a mask out of her, the better thing to do would've been to make an incision along the back of her head—that way it would've been easier to take off and on. By the time he finished muscling it off the way they assumed he did, via that single cut around her neck, her face would've been so stretched out and ruined that the end product wouldn't justify the means.

"So then why would he want it in one piece if not to show it off?" I asked.

"Torture," Molloy replied.

<hr />

IV

THE NEXT ONE TURNED UP ABOUT TWO WEEKS LATER. SAME thing—young woman, mid 20s, presumably—fully clothed with a crimson mask. Molloy changed his beat now that we knew for sure there was a serial killer amongst us. A very deranged one, at that.

This town never had any real trouble with drugs or prostitution. No gangs. Hardly ever had any violent crime. In hindsight, it was delusional to think it could be anything else. It was too horrific. This town's too quiet; mobsters, if any existed, would've just dumped them into a lake with cement shoes on.

Det. Molloy stood with his back to them again—and again, I had to catch a glimpse of her.

THIS ONE I HAD TO PAINT. NOT FOR ANY BETTER REASON than the first one; it consumed me until I was forced to. It was not beautiful. It wasn't erotic. It wasn't fun. What the fuck was I going to do with it now? Hide it in the closet and hope no one ever finds it? This has to stop.

"SCHIEL!" SGT. WAYNE HOLLERED BEHIND ME, LOUDER THIS time. I was sitting in my cubicle with my headphones on—gamma waves, 32 Hz; I couldn't stand the sound of people typing and jabbering around me—and I was so startled I jumped and spun around. He looked angry. I swatted my headphones off as I tried to read his lips and catch the end of what he was saying: "I thought I told you to never let me catch you doodling at your desk."

"That never gets old, sir—"

"Please!" a woman's voice suddenly cried from across the station towards the front door. "Please! Someone help me!" she yelled again and we all ran over to her.

"What's happened?" Det. Molloy yelled, looking at all the blood.

"Are you okay?" I asked, taking hold of her hands and easing her down into a chair. I couldn't tell where she was bleeding from or if it was even hers—I couldn't think straight at all.

"She kidnapped me!" the woman cried. "She was going to kill me!"

It must've been a combination. I found two small cuts, one

on her hand and one on her elbow, but they wouldn't have made this much blood. She was filthy too, like she climbed out of a hole. There was a drawing in her though, I knew it. Time was of the essence, but she needed to be cleaned and bandaged. Maybe even sedated a bit.

"SHE HAD ME LOCKED UP DOWN THERE FOR THREE DAYS. IT was the flayer—she told me what she was going to do to me. She said she knew me—that we met before. She didn't tie the rope tight enough around one of my hands. She—"

"This was a woman who did this?" I could hear in Sgt. Wayne's voice that what he really wanted to say was, "just a woman."

"She had the faces. She showed them to me. Oh God, she had their faces—they were lit up with candles. She made me look at them—"

"What did she do to you? How did you escape?" pressed Det. Molloy.

"Where is she? Take us to her," demanded Sgt. Wayne as the girl cried.

"Sergeant," I spoke up. "She's not going to be able to recall anything if we traumatize her. The quicker you let me do my job and get this recorded, the better."

"Damnit!" Sgt. Wayne yelled. "Why don't you just use your mind-reading bullshit to tell us how she winded up here so the real team can go take care of it?"

"Sir," I stayed cool, "that's not what I do."

"SHE WAS... BEAUTIFUL," THE WOMAN SAID, STARING FORWARD, unblinking. Her voice was slow and distant—far off—the way they always are. "Sharp nose with high Russian cheekbones. Large round eyes, um—" her throat choked up and she began sobbing.

"What else?" I asked. "Where were you?"

"The room..." she said, still staring at the same spot, as if it were in front of her. "She was keeping me in the basement. There weren't any windows, but I could hear her walking upstairs. I remember thinking, please God let someone knock on the door and I could scream. She... tried to kiss me. I didn't know what to do and—I pushed her. I didn't mean to—it was an impulse—but before I could apologize, she tased me until I went unconscious."

"What did you see when you woke up?"

"There were paintings on the walls and... art books every-where. Like, different painters. She told me I had to read them."

"Describe the paintings."

"Some were just nude portraits—but old ones—the kind you'd see in a museum. But some were... One looked like a goat that was being skinned alive."

The Flaying of Marsyas, I thought. Titian.

"I remember she had a David, too—like the sculpture, but just his head. It was on a shelf by the record playe—" the woman suddenly contorted and started screaming. "The shelf! Please! Make it stop! I don't want this—make it over, make it over—"

"What do you see? What is it?" I pressed on. Her arms and legs began flailing, but I knew she was unable to get up.

"The faces," she cried. "She unbolted the door on the night before she said she was going to kill me and took me outside of the room. I could see the steps, but I couldn't make my body move towards them. There was a dirt floor and she made me kneel. When I looked up, I saw the shelf. There were fa—" tears streamed down her cheeks from her wide eyes. "Faces. She cut their faces off—she cut their faces off! They were glowing! Oh God, please—"

V

"You did great, Joe," Sgt. Wayne said. For a moment, I believed the sarcastic sincerity in his voice.

"She told me that the killer said she knew her."

"Isn't that something? Too bad we can't ask her from where, now." He kept going before I could interject. "That sure is a real pretty picture you made though. Let's all give it up for Officer Schiel, everyone," he said, clapping his hands in front of the entire office. Thankfully, no one else joined in.

"Sir—"

"Let's all thank Schiel for getting the only witness we had on this to go mute—catatonic, they said—before we could get a location."

"Sir, nothing I did in there was going to change anyth—she was severely traumatized already! She saw the faces—"

"Joe, I'm gonna make this real simple for ya," he said, leaning in. "If this sketch doesn't bring us a lead by tomorrow night, I'm gonna take one of your pencils here, the longest, sharpest one you have, and shove it directly—"

I think he said up my ass first, and then through my neck. Maybe it was the other way around, I can't remember.

I didn't take her too far. She would hardly even talk before I spoke to her. Sgt. Wayne and Molloy wouldn't have been able to get shit out of her. They're lucky I was able to get what I got before it went sideways. As a thank you, I was ordered to go around every storefront in Tok and hang up one of my flyers personally—petty punishment. I already posted it all over social media after it was finished.

The sketch will work. They always do. Someone will recognize her.

By 10:30 PM, of course, no one had. It usually takes about 48–72 hours. We were only sitting at a little over 24.

Maybe tomorrow. After that, most times they disappear forever. And those are usually just thugs; I can't imagine the type of precautions a serial killer like this must take.

Sgt. Wayne had been buzzing my phone for the last couple hours—probably to fire me, but I was already three lagers deep by then, plus a snakebite someone bought me. I've never felt like this after a drawing—like I failed. And it was too early to think so anyway. It's normally always a feeling of calm afterwards—resolve—patience, even. Trusting that the drawing would catch someone's eye. This wasn't supposed to happen—

"Hi," someone said beside me; it almost sounded like a question. "You've been really mean-mugging that countertop for about 20 minutes now." I was—shit. I looked up to see who it was. "And your beer's empty," she said, suggestively, before I could apologize.

"Someone already bought me a drink—I'm fine, thank you," I said.

"Woa," she said, pretending to back away. "Real standoffish, huh?" I sighed deeply.

"I'm sorry, I just... had a bad day."

"So, what are you going to do about it?"

"I'm sorry?" I turned to get a better look at her.

"Well, I have my book," she said and flashed the cover at me —Velocities by Stephen Dobyns. "The guy beside you has his earbuds because the guy next to him keeps putting Van Halen on over the jukebox." I forced a smile but was unsure of what to say. "Those people are playing pool," she continued, "and, I can't tell, but I think that woman down there is flirting pretty hard with the bartender."

"Alright," I said, "so, what should I do? Go play shuffleboard so you can read your book?"

"Order a fucking drink. Stop sulking. You're weirding everyone out just sitting there crying."

"I'm not crying—"

"You're at the least brooding."

"I—" I struggled, "am not." Was she hitting on me? I've had women buy me drinks before—bought them a round or two, too —but I never had one tell me to order a drink for myself. I guess she was right. I sighed and turned the buzzing illuminated image of Sgt. Wayne's face over and raised my hand to flag down the bartender.

"You're not gonna answer that?" she asked. "Looked urgent."

"Not right now," I said, removing my hands from the counter.

"Wait—what's on your fingers? Is that blood?" she asked, a bit concerned.

"Oh," I said, "I was painting earlier."

"Wow, that's a bold, dark color. Must be for a good, warm study, I presume?"

"You like poetry?" I asked, looking back to the book of poems that she had marked with her finger. She ignored the question—it was obviously stupid—and continued talking about how she needed to add a fresh coat of paint in her own study until I was able to elaborate.

"Oh—you meant—you're an artist? What do you paint?"

Oh you know, mostly just dead girls with their faces torn off—

"The auroras," I said. "Mountainscapes, hinterlands—cheery, arctic adventures."

"Sounds like boring kitsch for dipshits, no offense. You never make anything real?" I could see all the drawings I crumpled up of the first crimson mask in my mind. The lidless eyes. The exposed teeth. The red skull and—

"Two gin and tonics," she said before I could answer. I didn't realize the bartender had been standing next to me waiting.

"I mean, I—" I tried to defend myself, but couldn't. "My paintings are real."

"Eh," she said, "maybe you could use some help with subject matter."

My watch started beeping at 5:00 AM, as it always does, but I couldn't reach for it with my other hand. It was stuck on something. I tried to open my eyes and investigate, but my shoulder was tight against my face. I tugged, but there was no give—it was tied to something.

I bolted up as quickly as I could—my head was still heavy and spinning—and I saw the large round knot around my wrist. Jesus. I didn't even remember drinking that much. What was the last thing I remembered? The lady at the bar. She helped me out to my car. She must've slipped something into my drink. I could barely even walk.

That's when she tased me. My legs buckled immediately and I fell down on my knees. I pissed myself.

"Yuck, I can't believe I kissed you," she said before tasing me again.

Then I woke up here.

No windows, just like the girl described. There was David on a shelf full of books: Vermeer, Sorolla, Goya, Van Gogh—dozens. And the record player. And the toilet behind the *tsuitate* partition. The only thing I didn't recognize; the girl never mentioned anything about an easel in the corner. My heart started pounding. And then the rope was gone.

I grabbed my wrist—nothing. Did I hallucinate it? I half expected the woman from last night to be sitting on the edge of the bed when I turned, but there was no one there. Just me. I swung my legs over the side of the bed and tried to sit up for a while until my vision straightened. What was this? Ketamine?

The door was miraculously unbolted when I finally managed to wobble over to it. A wave of sobriety washed over me—I was getting out. I used all my strength to slide open the large steel door and there she was, standing casually on the other side.

"I didn't want to wake you," she said softly, but with a coy, giddy look on her face. "You were sleeping on your arm weird, surprised it didn't go numb." I had to consciously stop myself from looking down to my wrist and rubbing the pins and needles. I had to keep my eyes on her. She still had her glasses on. And the wig—which she started to remove as she spoke.

"I was so afraid you were going to recognize me last night." Don't say it. Don't—"From your drawing."

It was her. The woman I had drawn two days ago. A murderer. There was no mistaking any of this now.

Another wave of foolish confidence overcame me and, defying my condition, I charged through the doorway. My knees buckled instantly upon reaching her and the next thing I knew my blood was boiling in my veins. I didn't lose consciousness this time though. She pulled the taser away and began booting me repeatedly in the ribs as I laid out stiff as a board.

"What the hell are you doing?" she yelled. "Do you have any idea how lucky you are I wasn't holding a knife in my hand? Asshole!" she yelled again, this time kicking me right below the ribs. She flung her hair back, straightening up, and seemed to take a minute to breathe. "Goddamnit, man! What's wrong with you?"

I could feel a hot tingling sensation in my fingertips and she could see that I was starting to get motion back. This time, she kicked me higher, an inch away from my armpit, and I had just enough strength to roll over and curl.

"Now we're gonna have to do this the hard way," she moaned above me, very disappointedly. By the time I raised my head to locate her, she already had my ankles hoisted up to her hips and was dragging me across the dirt floor back into the sealed room. That's when I looked up and saw the shelves of faces. Glowing flesh, mottled with dark reds and blacks—like dehydrated pig ears—from the candles burning inside them. There were so many. Where were all the bodies?

The rope that I imagined turned out to actually be a chain that was firmly cemented into the floor. The other end was locked securely around my neck.

"I did that myself," she said proudly. She saw me looking at the thick steel eyelet in the concrete where the chain was connected. "I'm a handy woman, alright, Joe? So don't try anything again and this will go a lot better for you, okay?" I nodded, raising my hands up to the chain that was padlocked around my neck. It was loose enough where it wasn't choking me, but far too tight to slip over my jaw. "If you're good, maybe we'll try something else; but the chain has to stay for now. Come on, stop mean-mugging me like I'm that bar top from last night. Aren't ya gonna say anything?"

"What is this?" I asked her.

"I didn't want it to be this way for us, Joe, but it's your own fault. I had high hopes for you—I saw this going completely different." How the fuck did she want me to react, thrilled?

"What do you want?" I asked.

"I really want to let you go," she snickered, but there was something genuine in her voice.

"Then do it," I tried.

"Not that easy, bub," she laughed again. "I need to trust you first. For now, I just want you to do a few things for me."

"Like what?"

"Well, I'm still trying to figure it all out, actually," she said and looked away from me toward the open door which led to the dirt room. Which led to the stairwell. Which led to a door. "But don't worry, I'm gonna get it all together soon. I need you to see some things first though, I guess."

"I've seen enough."

"I need you to see me, as I really am."

"I can see exactly who you are."

"No, no," she said, waving her hand in the air, "you don't understand. I want you to paint a portrait for me, Joe."

"Of who?"

"Of me, you dumbass!" She stood up enraged. I winced, thinking she was going to kick me again. "What would you prefer to paint, hm?—a topless woman or maybe some skinless corpses?" I was never so terrified of someone before. I had to get out of here.

When she calmed down, she turned and took a few steps away—but not far enough. I could tell by the slack in the chain that I could reach. Running entirely on a mixture of instinct, anger, and fear, I leapt over the bed like a greyhound and tackled her to the linoleum with the chain rattling behind me. My hands were squeezing around her neck, strangling her until her face turned red.

"Go ahead," she struggled to get out, a smile on her face despite the veins bulging in her forehead. I felt a stab of apprehension and I released my grip—just a bit. Just enough to let a little more air pass through. "Kill me," she said, "then you'll never get out."

I tightened my fingers back around her throat, trying to lace them behind her neck, and choked her for another minute as I thought about it. Until her face was almost blue. When I finally decided to let go, I couldn't tell if she was coughing or laughing, but I immediately began pressing her all over for the key—starting with her pockets. The coughs and other desperate choking inhales conclusively became laughs as I felt between her legs and breasts. I had to check everywhere.

"You're gonna be fun," she coughed as she looked up at me, the normal tone returning to her face.

VI

"ARE YOU AWAKE?" SHE CALLED DOWN THE STEPS A FEW DAYS later. I rang my bell. "Are you sure?" she asked again; I could hear her already running down the steps. The giddiness was back. "I know how you artist types like to sleep all day and not contribute." I rang the bell again, twice—more forcibly. "Oh, this is wonderful!" I heard her exclaim as she unbolted the door. "You didn't eat your soup," she said with dismay, stepping into my chamber, which is what it was. She decorated it a lot more since the first night, but it was still a prison cell.

"I'm not hungry," I said.

"Oh, don't start this again."

"Look, Nora," I said, tossing away one of her art books— John Singer Sargent. I could tell this bothered her; her eyes widened as it bounced and slid to the edge of the bed.

"Did you read the one about the guy who cut the woman's head off yet?—Caravaggio!" she asked, her eyes darting back to me once she saw that the book wouldn't fall to the floor.

"No." I did. He "photographed with paint," according to the author.

"Oh, it's one of my favorites," she said, taking a step closer to me. "They say he really painted it in his portrait of Medusa."

"That's not a portrait."

"Joe," she changed her tone—dawdling with me. "I want us to go slow tonight, okay?"

Oh, God.

"Nora—"

"I got you all your charcoals and crayons—" she laughed. "You didn't really think I was going to start off giving you pencils and brushes, did ya? Something to stab me with? We have a long journey ahead of us, Joe."

"I would never do that, Nora." I tried my best to make the affection I put in my voice sound sincere. Not until I get you to trust me.

She went over to the record player and put on a live '78 performance of Bruce Springsteen doing "Because the Night" with the E Street Band and then walked back out into the dirt room. When she returned, she was dragging someone in by the ankles—just like she dragged me. It was a girl, indistinguishable from her other victims—the same age and build, at least.

"Nora," I sat up; the little hairs prickled down my back as I watched the unconscious girl's chest rise and fall with her breath. "What are you doing?"

"Well, you know all the work I put into getting this tub down the steps," she said, dropping the girl's feet just outside the radius of my chain. It was sometime after my second or third night here when I heard her wrestling with it. It was porcelain, with feet. I couldn't believe she got it down here in one piece. "I guess I told a little lie when I said it was for you. I mean, I do want you to be able to bathe down here—that part was true. I never usually keep anyone this long; the hose is normally more than sufficient. However—"

"Nora, please—"

"Don't worry, she'll be dead in a moment."

"You don't have to do this," I begged as she bent over the tub and plugged the drain. I don't want to see this.

"Do you think she's pretty?"

"What?" I asked.

"I said, do you think that she's pretty?" she repeated.

"What are you going to do to her?"

"Ugh, men," Nora groaned as she lifted the girl up from under her shoulders. "Can't answer a simpl—you're not gonna believe it, Joe. Tell you the truth, I don't know if this is even gonna work," she laughed. "Hopefully this doesn't just rip her head off. Normally, it's a straight shot," she pointed out with her finger as if that cleared it up.

"What are you talking about?"

"I'm talking about capturing my essence," she yelled back at me. "Am I going to have to hold your hand?"

"Please don't do whatever you're about to—" I tried.

"Joe, you need to get it together, okay? I'm about to cut this girl's face off and I need you to be here for it."

"Nora, please, I'm an artist, remember? I can make it up! Just tell me what to draw and I'll do it!"

"No, no-no, you have to see how it works," she said with her back turned toward me. She was crouching down over the girl in the tub. "In order to get all the blood," she said, "you have to make a little superficial incision around the neck—like this,"

"Please, stop!" I cried.

"It's actually attached a lot looser than it looks. If you go too deep, they'll die before the heart can fully bleed out—and we can't have that." I couldn't see inside the tub, but I knew what she was doing. I began frantically searching all over the room for some way to stop her, but there was nothing. The chain wasn't long enough for me to reach her and I had nothing to throw but books and crayons. That's when I noticed the pulley system that was newly installed into the ceiling above the tub. When the hell did she—

Eat your soup, Joe. She drugged me again.

"The hardest part really is putting the hooks in," she said over her shoulder. "You have to use these big-game hooks—y'know, for halibut—and you got to place them evenly around the top of the head. Two in the front," she said, struggling a bit to pierce the next one. "Two in the back, and one in the middle. If you go too deep, you'll hook the fascia, and that's never good."

I could hear the girl beginning to wake from her daze as she started to stir and moan in the tub.

"Alright," Nora said, standing up. "Just have to fasten her feet to the pulley and we can get started—Joe? Joe. Joe!" she yelled. "This is very important that you pay attention right now and stop crying."

She began tugging down hard on the rope just as Bruce started tearing his guitar apart. She must've planned the timing. For me. This was all a show to her.

As the semi-lifeless girl's legs rose above the tub, her arms hung down beside her head. What I thought was a large amount of blood began pouring down her face until Nora let out a piercingly loud whistle, as if calling a pack of wild dogs.

I couldn't believe what I was seeing. Something upstairs yanked the rope around the corner and it went taut, jerking the girl's head over to one side. I heard glass smashing upstairs and then the sound of something very heavy screeching and skidding across the floor.

"Shit!" Nora blurted furiously. "I was afraid this was going to get caught like that—it's too much doing it through the house, damnit."

But before she could find a solution to the kink, the girl's entire body swung up in the direction that her head was being pulled and crashed into the shelf which housed the bust of David, sending it toppling to the ground where it shattered.

"Damnit to hell!" Nora yelled again. Everything began to get blurry after that.

The girl began to scream. There were changes in her face every time she shifted a bit—when whatever was pulling on her gained another inch or two. Her eyeballs looked like they were about to pop out of her skull and the corners of her mouth began tearing into a wide horrific smile—just like her collection.

"Stop it!" I yelled.

A broad red band began to open around her neck until her entire face suddenly snapped right off—spraying blood all over both of us—and flapped up the steps.

"Okay!" Nora cheered with satisfaction as the faceless body swung back over the tub. "I am so sorry about that, Joe," she said, spinning around and looking at the blood all over my face. "Normally, it does not go that way. This is kind of on you though for making me do it down here. They usually pop right off! Alright, we better clean up." She raised her leg over the side of the tub and steadied the body with her foot as it bled out—some final twists and jerks still firing in the girl's arms. I suspect it was a little over 5 liters—just enough to fill the bottom.

Nora handed me a wet towel to wipe off with and then drew the hot water on and left the room. When she returned, she was cleaned up—and naked.

"I know you could just make it up, stupid," she said, stepping into the room. "But I want you to see... I'm sorry, Joe, I should've specified this from the beginning—I'm gonna need you to be more of a photographer than an artist, okay? Like Caravaggio," she smiled. "Otherwise, I'm gonna have to let you go."

At that, she raised her foot up over the tub again, but this time, it slid in. As she lowered beneath the surface, I found myself starting to vomit—dry heave, rather; there was nothing in my stomach but bile. No drugs to make this easier to process.

"Come draw me," Nora called, as she lay there soaking in blood.

VII

"I'M SORRY ABOUT LAST NIGHT," SHE SAID THE NEXT MORNING —clean, dry, and clothed in her blue jeans. She almost looked normal with her white tennis shoes. I was still smeared all over with a stranger's dried blood. "I got so tired afterwards I just went right out," she laughed. "Here," she said, handing me a hot wet towel. "I'll wash your clothes, you know where the clean ones are."

"I don't want them back," I said.

"You know," she began, "you really oughta just take a bath. I made a bit of a mess with you. I mean, it's there," she said, looking over to the tub, and I glared at her full of hatred. "With water, Joe. I wouldn't do that to you... yet," she laughed again.

What else could I do? I had to get it off of me.

A couple months must have gone by like that. It was hard to keep track of time down there. She smashed my watch because she claimed that the beeping would wake her up. I know she just wanted to take it away from me—torture me a little. I guess that sounds obvious, but sometimes she actually seemed human.

Sometimes she would bring me things. New paints, new sheets, new books that she would make me read. Never any new albums; it was always Springsteen with her.

"Ooo, have you heard this one?" she asked one day. "It's about the Starkweather murder spree. Still gives me chills—I wish a man would come sweep me away like that. Wouldn't that be fun?—One day," she sighed and laughed, "not with you of course."

"Of course," I said meekly, holding up my hands—trying to show appreciation for my new handcuffs, which replaced the heavy chain around my neck—while also fantasizing about her death.

She would bring me food and water. Clean clothes. Not big on making coffee. I eventually convinced her to get a Rilo Kiley record. I thought she would appreciate it. She smashed it halfway into "Portions for Foxes." She mostly kept her temper as long as I went along with everything and pretended to read The Life of Modigliani or Botticelli again.

But then there were nights like before. When she would bring another girl home again. Always a girl. A very pretty girl. Det. Molloy was right about one thing, it was deeply personal.

Then of course, there was everything she forced me to do afterwards. At any rate, it meant she wouldn't kill me—or that I still had some time, at least. That really didn't make it much easier though.

"What's wrong, Joe? You don't want to fuck me?" she'd tease at first, lips red with another girl's blood, then get angry.

And the paintings—

"What did you think when you saw the first one?" she asked from the tub one night.

"First what?" I asked, smudging some charcoal around with my thumb.

"The first body you guys found." How do I answer that without making her mad? "Did you draw her?" she asked, turning her head around. I almost told her not to move, but then realized that I didn't give a shit how her fucking drawing turned out. "You did, didn't you? Admit it!" I thought she was going to splash me for a second and I almost got sick. "You're nuts, Joe."

It just then occurred to me that my apartment had most certainly been searched by now—meaning Sgt. Wayne and Molloy would've found my drawings. They must've loved that.

ONE DAY SHE STARTED ACTING DIFFERENTLY TOWARDS ME. More things were my fault than usual. Something was bothering her. She was spending less and less time in the basement with me and whenever she did, she was always snapping nasty remarks.

"What is it?" I asked her.

"Nothing," she said, like a child. She was being fucking coy with me again.

"Alright," I said, not too firmly. "How about you tell me what... pulls them off?" I caught her look over to me, curiously. "Upstairs. When you whistle."

"Oh," she hiccuped. Has she been up there drinking? "That's Shadow."

"Shadow?"

"Yeah, I would've loved for you to meet him—paint him— but you were a bad boy and lost your upstairs privileges."

"But haven't I been a good boy since then, Nora?" I asked. Her face tried to deny it but failed. "Admit it," I almost shouted. "I deserve it—I haven't seen the damn sun in months!" I was shouting now. "I've been trapped down here chained to a wall like a dog with no one but me—and Vermeer, and, and—you killing people." I fucking begged, "Please. Tie me up—gag my mouth—just let me out of this goddamn room!"

"Fine," she said. Why did I feel defeated? "I'll go get a rope."

THE WINDOW WAS OPEN IN THE LIVING ROOM. I HAD NO PLAN of jumping out. That would be stupid. It'd be difficult anyway; there was a cherry tree growing too close to the side of the house and the branches were nearly reaching in through the window.

"I planted that there just so I could do this," she saw me looking and then put her glass of wine down and plucked a few cherries off the closest branch. I nodded and tried to smile with my eyes. I couldn't help but find her attractive so I looked away.

She had a beautiful stone fireplace—complete with fire pokers. She left them out. She still trusts her knots. A large round woven rug on the hardwood floor in the center of the room. A wicker chair. No paintings. There was a very different feel compared to—

"Come—but don't get any ideas, Joe," she said, and I shuffled cautiously over to the window. I tried my best to look comfortable. "I'm going to lower your gag," she said, "so you can have one. But just so you know, there's no one around here for miles; you can scream bloody murder if you want and no one will hear it. But, if you do, I'll shoot you," she said, and pulled out a .44 Bulldog from behind her back and held it in front of my face. I tried my best not to flinch by averting my eyes until she put it away.

She did as she said and pulled the gag down and then pushed one of the ripe cherries into my mouth. I bit down on it and it popped with dark red juices.

"You don't like me anymore," she said, looking down.

"What?—Nora?—"

"You're bored with me."

"What are you talking about?" I asked, struggling to lick my lips without the use of my hands.

"I keep bringing you the same thing over and over again to paint—"

"What? No—I don't—" How the fuck was I supposed to respond to that? I couldn't think of anything and she looked away like she was about to cry. Maybe blow a .44 Special through my head, I couldn't tell.

"You're an artist," she muttered, "you need inspiration."

"No," I tried to interject. "I'm not. I'm a sketch artist. I'm a cop, remember?"

"Don't talk like that," she frowned. Don't piss her off. Try again.

"Nora—"

WE BOTH TURNED AT THE SAME MOMENT FOR THE FRONT door. A motor. In the distance, down her dirt road. There was a car coming.

"Oh, damnit!" she yelled, fumbling for her fake glasses. "Quick, get downstairs!"

I took a step backwards toward the door, but then stiffened.

"Joe, go! You want me to blow your brains out and them too? Move!" She shoved me towards the basement door. "Now, listen to me. I know you know that these walls are thin, so, if you even have the dumbest thought possible that you were gonna make some stupid noise while I handled this—I'll come right down there after I kill them and tear your fucking face off too. Do you understand me, Joe?"

As I went to nod, she kicked my back and I tumbled face-first down the stairs with my hands tied behind my back.

"Alright, shut up!" she called down the steps as I was groaning in pain. I was lucky for the dirt floor at the bottom of the steps, but I'm pretty sure my elbow was broken. Maybe my ribs too. My forehead was busted open for sure—I could taste the blood. The taste of her kissing me. "He's almost here! Do right, Joe!" she said, slamming the door shut.

Luckily, the rope busted somewhere between the steps and the floor and I was able to free my hand from underneath my body and jam it between my teeth. I don't know how else I would've been able to keep quiet. Every time I breathed it was excruciating. I thought for sure I punctured a lung. But I couldn't risk being responsible for some innocent person's death. She was crazy—I believed her. If I'm going to die, it's going to be in the process of taking her down. No innocent lives. Plus, if she was willing to shoot them, just imagine what horrors she'd plan for me. I bit down.

"Pardon my intrusion, miss," I heard a familiar voice say as she opened the front door.

"Oh, hello? Officer?" she tried to sound surprised.

"Detective Molloy—no cause for alarm. Are you Miss Nora Kloskov?"

"Yes," she said, "how can I help you?" I could tell by the sound of her voice that she was smiling at him now.

"I just wanted to see if I could beg a moment of your time?"

"Of course, officer! Come right in, what can I do for you? Would you like a glass of water?"

"Cup of coffee would sure go a long way for me, miss—it's been a rough few months lately. Seems like it's all I'm running on these days—if it ain't too much trouble."

"Certainly, I'll get a pot going." I could hear disgust in her voice and then her footsteps towards the kitchen. I tried to shift my body to hear better and almost let out a groan of pain from my pinned elbow. It was definitely broken. "So, what is this all about?" she asked, coming back where I could hear.

"Well," Molloy said. "I'm sure by now you've heard about the —" he wouldn't say flayer. "—Girls."

"It's so awful. How could someone do that?"

"I don't know, miss Kloskov, but we believe there's gotta be a connection between the girls somehow." Pull out your gun and fucking shoot her. "So far, we don't have much. Two of the girls went to school together. Another couple, church—the one who escaped went to the same bar on the weekend as a few of them—"

The Little Goat.

"This last one belonged to a yoga club, Athena's. You're familiar with it, right?"

"Oh, God—yes, I go there every Wednesday—who was it?"

"Do you know a Leslie Carmichael?"

"Yes, I think so, the pretty little blonde girl?"

"I believe that'd be her. Well, I figured I should touch base with you and—"

"Do you think I'm in danger?" Nora tried to sound panicked.

"Well, no—not exactly. It's not a bad idea to keep your eyes open though—which brings me to why I'm really here. Do you recall ever seeing anything out of place with Miss Carmichael? Maybe seeing her in the parking lot with someone not in the group or maybe she was acting odd one day?"

"I'm sorry, detective. Honestly, I don't think I ever really even spoke to her. Maybe a 'hello' or 'see you next week.'"

"Alright," Molloy said, followed by the sound of a chair screech across the floor—not as hard as Shadow. "I won't hold up anymore of your time then, miss, I appreciate it. If you happen to notice anything not on the up and up, you call the station and ask for me, alright? Here's my card, if it's late."

"Thank you, detective. I'll pray for the victims—and that you find him."

"Appreciate it, miss," he said, and then I heard the door close.

"What the fuck, Joe?" Nora screamed down the steps and kicked me hard in the ribs. If they weren't broken before, they were now. "What the fuck did you tell them about me? What do they know?!" She pressed my face down into the dirt until wet brown clouds puffed up on either side of my face and I choked on dust.

"You told the one that got away," I coughed, once she let me regain my breath, "—that you knew her. They know it's not random."

VIII

I DIDN'T KNOW WHAT TO EXPECT. I THOUGHT SHE WAS GOING to get angry again. Wreak havoc downstairs. Break things—maybe my legs. Stop feeding me. The only thing that really changed was the books, though. No more artist collections and biographies. She started bringing me some really weird books.

The Mysteries of Numerology was the title of the first one. Then came one on daemonologie—as it was spelled. "Arithmancy," that was a new subject for me; I had never heard that word before. They kept coming: various texts on astrology, polar radiation, a multitude of credible resources on geometry; but then came The Symbols and Patterns of the Unholy, and Esoteric Formulas for Necromancy.

I noticed something else too. It had been about a month since she last killed someone—at least, that I knew about. Molloy had gotten to her.

"Nora," I said one day. "What's wrong?" She was my life support. "He left, remember? There was nothing here. You covered your tracks—"

"Shut the fuck up, pig!" she snapped. "I'm sorry—I was just lost in thought about what we're going to do."

"What do you mean?" I asked. "Do what?"

"To make it more interesting for you—so I'm not boring you."

"Please, Nora, no more!" Maybe it was an opportunity to work on her growing paranoia? "In fact, maybe now is the best time to turn yourself in, you know? Before it gets any worse, before your Starkweather spree ends like Bonnie and Clyde—you don't want to go down like that, right? We could both escape."

"Joe," she said, and there was a look of such admiration in her eyes. "When I first saw the drawing you did of me in that ad, it was like I knew who you were and that you knew me. We just had to meet. It was the most beautiful thing in the world. Wasn't it like that for you?"

"Of course—" She slapped me before I could finish.

"Don't you ever lie to me again, Joe! You don't know anything —you're just some dumb cop. This is going to be the best painting you're ever going to be known for, and you're off pissing your pants again."

"Nora—"

"Do you know how easy it is to still get lye?" Nora asked, putting on a respirator and rubber gloves. "Dahmer made it a little harder, of course, but it's really no worse than trying to buy spray paint or cigarettes."

She stepped back and got down into a squat, moving her face away from the bucket as she opened the lid. "The problem is the fumes. They can be caustic—anywhere from a minor infection to neuropathy, if breathed directly. I think you're probably gonna be fine, though—I've given you stronger stuff. Now, the last time I did this, they were already dead, so you might want to shield your eyes—who knows what she's going to do?"

"Nora, please don't do this—" But she started pouring the bucket down the underside of the inverted hanging girl's chin. The girl began screaming immediately, but nothing was happening—so far as I could tell. I can't imagine what it must've smelled like; I was standing across the room and it was still making me sick. Once the water began reacting with the sodium hydroxide, the girl started a different scream altogether. Her lips began bubbling. Her eyes swelled shut. Steam and smoke billowed off her cheeks and scalp.

"Try not to breathe that in," Nora said, turning around to make sure I was still paying attention.

After the last bucket was poured, she said with great disappointment, "Well, it doesn't look like there's going to be any blood tonight. I'm just going to go to bed; I'll leave her there for you." My eyes were burning and I was coughing up a storm, unable to protest. "I'll let you keep the door open tonight so it can air out down here, but that means you have to wear your naughty boy chain. If you try to escape, I'll cut your balls off and go over them with the lawn mower. Goodnight, Joe."

I wiped my eyes and looked over to the tub. There was hardly any more than a skull left of the girl's face, with some red and white foam falling off it into the drain.

NORA BECAME EVEN MORE DISTANT AFTER THAT. SHARP-tongued, worse than before, even just to drop off my food and leave. She hadn't cared about my trash in weeks. Nothing but me and The Boss and a heap of books on sex-magic, blood treatises, and un-sacred geometry.

One day she barged in unexpectedly while I was contemplating "Highway Patrolman" and what it would be like arresting someone you loved. She slammed the bolt back with its customary clack and raved, "I figured it out!"

"Figured what out?" I asked.

"Look!" she said and opened up one of her art books. There was a side-by-side comparison of Michelangelo's Creation of Adam and an autopsy photograph of the inside of a human brain. It was really remarkable; I couldn't believe it. Everything lined up perfectly—the top of the skull with the creator's robe, the pituitary stalk and one of the angel's feet, even the cerebellum and the vertebral arteries were represented. It was so obvious—you could cut one image out and lay it right on top of the other. But I was still confused as to what sick idea she'd come up with.

"That's fascinating, in a disturbing sort of way, I guess," I said, hoping she wouldn't slap me.

"You know I don't like it when you say things like that. If you would do your homework and read more, you would've already known about it. Firmitas. Utilitas. Venustas."

For a split second, I thought she was actually trying to put a spell on me.

"Strength. Utility. Beauty," I responded, recognizing that she was quoting Vitruvius.

"Good boy!" she said and threw a new book on my bed:

Egyptian Mummification and the Forbidden Equations in the Pyramids.

"Nora," I said. "These books are getting—I don't understand what you want from me."

"I told you already, I figured it all out. I did the math," she said, as if that was supposed to comfort me. "You just need to smear the paint around."

She threw another book down at the foot of my bed and shouted, "I'll go prepare your canvas!" and ran upstairs like a lunatic. She's becoming more unstable every day.

"There's no way that this is actually going to work," I said. "You know that, right? This is crazy, Nora—you don't even believe in any of this bullshit."

"I don't think that matters, Joe—that's not the point. As long as we do it right. Plus, just think, if it does work, I won't need to take any more blood baths." I didn't believe that. I didn't believe any of it. She would never stop.

"Come on," I said, "all these books are from Barnes & Noble, aren't they?"

"Not that one," she said, pointing to the leather-bound codex in my hand. "Faith is only required for God, Joe—the devil doesn't need you to believe. He's always there, waiting for someone on the square. All he needs is a little invoking."

She hung up a canvas she had primed herself, complete with an elaborate geometric drawing in the center that she must've made with a ruler and a compass—I tried to look impressed. I presumed it was made in blood—probably even her own. There was a pentagram hidden within some angles in the center and other symbols I recognized from her books.

"This is how the composition has to stay," she said, pointing around the complex geometric patterns, "for the underpainting. You're free to do whatever you want color-wise, as long as you stick within the palette." Nora grinned at me for some reason and then turned back to the canvas. "But everything must be laid out perfectly in this arrangement. Is that clear, Joe?"

"Nora, this is silly—a painting can't make you younger, or prettier, or live forever—no matter how much you desecrate it with spells and blood. That's the purpose of a painting—it lives on, not us. These books are for sad people who don't go outside." I could tell she wasn't budging, so I tried another direction. "This isn't a good escape plan for when Detective Molloy comes back—"

She whipped me across the face with her Bulldog. It split my brow open and gushed hot blood down my face.

WHEN I WOKE UP, I WAS TIED TO A CHAIR IN FRONT OF THE easel. There were no paints in the palette tray, just differently concentrated vials of blood.

"It's going to work," she said. "I trust you, Joe. You wouldn't ruin this for me."

I never painted with blood before. It didn't go well. I had to keep redoing it. I wasn't aware of its challenges. Blood dried too fast, for one thing. And rotted. I thought I'd heard there was glycerin in it, but it kept coagulating and gunking up the brushes. Each painting was ruined, and she was getting very tired and annoyed.

"Joe, I swear, if this is some kind of way for you to—"

"It's not my fault, Nora, please—it's these vials, I swear. They need to be mixed with a solvent or something; otherwise, they're going to just keep rotting like this. It'll have to be a little bit different than imagined, that's all," I said as she bandaged her wrist. "It won't work like oils; they'll have to be thinned out with turpentine. I'll be able to use them more like in a watercolor—like Blake." I tried to convince her.

"Joe," she said. "If you have to restart this painting one more time, I swear I think I might cut your dick off."

It ended up reminding me of a Blake more than I cared to acknowledge. But it was her all right. Slightly larger than full scale. Rising above the tub, sheened in red. The faceless body hanging behind her.

"How much longer?" she asked.

"A few more layers," I said. "Then the varnish. It's going to need to be thick. I would give it a week or two after that before framing it—you don't want it to stick." I truly lamented the thought of it getting ruined, as much as it sickened me. I'd put so much damn work into this one, but I also felt like I was trying to buy time for some reason. Like she didn't need me anymore. "I made all the measurements for the frame too; I could help put it together for you. I was thinking something dark, like rosewood or cherry even."

"I feel great, Joe," she said. She looked it too, in her depraved way. I guess it wasn't just to make her immortal—it made her younger too. Stop it. "I can't believe it; I think it's working already. Do you still need me?" she asked, not waiting for my answer before breaking the pose.

"No," I said, dipping my brush into one of the vials of her blood. "I should be able to get the rest done on my own."

"What would I do without you?" she asked. There was a timer now—a deadline.

IX

SHE CAME DOWN THE BASEMENT EVERY DAY THAT WEEK TO SEE if it was done yet. She wouldn't stay for chitchat anymore. Stopped asking me about the books. Took the record player away; she said it was distracting me from finishing—I didn't bother telling her that I'd stopped listening to her Springsteen albums weeks ago. In fact, the only times I ever really saw her were when she was bringing me food or water—and a few times she forgot that, or was spiting me for taking so long.

"You have to finish the painting now, Joe," she said one day from across the room. "It's time."

"Well, I mean, we want it to be perfect, don't we? What if it doesn't work?"

"Joe, honey—I'm running out of use for you."

"What does that mean?" I asked.

"You're becoming a burden for me. I think I'm going to have to kill ya. Plus, I miss my ritual—it's so stuffy down here. Back when I had the tub out in the barn, I could lie naked under the sky and watch the moon rise into the night sometimes—or the clouds roll below the stars—listen to the wind blow between the sunflowers—hear the crickets. I'm just a simple woman, I guess. I'll do you quick, though."

"Wait—no, you promised. You said you wouldn't kill me as long as I did whatever you asked. You said you wanted to let me go!"

"I don't have anything left to ask of you. I don't need any more paintings, Joe, not now that I have this portrait. And come on, who was I kidding? You knew I could never let you go. I mean, come on—you of all people." She then impersonated Det. Molloy: "Pardon my intrusions, missy, would you be so kind as to make me a cup of coffee and then I'll just mosey on out without even taking a sip? Come on, Joe. That cop showing up here signed your death warrant, I'm afraid. You know, I was actually considering it before, but I could never let you go now. Do you think I'm stupid?"

"Wait—wait—wait, wait a minute," I stammered. "Hold on, hold that—hold that pose. Let's do another one—a better one! I've got the mixture down now—let's make some more art!"

"Oh, Joe—no, I'm sorry," she said sadly. "Not right now, though. I won't kill you like this, but soon—I have a date tonight! I'm gonna go get ready and kill her and then I'll come back and kill you."

"Wait, Nora! Don't go!"

The steel door slid shut and the bolt dropped on the other

side, and it was just me again with the painting. I thought about destroying it, but I feared what she'd do to me—what she was already going to do to me.

There are worse things than death in this house.

She's never out this late. I sat up all night listening for her truck to come back until I couldn't. I was hungry. She didn't leave any water for me before she left either.

I was starting to drift off when I finally heard a crash upstairs. It sounded like someone may've broken in through the back door, and I thought about yelling out for help, but I had to be sure first. Anything was possible with her. By the sound of it, they nearly tumbled down the steps—I couldn't tell if it was her gait. Once the bolt swung open and I saw Nora hunched over holding her stomach, I knew something was really wrong. Her yellow blouse was red with blood.

"Oh my God. What happened?" I asked.

"That fucking bitch," Nora moaned. She was pale. "That skinny bitch had a knife in her purse." I didn't dare try to help, of course. Maybe she'd bleed out. Maybe she had the key to the handcuffs on her. She began to crawl across the floor toward the painting, leaving a trail of blood behind her—one hand pressed against her belly—until she fell on her side.

As she lay there under the portrait breathing heavily, she pulled her shirt up and began smearing the blood around, trying to find the wound. That's when I saw it—the split skin closed under her fingertips.

"Oh my God, Joe—I think it really worked! Did you see that? It's gone! She stabbed me right here, but look—it healed!"

"What the f—" Above her, on the portrait, a small knife wound appeared on the figure's abdomen that I did not paint.

"It's so beautiful, Joe," she cried. "You did it."

I could swear the painting was watching me as I paced around the room while she was gone—she ran upstairs to look at herself in the mirror and never came back.

None of this was possible. She had to have drugged me again.

Only problem with that was I felt incredibly sober. And afraid. But I know what I saw. What the hell did we do? Patterns of the Unholy.

Nora called down the steps to say that she was running out again. She said she needed to grab some things for our goodbye. It disturbed me, thinking about what that could mean, knowing it wasn't cake and sparklers.

"It's been so much fun, Joe," she said, putting her hand over my heart before she left. "I forgot what it was like having a man around. I promise, I'll be right back." She didn't take the painting with her when she went back upstairs, so that was reassuring—not that I was afraid of her taking off. I wanted to tear a hole in the painting—take it off the wall and smash it over my knee.

That would not go well for me.

There was only one thing left to do. The only thing I had yet to be desperate enough to try. I began tugging down on the chains with all my weight until my palms began to separate from my wrists. I didn't hold back; not from the pain or the fear of her hearing my screams.

There weren't any squirters, which was good—that'd mean an artery. No, just the normal profuse bleeding one would expect from being de-gloved. There was an agonizing grating on the backsides along my knuckles as the cuffs scraped along my bones. I'd have to squeeze all my fingers together in order to pull them through the cuffs. It made me panic. I was afraid, after all the damage that I had already caused myself, that the bones wouldn't even fit.

Once my blood lubricated everything, I was able to wrench and twist my gnarled hands through the steel shackles much easier. I didn't know I had it in me to carry out such horrible self-mutilation. Most of my fingers still had some flesh attached to them when I was finished—maybe they'd be able to reattach the rest. My palms were a different story. The right one was still hanging off, but it was safe to say that I'd never paint the same again—if ever. But it wasn't time to cry about that. I needed a plan.

What the fuck was I going to do now? Free from the chain, but my raw, throbbing hands were bleeding all over the place. Not exactly the best condition to catch her off guard when she returned. I might even lose consciousness by then if the bleeding didn't subside. I should've thought this through more...

Bang!

I didn't hear her truck come back, but then again, I almost didn't hear it at all. I thought it was the blood pounding from my temples.

Bang-Bang!

Someone was there. I'd normally know better than to make noise, but I knew she wasn't knocking on her own door. Plus, I was already a dead man.

"Here!" I tried to yell. "Down here!" My mouth was dry and I could feel how pale and sunken my face must be—there was a puddle of blood in my lap. "I'm down here!" I tried to call out again, and my vision tunneled and then went black.

The bolt flew back with a loud metallic clack.

"Schiel!" Det. Molloy shouted. "Jesus! What happened?— What did you do?" For a second, I thought he was accusing me of something—which would be just like him—until I remembered that my hands looked like they were shoved down a garbage disposal. His eyes followed my trail of blood back to the bed and the bloody handcuffs and then looked all around. "Where is she?" he shouted. I could see the dirt room behind him—the illuminated faces.

"We need to leave," I said, grabbing him around the collar with my bloody hands. "She'll be back."

"Let's count on it," he said and holstered his weapon to help get me to my feet.

"No, you don't understand," I tried, "she won't die."

"What are you talking about?"

"I can't explain—just trust me. We need to destroy that

painting," I said, and he looked over to the red monochrome of her rising naked above the tub.

"We did something awful. I didn't think that it'd... There's something evil in her."

"Good God," Molloy said, stepping away. "She made you paint these?" he asked. "Don't worry, we'll destroy them later, I promise—no one will ever see them—that bitch."

"No, we have to do it now!"

"Son, right now is really not the time. Look at yourself—you're gonna lose those hands if you don't bleed to death." Fuck. "Let's go," he said and tugged me toward the stairs.

"How did you find me?" I asked as he swung my arm over his shoulder.

"You don't need to be high and mighty, Joe. Come on," he said, grunting a bit as we ascended the first step off the dirt.

"What?" I asked, confused.

"Someone recognized your drawing, of course," he said, using his other hand to grip the railing.

"Who?"

"Me," he said, almost shamefully. I tried to look over to him, but I was starting to feel dizzy again.

"A woman was attacked outside of The Little Goat the other night. She said she tried to defend herself, even managed to stab her assailant before they got away. When I asked her to describe them to me, I got a flash of your drawing. She was describing the same woman. Then something about it reminded me of when I left here the first time—her eyes. I guess you are good. I stared at it long and hard. It was her."

"Really?" I asked.

"I figured she was worth checking out again."

"Sir, that's—"

"I mean, there were a lot of inaccuracies—the nose wasn't as pointy, her hair was quite a bit off." Even after finally acknowledging my importance, he still couldn't resist jabbing me as we struggled up the stairs. "Of course, I was suspicious of you being involved somehow when we found those drawings in your apartment. You're a sick one, for sure—she picked the right man for the job."

The small corridor that turned at the first landing became much narrower—only room for one person at a time—so Molloy pushed me up front so that he could stabilize me with my tailbone in the heel of his palm. In his other hand, he took out his gun. It didn't occur to me that he might be using me as a human shield until the back door opened.

X

"JOE!" NORA YELLED INDIGNANTLY. "WHAT THE FUCK ARE you doing up here? You scared the shit out of—"

"Hands up!" Molloy shouted as his shoulder catapulted me onto the kitchen floor. Nora stood there smiling innocently, holding a full grocery bag in each arm.

"I—" she said, motioning politely to the bags.

"Put the bags down very slowly," Molloy said. "You alright, Schiel?"

"Joe, what happened to your hands?" she asked.

"I said put the bags down and put your hands behind your head!" Why at that moment did I want to say "I'm sorry"? And to whom?

"Do what he says, Nora," I tried.

She stood there still for a moment, a slight bend in her knees, her chin down, staring back and forth between us. And then came the blood.

She threw down both of the bags with a smash and reached for her Bulldog, but Molloy was faster. He blew a single round right through one of her perfect cheekbones, and she flew backward into the counter, knocking an oval mirror off the wall behind her, and slid to the floor.

"She's going to heal," I cried as Molloy holstered his weapon and began lifting me back up. "Jim, I'm not crazy—please!" I begged as he tucked his neck back under my armpit.

"It's okay, Joe," he said calmly. "It's over."

"It's not ov—!"

A metallic tinkling noise on the tile behind us. We both turned around and saw the bullet rolling in a circle before resting in a puddle of Nora's blood. We both looked up to her face just as her eyes opened. Her neck straightened first, and then she turned to us and began to move.

"Get down!" Molloy yelled, flinging me back into the refrigerator. Three more pops this time. One in her rib, shoulder, and forehead.

"What the fuck?" Molloy screamed.

"Please! We need to destroy the painting," I cried, regaining my balance.

I couldn't tell if Det. Molloy was suddenly thinking clearly or just done with thinking entirely when he turned to me and said, "Go. Burn it."

I scrambled downstairs as quickly as I could without falling onto my face. When I reached the dirt floor, I stumbled over to the shelf and forced my bloody hands to retrieve one of the candles from under the row of glowing flayed faces.

Bang!

Another gunshot from upstairs. There was hardly any time left. I ran over to the painting and saw that it had bullet holes on it now, accompanying the stab wound. As a new one opened right in one of the portrait's eye sockets, I held the candle under a corner until flames began licking up the side of the canvas.

Then I ran.

"What the fuck is happening?" Molloy could hardly find the words to ask himself as I struggled to the top of the steps. He was standing right above her now with his pistol aimed directly at her forehead. "She won't—"

"Come on!" I could smell smoke now. It was our chance.

"How does she keep getting up?"

"It doesn't matter, we need to leave." Molloy looked up to me from the iron sights, and after a moment of consideration he reluctantly lowered his gun.

"Alright," he said, but before he could take a step back, a long shard of broken mirror sank through his thigh above the kneecap. He gasped in shock and snapped back on his trigger, but there was no explosion this time. Nora ripped out the sharp, jagged glass from his leg with a geyser of blood. "Run!" Molloy yelled as he started whipping her over the head with his pistol.

But she was up in an instant, on his back, stabbing him repeatedly as he screamed, trying to wrestle her to the floor. I found the fire pokers and spun back around in time to jam one into her face until I felt it hit the back of her skull. The steel made a clang as she dropped to the floor. Molloy was motionless on his back, and she could be up any minute if the painting wasn't consumed yet. I had to get the fuck out of there quick.

I fell through the screen door and tumbled down two wooden steps before landing on gravel.

Molloy was dead, fuck, Molloy was dead—I couldn't help him.

"Don't go, Joe," I heard Nora's voice echo from inside the house.

Across the gravel to the left was a field of frozen sunflowers covered in dull blue frost. To the right was an old barn, with a backdrop of dense woods as far as I could see. I couldn't afford to run. If she caught me, she'd kill me. I needed to take cover— needed to take arms—before she knew the painting was on fire. Kill her myself. Barn it is.

"Joooeee," she called mockingly. "Where aaare you?"

Tools—something sharp—my eyes darted all over looking for a hammer or a screwdriver; a pipe wrench would be great. Nothing but bales of hay. There was a pair of rusty shears on a workbench—too impractical. A chainsaw hung on the wall; too loud. Shovel; not lethal enough. In the back corner of the barn was a small stable with a quiet black horse in it.

Shadow. Must've been sleeping. On the other side of the stable was a tractor with a loft above it. I was able to get up the ladder just as I heard the large barn door creak open.

Nora was naked again, covered in blood—her own for a change. Even from where I was hiding, I could tell she was still healing.

"Come on out, Joe. You know I'll find you." I started to get nervous when she came near the ladder—I must've been shaking. Underneath a pile of hay, my foot struck something solid. "Oh, Joe, please stop," she said. I could see her through the floorboards as I tried to tighten my grip. "Come down here," she laughed, "or I'll come up."

"Stay where you are," I threatened. The painting must be close to immolated by now. She didn't have to die. There was still a bit of me that wanted her to face justice. I don't know if that was actually me thinking that or just my sorry, weak, blood-stained, skeletonized hands.

"What are you going to do with that?" she giggled, watching me stand up from the hay holding a scythe, her hands ready on either side of the ladder. She was right. Even if my hands weren't destroyed, I'd never swung one of these before in my life—not even a golf club.

"You know what?" she asked, and I wearily lifted the scythe above my head and she started laughing and scaling up faster. "I want you to do it, Joe. Why not, right? Just imagine me rising back up after you mutilate me. Now that would be some art. Go on! Swing it!" she yelled maniacally as she sprang closer to the top. "Oh, I wish that I could just let you do one more pai—"

The left side of Nora's face suddenly lit up with an orange glow, and I saw what she saw. A shaft of waving light was coming in through the barn doors. The house was engulfed in flames. In that instant, we both knew that the portrait must be burning too.

Quickly and mercilessly—before she could turn—I swung down at her neck with every last ounce of energy I had, and at the end of the swing the scythe flew out of my hopeless hands and spun like a boomerang across the barn. For a second, I was afraid; I thought I missed. It was so sharp; all I heard was the slice. Nora's head lobbed through the air as her body fell lifelessly into the hay below, and blood rained over my eyes.

XI

I WALKED OUT OF THE BARN INTO THE FIRELIGHT. IT WAS beautiful. Orange flames dancing and licking all over the roof of that awful house. All that evil within it burning away. A window smashed on the top floor; a ball of smoke and glass flew all over the lawn. I sat down on the frost-covered grass and looked to my gnarled hands. Life would never be the same, but they'd held up for everything they had to.

"Joe," a low voice said behind me. I was in a daze watching the fire—depleted of blood and all mental fortitude. I turned slowly around toward the black rectangle that separated the inside of the barn from the pasture. In the glow emanating from the flames, I first saw a puff of steam—I thought it was smoke—but then the large black beast's head emerged—Shadow.

"Did you really think that was going to work?" the voice, only distantly reminiscent of Nora's now, asked. Shadow's other hoof emerged from the barn and stepped out onto the grass at the top of the hill. In the hot flashing light of the fire, I could see Nora mounted on his back. She was naked, bloody, and headless.

And she was holding a long, coiled rope by her side.

"Please," I begged.

All was quiet except for another puff from the horse's snout. Then suddenly Shadow jumped up and stood on his hind legs, neighing loudly.

And the rope was taut around my neck.

THE FEAR

ELLIS HART

I don't know you. I don't know your name, your age, the state you claim on forms, or whether you butter toast to the edges. But I do know one thing, and I'll stake the eleven dollars in my savings account on it: you know The Fear.

Not fear in general. I mean the specific late-night moment—the ritual—where your house goes dark and you go soft inside. Everyone has their version, but it goes something like this: the TV finally threw up its slate of reruns and infomercials, the laugh track coughed itself out, and the living room settled. The last plate covered in pizza rolls grease slides into the sink. You checked the deadbolt the way Dad taught you—twice, tug, good. Then it was just you, one light on downstairs, the stairway up to safety, and the cheap plastic switch under your thumb.

That's when The Fear awoke, deep inside your chest, like it had been asleep somewhere behind your ribs and sat up the second your fingertip found the switch. It warmed the back of your neck. It had a smell too: sour, penny tin, old gym shirt.

You've been there. You stare up the stairs and run the math. You know your count. Four to the first landing, twist, nine more to the top. Thirteen in total. Socks on. Bad plan. The wood on your stairs had that glossy finish your Dad was proud of

—"waxed, like a proper house"—which meant it was basically an ice rink with corners. So you considered peeling the socks off for grip, but the air had that midnight AC bite, and you didn't want to risk the darkness seizing you as you balanced on one foot.

Upstairs: parents sleeping, sibling wheezing through their sinus battles, the aquarium filter in the hall giving its soft, constant hush. Downstairs: you, exposed floor, hum of the fridge turning into a different hum when you notice it. The TV screen transitions from a clear picture to a gray smear and then to black. Every light was off except for this last one, and the way it made the hallway look like a throat.

Here's what's always illogical about The Fear. Only a moment ago, you were fine. No monsters while you microwaved pizza rolls. No monsters when you were singing the Buffy theme under your breath. Then you put your hand on a light switch, and the house converges on you like a trap. The room hadn't changed. You had. The Fear made sure of it.

You try a rehearsal. Palm on the banister, knees bent, take two slow steps up with the light still on, feel the wood, look back, check your landing route. The plan was simple: flip the switch with a fingertip, explode up, hook the turn at the landing, and take the last nine on hands and feet if needed. Door to your room, close, click, shoulder against it, exhale. A clean sprint. No dawdling.

You take a breath big enough to taste dust and plastic and flip the light.

Dark.

Not full dark yet—you can still see the outline of the room in your mind's eye, but quickly, too quickly, you let the room invent shapes. That was enough for you to make the first move: right hand to the banister, hip into the rail, whip around, skip two steps, plant a heel on the first landing, haul.

Three steps, a groan in the wood that always gave a parent away as they approached your room. The VCR clock is a square of sick green. The aquarium filter blinked the tiniest orange

LED, like a weak eye. The kitchen had its window over the sink, and that showed a lighter kind of dark, the kind that held the yard and the world and other people's houses. But the stairs were their own unique brand of sickly black.

The pattern had always been the same: a push in the back. You never saw anything. That's how you preferred it. The Fear was a promise with no face—*move now or something bad arrives.* That worked on you. It worked so well, you had rules (I bet the same ones we all did). No looking over your shoulder. No stopping to grip the rail tighter. No trying to parse the sound that might be breath but could also just be AC. Just go.

But tonight, the pattern broke. Halfway to the landing, you slip. *Those fucking socks.* A cartoon movie. Your knee bangs the riser, and a muffled bark jumps from your mouth before you can swallow it.

You want to freeze. Every cell in your body wants to pull turtle and wait for the feeling to ebb. But your senses are already blacked out. The house hushed like someone hit mute. The fridge compressor cut off. The aquarium filter choked, burped, and kept going. In the gap, you hear everything—your shirt leaking armpit sweat, the blood drum in your ears, the tiny hiss of AC hitting a vent and sending dust mites across the darkened home. And under it all... a breath that isn't yours.

You bolt.

Hands and feet now. You go full spider and scuttle. The banister stings your palm, rubbing skin away. Eight... nine...

You top the landing, and the intensity is almost too much for you to blink. Your door sits three steps to the right. Safety, click, breathing into your pillow, reflecting on how silly you are. *Only babies believe in monsters.*

"Hey!"

Every muscle stalls like a blue screen on an old laptop. You keep your hand on your doorknob and treat stillness like a power. You do that, right? You freeze so hard you think you've gone invisible; the problem will just... go away.

"I hear you," Dad says, clearly this time. "Get in here."

You stand there with your forehead leaning on your door. You curse yourself for making the oldest mistake there is: never wake a sleeping father. The Fear steps back in shame, as if it's holding the door, giving space for embarrassment.

You turn to cross the landing.

Straight across the hallway, across the landing you just leaped from, is your parents' room with a rug your Mom says ties the hall together. The rug's corner has a frayed little knot you kick three thousand times a month. You put your heel on that knot.

And then... the misread cue. You don't clock it. Too busy being a good kid now that you've been caught barreling up the steps like a god damn elephant. You start your apology walk, preparing for your punishment. *Dishes for a week, no TV, no phone? What will it be this time?*

You take two steps across the square without looking left. If you *had* looked left, you would've see a pale set of eyes, almost invisible in the darkness. One more step, and something exhales where the stairwell mouth opens. Not loud. Wet. Close to the floor. It pulls air in through a throat raspy from little use.

The Fear goes full chemical then, but it's too late. The sirens in your brain and the panic in your chest can't save you.

Your father's voice—his exact words, his rhythm—comes again, not from his bedroom, but from two inches to your left.

"Got you."

The had really isn't a hand at all. Cold. Wet. It is breath and spit and something thicker that strings when it stretches. Fingers take your ankle just above the sock and push into the meat like a blood pressure cuff.

You go sideways without permission. Your hip hits the floor. Your palms bark. You grab for a banister spindle and miss it by a millimeter. The tug isn't a jerk. Instead it's strong and steady.

You kick, though your heels find nothing but air. The frayed knot on the rug rolls under your other foot, and suddenly you are on it, sliding, doing a controlled split you haven't trained for in the gym. The banister post slides past in a blacker black. The breath in the stairwell thickens with you, and a soft, animal whine that hurts your throat escapes from between your lips.

"Shhhh," your father's voice says from the dark.

The stairs take you. Kneecaps first. Shins whining. You get a palm around the newel post and buy a heartbeat. The thing on your ankle squeezes in, not around. That is the worst part. It knows your shape already. Not talons, not pincers, nothing easy to fight. Skin that sticks. Pressure that understands your bones. It adjusts to you the way a mouth does when you drink from a bottle making it impossible to wiggle free.

A post squeals in its socket. Your fingers burn. You slip and scrape, and you are no longer on the rug knot but on the lip, and then the stairwell eats your view of the hall, and you learn an awful truth: darkness doesn't need teeth to eat. It can simply swallow you whole.

Everything from here gets small. Not the way memories fade. The way they compress to beads you can slide on a string. You don't scream. You want to. What comes out sounds like somebody working a zipper with no tongue.

You make yourself look once. Just once. People say you should look once, so you don't have room for your brain to invent worse later. You turn your head and try to look at the hand, except you don't see a hand but rather a face that steals the very oxygen from your lungs.

An elongated face that's been flipped upside down; bulbous eyes existing where a chin should, and above them, a menacing, gapping hole with exaggerated lips, intentionally covering yellow teeth so your skin doesn't rip on the way inside. This isn't a creature hanging upside down in the darkness, no, this is the absence of anything good, a broken, mangled, contorted face bearing down on you.

You hit the carpet at the bottom of the stairs and get a lungful of cool air that tastes like shoes. Then you move sideways without wanting to, and the world brings your ear to something warm.

Eating doesn't always have to be a crunch. It can be a fold and a pull and a wet patience that undoes the idea of you inch by inch until you simply don't exist.

If your snotty sibling had awoken at this very moment in time to get a glass of water, they would've stopped and listened. They would've pushed their hearing down the stairs, around the bottom landing, across the living room floor, and into a corner where mixed in with the darkness and shadows, they would hear a soft, sloppy eating sound. A feast The Fear works so hard to avoid, and often, does.

But unfortunately for you, your sibling does no wake up. And so your parents will awake in the morning to find the dishes you left behind, the single sock that flew off at the top of the landing, but no other sign of you. No blood, no hair, just the mild stench of The Fear that flowed from your pores only hours before.

The faint smell lingers. It slides in where grief would live but arrives early, a placeholder. Mom cracks the windows because she thinks something spoiled in the trash. Dad checks the sink trap. Your sister covers her nose with the sleeve of her sweatshirt and says the house smells weird, like pennies and lunch boxes after August.

By the time they call your name, the peculiar odor dwindles quickly with the windows now open, air running, and lemon cleaner on the banister. And as your family goes through their morning routine, they carry a little of you with them on their clothes without even knowing it.

At least, that's the way it *could* go if you don't listen to the Fear. So *please*, just remember, when you're faced with turning your light out or leaving it on before you head to bed tonight, perhaps think about it a moment longer. You're never entirely sure what's waiting for you just beyond the point where the light stops reaching.

COLD AS ICE

ALEX FRANKLYN

For Nicola and Megz

Climate Change Is Real!

"Who'd have thought it?" Roman muttered, eyeing the newsstand. One tabloid screamed that the polar ice caps had accelerated after a freak solar flare event. A slightly less dramatic broadsheet read:

> ...*With the current escalation of ozone depletion over the Arctic, combined with last month's unprecedented weeklong solar flare, the impacts are more severe than reported. Radiation affected the surface ice and heated the water beneath it—microwave-style. Heat above and below the glaciers is driving a polar melt unlike anything recorded. Increased fossil-fuel use and other pollutants led to the atmospheric hole that*

should have protected the Arctic, according to marine climate scientist Dr. Roman Blake and his team.

As Roman read on, he squinted. Were they implying he made it up? Truth didn't bow to preference or politics. The article referenced "other sources," calling him a crackpot, many of them government representatives with money tied up in big oil. Funny how that detail never made it to print.

> *...Dr. Roman Blake states he will prove the impact during next week's expedition to the Arctic, where he intends to find evidence for the sudden changes. As previously reported, multiple Arctic bases built on ice were swallowed when the ice gave way; no bodies have been recovered due to an unstable ice floor and fast-moving icebergs that can crush boats. Yet Dr. Blake and his team say they will risk the journey to obtain critical readings and search for possible survivors.*

His phone buzzed. Where the hell are you? Shit. He was late for the airport pickup. He slid the paper back and flagged a taxi. An orange cab with a turquoise hood pulled to the curb like an old friend. The driver leaned over.

"Where to?"

"Toronto City Airport, please." Roman sank into the seat and texted Grayson: You go ahead. I'm grabbing a taxi straight there.

He could hear Grayson's reply without opening it: for fuck's sake—you're never a team player, are you? Gray said that a lot, accusing Roman of being a maverick who rubbed people the wrong way. Roman thought of himself as an independent thinker who didn't need hand-holding.

Leading a team, though, was easier than being on one. He liked being in charge and hated being questioned. He combed his blond hair with his fingers—a small comfort—and closed his eyes for a steadying breath. Tightness pressed his chest. This expedition was the most important of his life, and Grayson never missed a chance to remind him. Roman sometimes fantasized about cloning himself instead of managing a team. He liked Gray—college friends—but familiarity bred contempt. Late thirties, no family, no kids. Sometimes he longed for it; time with other people usually cured the feeling. Screaming children, swallowed tongues, the endless compromises of making a relationship "work"... nah.

The taxi stopped. Roman tipped well—he wasn't stingy with money, just everything else—and hoisted his backpack.

"Hey, man, no other luggage?" the driver called.

"Yeah—no. Most of my clothes count as equipment, buddy."

The cabbie shrugged and drove off. Inside the busy terminal, Roman spotted Grayson near the front of the check-in line. Roman slipped through the queue, murmuring that his friend had the travel documents. Gray, earbuds in and paperwork ready, jumped when a hand smacked his shoulder.

"You just can't wait, can you? You can't stand in a line like everyone else?"

"You wanted me here; I'm here. What's the problem, Gray?"

Gray rolled his eyes. In his early thirties, he was a prodigy who liked order and process. His wife did too. She'd already coordinated most of the trip.

"The wife already in Svalbard?" Roman asked. Gray's left eyelid twitched. Roman didn't have an issue with women, per se —just with married people on his team. They felt less likely to follow his rules and more inclined to team up against him.

"Yes. She's finalizing the arrangements so the expedition can happen. She's organized like that—which I love." The words carried a pointed look.

"Well, I'm here. So can we just—Ah! Look. Free check-in."

Gray's chest thumped at the cut-off sentence. Roman did that to get under his skin. The nineteen-hour travel stretch was fine: work, then sleep. On their laptops, they reviewed weather and sea temperatures, which led to news.

> *...A small fishing boat was found empty off Greenland's*
> *northern coast. Logs show it ventured farther into*
> *the Arctic Sea than advisable for a better catch.*
> *With no damage to the hull, authorities are searching*
> *for survivors. This comes a week after a trawler*
> *likely crushed by moving ice...*

Gray shivered. Their tech was better than a fishing boat's, but no one was immune to the elements. Roman glanced over and caught the gist. His face softened.

"Stanley's a brilliant geoscientist," he said. "Specialist in radio glaciology. She's been out there for years. With her and the gear, we'll be fine."

"Doesn't mean we won't have to move fast. The ice flow is pushing hard, bergs moving quick."

There was that tightness again.

"Gray, we'll be on stable ground. Stanley will make sure of it." Roman wasn't sure whether he was reassuring Gray or himself.

"Why don't you call her Meg?" Gray asked. "Why 'Stanley'?"

"Professional." Gray snorted and turned back to his screen. Sure, he thought. No reason at all.

Svalbard Airport air felt oddly warm for the season—ten degrees—and the wind carried a faint, unfamiliar smell. Meg Stanley had arranged their pickup. Roman cracked a window, chasing the scent. Something familiar, but he couldn't place it. The faint trace calmed him; he exhaled like he'd taken a hit off a joint, breath fogging in the cold. He shut the window, blaming it on a lack of sleep and the poor coffee. Hopefully, Stanley had sourced something drinkable.

As they neared the docks, more people than usual filmed the horizon. From the coast, massive icebergs sailed past, torn from larger glaciers. When the wind shifted north, the smell returned, a touch stronger. Gray tapped Roman's arm.

"Are we going, then?"

The docks were a hive. Gray's wife, Maja, directed the loading, barking fluent Norwegian.

"Handy having a wife who speaks... Svalbardian," Roman said.

"Norwegian. These islands are part of Norway. Do you retain anything outside work? We've been married two years."

"I knew she was Norwegian. I didn't know the language was... look, forget it."

They headed down the deck as Maja's voice carried: "Bare legg det der borte, takk."

"Heya, honey!" Gray hugged her. She kissed him quickly and resumed issuing orders.

"We're close," she said. "Three more people inbound. Once their gear's stowed, we go. No need to wait for tide anymore, apparently." With the great melt, tides had gone to hell, fish were confused, and other research boats were already on the water with dive crews.

Roman's team wasn't following them; they alone were going far north—or so they'd planned.

"What the actual fuck!" Maja pointed at a larger, well-funded vessel slipping past.

"Fucking MacDonald and his shitty ecosystems team! Oi! Fuck you! Bastards!" She flipped them off. Their rival, happily sponsored by oil and tech, loved calling anomalies "freak occurrences" and undercutting Roman's findings. At the prow, MacDonald cupped his ear theatrically and laughed, then signaled his captain to punch north. The wake slammed their smaller boat against the dock.

"Fuck you! Fuck you! FUCK YOU!" Maja kicked the gunwale. "They'll publish first with bullshit and bulldoze whatever we do."

Gray tried to calm her. "If they don't do the work, their readings won't hold."

Roman shared her worry. "If they start first and find something, they announce first. I told the press about us. We'll be a laughingstock."

"Which is probably what they want," Gray said. "If you hadn't told anyone, they wouldn't know. So let's get our shit together. Ah—about time. The rest are here."

Down the slip came Meg Stanley with Bill and Andy. Fist bumps all around. Maja dropped her clipboard to help haul cases, urgency lost in the greetings.

"Anyone who wants to help me catch that bastard MacDonald is more than welcome!"

They were underway within the hour. They couldn't match MacDonald's speed, which drove Maja to take a shot of aquavit. She and Gray, like Roman, had put personal money behind this venture; prestige mattered. No one remembered the second team unless they found what the first missed.

The swollen sun sagged toward evening. Sonar ran constantly —surface and below. New currents tugged the boat upstream; winds swung without warning. The ship rose and fell like in a storm, though the sky was clear.

BANG.

Something slammed the under-starboard side, lifting them. People yelped. Maja kept her gin from spilling and moved with the roll, the sailor's daughter steady on her feet. As the hull slapped back down, she stalked to Stanley.

"How the fuck did you miss something that size on sonar?"

"It wasn't there a second ago!" Meg said. "This refreshes every second. First there was nothing—then there was—and then it hit us. That fast."

The reply backed her up. Maja's mouth fell open. "What the hell was that?"

Bill hurried in, shaken. "Was that a rock?"

"See anything?" Maja asked.

He shook his head. Nothing above the waves. If it had been an iceberg, it would've resurfaced. With the bright moon and clear sky they'd have seen it. The sonar shape hadn't looked like a whale. It looked like... something big.

Crew checked the hull. No breach. Norwegian boats were built for this, if not invincible.

"How are we okay?" someone asked.

"Whatever we hit was flat," a crewman said. "No sharp edges. Maybe a whale?"

Maja frowned at Meg. "Recalibrate. We should've seen a whale long before impact—even from below."

Meg pressed her lips thin and reset.

The rest of the night passed without incident. Sea air and adrenaline ebbed; they needed rest. There are only a few hours of night this time of year. By morning, they'd be within range and move slowly after the near miss.

Roman drifted between sleep and waking behind an eye mask until Meg shook him hard.

"What? I'm up."

"Roman, you've got to see this."

He pulled on a thermal jumpsuit and climbed to the deck. The smell hit him—strong now. Coffee and sleep deprivation, mixed with the scent, nearly dropped him. He slapped his cheeks, adrenaline clearing his vision. Icebergs drifted like twenty-foot cathedrals; their unseen depth made him uneasy. On the port side, the crew clustered, staring.

MacDonald's boat listed, lifeless.

"What the hell happened?" Roman asked. Andy just shrugged; Bill filled the silence.

"Whatever we hit last night came back, maybe. There's a

bend and break in their hull. All lifeboats still aboard. No radio response. No movement."

Even Maja, who loathed MacDonald's, looked unsettled. Roman forced himself into leader mode.

"Bring us alongside. Check for survivors."

Andy balked. "Shouldn't we wait for the authorities? Whatever happened might happen to us."

"The authorities will take time," Roman said. "Every second counts. What would you want if it were you?"

He didn't like Andy's instinct to sacrifice others to save himself. If Andy hadn't been good, cheap, and available on short notice, Roman wouldn't have hired him.

Grayson appeared with Meg, carrying a large first-aid kit. "The question is who's coming."

They loaded the dinghy. Roman went first. Bill followed. Gray kept Maja from climbing in.

"Not you. I need you here."

"Why?" Maja asked, calm enough to be alarming.

"If you come, the only one left to direct our crew is Andy," Gray whispered. "You okay with that? Meg's first-aid trained, and we may need to carry people."

Maja glared. "Fine, dear."

She watched, eyes wide, as the dinghy sped off, then narrowed her gaze at Andy, chewing his nails. Never again, she thought.

The inflatable thumped against MacDonald's hull. A crewman lashed it fast. Roman climbed the ladder and peered onto an empty deck, careful of surface ice. The silence was wrong. The smell was strong. A light haze hummed around his team.

"What is that?" he asked.

Gray sniffed. "Been wondering. Slightly sweet... chemical? I figured with the atmosphere changing, who knows. But it's stronger here."

Meg and Bill nodded, following Roman inside as the hull

gently swayed.

Back on their boat, Maja hounded the coast guard for an ETA and tried to ignore Andy's pacing. Fieldwork had never been his plan. He preferred quiet and data collected by someone else. Taking credit for others' research had wrecked his reputation; only one lawsuit had been smothered for the university's sake. Ironically, the project he'd cannibalized was MacDonald's. MacDonald took the payoff and his work back.

Roman's team hadn't checked references closely enough.

"They're on their way back!" a crewman shouted.

Maja and Andy ran out as the dinghy approached, dodging sheets of ice. Maja squinted through binoculars. "Do they have anyone with them?"

"Hard to tell," Andy said, trying to count heads. Looked like five. Relief loosened his shoulders.

Meg came up first, shivering despite the insulation.

"Well?" Maja demanded. "What did you find? Where the hell is the crew?"

"We only found one," Meg said.

They winched MacDonald up in a harness, wrapped in foil blankets. A wind gust yanked the sheet aside. His head lolled, revealing swollen features, bitten lips, sunken eyes.

"Jesus fucking Christ in a hand-basket," Maja whispered. "What happened to him?"

Roman and Gray helped carry him inside. "He's been attacked," Roman said.

"Bled out, a lot," Bill added, trailing them. "We'll use the lab as a sick bay."

"Bled out? Those bite marks aren't bleeding now. Why is he so swollen?" Maja asked.

Bill only shook his head.

Meg cut away MacDonald's clothing. Bite marks punctured thick insulation. His breathing was shallow, pulse weak. His pale, bloated skin felt cold and spongy under Roman's hand. Meg reopened one wound: thin, watery blood mixed with a stagnant seawater smell oozed out.

"Sea water?" Roman asked. "How is he alive?"

Meg shook her head. She pressed for a pulse—weak but there—and swabbed a wound with antiseptic. MacDonald gasped; fluid gurgled into his lungs. He spasmed and vomited a briny mix. They rolled him to prevent choking. Bruises mapped his back like he'd been slammed against metal. He convulsed, then went rigid.

His eyes snapped open, arms straining toward Meg, fingers twitching, eyes rolling—and then he let go. Quiet.

Roman eased him onto his back. The dead eyes stared. Meg began to cry. Roman, not prone to there-there, pulled her against his chest, stroking her hair.

"It's okay. There was nothing you could do. No one should have to see that. You tried. We tried."

She sobbed harder. He took her by the arms and looked her in the eye.

"Listen to me. It happened. It was horrible. You did what you could; that makes you a good person. We'd be bad people if we'd done nothing."

Meg's tears dried to a flash of anger. She pulled free and stomped out. Roman exhaled—probably not the best approach.

Maja burst in mid-call with the coast guard. "Their chopper's down for maintenance; another is tied up with an iceberg collision. What the—" She stopped, seeing the sheet.

"He woke, went into shock, and died," Gray said softly.

Maja stared a moment, then marched to the chest freezer. "We keep him cool until pickup." She heaped bagged ice on the body, then gagged at the sour puddle on the floor. "Out. All of you. Get out of my lab." The men fled while she cleaned.

Up in the observation deck, silence pressed in until a crewman set down a tray of sandwiches. No one had eaten since morning—a bad idea in the Arctic.

Meg looked and turned away. Maja sipped aquavit from a hip

flask—Gray had once believed aquavit was vitamin water. Bill ate, ignoring looks.

"What?" he said. "Starving in the cold won't help. We're not doctors. The best we did was keep him from dying alone. We tried." He grabbed a few more and escaped to the comms room. Andy slunk up, fistfuls of sandwiches clutched, and vanished.

"I should eat," Maja said. "Wouldn't do to be drunk on an active expedition." She wrapped a few for herself and Gray, motioning him along. Roman and Meg were left.

Roman chewed. "I don't think I've seen you eat. You should. Not great, but it does the job."

"I thought you hated him," she said.

"What?" He blinked.

"MacDonald. I thought you said you hated him—wished him dead."

"Oh no. You're not pinning your guilt on me. I've had women try that—blame me instead of owning their feelings. But I don't think this was your fault either. Survivor's guilt isn't healthy. Drop it."

She scoffed. "Clarifying, that's all. If I misread you. He could have wrecked your career. If he got there first, you'd be ruined. So would Maja and Gray. All your money, gone. Am I wrong?"

Roman rubbed his temples, forcing down dry bread. "I didn't like him, no. But I wouldn't wish that on anyone. If you think I'm happy about this, you're mistaken. I'm not hardened to this kind of thing. And if you think I think this is good? No."

She stood abruptly and left. He told himself grief looks different on everyone. Also, cultural differences. He finished eating and considered a nap. They weren't going anywhere until the coast guard arrived.

In his cabin, Andy and Bill were already sleeping. Roman sealed the door, unsettled by the memory of dented metal on MacDonald's galley door. Bill—usually an insomniac—snored. Odd. The sweet, chemical scent threaded his dreams.

He woke to Andy shaking him hard. "Jesus, Roman, wake up!"

"I'm awake. What?"

"They're gone. They're all gone."

"Who?"

"The crew. We're alone out here."

Roman's heart hammered. He shoved past Andy, ripped off his eye mask, and slammed the door open. The smell was strong. He shouted for anyone. No answer. Gray and Maja's bunks were empty. He froze, turned, and sprinted to the lab.

The table was bare. The stained sheet was gone. Nobody. Meg. He ran to the comms room. The door was sealed—from the inside. Someone was in there. He pounded, then stepped back as the wheel slowly turned. Cold dread rippled through him. Who—or what—was on the other side?

The wheel spun free. The door cracked open. Meg stood there, tear-puffed eyes rimmed red, blood on her clothes. He grabbed her, more in his relief than for hers.

"Meg, what happened? Where is everyone?"

"There was a fight," she said, voice flat. "Maja and Gray argued. The crew wanted to leave when the coast guard arrived. Gray said it made sense. Maja didn't. There was shouting. I don't like shouting." Shock had emptied her tone. "When I went to get you, I heard them say bad things about you. That all this was your fault. That they'd lost their savings. I didn't want to hear, so I left. Then a terrible noise. I was scared. I hid in here. I don't know what else happened. I'm sorry."

"So what happened next?"

"I fell asleep. I've never felt so tired. There was that smell. I've only just woken up."

He didn't challenge her. He knew the smell. He led her to his cabin and sat her on the bunk.

"Rest," he said, tucking the blanket around her. She grabbed him and kissed him. He kissed back, then pulled away.

"You're... rejecting me?" she asked, hurt.

"No. This isn't the time. You're in shock. We'll talk later. I have things to do, and you need sleep."

Tears welled. She lay back and muttered, "Foolish. Stupid," and thumped the wall with her fist. Roman stepped back and closed the door. She needed help. He required the coast guard.

In the comms room, Andy yelled Mayday into a dead mic. Roman shoved him aside and flicked the transmit.

"This is Dr. Roman Blake—coordinates as follows—confirm you have our crew," he demanded.

"We do not have your crew," the reply crackled. "We're en route now. We were told we were no longer needed—that there had been a mistake and—" Static swallowed the rest.

Roman stared at Andy, curled on the floor, sobbing.

"Where are they?"

"I told you—I couldn't find them."

"What have you been doing for the last couple hours?"

"I was asleep. Nightmares. I got up for water—no one around. I searched the whole boat. Then I woke you."

"I found Meg. In here. How did you miss her?"

"What? No. I swear to God the door was open and this room was empty."

"Just because you couldn't open the door doesn't mean—"

"It was open. She wasn't here." Andy clutched his head. "I ran deck to deck, screaming. She was not here."

Roman smiled without humor. "How do you account for the fact I tucked her into my bed?"

"Fine. Let's go see her."

They went. Roman threw the door wide with a flourish.

Empty.

"Are you sure she was here?" Andy whispered.

"What? Of course. Do you think I'm crazy?"

"You're acting weird. Do you have any history—"

"Don't." Roman lowered his hand, trying to steady his voice. Andy backed away and bolted. If he locked himself in the comms room and did something stupid—

Roman chased him up to the main deck. Andy slammed a door behind him, failed to latch it, and skidded on ice. He scrambled up the ladder leading down to the dinghy. Roman burst through the door.

"Andy! This is ridiculous. You're panicking—we both are. Come back up. We'll sit in the observation room. The coast guard will be here in forty-five minutes."

Roman forced sincerity into his voice; his eyes betrayed him. Andy climbed down anyway. Roman edged toward the rail, careful of the slick deck.

The scent rolled in, strong. Roman swayed. Andy blinked up, and they both smiled. Laughter bubbled. Fear slid off like ice melt. The sky's colors were exquisite; the sea was a calm, brilliant blue. Roman marveled at the beauty of everything and at Andy's bright, happy face.

They hardly noticed when it rose from the water.

It was big, wet brine slicking oil and seaweed that streamed from its hide with a grace Roman found beautiful. Its teeth gleamed like diamonds. Its eyes—so deep, so restful—were veined blood-red against a putrid yellow, like a perfectly rendered oil painting.

Tentacles slipped around Andy's waist. Andy laughed. "It's hugging me, Roman! It's hugging me!"

"It's going to give you a kiss, Andy! Oh my God—so beautiful. I'm so happy for you. It should have been me. You're so lucky!"

Blood spattered Roman's face. He clapped, impressed by the force. The thing chewed until Andy's laughter stopped. Roman breathed deeper, feeling freer than ever. It looked up at him, expression familiar somehow. It lifted him by the legs, hanging him upside down, drawing him toward its mouth. Roman giggled.

"Oh my God! Like a fairground ride! Weeeee!"

Then the smell snapped away. Cold air knifed his lungs; fear flooded back. Blood rushed to his head. The thing turned him to face her, and he saw the contorted truth. The eyes were not beautiful. Slime ran from the warted, scale-like mass.

He knew her as he screamed.

Silence.

The coast guard later reported two empty boats, intact but deserted. International search protocols were triggered.

On shore, Meg watched until a reporter approached. "So what made you leave the boat when you did, Miss Sirene—is it?"

"Yes. Meg Sirene. It's embarrassing. I'd argued with my boyfriend—my first. He rejected me, so I left. I mean, I'm here now but I left when I was there." She frowned, groping for words. "My English isn't very good. He didn't understand me. I tried to please him, sometimes at risk to myself, but he didn't appreciate it. Nor did his friends. So I left. I took a dinghy. One of the boats picked me up."

"You realize you risked your life, don't you?"

"I know. But I had to get away. I couldn't stay. And now I'm glad I didn't."

The reporter studied her unusual amber eyes—yellow-brown, common among islanders, a likely genetic quirk. A quiet people, uneasy with outsiders, yet newly welcoming to many foreigners.

The reporter inhaled the breeze. "I do think your people are getting a taste for us, though, aren't you?"

Meg smiled.

THE GHOST OF MOUNT DORA

ELLIS HART

At Mount Dora Middle, the third table from the left against the cafeteria wall, the new kid learns the rule: Halloween night. Three knocks. Look up. Don't speak.

The school's bully, Trent Harker, tells it as he always does. He's the kind of kid who lounges across the bench like it's a throne—shoulders squared, voice stretched thin with performance—but the illusion can't hide the soft belly cinched into his hoodie or the angry constellations of zits scaling his jaw and cheeks. He smells faintly of cheap deodorant and energy drink, the sour, nervous reek of a kid boiling in his own insecurity and ladling it onto other people to cool himself down. He makes the story bigger than it needs to be, mouth rounding on the important parts, stabbing the air with a plastic fork for punctuation.

"Only on Halloween," he says, leaning in so the whole table leans with him. "Three knocks on the door of the old Brendamore place. Then you say, 'I'm sorry for your loss.' She'll then let out a horrifying, terrible scream. If you blink, if you look away, if you do anything at all, you die. If you see her and keep your cool, you're in."

"In what?" the new kid asks. His tray sweats under congealed cheese fries. The banner for Friday's game sags above them like a tired mouth.

"In with us, idiot," the bully says, and the table laughs, but he doesn't. He pins the new kid with a smile that is not a smile. "Halloween or never. You got one shot."

The new kid looks at the exit but doesn't let himself look long. He is not brave; he is new. New is hungry. Hungry says yes.

"Atta boy," the bully says, clapping his shoulder too hard and leaving his hand there a second too long. "Tonight, we make you a Dora local."

Word spreads in the dumb, miraculous way it does at school —hiss to giggle to stampede. Phones are already out. By last period, the lake light is tilting gold and sticky across the floors and the new kid has memorized the dare without meaning to: three knocks, look up, don't blink.

They meet at dusk. The walk down Ninth Avenue feels rehearsed: Frankie spinning her BINGO sign, the Historical Museum glass taped with CLOSED EARLY FOR HALLOWEEN, glitter dusting the mat. The hill behind town is already a darker black, the big house on the ridge cutting its silhouette across the sky. On the outskirts of town, the Brendamore house squats behind its leaning picket fence, door flayed by weather. Upstairs, several window panes look out, but only one catches the new kid's eye.

"Positions," the bully says, suddenly businesslike. He assigns with a conductor's certainty. "Everyone film from the sidewalk. New kid, porch. It only works if you're at the door."

"What about you?" someone asks.

The bully flashes a grimy, yellowing smile before whispering so only a few hear. "I'll be making sure our guest shows up."

The gate complains. The walkway bucks with roots. The house smells like soil and damp paper, like a library that drowned politely. The new kid stands on the porch where the wood is cold and splinter-humming under his soles. Behind him, phones whisper open. His hand hovers over the door shaking no matter how hard he tries to control it.

He knocks.

One. The sound thuds into the house like a stone tossed down an empty well.

Two. The porch light flickers, fails, leaves him colder.

Three. "I'm sorry for your loss," he says, although he isn't exactly sure what he's sympathizing with or what tragedy befell them to create such a scary urban legend such as this one.

The door unlatches—far too slowly—opening by inches, and an old-house breath cold as lake water sighs from the seam. From somewhere deep inside, a scream tears up: long, wet, high, the kind that grabs your ribs from the back and yanks.

Phones jump. Kids shriek. Adult words are used. The upstairs window throws a sudden amber candlelight, thin and alive. In it, a woman's shadow rises into view, shoulders and bobbed head and lifted hands splayed on glass. The silhouette's mouth opens and opens and opens.

The sidewalk detonates into motion. Sneakers slap. A little brother's witch hat flies. Someone sob-laughs. The new kid can't recall moving, but he knows he did because the porch steps are already behind him, and the gate is already banging back, and the street is already a river of retreating children.

He turns once, because something in him believes what they just saw can't be real. The window holds the shadow, perfectly framed, perfectly terrible. The scream keeps going. And then, cutting the scream off like a track fading to zero, the house goes still again.

The kids don't. They scatter and thin and vanish around hedges and corners and into the loud tenderness of their own mothers calling from porches. The sidewalk empties.

The house remains.

The front door opens as Trent steps out and thumbs the speaker off; the last of the canned scream dies. He holds the wig to his head and preens in the blank window of the house, tilting, pursing his lips. "Like a movie," he tells himself. He's giddy, fizzing with the pleasure of shrinking someone else so he feels bigger. He tucks the wig into his backpack between a coil of fishing line and a battery pack and flicks candle stubs in the front room with his sneaker until they gutter and smoke. When he steps onto the sidewalk, the night has settled into its cool, familiar weight, a cat reclaiming a lap.

He walks home easily, keeping to shop windows for the accidental mirror they offer. He wants to see himself laughing. He wants the shape of himself laughing to be permanent.

In the glass of the antique store, something tall and wrong stands behind him, far down the sidewalk. A trick of the streetlamp, of course. He banks a corner; his reflection slides and breaks into three. The wrong tall thing slides with him, closer now.

He turns. There's nothing on the street except a plastic grocery bag snagging itself free, a roach that knows the seams of the curb, a sprinkler switching on with a spit. He laughs at himself and the laugh rings a little brittle in his own ears.

At home the bathroom fills with steam. His mother's voice travels up the hall: "Don't use all the hot water!"

"Five minutes," he lies.

He drags his hand across the mirror and the clearing streak fogs back slow. Behind the milky veil, a darker oval paces toward him, a head tilt with a blunt cut of hair, a mouth drawn too wide, too red. He leans closer. The mirror beads sweat. A thumbprint appears in the fog and pulls downward, one glossy track like the path a slug leaves on a patio after rain.

He spins so fast he pops his hip. Shower curtain, towel, door —only the mess of a boy who thinks he is a man and a line of purple on the sink where his mother's lipstick rolled and paused. He laughs again and it comes out wrong. He opens the door and lets the steam spool down the hall. He does not return to wipe the mirror clean.

In the morning the kitchen is sun-bright, a good Florida lie. The bay window in the breakfast nook turns the yard into a painting. His mother stands at the stove with a wooden spoon, hair up, robe tight, the towel under the plant still damp where she overwatered it three days ago.

"Eat," she says. "You look green."

He forks eggs in mouth, jaw working on autopilot. He half watches the glass, half watches her. Across the street Mr. Delaney drags a black bag to the curb. In the window, in the slice of reflection near the latch, a woman stands just behind his shoulder. Bobbed hair. Smeared lipstick like a bruise across her mouth. Her face is turned to him, not to the room, as if the glass is a door she's pressed her cheek against to hear better.

He drops the fork; metal jitters tile. His mother looks; she sees a teenage boy jumpy about something he will not explain. "Big test?" she says, but it is not a question that expects an answer.

He blinks and the reflection is his alone again. The eggs go cold. The bus barks twice and leaves him ten seconds to grab his backpack and bolt.

At school, at the third table from the left against the cafeteria wall, the bully's friends crown him with a dozen open palms.

"Legend."

"Dude."

"You broke him, for real. He looked wrecked."

"Get on my story," someone says, and the bully's name shoots across screens smeared with grease and joy. The videos are a cheerful montage of other children's fear. He nods and shrugs and throws a little smile and the whole time his eyes keep cutting to reflective surfaces—phone, tray, the metal strips in the ceiling that hide a line of wire.

In every one, he thinks he sees a shoulder - not his shoulder - a flank of dress - not any dress these girls would wear - a gray wig bob that isn't the thrift-store thing he stuffed in his pack. The old lady's lipstick is wrong, too purple, too high on one side like she put it on with shaking hands. She is closer now in glass than she felt last night in air.

Questions crowd him and he can't hear any. He pushes away from his own coronation. "Bathroom," he says to no one who's listening.

He almost runs into the new kid in the doorway. They both flinch and both pretend it's because of speed. Up close, the new kid looks like he didn't sleep inside at all, but rather wherever fear put him down.

The bully opens his mouth; apology rises like a hiccup he could let out and be done with. A thing loosens in his chest, a knot his whole family has handed down tied by bruise and joke. He imagines saying, "It was me," and then he imagines the version of himself that gets smaller under the words. He stiffens.

"Watch it," he says instead, and shoulders past.

In the boys' room, he drops his backpack on the dry patch under the paper towel dispenser because he still believes there will be a normal after this. He opens the faucet and lets the water run too long because the sound is louder than his thoughts. He splashes his face and counts slow—one, two, three—and forces his eyes up.

Nothing.

Tile. Fluorescent tube. A cracked pimple on his cheek he planned to cover with a hoodie shadow. He huffs, maybe laughs, maybe sighs; it blends. He cups water again, cold knifing sore skin awake, and throws it on.

He looks.

Nothing.

"I'm fine," he says, and the empty room returns, "You're fine," in the voice tile has.

A hand lands on his shoulder.

Not a friend's slap. Weight, but too light to be male. He looks down. The hand is pale, too pale for your average Floridian; the back a map of small, purple rivers. The nails are short, ridged, painted a color so bright it looks like candy—purple, though chipped, and a smear of the same color high on the middle knuckle where someone painted carelessly and never fixed it.

He knows.

The mirror waits. He turns for it because that is what you do when you can't turn anywhere else. In the glass, the woman stands where no person stands, close enough he could count the tiny lashes that stuck together when she blinked. Bobbed hair like a helmet. Lipstick a shade too young for the mouth it tries to claim, filling in the wrinkles around her lips. Her eyes are not cruel. That is what makes the breath leave his body in a rush.

He opens his mouth to scream. It comes out all the way this time—loud, bright, animal—and ends like a wire cut.

A JANITOR BARRELS IN, KEYS JANGLING, RADIO CRACKLING, eyes wide. "What. In. The. Hell?! What's going on?"

Trent blinks into the mirror's hard rectangle and in that moment he knows his life is forever changed. No old lady at his shoulder. No dress, no lipstick, no second shape in the glass. Only a boy with water on his face and a trembling mouth, standing in a room that looks perfectly, boringly normal.

"Kid?" the janitor says, taking him in. "You okay?"

Trent's voice snaps into the wrong register. "She was— She—"

"Do you need me to call someone?" The janitor says worried while checking stalls, peeking behind the door, waiting for an explanation to appear.

Trent looks crazier the longer he mumbles, the more effort he puts into sharing what he saw. He's hyperventilating now. The janitor softens, guides him to the sink, presses paper towel into his hand. "It's all right. Breathe. Dry your face. Come on now."

Trent nods too fast. He can't make himself look at the mirror again. The janitor lingers, then leaves with a last, careful glance, the door sighing shut. Water runs. The radio murmurs: all clear. The room is empty except for Trent and the fact that nothing is there.

THE DAYS AFTER COME ON LIKE FEVER. HE STOPS LOUNGING. He stops laughing. He stops. He becomes the kid who sits at the end of the bench and peels the label off his chocolate milk and lines his mini Oreos along the tray's rim, keeping out all the bad thoughts. Teachers call on him and he shakes his head no. Jokes come and he doesn't swat them back. He gives the hallway its right-of-way.

The new kid notices the space where power used to sit and tries it on. First a light shove at a locker—kidding, bro. Then a louder story at lunch that lands sharp. A brave, mean laugh that gets echoed. Phones find him; hashtags and mentions climb. By Thanksgiving he's the one who decides who sits where, who makes the nicknames, who fakes the friendly arm over a shoulder that ends in a dig. By Christmas, he's learned to enjoy the hush that falls when he enters a room. By spring, he knows what Trent used to know: you can put your fear in other people and it feels like relief.

Trent moves through school like a ghost. He keeps his eyes low because every glint—vending machine glass, trophy case, bus window—threatens to throw back more than just him. The few times he checks, the mirror gives him only his own face, which is somehow worse. The bathroom becomes the longest walk in the building. He times it to the bell so no one can follow and no one can see him freeze on the threshold, counting one two three before stepping inside.

He does not tell the story. He does not tell any story. Weeks unspool. Months. He never sees her again.

IN A YEAR'S TIME, ON HALLOWEEN, AT THE THIRD TABLE FROM the left, the cafeteria hums like a kicked beehive. The banner for Friday's game sags. The fries congeal. A new, *new* kid has found his way into the seat of orbit beside the new, *old* kid, who is not so new anymore and wears approval like a team jersey.

Someone at the far end says it, easy, a tradition tossed like a crumpled napkin: "We should hit Brendamore tonight. Three knocks. Make him local."

Trent Harker—who has not spoken above a whisper in eleven months—knocks his knee on the underside of the table so hard the trays jump. The sound that comes out of him is too loud for a cafeteria and too raw for school. "NO!"

Heads turn. The room pauses, then leans.

"Don't go there," he says, voice fraying to wire. "Don't. Don't knock. Don't say a god damn thing there."

His eyes are wild, hands trembling as he laces his fingers back and forth to release the horror he feels building in his chest.

"They need to tear it down! Knock the whole thing down! Do you hear me? DON'T GO, KID."

He's on his feet now, chair skittering, breath hitching like a sputtering engine. Teachers converge, hands out, voices soothing, as if they are approaching some panicked animal. He kicks once, twice, not at anyone, just at the idea that someone else could experience what he had, or worse, wake up what had gone to sleep almost a year ago.

"Listen to me," Trent pleads as they take his arms. "Don't let him—don't let anyone—just don't—"

The room shifts to let the little parade through: kid, two teachers, radio whispering, door opening. His voice echoes down the hall and then is taken by it.

When the old bully is gone, the group draws in naturally, shoulders closing a circle the way kids do when the weather changes. The new old kid—who learned this posture from someone else—leans to the new new kid with a smile that is not a smile.

"Okay," he says, conspiratorial, generous, predatory. "Here's the rule. Halloween night. Three knocks. Look up. Don't speak."

ACKNOWLEDGMENTS

This collection would not exist without the extraordinary group of authors who jumped in headfirst with me. What started as a wildly impulsive, poorly timed idea somehow turned into a finished book because they poured their talent, heart, and late nights into these pages. Every story here is a testament to their creativity—and I'm grateful to now call many of them not just collaborators, but friends.

Endless gratitude also goes to my editor, Megan Haymans. Her meticulous eye and thoughtful feedback have saved me from more than a few disasters. Megan, thank you for caring about every misplaced comma and every knot in the plot—you've sharpened this project into something I'm proud to share.

To the readers: you are the reason this book exists. From the early, scrappy little stories I posted on Bookstagram to this full anthology, your encouragement gave me the courage to dream bigger. Every comment, share, and word of support mattered more than you know. You're the best kind of chaos crew, and I love you for it.

And lastly, to my family—thank you for letting me chase down ideas at odd hours, for putting up with endless drafts, and for reminding me that the stories we live are just as important as the ones we write.

Here's to more stories, more scares, and more late-night ideas that sometimes blossom into something special.

ABOUT THE AUTHORS

Alessandra Benini is an indie horror author whose work explores the intersection of supernatural fear and emotional truth. Her work often explores haunted houses, blurred realities, and the lingering weight of family secrets. A lifelong fan of the paranormal, she is the author of *The Inheritance of Giuliana*, *House of Ash and Spirit*, *Dead Line*, and *Preferred Reality*, a collection of paranormal short stories. Alessandra lives in El Salvador with her husband, their three children, a very needy cat named Loui, and their sweet dog Bimba. Connect with her on social media @alessandrasbookreviews

Shawn Brooks is the author of a Japanese folk horror series with four books out now: *Endless is the Night*, *Under the Amber Wave*, *Iomante*, and the newest released in September 2025, *Dead Roots of the Earth*. He has also written two small town American short horror story collections: *Pine Haven* and *What Dances in the Dark*. He lives in Japan with his wife and psychotic Siberian Husky and has dreams of owning a ranch full of wolfdogs and cats, with maybe a llama or two. Connect with him at shawn-brookswrites.com or via social media @shawnbroookswrites

Cailin Cecchini is the author of *Moon Day*, its prequel, *Wolf Star*, as well as *The Ghost Story of Tristan & Dolores* and *Us When We're Apart*. She is also the host of Fang Girling, a rewatch podcast of all things creatures of the night. She writes from Massachusetts, usually with an overly sweetened iced coffee (even in winter) and a black cat named Damon fighting for her attention. Connect with her on social media @thecailin

Aurelie Duncanson is the author of three psychological fictions, *The Mind's Appetite*, *The Neighbor She Never Knew*, and *Whispers From The City Of Light*, all released in 2025. She's from France and moved to the US when she was 26 years old. She lives in California with her family. She loves reading thrillers and classic french literature. She also collaborated on a supernatural story, *Human By Day* released in July 2025. Connect with her on social media @aurelieduncanson.author

Alex Franklyn is a UK-based author and actor whose work spans psychological thrillers, crime comedy, and speculative fiction. She is the author of *The Empathist* and *Cleaners Wanted*. Her film credits include the Nigerian feature *Ireke*, which premiered at Cannes, and she also writes for upcoming indie projects. Current works-in-progress include *Arte-culture* (a sci-fi conspiracy), an untitled horror collection, and a historical psychological drama planned as a series. When she isn't writing or at book cons, she's geeking out over graphic novels and hanging with Noodle, her very opinionated rescue cat. Connect with her on social media @alex._.franklyn

Ellis Hart is an independent author based in Orlando, Florida. His debut novel, *The House That Held Her*, was released in May 2025 and has already garnered attention for its gripping psychological suspense and puzzle driven plot. He is already at work on his second thriller, *Make Me Forget Again*, which can be expected in the Spring of 2026. He shares his life with his wife, three children, and a delightfully curious cat named Jovie. When he's not crafting twisted tales, you can find him swapping book recommendations or goofing off on his author platforms. Connect with him at ellishartbooks.com or via social media @ellis_hart_author

Julia Jackson is the author of *Powder & Poison*, is featured in various international horror anthologies, and is a member of the Horror Writers Association. After a near-fatal car accident, Julia turned to writing as part of recovery and now crafts chilling stories that strip away the masks women wear, revealing emotional depth and damage. Julia has had more surgeries than Frankenstein, is a creature of the night like Batman, and creates memorable heroes and monsters of her own. Julia teaches mindful writing at Kristin Dwyer's Breaking the Story Retreat, as well as to the online writing community. When Julia is not writing, she works in Corporate Communications and watches an unhealthy amount of ghost hunting shows and horror movies. Connect with her at @juliajacksonauthor

A.D. Jones lives in the North of England; where he spends his time favouring books over people and can be found writing or devouring said books to review online. He loves Coca-Cola, Twin Peaks, all things horror, and cult movies. He dislikes the movie *The Karate Kid* with a passion that burns brighter than the sun. His debut novel – *Umbrate* was released in October 2023 to positive feedback, as were his following 2024 releases: *Sacrificial Waters*, and *Born of Bloodshed*. His latest novel, *Little Horn* was released in April 2025. Connect with him on social media @the_evergrowing_library

S.J. King is the author of two dark psychological thrillers - *Where You Belong* and *Lauren Is Missing* (2025). She has a brother named Stephen King (*not that one!*) whom she blames/thanks for her lifelong obsession with horror and dark thrillers. As a global Public Affairs director, she has a rather responsible day job. But by night, SJ writes unsettling fiction to unwind and escape. SJ especially loves Halloween, having met her husband at a costume party in Hong Kong. When he fell off a speaker, she took him to hospital in a police speedboat. They now live with two teens and an Indian street-cat on Prozac. SJ's third novel is due out in 2026. Connect with her on social media @sjking_writes

H.H. Mika is the author of *Something in the Blood*. He is currently living in Alaska with his dog Chili where they are hard at work on his second novel. When not writing, Mika tries to stay warm and pets his dog as often as humanly possible. Connect with him on social media @h.h.mika

Victoria M. Sorenson is the USA's best-smelling author; she exudes the blended fragrance of melancholy tones and a hint of rich sarcasm, paired beautifully with individual notes of floral. Her works include *The Sacred Vine*, book one of *The Tendrils of Light Series*, as well as book two, *The Soul Shield*, which releases November 6th, 2025. Connect with her on social media @victoriamsorenson

Amy Tackett is a psychological thriller author who was born in the heart of Appalachia before later relocating to the Midwest. She is most known for her Christmas slasher, *Secret Santa*. When Amy's not writing, you can find her playing with her wild (lovable) children, hiding her book purchases from her husband, or rambling way too much on her Instagram stories. Connect with her on social media @authoramytackett

David Washburn lives in the Greater Cincinnati area (in Northern Kentucky for any locals who choose to argue about geography) where he lives with his two teen sons. When David isn't fighting imposter syndrome as a writer he is probably working out, watching horror movies, baseball, or wrestling.

Suspense and tension are David's playground and he has

independently self-published multiple books in addition to having short stories published in several anthologies. His novels include titles such as *Where Pop Stars Go to Die, DIY Exorcism,* and *Devils That Prey*. You can find his books everywhere books are sold. Connect with him at washburnwrites.com and on socials @washburnwrites